A Fractured Song

HEARTSONG BOOK TWO

For anyone who has the talent of making magic through music. You inspire me!

ONDFORD
RIVER OND
OLEAND
SUNDERING CANYON
PORT TARAN
ZEV'S HOLDINGS
TARANDON
AELTAS
The SOVEREIGN REALMS
N
S
W
E

CHAPTER
ONE

Marieke

Marieke splashed water onto her face, taking a moment to consider her reflection in the looking glass above the basin.

She looked tired.

She had no business looking tired, she told herself sternly. It wasn't as though she was traveling, or preparing for examinations. Life in her parents' home didn't involve much idleness, but it wasn't particularly arduous either.

The trouble was that she wasn't sleeping very well. She'd been home for a month, and she still found it difficult to settle. During her waking hours, her mind was consumed with the questions that Gorgon's death hadn't answered.

And at night, when she laid down, supposedly to sleep... well something else filled her thoughts in those moments. Or rather, someone else.

To be fair, Zev crept into her thoughts during the day as well. Such as right now, as she stared at her dripping face in the looking glass and wondered if he thought about her half as often as she thought about him. Was he also kept awake by memories of the passionate kiss they'd shared in the unguarded moment of relief that came after surviving Gorgon's attack?

She hoped so. She felt no noble desire for him to be free of the emotional turmoil in which she found herself.

In fact, she thought, her brow creasing in an irritated scowl as she stared at her reflection, she hoped he was positively pining. In her less generous moments she was still annoyed with him for walking away from her. For declaring—quite reasonably—that whatever was going on in Oleand wasn't his fight, and then leaving it at that, as if their own situation didn't even merit being addressed.

But her annoyance was softened by the memory of those cloud-gray eyes when he'd said goodbye. He'd been conflicted, she was sure of it. Walking away hadn't been easy for him, and it wasn't as simple as doing what he wanted. And it wasn't as though they would never see each other again. She grabbed a nearby towel with a decisive motion. She would make sure of that.

Her face dry, and her mind as awake as it was likely to be, Marieke made her way out to the kitchen of her family's home.

"Good morning, Mari." Her mother's bright voice greeted her, and her father smiled absently without looking up from the letter he was reading.

"Good morning," Marieke said, the greeting encompassing them both. She hastened to her mother's side, carrying the milk pitcher to the table as her mother did the same with a plate of eggs.

"It's certainly nice to have your help around the place again," her mother commented.

Marieke smiled in response. "It's nice to have you cooking my meals for me again."

"There's always a role for you at my clinic," her father

reminded her, lowering the letter. "We could use your initiative and hard work around the place."

"Not to mention my songcraft?" Marieke challenged.

"No." Her father lifted the letter again with a sage expression. "Except maybe for cleaning. You'd have to undertake much more rigorous study before I'd let you get your magic anywhere near my animals."

Marieke laughed. "Wise man."

He was absolutely right to be cautious, since using magic on animals was a nuanced and specialized business which she wasn't equipped to do. Naturally she refrained from mentioning that her decision not to specialize in that type of songcraft had been motivated by a desire to *avoid* spending her life assisting her father in his role as a horse doctor and farrier.

"Well, as I told you when I came home, I'm not here to stay, I'm afraid," she said, settling at the table beside him. "Just for a little while."

"Yes, but that was a month ago," her father said in a practical spirit. "And it doesn't seem to me that you have any clear plan about what to do next."

"It's a shame that earning that place on the delegation to Aeltas didn't raise the further opportunities you hoped." Her mother's tone was softer and more sympathetic. "I'm sure you acquitted yourself well." She frowned slightly, the expression sitting poorly on her pleasant face. "Besides which, you'd think they would feel they owe you something after your place on the delegation almost got you killed."

Marieke laughed weakly. "I don't think that means they owe me. And perhaps opportunities will come up yet."

She hadn't told her parents that she'd gotten on the wrong side of the Council of Singers by pursuing unpopular lines of inquiry. In fact, there was a great deal she hadn't told them about her most recent time away from home, and she didn't feel inclined to share any of it. No need to alarm them with her suspicions that some sinister magic continued to target their country.

After all, even she was beginning to doubt herself. In the month she'd been home, she'd made a point of seeking every opportunity to get news from the capital. She knew from discussing it with her parents that the series of accidents that had befallen singers previously—accidents which turned out to be attacks orchestrated by Gorgon—had been big news locally. Yet there'd been no whisper of any further incidents of that nature since she'd left Ondford. Perhaps she'd been wrong to read some kind of deeper, more sinister magic into Gorgon's attacks. Perhaps he really had been acting alone, and the threat was now over.

There was no obvious improvement in the fertility of the land, but after all, no one had ever confirmed a connection between Oleand's increasing barrenness and any kind of magic. Maybe her conviction that it was connected to the long-ago deaths of Oleand's former monarchs was nothing more than a sign that she'd become too suspicious.

"That letter has you engrossed," she commented to her father, who was once again poring over the parchment.

"Yes," he said. "It was delivered with the market cart early this morning. It's from an old neighbor who lives up near Bull Creek now." He glanced up at Marieke's mother. "I think I'll have to move things around today and pay a call to him."

"In Bull Creek?" Marieke asked, surprised. "That's pretty far away."

Her father nodded. "It's outside my usual area of service. But the closer horse doctor is out of town, apparently. And they're in some difficulty with a pregnant mare who's in a bad way. They can't afford to lose the mare or the foal, not with things so tight."

"The journey there and back will take the better part of the day," Marieke's mother said, looking worried. "Can *we* afford the loss of your other work?"

Her husband sighed. "Better than they can afford for the mare to die, I think. I'll leave at once, the sooner to be back. Maybe I'll still be able to open the clinic here for a couple of hours before sunset."

"I'll come with you," Marieke offered. "For company on the drive if nothing else."

"That would be welcome," her father told her. "And I'm sure we can put you to more work than that."

Marieke nodded, not averse either to the change in scenery or the opportunity to be useful. She busied herself helping her mother pack a hamper for the struggling family while her father hitched up their wagon. Before long, she was sitting beside her father on the broad bench seat, bumping along the road westward, away from the coast.

The pair chatted easily on the journey, but Marieke's heart was heavy. The landscape they passed through seemed to mock her optimistic earlier thoughts that perhaps no great threat still hung over Oleand. The dry fields and scrawny trees were such a stark contrast to the thriving, fertile land she'd seen on her visit to Aeltas. Zev's family holdings had been particularly rich.

And her mind was back on Zev. She forced all thoughts of the inconveniently captivating farmer aside, determined to stay focused on where she was and what she was doing.

When they arrived at the farm near Bull Creek, there was enough to do to keep Marieke fully occupied. But her heaviness of heart didn't ease—the struggles of the family in question might be a distraction from dwelling on Zev, but they were a further indication of the generally deteriorating state of Oleand.

The silver lining was that her father was able to diagnose

the mare's ailment, and provide treatment which offered reasonable hope of survival both for mother and foal. They were just packing up their supplies, optimistic about making it home in good time, when a shout went up from the lane leading to the farm.

Marieke paused in the act of loading her father's old leather bag, looking up in concern.

"Stay here," her father said, as if she was still a vulnerable child, not an adult and a trained singer. "I'll see what's happening."

He strode out of the barn, his lean form disappearing from view. Finishing her task quickly, Marieke stood and made her way to the doorway, hovering there in half-hearted obedience to his instructions. But she didn't need to emerge to hear the shout that was going up on all sides.

"Fire!"

Fire? Marieke froze, her eyes wide with horror as they flicked to the farmhouse nearby. But she could see no sign of billowing smoke or licking flames.

"Fire in the fields!"

Marieke let out a gasp. Having grown up around farmers, she understood how those four words contained a nightmare of the worst kind. If someone's crops were on fire, not only homes would be threatened, but whole livelihoods. And in a field of dry wheat, the flames could spread with terrifying speed. If not stopped quickly, it would be near impossible to quell them.

At least with normal methods.

Disregarding her father's orders, Marieke hurried out of the barn, joining the group gathering at the gate.

"Where's the fire?" she demanded.

"Out in Mosley's wheat field," a stranger said, oblivious to the fact that Marieke wasn't from the area and that description meant nothing to her. "It's spreading fast!"

"What caused it?" demanded Marieke's father, gazing up at the cloudy sky. It wasn't exactly peak fire conditions.

"No one knows," the man said. "Smoke was first spotted out in the middle of the field, nowhere near any dwellings. It's fields on all sides, and no one was out there that we know of. Half a dozen families stand to lose what little crops they have."

"No time to waste, then," Marieke said briskly. "Does someone have a wagon ready?"

"Marieke." Her father turned warningly to her. "You're not going near there."

"Of course I am," she said, staring him down. "Unless there's anyone else here who's a singer trained specifically in agricultural song."

"You're a singer?" One of the locals leaned forward, looking ready to seize her shoulders in his relief. "You have to help us!"

"I'll do whatever I can," she told him seriously, her insides crawling with nerves. In spite of her bold words to her father, her theoretical studies in agricultural song felt feeble in the face of a real-life crisis where people's livelihoods might depend on her.

"Come on," said the man who'd brought the news. "We shouldn't delay."

He led the group to where a wagon stood at the end of the lane, Marieke and her father clambering into the vehicle alongside the others. Marieke could tell that her father still didn't like the idea of her going into danger, but he didn't protest again in face of everyone's eagerness for her help.

The smell of the fire reached them well before the sight. Smoke filled Marieke's nostrils, suffocating and terrifying because of all it represented. When they reached a crossroads near the affected field, they paused to let another wagon through, this one loaded with barrels of water. Marieke's heart sank as they followed the wagon around the corner and got a good look at the thick plume of smoke. The sheer size of it told her that the water would do little good.

"How close do you need to be?" demanded the man driving the wagon.

"You can work from a distance, can't you, Mari?" her father said quickly.

"A bit of distance is helpful," Marieke agreed. "But closer than this. I need to get a feel for what's going on."

"Tell me when to let you out," the man said. "The rest of us will continue and help unload the water from that other wagon."

Marieke nodded absently, her senses already focused on trying to test the magic in the ground. Confused, she began to hum softly, not pulling much magic into herself, just probing what her extra sense encountered. This area was much like her home, and the magic in the ground should feel similar to what she knew. But something wasn't right. There wasn't enough dormant magic ready to respond to her, but there seemed to be plenty in the air. And it felt...angry. Like fire.

Marieke drew in a breath, ready to sing, and instead let out a choking cough. Much closer and the smoke would inhibit her songcraft due to purely practical reasons.

"Here," she told the driver, and he pulled the wagon to a stop. She climbed down, her father close behind her, along with another man.

"There's only so much they can do with the water barrels," he said by way of explanation. "You may need assistance here." His voice was grim. "If nothing else, assistance to get out if it comes to that."

Marieke nodded distractedly, her focus back on the magic. "The wheat field where it started is that way?" she asked, pointing to their right.

The man nodded, seeming surprised. "How could you tell?"

Marieke just shook her head. She didn't want to tell him what she was thinking, not until she knew whether it meant anything. But the truth was, that was where the angry magic was swirling most strongly. It was distinct from the familiar magic of the farmland, which was behaving just as magic in this type of terrain should.

She put this mystery to one side for the moment, focusing on the fundamental practices of agricultural songcraft that she'd been taught. Keeping her voice low and steady to conserve her energy, she sent out an assessing song, designed to identify areas of danger in farming conditions. As expected, her awareness burned fiercely with the presence of the fire, the sensation of it in her mind uncomfortable almost to the point of pain. She quickly cut off that song, scolding herself for using a strategy that was far too basic for the situation. If there was any other danger of relevance to farming, she wouldn't be able to find it under the overwhelming influence of the fire.

"What did you learn?" her father asked frantically, noting that her song had finished.

Marieke grimaced. "That the field is on fire."

He looked at her like she'd lost her mind, but she was too focused on her next move to explain herself. The situation was well beyond diagnosis. She needed to use her song to try to craft a remedy. She closed her eyes, drawing a deep breath as she once again let out a hum to assess the magic of the land. There still wasn't as much in the ground as she'd expected, but there was certainly enough for her to access it.

Agricultural song was intuitive, she reminded herself, especially for someone who'd grown up on the land rather than in a big city. It was all about the natural elements, and since magic was itself part of nature, nature was more responsive to its influence than, say, a human-built structure.

Keeping her eyes closed, she let her hum grow into a proper

melody, putting words to it. The words were according to a formula from her studies, seeking to assess the natural forces of the air, including wind and rain. There were plenty of clouds overhead, but none seemed heavy enough to promise immediate rain, unfortunately. And the wind was behaving in the worst possible way, blowing a dry and steady gale outward from the center of the fire, urging the flames on toward the surrounding fields.

That she should be able to influence, she thought, steeling her resolve. She'd never had to do it on this magnitude before—or with such high stakes—but she'd performed well in her examinations regarding the manipulation of wind. She drew in a quick breath as the words of her song changed, turning to an invocation to the wind. Controlling, or even creating, wind was merely a matter of remolding power from one natural form into another. She wouldn't usually try to change the course of such a strong wind for fear of the potential unintended consequences, but in this case she didn't hesitate. The consequences of leaving it unchecked were worse.

Pulling power from the ground and channeling it through herself as swiftly as she could, Marieke sent magic streaking outward, directing it with her song to infiltrate the wind and become part of it. With the magical awareness of the fire still burning dully in her mind, she directed the wind to curl back in on itself, sending the flames toward the already blackened patch of field, where there was nothing to fuel their onward journey.

The effort cost considerable energy, which was no surprise, given the strength of the wind and the large area she was trying to impact. But provided she was up to the task, it shouldn't have been complicated. To her confusion, she found that the wind was resistant to her direction, fighting the tugging influence of the magic still under her control. Marieke's voice increased in volume and intensity as she doubled her efforts, refusing to let the power she was channeling yield before the opposite force. She opened her eyes, trying in vain to see through the smoke as sweat beaded on her forehead.

"Mari, what's wrong?" Her father gripped her arm. "Are you all right?"

She waved him off, unable to speak without breaking her song. With the inexplicable sense only singers were born with, she reached further afield through the ground behind her, finding more reserves of magic to pull on and send to aid in her task.

Gradually, exhaustingly, she felt her songcraft take effect. The wind slowed, then shifted, changing direction as her magic was coaxing it to do. As it turned on itself, Marieke suddenly felt the resistance disappear, not gradually, but all at once. Part of her mind understood something that sent a chill over her, but she pushed it to one side, knowing she still needed to give her full focus to the task at hand. The flames had slowed considerably with the wind no longer on their side, but that wouldn't be enough to put them out. And nor would the efforts of the humans whose shouts could be heard faintly from further into the field.

Satisfied that the wind was on course and no longer needed her to sustain it, Marieke let her voice drop, drawing in a shuddering breath as she prepared a new song. Once again, her voice reached out in assessment, this time seeking only one natural element: water.

With the use of her magic, she could feel the barrels of water in the out-of-sight wagon, as well as the more dissipated moisture in the low-hanging clouds above them. She hesitated, unsure both what she was capable of, and what was safest. But there was no time to second guess herself.

She knew, as the farmers surely must as well, that the

barrels of water weren't going to do anything on their own. It was a desperate effort because they couldn't do anything else, and they couldn't bear to do nothing. Fortunately, Marieke *could* do something else.

Taking simple control of an element such as water was advanced magic that was taught as part of agricultural songcraft with much cautioning. It was dangerous both for the singer and for the environment around them. But Marieke couldn't think of any other option. With a song which was more like a chant about the power and strength of water itself, she sent magic curling up into the barrels, seizing the water that filled them and shooting it into the sky like a jet. It joined the clouds, losing far more of its volume on the way than she would have liked.

Stretching both her energy and her magic past what was comfortable, Marieke reached for the clouds further out, directing power to surround the water in them and pull it inexorably out. Again, she didn't know what atmospheric ramifications there might be of this redirection of nature, but given she was only capable of reaching the nearest clouds, it hopefully wouldn't be anything too dire.

The water pulled from the nearby clouds joined that from the barrels in the cloud bank right above the fire. To her immense relief, it was enough. The balance tipped as the moisture gathered, and the cloud began to release rain.

With a gasp, Marieke broke off her song again. As soon as she wasn't actively singing, she realized just how much her songcraft had taken from her. She'd channeled far more magic than her limited experience had prepared her body for, and she was barely conscious. She swayed on her feet, her father steadying her with strong hands.

Marieke's eyes drifted closed, salty sweat stinging them as it dripped down her face. All she wanted was to sleep, but the job wasn't done yet. The rain was a good start, but it wasn't a torrential downpour. She needed to enhance it if she possibly could.

An expert in agricultural songcraft might be able to increase the volume of water with only their song, but Marieke didn't know how to do that. She needed to swell the rain with water she found elsewhere. And there wasn't any in the immediate vicinity.

With an effort that kept her too exhausted to open her eyes, she sent her assessing song further afield, trying to find water with the desperation of a dying man in the desert.

There. A body of water just on the edge of her awareness. Likely a dam belonging to the nearest farm, for livestock to drink from. Marieke sent power surging through the ground, calling on the water. She didn't try to make it fly impossibly through the air like she'd done with the water from the barrels. It was easier magic to simply increase natural processes—in this case, evaporation. She sent it up into the clouds, urging it to swell the rain already falling.

She enhanced the natural evaporation process far beyond what would ever happen without magic. The dam was almost drained when she caught the cries of joy from the farmers battling the fire. She permitted herself a smile. Her eyes were still squeezed shut, but she could hear the steady thrumming of what was now a heavy—albeit isolated—patch of rainfall.

As much of the water as she could manage was in the clouds now, and it would fall without her continued intervention. That was part of the benefit of utilizing natural processes as much as possible. She could afford to stop singing.

"You did it, Mari." Her father's voice, hushed in awe, filled the sudden quiet created when her song cut off. "You did it all by yourself."

She tried to muster a smile for him, but she was barely

awake. She'd undertaken a task that should really have fallen to a team of singers, and taken control of much more magic than was safe for her body. She felt blackness creeping in at the edges as she let her weight fall against her father.

It wasn't an entirely peaceful descent into unconsciousness, however. Her mind tried to fight against oblivion, insisting on solving the agitating question of the resistance to her attempts to direct the wind.

Only now it was all over did she recognize what she'd felt in the moment. As the wind resistance had suddenly died, so had the angry magic she'd felt when she first assessed the fire.

Even in her befuddled state, there was only one conclusion to draw. This blaze hadn't been natural. It had been created—or at the very least fueled—by magic. And not the dormant magic of the land. The intentional, channeled magic of an active enchantment.

Her last thought as she finally succumbed to unconsciousness was anything but reassuring.

She wasn't the only singer present.

Marieke

Marieke woke slowly, her mind reluctant to return to consciousness. Probably because of the steady pounding in her head. Who was knocking against her skull, and why?

She let out a soft groan, and heard rapid movement next to her in response.

"Mari!" Her father's familiar voice was laced with relief. "That's it, nice and slow. Don't push yourself."

"My head hurts," Marieke groaned, wincing as she sat up. She put a hand tentatively to her temple.

"I don't know anything about magical ailments." Her normally collected father sounded anxious. "What do you need? Is there something I should be doing?"

Marieke smiled in spite of her pounding head. There was something very endearing about her father's concern.

"It's not a magical ailment," she said. "I've just overextended myself."

"From using magic," her father insisted.

"Well, yes." Marieke gave a weak laugh. "But I'll be fine, once I've had a chance to rest and recover my energy. As for what you can do…" she winced again as her temples throbbed, "a drink of cold water wouldn't go amiss."

"There's a glass just here."

Marieke downed the liquid gladly, looking around her. The room was completely unfamiliar.

"Where is *here*, incidentally?" she asked.

Her father leaned back in his chair, his eyes on her face. "The farmhouse of the Mosleys."

"Who?"

"The family whose field was the first to catch fire."

"Oh." Marieke put the glass down, full memory of the incident rushing unpleasantly into her awareness. The fire. The fire fueled by angry, intentional magic. "Is the fire out now?"

Her father nodded. "They're still out there, using barrels of water to make sure the last of the embers are extinguished, but it's all contained."

"Well, that's a relief."

Her father raised an eyebrow at her. "You sound subdued for a heroic rescuer."

Marieke snorted. "A what?"

"A hero." Amusement glinted in her father's eyes. "If I'm not mistaken, the locals will be building a statue of you before the week is out."

Marieke shuddered dramatically. "Song and power! Let's get ourselves home before anyone can do anything so horrifying."

Her father laughed aloud at that. "Good plan." His gaze softened as it rested on her. "Jokes aside, Mari, what you did was incredible. You really were heroic. I'm proud of you."

Marieke felt her cheeks heat, and made a scoffing noise to hide her pleasure. "Don't you start, Father." She closed her eyes against the aching in her head, trying to marshal her thoughts. How much should she tell her father? She needed to tell *someone* what she'd felt. But he wouldn't know what to do about the information. "How long was I out?"

"At least half an hour," he said. "Maybe closer to an hour by now."

She nodded. So it was highly unlikely that whatever singer had fueled the fire with that angry-feeling enchantment was still within reach. Presumably they would have slipped away when their scheme was thwarted. Part of her was disheartened by this information, while the other—more cowardly—part was relieved a confrontation was unlikely to be possible.

"I've held you up," Marieke realized aloud, her eyes shifting to her father. "You were hoping to be home this afternoon with enough time to open the clinic."

He shook his head, his smile amused. "Obviously there won't be time for that now, but I don't think you can take the blame, Mari. Unless you lit the fire in an attempt to display your skills to an admiring crowd."

The words were spoken lightly, but Marieke felt her brow lower.

"It was a joke, Mari," her father said. "Obviously no one would suspect that, least of all me."

"I know it was a joke," she said quickly. "It's just..." She put a hand on her still-throbbing head. "Naturally I didn't start the fire. But I think someone did."

Her father's frown now matched her own. "You think it was arson? What makes you conclude that?"

"I felt..."

Marieke hesitated, reluctant even with her father to say what she'd felt. Some farmers felt strongly that magic shouldn't mix with generations-old farming traditions, and would rather singers stayed away from their fields altogether. She hated to reinforce any mistrust they might have by making allegations that magic was used to nearly destroy a farm.

But there was no help for it. She drew a breath.

"I felt magic. In the fire. Or fueling the fire, or something. I don't exactly know the form it took. It wasn't a familiar enchantment to me. But it was targeted magic of some kind, not just the magic of the land taking its natural course."

Alarm flashed across her father's face as he considered this information. "Are you sure?"

Marieke nodded. "When I first assessed the situation, I could feel this angry kind of magic that I didn't identify at first. But when I was using songcraft to change the direction of the wind, I felt it again. The wind was fighting my efforts, and eventually it gave way to the wind under the control of my magic, and then the angry magic disappeared altogether, like its grip had been broken by my opposing magic."

"You could change the direction of the wind with your song?" Her father's voice sounded strange as he latched on to the unimportant detail. "Just...anytime you want? You can control the wind?"

Marieke bit her lip, not liking his expression. She'd been pleased when he said her magic was incredible. But something about his reaction now—almost awed—didn't sit as comfortably.

"Not just whenever I want," she said. "There are limitations on what songcraft can do, and we have to be very careful that we don't create unintended consequences of messing with the weather." When he still said nothing, she forced a reproachful note into her voice. "I have tried to tell you about my studies in agricultural song before, Papa. Lots of times."

His face softened into a sheepish smile, dispelling the unfamiliar expression he'd worn. "I know, but I never took much in. It never felt real when you talked about it as something you'd learned in a classroom far away. Seeing it in action today..." He shook his head. "Well, it was different, that's all." He ran a hand over his chin. "This is concerning, though. If some singer is targeting farms, the situation is serious. We'll probably have to report it to the Council of Singers, I suppose."

Marieke didn't miss the reluctance in his tone, and she understood the reason for it. The Council of Singers ran the country effectively for the most part. But coming from a rural area where singers were scarce and the land's deterioration hit hardest, she knew as well as anyone that there were valid reasons to feel frustration toward the privileged leaders.

In fact, she knew better than most, given the events of the last few months.

But this wasn't about her, or about the fact that the council may still hold her in suspicion. It was much more important to find out who'd attacked the farm, threatening to destroy what little harvest the region had.

"Yes, I think we will," she agreed. "But it's probably worth finding out more first."

She didn't intend to tell her father everything she was thinking. But she suspected that once the council got involved, she would be pushed to the side, and it would become considerably harder to gain information. If she wanted to know what was going on, she'd be wise to find out as much as she could before telling the council anything.

And she did want to know what was going on. She felt personally invested. She could still feel in memory the pressure of her magic grappling with the other magic. It had been a raw and desperate struggle, and it was probably for the best that at the time she hadn't realized she was fighting another human rather than just the natural elements. She might have lost her nerve if she had.

"Let me speak to the Mosleys," she said abruptly, pushing herself to her feet.

"Whoa, steady there." Her father held out a stabilizing hand as she wobbled, but she waved him off. Her energy was still depleted, but not so much that she couldn't move.

She'd barely started toward the door, however, when it swung open, and a woman with a round face and a friendly air bustled in.

"You're awake, child!" she said, nodding from Marieke to her father. "Well, that's a mercy. I was getting worried." Before Marieke could reply, she surged forward and enveloped her in a hug. "We're indebted to you forever, my dear. From all I hear, you saved us, and we're grateful."

"I just—it was nothing," Marieke stammered, embarrassed, but strangely comforted by the embrace.

"Nonsense." The older woman drew back. "None of it is nothing." She sighed. "It's still a disaster, no doubt about it. But it could have been infinitely worse. Would have been, if you hadn't happened to be here! And that's something to celebrate."

"Here comes the statue."

The murmur from Marieke's father was so low that the farmer's wife didn't hear it. Hopefully.

Her lips twitching traitorously, Marieke turned away from her father in a pointed way, addressing her question to the woman she assumed was Mrs Mosley.

"I hope I won't seem impertinent, but can I ask you some questions?"

"Of course you can, dear." The older woman chivvied her back toward the bed. "Once you're resting, and I've brought you some food."

Marieke's protests fell on deaf ears. She had no choice but to sit meekly on the edge of the bed and wait until Mrs Mosley had returned with a tray full of enough food to feed a whole family. Marieke had thought herself too tense to be interested in food, but as soon as she saw the steam rising from the home-baked goods, her stomach grumbled eagerly. She'd forgotten how much the exertion of magical energy could deplete the body. She remembered being constantly hungry when preparing for practical examinations at the Academy of Song. And even in her final year, she'd never undertaken anything on as large a scale as what she'd just done. It was no wonder her body was crying out for sustenance.

She picked up a scone, downing it in three mouthfuls as her hostess watched on with a faint air of smugness.

"There, I knew you must be famished. Why are people always too polite to admit they're hungry? Myself, I love a good feed."

She lowered herself into a chair, her round cheeks warmed by a grin that Marieke couldn't help responding to in kind. The food was good, and it wasn't at any risk of going to waste, not with the way her father was also helping himself.

"Now what questions did you want to ask me?" Mrs Mosley pressed.

Marieke straightened where she sat, lowering the apple she'd just raised to her lips. She was no investigator. Her questions would probably be clumsy compared to someone trained by the council to look into incidents like this. She'd just have to do her best.

"Have you ever had any accidents or disasters like this before?"

"Nothing like this," Mrs Mosley said. "Of course we have our share of little accidents around the farm, and setbacks in our harvests. And we're suffering under this blight like everyone else. But we've never had any catastrophes on a scale that threatened the whole farm until now."

Marieke nodded slowly. "And...can you think of anyone who might wish to do you a mischief?" She saw the other woman's brow crease, and hurried on. "Have you had any recent conflicts, I mean?"

"No, not to speak of," Mrs Mosley said slowly. "We get on with our neighbors in the general way."

Marieke fidgeted as she thought how to word her next question. "Do you know any singers? Have you ever had problems with magic of any kind?"

Mrs Mosley leaned forward. "Are you suggesting this was not only deliberate, but caused by magic?"

Marieke exchanged a look with her father, who'd also stopped eating now. "I don't know anything for certain," she said cautiously. "But I suspect it might have been."

Mrs Mosley looked genuinely astonished, her eyes wide with dismay. "Heavens preserve us! We can't fight against magical attack. Why would anyone use songcraft to set our farm on fire?"

"I don't know," said Marieke helplessly. "There's no benefit I can see. Which is why I wondered if someone did it purely out of spite."

"I can't think of a living soul who'd be so motivated to hurt us that they'd try to convince a singer to burn down our fields!" Mrs Mosley protested. "We don't have any quarrels like that with anyone, at least not that I'm aware of. And even if we did, why would a singer agree to attack us?"

Marieke shook her head slowly, fairly certain the woman wasn't hiding anything. "They wouldn't. The council regulates song-related services offered for hire. As you'd imagine, arson isn't on the approved list. Any singer who took part in something like that would be locked up."

"So I'd imagine," Mrs Mosley agreed.

"In any event," Marieke went on, "the fire should be reported to the Council of Singers." She couldn't restrain a sigh as she added, "I suppose I ought to travel to the capital with the messenger and give my own report directly."

She caught the swift look her father threw her. He could obviously read her reluctance about the idea, and would surely have questions. After all, last she'd told him, she'd been hoping to be offered a position in the capital, and working for the Council of Singers had been her ideal option.

"Well, a messenger already went," Mrs Mosley said, smoothing her apron distractedly. "They won't report your suspicions, of course, but they'll tell the council about the fire." She must have seen her listeners' confusion because she added with a slight frown, "Every farmer I know is under instruction to report anything that threatens their crops. In case you hadn't noticed, our whole country is becoming more barren by the season."

"We had noticed," Marieke's father said heavily. "We'll be headed for a famine if something doesn't change."

"Well, we can't do anything to change it," Mrs Mosley said, her frown deepening. "That's the council's job. Singers are supposed to be the ones who can manipulate the land and keep things healthy." Her face softened a little as she nodded at Marieke. "It's possible, as this one's proved. It's just a matter of willingness."

Marieke sat stiffly on the edge of the bed, all her earlier discomfort returning. "The Council of Singers do want to resolve the blight on the land," she felt compelled to say. "It's not that they aren't willing. But they don't know what's causing Oleand to deteriorate, and they don't know how to magically fix a problem this pervasive."

"Don't you worry, dear, we're not going to march on your council or pull down your academy." There was a hint of indulgence in Mrs Mosley's voice as she stood. "I'll go and double check whether the messenger already left."

Marieke watched the older woman bustle out of the room, aware that she placed no stock in Marieke's reassurances. Mrs Mosley would assume that Marieke spoke out of blind loyalty, duty-bound as a singer to defend their ruling council.

And she wasn't entirely wrong. After all, it wasn't as though Marieke was rushing to share all her thoughts. She believed she'd spoken the truth that the council didn't know how to fix the affliction on the land. But was it really true that they had no idea what was causing it, and would do all in their power to find out if they could?

Marieke turned the apple over in her hand, her eyes on its smooth red skin as her thoughts flew back over the months. Apples always made her think of Zev now. This one surely couldn't be as sweet or juicy as the ones she'd eaten at his farm. Was his beloved orchard continuing to thrive? No doubt it was, given Aeltas wasn't affected by whatever was eating Oleand away from the inside.

Marieke's unease grew as she remembered all she'd learned during her time with Zev—and all he'd continued to withhold. Most troubling was the ruined trade city of Port Taran, from which the deposed royals had supposedly fled to exile on the far-off continent of Providore. Even after generations, the marks left on the city seemed to support the version of history Zev had been taught—a version in which the royals weren't exiled but hunted, pursued as they fled to the port and massacred in cold blood.

Marieke put the apple back on the tray, her appetite gone as cold fear stole over her, just as it had done when Zev had first challenged what she'd been taught. Could Oleand be under a curse, caused by the slaughter of the royals so long ago? A slaughter carried out by singers—the predecessors of the current council.

If that was so, she wasn't certain that the council would

truly wish to identify the cause of the blight, or be willing to do all in its power to resolve it. Not anymore. Not since she'd experienced the council's treatment of her for the crime of being exposed to information they might not wish her to have.

But she couldn't say all this to Mrs Mosley. She couldn't even say it to her father. What would they do with the information? With nothing certain, it would be not only a burden to them, but a dangerous one.

Marieke pulled her thoughts away from the spiral they'd been stuck in for the last month, the one where she battled with the uncomfortable realization that if the council couldn't be trusted to genuinely pursue the truth about what was happening to Oleand, someone else would have to.

And she seemed to be the only one who was asking the right questions, with the exception of a former student, Jade, whom she very much feared had been permanently silenced for her questions.

At least, she was the only one in Oleand. Inevitably, Marieke's thoughts flew back to Zev and his family, so unlike the other farmers she knew. They weren't exactly asking questions, but he'd certainly seemed to know a great deal she didn't.

Most of which he'd declined to tell her.

Scowling, Marieke once again tried to push him from her mind. However much her heart ached over his absence, he'd made it clear that whatever Oleand was suffering wasn't his fight. There was no use looking to him to help her figure things out. Which meant that she would have to pursue other means of helping her country. She couldn't do it alone, and whatever risks were involved in seeking out the council, everyone who could help her was in the capital.

"What will you do if the messenger has already left?" Her father's quiet voice broke into her reverie.

She looked up to find his eyes on her, his gaze unusually piercing.

"I think I'll need to travel to the capital anyway," she said.

He sighed, the sound resigned. "You're not coming home with me today, are you?"

She gave him a twisted smile of apology. "I don't think so. I won't leave for the capital until I've had a chance to have a proper look around here, though."

"Well, I don't doubt the Mosleys will be happy to house you," he said, pushing himself to his feet. "But I imagine our friends would also be willing."

"That's a good idea." Marieke brightened at this mention of the family whose horse her father had just treated. She had a feeling the Mosleys' gratitude could get stifling if she stayed where she was. "I'm not the expert you are, but I know enough about horses that I can probably be helpful in monitoring the mare's progress."

"True." Her father nodded. "You can send me a report in a day or two. I'll speak to them before I leave, if you like."

"I'll come with you." Marieke stood as well. "I won't be around more than a week, I'm sure."

With a final glance at the apple lying abandoned on the tray, she followed her father from the room.

As it happened, she was in Bull Creek for only half the predicted week before a group from the capital arrived. Marieke was surprised by the efficiency—the singers must have been dispatched the moment the report regarding the fire was received.

She had mixed emotions when news of the arrivals reached her. It would probably be safer for her to make her report to these envoys than to the council itself. But she'd been hoping for more time. She'd learned very little from her inexpert investigation. No natural cause for the fire had been identified, yet no one had seen or heard anything unusual. And she'd spoken to what felt like half the town.

Most people seemed to have concluded that the fire had a natural cause, but Marieke knew what she'd sensed. Magic had definitely been involved. And it had felt much stronger and more targeted than the magic she'd sensed when Gorgon had almost drowned her from a distance. She still had no explanation for how magic had been involved in the attack from the canyon-dwelling rebel—who definitely wasn't a singer. But the trace of the magic had been faint and confusing. By comparison, the magic in the fire had been familiar, at least in form. It was surely the targeted magic of an active song, which she'd experienced countless times when training with other students at the academy.

In any event, whoever was behind it must be smarter and more careful than Gorgon and his group had been, to leave no trace of their presence. If Marieke hadn't happened to be there and to have felt the magic herself, there would be no reason whatsoever to think a singer had been involved.

Marieke joined the group of curious locals trickling into the center of town to see the arrivals from the capital. She told herself that her nerves were unjustified. The council wouldn't have sent anyone senior or important in this little group. It wasn't as though she was about to see the Head Instructor. In fact, no one from the academy would be sent to investigate a fire.

The thought had barely crossed her mind when she emerged into the town square and caught sight of the delegation. She paused in surprise as she realized that the group did indeed include an instructor from the Academy of Song. But

Instructor Oriana was one of the friendliest people Marieke knew, and her presence was no cause for anxiety.

Marieke started walking again, her eyes scanning the group and widening further as they landed on yet another familiar face. Thankfully, this one was even more welcome than Instructor Oriana. Marieke picked up her pace as she strode across the clearing, her hand raised in greeting.

"Solomon!"

THREE

Zev

Zev's muscles strained as he lifted the bale of hay, depositing it on top of the others in the corner of the barn. Four more to go and he was done.

The impatience wasn't like him. He wasn't generally in the habit of counting down his tasks. But lately he'd been finding indoor work increasingly oppressive. He wanted to be out in the open air, where he could breathe and think.

Or at least that's what he told himself. It was better than acknowledging that what he really wanted was to be back on the road, heading northward. Never before had he felt restricted or trapped on his family's farm, and he hated that he felt that way now.

But he didn't hate the cause of his restlessness. He didn't even resent her. None of this was her fault, after all. If anything, she was the one who should resent him. She probably did.

Not for the first time, her face appeared in his mind's eye, her voice clear in his ears, right down to the shyness of her tone, uncharacteristic as that was for her.

I'm not really done looking for answers. Perhaps we can try to unravel it all together.

She'd looked so hopeful as she said it. Zev didn't think himself conceited, but he would have had to be blind to miss her meaning as she'd shifted toward him in that moment. She'd been so near, her skirt swishing against his legs with the movement as she'd tilted her face up toward his.

She'd wanted him to stay with her, to help her with the overwhelming task of trying to solve Oleand's troubles. But it was more than that. She'd wanted *him*. Unless he was mistaken, she'd wanted him to kiss her again, like he had after he'd almost been too late to stop Gorgon from killing her.

A thrill that was some tangled mixture of pain, elation, and regret passed over Zev as he heaved the final hay bale into place. It didn't feel conceited to acknowledge what Marieke had wanted. He'd wanted the same thing, after all. But instead he'd walked away, constrained not just by his own circumstances, but by generations of complexity.

And he wasn't conceited enough to assume she was pining for him. It had been a month—a long and restless month—since he'd left her. She may be angry with him for entangling her in whatever had started to grow between them and then just abandoning her. Or she may have gotten past any attraction she'd felt. She may be too consumed with trying to solve her country's troubles to think of him at all.

Or, a hard, cynical voice said in his mind, *she might have gotten herself hurt, imprisoned, or even killed by her council in her attempts.*

He tried to push the dark thought aside, as well as the guilt that came with it. When he'd left Marieke, he hadn't thought her in imminent danger from her country's Council of Singers. Not if she kept her head down. But as the weeks had passed without any contact with her, his certainty had ebbed. How long would she lie low for? If he knew her, not much longer. And he'd left her all alone in her fight, in spite of knowing that at least one member of the Oleandan council would be untroubled to see her dead.

But what could he have done? If he'd stayed with her, he'd be embracing a fight that wasn't his. And he'd be consumed with guilt over abandoning his family instead of abandoning her. After all, they had just as much to lose. More. Surely his first loyalty should be to his own flesh and blood, not to a girl he'd only known a matter of months, no matter how captivating.

So why did he feel like he'd betrayed himself by leaving Marieke behind?

"Zev!"

Azai's voice from outside the barn broke into Zev's thoughts, the sharpness of the tone catching his attention. Something was wrong.

Zev strode from the building, his muscles tensed as his eyes scanned the area. He spotted his brother quickly, standing near the front gate with his eyes fixed on something outside the property. Zev joined him in a few swift paces, searching the trees on the far side of the dusty road.

"What is it?"

"That." Azai pointed.

Following his gaze, Zev squinted at the object caught in the trees. It was a large, white rectangle, although it had lost its shape somewhat, tangled as it was in the branches.

"Is that parchment?" He frowned at it.

"Looks like it, doesn't it?" Azai agreed.

Zev raised an eyebrow at his brother. "A loose bit of parchment is what made you call for me like you were under attack?"

Azai rolled his eyes. "You're exaggerating. And it's not just a loose bit of parchment. There's something not natural about it."

"Why do you say that?" Zev asked.

"I saw it get tangled up," Azai said. "It was wafting back

and forth, like a kite on a string, but there's no string, and there was no wind. Barely a breeze, definitely nothing that matched the parchment's movement."

"That is strange," Zev acknowledged.

Maybe Azai could hear in his tone that he wasn't entirely convinced, because he added, "It's not just that. I could feel something when it was approaching. Something in me responded to it."

"Something in you?" Zev repeated.

"Not in me, exactly." Azai seemed to be searching for words. "In…"

"The land," Zev finished for him. He turned his eyes back to the parchment, taking his brother more seriously. The connection he felt to the land didn't belong just to him. It played out differently for other members of his family, but it was just as real. If Azai said that the land had given some kind of indefinable response to the presence of the strange object, Zev believed him.

"Come on," he said, vaulting the section of fence on which he'd been leaning. "Let's have a closer look."

Azai followed him across the wide strip of dirt that served as the road to their farm. Zev pulled himself up onto a boulder lying on the far side, to better search the branches above him.

He knew instinctively where the family's property ended, and it didn't seem coincidental to him that the parchment was just outside the boundary line. Squinting at it, he realized that it didn't look like normal paper.

"It's sort of waxy," he commented to Azai, who was climbing the boulder. "To make it weatherproof, I suppose."

"Is it a proclamation of some kind, intended to be posted in a village square or something?" Azai speculated.

Zev shook his head slowly, grabbing a nearby branch to steady himself as he leaned upward. "I don't think so. Look—

there's writing on it, but it's too small for a proclamation. It looks more like lists."

It was hard to read any of the words, especially with the way the parchment was twisted around a branch, but Zev could see that the page was about half full. Straining his eyes, he caught a few words.

"It looks like an inventory of the area," he said. "Crops, acreage..."

He trailed off as Azai swung himself into the relevant tree, climbing up until he was close to the parchment.

"You're right!" Azai declared, scanning a line of the neat, even writing. "I think this last part is describing the farm just west of here! And—" Azai's words cut off with a gasp after this mention of their neighbor.

"What is it?" Zev asked sharply.

"More words are appearing!" Azai said. "At the bottom here! But it's slow, like the words are struggling."

Zev scaled the tree quickly, holding his balance on a branch just below the parchment. "You're right," he breathed. It was like watching someone trying to write by the light of a candle that was sputtering out. Except there was no someone. The words were just appearing.

And disappearing, he realized with a start as he watched a word erase itself letter by letter, replaced sluggishly with a correction. Zev's gaze was drawn to his brother's movement, and he held out a restraining hand.

"Stop, Azai! Don't touch it."

Azai paused, his fingers an inch from the edge of the parchment. "Why not?"

"There's obviously magic involved," Zev said. "A singer must have enchanted it. Possibly multiple singers, who knows?"

"All the more reason to get hold of it and destroy it."

Zev wasn't looking at Azai, but he could hear his brother's scowl in his tone.

"I think it's some kind of tracking document, Azai," he said impatiently. "If it has a description of the next farm over, it must have some magical method of taking in information from what's around it. Who knows what it might record about you if you touch it?" He sent his brother a piercing look. "Or about our family if you take it into our home?"

"I don't need to take it inside in order to burn it," Azai muttered. But he'd already withdrawn his hand. "So what do we do with it? You want to just leave it there?"

Zev considered the matter. "No, I don't like the idea of it hovering here," he said. "Not if it's recording information." It would be like having someone hiding in the tree, spying on them. "Let's prod it free with a stick and see what it does."

"You want to free it to enter our property and make notes of everything it sees?" Azai protested in outrage.

Again Zev took a moment before responding. "No," he said at last. "If it enters our property, I think we should destroy it rather than let it leave again."

"Finally you're talking some sense." Azai wrapped a leg around a thick branch to steady himself as he pulled a dagger from his hip. With a few swift strokes, he hacked himself a stave of sorts from the tree.

Zev watched as Azai pushed and poked at the parchment with his stick, trying to get it loose. It was properly tangled in the branches, but eventually he managed to free it. At once, it took to the air, and Zev instantly saw what Azai had meant. The way the parchment darted from side to side definitely wasn't a natural response to any wind Zev had ever experienced.

As the parchment swooped toward the nearby road, both brothers tensed. But they didn't need to. The mysterious item didn't make it onto their property, once again thwarted by the line of trees that marked its edge. Zev felt a rush of what he thought was elation at this protection of his home. But as the feeling shifted and subsided upon the parchment going still, he realized it was more than just emotion. It was more like intuition, and it had seemed to come not from his heart or his head, but up from his feet.

Interesting. Just like Azai had said, the land had somehow responded to the parchment's approach. Specifically, *their* land. Their family's property.

"What do we do now?" Azai asked. His expression was disgruntled, but Zev caught the smile in his words. He was also pleased that their farm remained un-breached.

By way of answer, Zev snapped his own rod from a nearby tree, pulling himself hand over hand until he could reach the parchment. He deftly inserted the stick into the folds of waxy paper, flicking it away from the entangling foliage.

Again it flew toward their farm, and again it didn't make it. The brothers had to redirect it four more times before it eventually gave up and drifted off toward the north.

"It won't find much that way," Azai said in satisfaction. "It'll be at Sundering Canyon before long." He frowned. "Unless you think it will try to find another way onto our farm."

With a casual flick, Zev sent his makeshift rod spinning into the undergrowth. "If it does, I have a feeling it won't have any more success than it did here."

"It was more than just luck, wasn't it?" Azai said, following Zev as he strode across the dusty road and through their gate. "Do you think the land somehow kept it off our property?"

Zev ran a hand across the back of his neck in thought. "Seems that way."

"Huh." Azai sounded pleased, and Zev could understand why. "I guess generations of defensive power have had some effect."

"Of course they have," said Zev, a touch of impatience in his voice as his gaze darted over his shoulder, scanning the solid line of trees that bordered their property and taking in the glimpses of the closest circle of hills beyond. He knew his history. Neither feature of the land had been there when his ancestors first settled in this area.

He understood Azai's surprise, however. Subtle changes to the land over generations were one thing. Whatever had happened with the parchment was more immediate. More concrete.

Was their power getting stronger, or was the magic of the Council of Singers getting more aggressive?

"Too bad the defensive effect isn't broader. It would be great if it could keep out not just enchanted objects but the singers who create those enchantments," Azai said. His voice dropped to a mutter that he nevertheless clearly wanted Zev to hear. "One in particular would have been nice."

"Let it go, Azai," said Zev in irritation, his moment of fellow feeling with his brother fleeing rapidly.

Azai scoffed. "Let it go? I don't think I'm the one who needs to hear that advice."

Zev felt his face set like steel. He refused to engage with the conversation.

"Seriously," Azai pressed, unwilling to drop it as usual. "You've been moping ever since you came back from Oleand. If Ramsey hadn't spilled your secret, would you have even told us you were with Marieke the whole time you were across the border?"

Zev gave a grunt of annoyance. "Don't be a fool, Azai. None of it was a secret. And Marieke wasn't with us the whole time we were there. How many times do I have to tell you that I ran into her by coincidence, not design?"

"Then it's quite the coincidence," Azai said dryly. "You

know one Oleandan, and that's who you run into, in the whole country? You expect me to believe it wasn't by design?"

"Well, not by my design anyway," said Zev. "Or hers. So if you're determined to believe it wasn't coincidence, maybe we should conclude that the power of the land brought us together again. In which case, who are we to protest?"

Judging by his scoff, Azai was unimpressed with this argument. "You weren't in Aeltas, Zev. You were in Oleand. Even if that land had power—which I doubt, given the way it's dying and crumbling from under its people's feet—then it would have no reason to respond to your presence. It wouldn't bring you together with anyone."

Zev frowned. Something in Azai's words tickled at the back of his mind. More specifically, the part of his mind trying to understand what was happening to Oleand. He pushed the thought aside, reminding that corner of his thoughts yet again that it wasn't his mystery to solve. He would be wisest to stay well away from whatever was destroying Oleand from the inside.

Again that ghost of an idea wafted just out of reach. This time it was Azai's words which forced it further afield.

"So don't try to portray yourself as being thwarted of your fate or any nonsense like that."

Zev gave him a pitying look. "I'm not trying to portray myself as anything. What are you yammering about? It's that parchment we should be focused on."

Azai subsided with a grunt. "That's true enough. What are we going to do about it?"

"Tell Father, first of all," Zev said absently. That part was a given. With some glaring exceptions relating to a certain dark-haired Oleandan singer, he didn't keep important information from his family.

His conscience tugged at him, remembering how his

brother had just accused him of wanting to keep his interactions with Marieke a secret. Azai was closer to the truth than he realized. But Zev couldn't see anything to be gained from telling any of them about the kiss he and Marieke had shared—the one that still kept him awake at nights. And he couldn't bring himself to tell them that she was straying perilously close to investigating heartsong in her search for answers about Oleand's deterioration. Even though his family would undoubtedly want to know that information.

Traitor, whispered a voice in his mind. He scowled at no one in particular, wishing he could tell his conscience to either pick a side or shut up. It couldn't punish him both for abandoning Marieke out of loyalty to his family *and* for keeping things from his family in a bid to protect her.

Or at least, it shouldn't be allowed to. Clearly it had found a way.

"Yes, Father will know what to do." Azai was mercifully unaware of Zev's thoughts.

"How about you tell Father?" Zev said abruptly. "I'll try to follow it, see where it goes."

Azai stared at him. "I thought you said you didn't think it would be able to get onto our property."

"I don't," Zev said. "But it doesn't hurt to make sure of it."

He turned on the words, not waiting to see if his brother found his excuse convincing.

FOUR

Marieke

"Solomon!"

Marieke called his name again, and this time the assistant instructor turned. Recognition flashed through his eyes, and Marieke was relieved to see his face relax into a friendly smile. Whatever ill will she'd created at the council, Solomon didn't seem to be affected by it.

"Mari! What are you doing here?"

"I live here," she said brightly, crossing the last of the distance between them. "Or at least, not here in Bull Creek, but in this region. My home is only a couple hours' ride away." She directed her smile toward the woman standing beside Solomon. "Instructor Oriana. It's good to see you again."

"Marieke," the instructor greeted her. "You too. I didn't expect to find a graduate out here. I thought you were planning to stay and work in the capital."

"I've been visiting my parents," said Marieke. "I'm afraid I haven't quite figured out what I want to do with myself, so I'm not using my songcraft much yet."

The instructor looked surprised at this declaration from Marieke, who had been a determined and driven student. But she made no comment, perhaps thanks to Mr Mosley joining the conversation.

"Is Mari here being modest again? Don't let her tell you she isn't using her singing abilities! She used them to save my farm! And all our farms, probably. We'd be in true strife if not for her."

"Is that so?" Instructor Oriana and Solomon both turned interested faces toward Marieke, who felt her cheeks going pink.

"It was fortunate I was on hand and able to help, but Mr Mosley exaggerates my role."

"What poppycock!" Mr Mosley contradicted. "I ain't exaggerating anything."

Marieke was about to protest further when a memory forcibly asserted itself—of her having much the same argument with Zev when he tried to downplay his part in thwarting various of Gorgon's attacks. She snapped her mouth closed.

"She stopped the fire with her voice," Mr Mosley continued. "Changed the wind, made it rain...things I'd never believe if I hadn't seen with my own eyes. All by herself!"

"Goodness." Instructor Oriana spoke mildly. "That's advanced songcraft for a solitary singer just out of the academy."

"I was careful," Marieke said quickly. "I did no more than was necessary to put out the fire. And I've stayed in the area since, monitoring the elements. I don't think my intervention had any unintended impact on the weather or environment."

The instructor's smile was indulgent. "I wasn't criticizing you, Marieke. I'm impressed—I'd forgotten that agricultural song was one of your key areas of study. And frankly, I'm relieved. We left the capital in a hurry when we received the report of another huge wildfire. We didn't know what we'd find, and I admit I was expecting things to be in a much worse state when we arrived."

"What do you mean *another* huge wildfire?" Marieke asked with a frown.

"This is the third one in the last fortnight," Solomon said gravely.

"I haven't heard anything about that!" And Marieke had thought she'd been keeping her ear to the ground for any major reports from the capital.

"The others were in different parts of the country," Solomon said. "It takes time for news to travel."

"Were the others caused by magic?" she asked quickly.

Instructor Oriana gave her a sharp look—it sat strangely on her round, friendly face. "We'll just get settled in, Marieke, and speak with the town elders. Then we can discuss these matters more fully somewhere comfortable."

Marieke accepted this dismissal with a nod, not averse to having the extra time to gather her thoughts. She hung back as the other singers followed Mr Mosley into the town hall that sat just off the central square. She'd prefer to tell her version of events in private anyway, rather than in the company of the local witnesses.

When the group from the capital emerged, Marieke was waiting. She fell in with the small crowd trailing along behind as the newcomers were guided toward the site of the fire.

"I don't suppose you can repair any of the damage?" Mr Mosley asked hopefully, as they all came to a stop near the blackened field.

"I'm afraid not," Instructor Oriana said, sympathy in her voice. "I'm no expert in agricultural song, but I don't believe there are any songs that can revive plants this badly destroyed."

"No, the crop is gone, I'm afraid," Marieke chimed in.

Instructor Oriana nodded sadly. "What I do have experience with is storytelling song, however. I can't fix the damage, but I can assess it. And maybe get a picture of what happened." She turned toward the destroyed crops, a look of calculation on her face.

"How can storytelling assess damage?" The whisper came from a local man standing just beside Marieke.

"Storytelling is a broad term," Marieke told him, her own voice quiet as well so as not to disrupt Instructor Oriana's process. "And a misleading one, because it makes the area of study sound insubstantial or primarily for entertainment. It's actually one of the hardest and most powerful types of songcraft. There are very few fully qualified storytellers, and Instructor Oriana is one of them."

"But what do they do?" the man asked. "Tell stories?"

Marieke shook her head. "The discipline of storytelling songcraft isn't about singers telling stories to other people. It's about magic telling stories to the singers. A singer qualified in storytelling can get the magic to tell them the story of what's in front of them—or in mundane terms, to provide an assessment of what they can see. For example, they could walk into a room and use a song to discover what and who might be in the room, without needing to see it with their eyes. That's how she'll assess the damage—she can sing a song that will read the state of the field and report it back to her."

The man nodded, looking impressed, but Marieke wasn't done. That cursory explanation gave Instructor Oriana far too little credit for the true scope of her capability.

"That's the basic level of skill," Marieke went on. "A really experienced storyteller can manipulate the magic such that it will tell them not just the story of the current situation, but the story that led to it. A powerful storytelling song will recreate the events that led to what's currently visible."

"They can see the past?" the man demanded.

"Not literally, but sort of," Marieke said. "They can get enough information about the past to make informed speculations about what occurred to bring us from that past to this present."

She could see she'd lost her listener with her increasingly convoluted explanation, so she didn't add her final point. After all, there was no need to go into the most impressive form of storytelling song, given that as far as she knew, Instructor Oriana couldn't harness it. Marieke didn't think anyone alive could do so. The ability to coax magic into telling the story of what was yet to come was so impossibly difficult to attain that not all experts on singing lore agreed that it was even possible. There were tales of it happening in the past, but Marieke's fellow students had believed them or not as they saw fit.

She smiled as she thought about the first time she'd heard of storytelling song, in a class led by Instructor Oriana, incidentally. Dazzled by the prospect, many students had signed up for the three-week introductory course, which was designed to test aptitude. Almost none had gone on to actually study it, after discovering how very difficult the skill was and how slowly they were progressing in spite of their hard work. For her part, Marieke had enjoyed the course immensely. She would have been glad to continue to do a full semester, if not more. But given most students didn't pursue it, the academy had allocated a small capacity for the class. It had been full both times she'd tried to apply for further study in the area. So she'd focused her energies on agricultural song instead.

Her reminiscing was cut off as Instructor Oriana began her assessing song. Thanks to all the practice she'd had during the instructor's classes, Marieke managed to keep her reaction internal. The good folk of Bull Creek didn't have equal success. She saw winces on all sides, and a few people actually covered their ears with their hands. Others just stared open-mouthed at the venerable instructor, who was standing with eyes closed and arms upraised as she released a song that sounded closer to a bat's screech than a bird's melodious chirp.

Off-key, Marieke's choral instructor would call it. It was a concept very difficult to explain to the majority of the population who were born without the capacity to sing and could simply never learn to make their voices do that. Difficult to explain to some singers, too, she thought, one eye twitching as Instructor Oriana's song changed, swelling from a simple assessment to some more specific task Marieke didn't recognize.

Needless to say, Instructor Oriana wasn't the one who taught choral class. In fact, rumor had it that the class had been introduced because of the storytelling instructor's inability to carry a tune. She was the cheeriest of academy members, liked by everyone. But there was simply no getting around the fact that her singing voice sounded like a cat being forced into a bathtub.

At least it didn't affect her strength, magically speaking. In terms of her grasp of magical theory and her ability to manipulate the magic of the land, she was among the best in the country. The academy required students to study pitch and rhythm and such concepts in choral class as a matter of presentation and professionalism in their craft. It had nothing to do with the effectiveness of their magic. Marieke had learned on her visit to Aeltas that the southern country didn't even have such a class.

Instructor Oriana's voice petered out, leading to a relaxing of the posture of everyone around her. The instructor must have noticed it but, bless her, she never seemed to let it trouble her. There was something to be said for knowing your limitations and not wasting time bemoaning them, Marieke supposed.

"What are your conclusions?" Solomon asked as soon as her

voice was silent. There was a frown on his face. "I didn't follow all of what you did, but it seemed as though your assessment was targeting that way." He pointed.

"Yes," said Instructor Oriana slowly. "The magic had a strange story to tell about the land over there."

"But that's not where the fire originated," piped up Mr Mosley. "It was more that way." He pointed as well, his arm several degrees off the direction of Solomon's.

"But you said you could find no sign there of what the cause might have been?" clarified Instructor Oriana.

"That's right."

"Should we examine the area you were assessing?" Solomon pressed.

She shook her head. "No. The story is clear. Whatever was there at the time of the fire isn't there now. We should return to the hall." Her eyes flicked to Marieke. "Or somewhere we can talk more comfortably."

Not until the older woman was looking right at her did Marieke notice how weary she looked. She'd forgotten for a moment that drawing tales from the land—always a discipline that required a high level of both skill and energy—was more demanding the further back in time you were reaching. It had been the better part of a week since the fire. Instructor Oriana must be exhausted.

"Of course," said Marieke quickly, picking up the silent message the singer was sending. "I've been staying with some friends of my parents', and I'm sure they'd be happy for us to retreat there for a rest." To rest, and to talk more openly about what they'd all sensed in their various investigations.

Instructor Oriana was quick to accept the offer. Soon she, Solomon, and a handful of others from the group had followed Marieke back to her lodgings and settled in the parlor for as private a conversation as they could hope for.

The older woman—who was clearly leading the investigating team—let out a sigh of relief the moment her round form relaxed into a chair. Her eyes drifted closed for only a couple of seconds before they flew open again, settling straight on Marieke.

"Let's not beat about the bush," she said. "It caught my attention earlier when you asked if the other fires had been caused by magic. And after examining that field, I'm even more interested. Why did you ask that?"

"Because I'm almost certain that this one *was* caused by magic," Marieke said. Without embellishment, she gave her account of the fire, finishing by explaining her intention to make her way to the capital to report it to the council.

"So you coming out here has saved me a trip," she said.

"I doubt that," Instructor Oriana said thoughtfully. "I suspect the council will be very interested in what you witnessed, and will want to hear it firsthand. You'd better return with us, I think."

Marieke suppressed a sigh. She'd been afraid they'd say that. But perhaps it was for the best. Perhaps returning to the capital would offer her an opportunity to pursue her own inquiries about whatever was happening to Oleand. It wasn't as though she was likely to make progress hiding out at her parents' home. No one in her little town knew anything about curses or hidden history or mysterious heartsong magic.

"What did you sense out there?" she asked boldly.

The instructor's kind face lowered in a frown. "Nothing as concrete as I'd like. But it was odd. The land's memory of the incident didn't make a great deal of sense. It was like it was telling me that the fire started in one direction, but came from another."

"Could a singer start a fire from a distance?" Marieke asked.

"Absolutely," chimed in one of the other members of the

group. "Not from miles away or anything, but they wouldn't need to be right on top of it."

"All right, I need longer to recuperate, but the rest of you have no excuse for sitting around," said Instructor Oriana, her habitual friendly demeanor robbing the words of any imperiousness she might have been hoping for. "You all know what to do, get on out there and investigate. I want to be as efficient as possible in gathering whatever information there is to be had. Ideally, I'd like to be heading back toward the capital by the end of tomorrow."

There was a flurry of movement as the others obeyed. Marieke stood as well and followed them from the building, pleased when Solomon read her cue and paused in the doorway.

"Everything all right with you, Mari?" he asked. His delicate tone told her that he hadn't missed the tension the council had shown toward her.

She nodded. "I'm fine. Solomon, have there really been other fires as bad as this one?"

"Worse," he said. "And not just fires. There have been some unseasonal storms, and even a few tremors in areas that have never had them before. That's why they're drawing on singers from the academy to join the response teams. The council's own teams are stretched thin."

Marieke frowned. "And these mishaps are targeting singers like Gorgon's attacks?"

"No, not that anyone can tell." Solomon swept an arm toward the Mosleys' decimated field. "I mean, no singers live in this community, do they?"

"Good point." Marieke bit her lip, worried.

Solomon glanced around, then lowered his voice. "Officially no one is pointing out any connection between the various events."

Marieke snorted. "They're hoping people just won't notice that they're frantically dispatching investigative teams the moment news of any calamity reaches the capital?"

"Well…" Solomon smiled reluctantly. "I guess they are, but I doubt anyone really thinks no one's noticing. Unofficially the prevailing theory seems to be that these fires and storms and the like are further evidence of the land's deterioration. The next step in whatever ailment is making Oleand fail."

"It's a logical conclusion," Marieke said slowly. "But my account doesn't fit with that, does it? The magic I felt makes it look more like sabotage than an aberration in the power of the land."

Solomon nodded. "Which is why Instructor Oriana thinks —and I agree—that the council will be very interested in what you have to say."

"That would be quite the change."

Her muttered aside brought Solomon's head snapping toward her, and she grimaced internally. She'd only half intended for him to hear.

"Well," she forced her voice into a brighter tone, "it looks like we'll be traveling together again."

"Yes," said Solomon, still considering her thoughtfully. "It looks that way."

FIVE

Zev

In spite of his genuine curiosity about the parchment, Zev felt faintly cowardly as he entered the barn and saddled up his preferred mare. He could only hope it hadn't been too obvious to Azai that he had the secondary motive of avoiding being questioned by their father regarding matters of magic.

Azai wasn't the only one who'd been a little off in manner toward Zev since his return from Oleand. They didn't know the half of what had passed between him and Marieke, and it was still enough to make them edgy.

It all just reiterated Zev's opinion that his family's judgment of Marieke was unjust. He simply couldn't recapture the confidence he'd once felt in his father's wisdom—the same confidence that made Azai so sure that the older man would know how to handle this latest development.

By the time he rode out of the farm's gate, the parchment had a sizable head start, but Zev didn't doubt he could catch it. Sure enough, he was only halfway down the length of his property when he encountered it again, drifting along the boundary line. The way it moved was so unnatural, it sent an unpleasant ripple up the back of his neck. It reminded him of a puppet, jerking and jumping disjointedly as its strings were pulled. Except whoever was pulling those strings couldn't be seen.

Zev's thoughts flew to the member of the Aeltan Council of Singers whom he'd met when he'd accompanied Marieke to the capital, Tarandon. He'd been as insufferable and self-important as Zev had always imagined council members to be. It was easy to picture him smugly pulling on invisible strings, controlling the country as he liked.

Once the parchment reached the end of Zev's property, it picked up speed. It had apparently given up trying to enter their holdings, but it didn't continue on toward Sundering Canyon as Azai had predicted. Instead it turned west, heading toward the farm belonging to Ramsey's family.

Zev urged his horse onward, noting that the parchment slowed down again once it neared the boundary of Ramsey's property. It was as though it already knew where each farm began and ended, which was an unnerving amount of knowl-edge for an inanimate object. The parchment ignored the farm's gate, instead soaring up and over the small stand of spruce trees to one side of it. Unlike on Zev's farm, it had no problem clearing the trees. Zev had caught up enough to get a glimpse of the paper as it whooshed upward. There was defi-nitely more writing on it than there had been when it had been tangled in the branches across from his own gate.

Frowning, Zev turned away, making for the gate rather than pushing his way through the trees like a common thief. He felt an obligation to let his neighbors know that an unknown magical object had entered their property.

It was no surprise when Ramsey strode across the yard, eyes bright at the sight of his visitor. Zev had assumed the cheerful, talkative farmer would be there. It was rare for anyone in the region to go far from home, which was why Ramsey had been so unashamedly eager to join the group traveling to Oleand a short time before.

"Zev!" The younger man waved a hand enthusiastically over his head. "What brings you here?"

"Hello Ramsey," said Zev, swinging down from his horse. "I'm not entirely sure how to answer."

Ramsey raised an eyebrow. "Being cryptic, Zev? Does that mean Marieke is here somewhere?" He did an exaggerated sweep of the area with his head before returning his gaze to Zev, a grin on his lips.

Zev grunted, unimpressed when Ramsey's smile widened. Of course Ramsey couldn't resist baiting him—Zev had no difficulty recognizing the veiled reference to Marieke's complaints that Zev spoke to her in riddles.

Ramsey's banter didn't bother him. What bothered him was the possibility of Ramsey seeing how affected he was by the mention of Marieke.

"I'm not being cryptic," he said. "I don't know how to tell you what brings me here because I can't identify the item in question."

Ramsey frowned. "What item?"

"Some kind of magical parchment," Zev said. "It came to my property, then I followed it here. I just watched it fly over your property line and onto your farm."

"Show me," said Ramsey, his brows still pulled together.

He glanced around, spotting another man walking across the yard and summoning him with a whistle.

"Look after Zevadiah's mare, would you?" He sent Zev a swift smile. "Harvest is so good this year, Father's hired some extra hands."

Zev relinquished his horse before striding toward the back

of the stand of trees. It took only a minute to locate the parchment, which was speeding away toward a wheat field.

"What is that?" Ramsey demanded.

He sounded more intrigued than alarmed, his steps overtaking Zev's. When he reached the item, it was hovering over the crops, low enough to touch. Before Zev could discourage him, he'd reached out and snatched it from the air.

"Zev, look at this!" he called. "It's unbelievable!"

"I'm not sure you should be touching it," Zev said. "It's clearly magical."

Ramsey just laughed. "Trust you to be overly cautious, Zev. At least any time magic is involved. Look at it! It's recorded the size of this field. And look!" His voice grew in excitement as words continued to appear on the page apparently of their own accord. "It's calculating the likely yield! That could be handy."

Zev made a noise in the back of his throat. "I could tell you the likely yield without any magic involved."

"So could I, but this might save time," Ramsey said reasonably. His eyes were bright as he looked up at Zev. "This is incredible, isn't it? I've never seen anything like it." He scanned the page again, his head slowly shaking as he recognized details of their familiar region. His brow suddenly puckered, however. "Hold on, I thought you said it had been to your farm."

"That's right," said Zev cautiously.

"But there's nothing on here about your land," Ramsey said.

Zev cleared his throat. "It floated past on its way down the main track, but it didn't actually come onto our property."

"That's odd, isn't it?" Ramsey asked.

"Is it?" It wasn't hard for Zev to keep his expression neutral. He'd been keeping secrets all his life. Knowing that less was more in such situations, he didn't elaborate on his answer.

"Hm, looks like you're right," Ramsey said. "I shouldn't be touching this." In spite of his words, he didn't sound troubled. Zev followed his pointing finger to see a message written across the bottom of the parchment in bold letters.

Official survey of the Council of Singers. Please do not interfere with this item.

The warning was accompanied by an image of a budding tree in bronze and blue ink. It was the symbol of the Aeltan Council of Singers.

"So this really is a magical item," Ramsey mused. He frowned as he ran his thumb over the council symbol. "But I thought the knowledge of how to make talismans had been lost generations ago."

"So I understand," Zev said. "I don't think this is a talisman —I don't think magic is stored in it. It's probably a normal object being moved about by magic."

"You're probably right." Ramsey rubbed the back of his neck. "What do you think it means by an official survey?"

"They're obviously taking stock of the land," Zev said. "For what purpose, I don't know." He felt his brow furrow. "I'd like to find out, though." He jerked his head toward the parchment Ramsey still held. "Let go of it and let's see where it's headed."

After one last look, Ramsey complied. They watched as the parchment fluttered over the wheat field before circling back toward the farmhouse.

"Come on." Zev was already on his way back to the yard, ready to reclaim his mare. "You coming?"

"Of course."

There was a spring in Ramsey's step as he came alongside, obviously glad of any excuse to postpone his usual chores. He certainly didn't seem to share Zev's concern as to the intention of whoever had sent out this survey.

They were saddled up in no time, and able to follow the parchment as it completed its final circuit of the property and soared back over the boundary. To Zev's relief, it followed the road for some time, providing an easy route for their horses. When it did eventually turn and head across the grassy hills, they urged their mounts after it.

"This is the most exciting thing that's happened since our Oleand trip," said Ramsey with his signature grin.

Zev cast a pointed look around the quiet hills, bathed in sunlight. A light breeze was rippling the grass, and in the distance a flock of birds could be heard cawing as they took off from a stand of pines. Closer at hand, the slow flight of a passing honeybee was the only movement—barring the parchment.

"Would you call this exciting?"

"I would," Ramsey said staunchly. "It's like a chase. Especially now that our quarry seems to be in a rush."

Sure enough, the parchment had stopped wafting back and forth. It was moving forward steadily, a constant and targeted breeze urging it onward in a southwesterly direction. Zev had a feeling it was heading back to some kind of base, and he wanted to be on its metaphorical heels when it arrived.

They followed it for almost two hours before it finally reached its destination. By that time it had cleared the ring of low hills that surrounded the region. The plain area beyond sat between the rich farmland of Zev's home and the capital city of Tarandon, further to the southwest. It was a familiar area, and the presence of several large tents therefore stood out starkly.

"What's that?" Ramsey interrupted his own chatter to point to the tents.

"I think that's its base," Zev said.

As if in confirmation, the parchment sped forward and disappeared into one of the tents. Zev pulled his horse up a safe distance away, frowning as he scanned the set up. A few people were coming and going between the tents in a leisurely way. A second look showed Zev that each tent sported a banner with the symbol of the Council of Singers.

"Let's go." Ramsey seemed excited, but Zev put out a hand to stop his friend.

"Hold on. It might not be wise to show ourselves."

Ramsey just laughed. "It's an official group from the council, Zev, not a bunch of traveling bandits. What are you afraid of?"

He spurred his horse across the grass, Zev following with a sigh. He dismounted near the entrance to the tent where the parchment had disappeared. To his surprise, no one appeared to challenge their entrance. To his even greater surprise, when he tried to stride into the tent, he found himself bouncing backward as if he'd run into an invisible wall.

"Magically protected from intruders," Ramsey commented cheerfully. "That's proof these people are singers, in case the council symbols weren't enough." He eyed Zev sideways. "Oh, is that why you're reluctant to approach? You don't like singers, do you? Well..." His annoying grin was back. "With one exception."

"Of course that's not why," said Zev shortly. "I'm not reluctant."

It wasn't entirely true, but he tried to convince himself it was. Turning away from Ramsey, he raised his voice.

"Hello in there?"

After a moment, a stranger popped his head out of the tent, eyeing the two of them. "Can I help you?"

"Hopefully," said Ramsey before Zev could speak. "We followed that flying parchment here. We want to know what it is."

The man sighed, clearly irked at being interrupted from whatever essentially important work he was doing for the council.

"It's the surveyor." He took in Zev's posture, arms folded. "And you two had better not have interfered with it."

"We didn't," Ramsey assured him, his compliance only making Zev feel more mutinous.

"Although we could argue our right to do so if it enters our land without authorization or even notice," Zev said. Judging by the way the council worker's eyes narrowed, his mild tone wasn't fooling anyone.

"The Council of Singers has authority over all land in Aeltas," the man said crisply, blissfully unaware that his choice of words had his listener bristling. "The surveyor was sent under the council's express instruction and is fully within its jurisdiction to enter farms in this region."

"But what is the surveyor?" Ramsey asked.

The man's eyes flicked to the younger farmer, and his posture relaxed. "It's a document assessing and recording the state of the farms around this region."

"Recording what about them?" Zev pressed. "And why this region?"

"Their capacity, health, and yield." The man was growing visibly more impatient. "It's not just this region. We were instructed to start with this area, but we'll be undertaking a survey of the whole country."

"Is this because of that Oleandan delegation?" Ramsey asked, surprising Zev with the astute question.

The council worker also seemed surprised. "You've heard about the delegation, have you?"

"Of course we have." Ramsey laughed, glancing at Zev. "In fact, Zev here—"

"I heard all about it, too." Zev cut Ramsey off before he could describe Zev's involvement with the delegation. He'd drawn far too much attention to himself at the time, no need to repeat his errors. "Everyone was talking about it. Word is they were trying to find out if our land is failing like theirs, and if not, why not."

"That's about the sum of it," the council worker said, nodding in reluctant acknowledgment of Zev's accuracy, while Ramsey gave him an odd look.

"So your survey is trying to ascertain the same thing?" Zev pressed. His thoughts were tense underneath his impassive expression. This type of enquiry was precisely what his family had been afraid of when they learned the purpose of Marieke's delegation.

"We have no need to ascertain that our land isn't failing." A hint of stiffness had entered the stranger's voice. "Aeltas continues to thrive as it always has under the leadership of our council."

Zev ignored this propaganda, returning to an earlier comment that had troubled him. "Why were you instructed to start in this region?"

"No idea." The singer spoke with a tone of finality, clearly ready to end the conversation. "That's not my decision. But it was a very clear directive. We were to start a dozen leagues northeast of the capital, just south of Sundering Canyon."

"Well, it is Aeltas's most fertile region," Ramsey said, sounding smug.

The council worker just shrugged, both of them oblivious to the alarm racing over Zev. The man's description of the region precisely matched what he'd been obliged to tell the council member he'd met in the capital, when he was there with Marieke. The council member had been very interested when he'd heard where Zev was from. He'd called the region one of the country's crowning jewels. It had made Zev uneasy at the time to have his home recognized and singled out, but he'd told himself he was being overly cautious. Now all his misgivings came rushing back. Could this all be happening because of him?

"So our hard work and success is being punished by the council sending magic into our homes to spy on us without permission?" he challenged, his disgruntlement rising with his guilt.

"It's hardly a punishment," the man said, also irked. "And no one is being spied on. The surveyor merely gathers basic information about the land."

"Land that belongs to us," Zev said. "At least when the census happened, a real human knocked on our door, and didn't try to hide what they were doing."

The man eyed him with disfavor. "And a great deal of manpower it required. You should be glad that resources are being conserved thanks to the recent developments in communication songcraft—the enchantments on the survey parchment are newly designed. Now we don't have to send hundreds of singers all over the country to knock on doors."

"That's handy," said Ramsey, obviously feeling none of Zev's offense. "Much easier."

Contrarily, the singer didn't seem any more pleased with the praise than he had been with the criticism. "I wouldn't say easy," he sniffed. "It took a great volume of magic, and considerable finesse. The technique was only developed because there's been so much focus on the area of long-distance communication since the bridge was closed."

"How fortuitous," said Zev dryly.

"Yes, isn't it!" Ramsey had apparently missed his tone. "Does that mean parchments like that can be used to communicate with people in Oleand? Like a postal service that crosses the canyon using magic?"

"That's the eventual plan," said the stranger. "A formalized system is being developed. It will be much more efficient than going around by sea."

Not to mention your council won't want more people than necessary to explore Port Taran. Zev didn't speak the thought aloud. It would make no sense to either of his companions. Even the council representative probably didn't know the secrets hidden in the port city from which the long-dead royals had once attempted to flee the continent. But an astute person could find them. Especially an astute singer like Marieke. Given how determinedly the council taught an entirely different version of history, Zev could understand why it had been a priority to them to find a means of communication that would minimize traffic through the abandoned port city.

"We should go," Zev said abruptly, the words directed at Ramsey. He inclined his head stiffly to the council worker. "Thank you for your time."

The man gave an equally unenthusiastic nod before disappearing back inside the tent.

"That was bordering on rude, Zev," Ramsey said as they remounted their horses. His habitual cheerful tone robbed the words of reproach. "You really shouldn't judge someone just for being a singer."

"I don't," said Zev, directing his mare northeast. "I don't have a problem with singers."

He spurred his horse faster, not interested in exploring the topic. He had enough on his mind figuring out how he would break the news of this latest development to his family.

One thing was for certain—they weren't going to be happy.

And they would surely realize, as he'd done, that it was likely his initial assistance to Marieke that had instigated all of what was happening.

He had some uncomfortable conversations ahead.

CHAPTER

SIX

Marieke

Marieke had expected the rush of nerves she felt as the carriage pulled into the capital, Ondford. After all, she'd left a month before with the express purpose of avoiding further attention from a ruling council she no longer fully trusted. The same ruling council to which she was about to make an official report.

What she hadn't predicted was the other raft of emotions that tangled around her apprehension, muddying it. Last time she'd been in the city, she'd been with Zev. If she was perfectly honest with herself, she hadn't fled to her home just because she felt at risk from the council. She'd also been driven by something bordering uncomfortably close on heartbreak.

If only he was here with her now, she wouldn't feel as nervous about facing the council. His silent presence beside her last time she gave testimony had meant the world to her. She felt so much more vulnerable this time, all alone. She would really need to do something about that. After all, she'd told Zev she would be careful, and putting herself straight back in the council's target didn't feel careful.

Of course, she'd told Zev she'd be careful right before asking him to help her on her self-appointed mission. Which was also right before he rejected her appeal and drew back from her, both literally and emotionally. She was probably being foolish to think he'd be overly worried about her safety now.

What would he think of this latest turn of events? What would he think of her role? If he'd seen her stop the fire, would he be softened toward magic? Would he be impressed by her?

Embarrassed by her own thoughts, Marieke tried not to think about Zev at all. This task proved difficult when they alighted and Instructor Oriana led them right past the gardens that sat between the council and academy buildings.

The gardens where Gorgon had almost killed her.

The gardens where Zev had kissed her as though their very lives depended on the desperate movement of their lips. Where he'd held her as though someone would have to kill him to get between his body and hers.

See, that was the kind of thought that did nothing to help her peace of mind.

"Mari?"

She blinked, realizing belatedly that Solomon was speaking to her.

"Sorry, what did you say?"

"Will you be all right if I head back to the academy now? Or do you want me to stick around and help you settle in?"

"Thanks, but I'll be fine," she said quickly. His solicitousness brought back her earlier thoughts about her own vulnerability. "Actually, I was thinking I might go and find Kaine. Do you know if he's still stationed in the capital?"

"I believe so. I see him around occasionally."

Solomon seemed surprised at this mention of the singer who was a member of the council's guard. They'd both gotten to know him fairly well on their journey to Aeltas, but it seemed Solomon hadn't kept up the acquaintance since their return.

Marieke intended to, however. She didn't have many friends in the capital, and she could use all the help she could get.

Marieke barely deposited her bags in her allotted room in the council building before heading back out in search of the guard. She'd yet to be informed of when the council was likely to summon her, and she thought she'd be wise to make the most of whatever time she had. Who knew how quickly she'd be dismissed once her report was made?

She was fortunate to find Kaine walking out of the barracks. He welcomed her with a smile, gesturing for her to walk with him.

"Marieke! I didn't expect to see you. When did you return to the capital?"

"Just now," she said. "Where are you headed, Kaine? Have I caught you just as your shift is starting?"

He shook his head. "I've just come off duty, actually. Were you looking for me? Can I help with something?"

"I was," Marieke confirmed. "And I hope so. I was wondering if you'd be willing to teach me to defend myself."

He looked surprised. "Against who?"

She shrugged. "Anyone who might attack me, I suppose. I'm just regretting my decision not to ever take the combat elective at the academy."

"Of course you are." Kaine chuckled. "I said it to all my friends, everyone should study it for at least one semester. None of them listened to me."

"And now they regret it?" Marieke asked, falling into step beside him.

He laughed. "Sadly no, they still don't recognize my wisdom." He gave her a sideways look. "Apparently they don't anticipate the same dangers you do. That fall into Sundering Canyon really rattled you, huh?"

Marieke shuddered. "I'd rather not be reminded of it, thank

you very much." She still had nightmares about falling some-times. And it wasn't just the fall itself that kept her awake. That incident had been the start of all her problems.

Although, she admitted to herself, she wouldn't turn back time if she could. She wouldn't choose to return to her former ignorance.

"How long are you in Ondford?" asked Kaine.

"I'm not sure," Marieke admitted. "Possibly not long."

"Well, I've got a few hours now," he said amicably. "Give me ten minutes to eat something, and I can give you some basic pointers."

Marieke thanked him profusely, and met him in the training yard at the indicated time. She'd used the opportunity while he ate to check back in with Instructor Oriana. There had still been no summons from the council, so she assumed that in the meantime she was free to occupy herself how she pleased.

"All right," said Kaine, after he'd led her in a brief warm up exercise during which he'd scrutinized her critically. "Sorry to be blunt, but physical strength isn't your greatest asset."

Marieke grimaced in acknowledgment. She'd never under-taken any kind of training in combat, so it wasn't surprising.

"Since we have very little time, I think I'll focus on an area where you might have more success with less practice. Or at least, which you can practice later, without me here to help you."

"What area?" Marieke asked.

"Magic," he said simply. "I'll teach you some basics of combat song, rather than trying to teach you to be a physical fighter. You can't learn that all in a rush, anyway."

"But you can learn combat song in one session?" Marieke asked skeptically.

He laughed. "Of course not. But I can tell you some basics, and you can keep working on it."

"I'll take it," she said.

"I'm going to focus on one basic principle," Kaine went on. "I think it could be very helpful to you if you find yourself in a physical fight. And it's a concept you could keep working on without me, given you already have a graduate's level of magical ability."

Marieke nodded.

"It's called the principle of strategic distraction," Kaine said. "In concept, it's quite simple. It basically means using your body to fight in a certain way—like swinging your fist for a punch—but using your magic in a different way—such as causing a protruding root to shift and trip your opponent. The other fighter is focused on defending against your punch, and doesn't notice the moving root."

"But surely they'd notice I was singing," Marieke said, frowning.

"Of course," Kaine acknowledged. "But most people, especially those with no training in combat song, will subconsciously assume that your song is connected to what they can see—that is, the swinging fist. They'll think that you're using magic to enhance the strength of your fist."

"Which probably isn't a bad idea in itself," grinned Marieke, holding up that unimpressive part of her.

Kaine chuckled. "You could try that. But in your case, I think strategic distraction will be more, well, strategic."

"I suppose to sell the misdirection, I'd have to be careful what words I used in my song," she commented.

"Exactly." Kaine seemed pleased at her comprehension. "If you graduated, I assume you're proficient in basic masking skills?"

"Of course," Marieke said.

As Kaine knew, all students at the Academy of Song were taught the skill of masking their magic use from observers by avoiding using any words in their song which gave the task away. It required training and practice to mask song, because although the words of a song weren't actually the key to molding magic with it, simply telling the magic what to do with words was the easiest way when learning to control it.

"Good, because that's important in making strategic distraction work," Kaine said. "Really advanced combat singers will actually use masking offensively, but I won't try to get that detailed." He must have seen her confusion, because he explained, "They use words in their song that appear to tell the magic to do one thing while the power of their song directs the magic to do something completely different."

"That would take a lot of concentration," Marieke said. "I can't even imagine having that much focus while physically fighting for my life."

Kaine smiled. "Like any area of magic, it takes a lot of training and persistence to excel."

"Well, I don't need to excel," Marieke said. "Just to survive."

Taking her cue, Kaine moved from the theoretical to the practical part of her training. He very generously gave her two hours of his time, during which he taught her the basics of strategic distraction. Marieke understood the concept, at least. She wouldn't master it to assessment level, but she might be able to keep practicing it once she left the capital.

"That was good," Kaine said, watching critically as Marieke used her song to send a wind swirling through the training yard, blowing the punching bag out in the opposite direction from which she was pushing it with her arms. "It's a very solid start."

Marieke nodded in appreciation of the praise, letting her song peter out as she stepped back and wiped her brow with one sleeve.

"If I'm still in Ondford tomorrow, would I be allowed to use this training yard to practice more?" she asked.

"Absolutely," said Kaine. "Come find me, and I'll help you. If we have time, I'll get you started on some collaborative combat."

"Fighting in a team, you mean?" Marieke glanced around the yard, not eager to embarrass herself by joining forces with any of the experienced fighters currently training in the space.

"Specifically one aspect of it," Kaine clarified. "Since you're not a strong physical fighter—no offense—you might fight better in a team if you could focus on sharing your magic. As in, using it to give extra strength to the physical attack of another fighter."

"Interesting," said Marieke, her mind running through all the possible applications. "I have to say, I'm starting to think you were right. Every student should do combat for at least one semester. It's fascinating, and there are so many ways to use combat song!"

"Hah!" Kaine raised a fist triumphantly, drawing curious looks from the closest pair of guards. "A convert. I knew with training from a master such as me, you'd come around."

Marieke rolled her eyes, although she was grinning. "In my experience, boasting often hides inadequacy, or more specifically the fear of it being found out."

Kaine was undaunted by this dig. "Not in my case," he said. "My instructors all assured me I was the most promising student in my class. Usually when berating me for wasting my potential by not working hard enough."

"Hm." Marieke eyed him as they made their way out of the yard. "Do you think that's why you couldn't convince your friends to study combat with you? No one wants to sign up to be outshone."

"Whoa." Kaine gave her a look. "That must have been an insightful question. I actually felt that."

Marieke stared at him, bewildered. "What do you mean you felt it?"

"I felt the magic of it," he said. "You know that feeling, when the magic of the land sort of concentrates under your feet, ready for you to access it with song?"

"Yes," Marieke said slowly. "I know that feeling. I don't know what it has to do with my question, though."

Kaine shrugged. "It's not the first time I've noticed your questions having that effect. Magic pooled toward you when you asked about my friends. You weren't calling it on purpose, preparing to draw it out?"

Marieke shook her head, completely nonplussed. "Not at all. I have no idea how my questions could make magic pool. I've never heard of anything like that before."

"I have," Kaine said. "I believe it's a branch of storytelling song. You really haven't studied that skill? You must be a natural if you're doing it unconsciously. Did you take story-telling song?"

"Only the introductory course," said Marieke regretfully. "I wanted to continue, but the class was full."

Kaine raised an eyebrow. "That's unusual. I thought hardly anyone did storytelling. When I was at the academy, there were only about half a dozen students in that class at any given time. I can't imagine Instructor Oriana turning anyone away who wanted to study it. She was always trying to get extra students interested."

Marieke frowned, confused. The class had been equally small when she'd been a student, but she didn't remember ever hearing Instructor Oriana try to recruit more. She'd been under the impression that six was the absolute limit for the class. She vaguely remembered someone explaining that due to the complexity of the skill, the teacher needed significant one-on-one time with each student.

Kaine's experience and her own didn't quite add up.

She was so distracted by the mystery, she barely heard herself as she thanked him for his time and peeled away toward the council building. She made her way through the guest quarters, pleasantly surprised to discover that a meal had been delivered to her room. Along with it was a note requesting her to present herself in the council audience hall the following morning. Her heart jumped a little with nerves, but on the whole she thought it was good to get it over with.

She had difficulty falling asleep, her mind still turning over Kaine's comments. Had she really drawn magic toward her simply by asking a question? She hadn't been aware of it. But then, she found magic to sometimes behave unpredictably in the land beneath her feet, gathering and dispersing with no apparent logic. Was it possible she'd had more to do with that process than she'd realized? What a pity that she'd been unable to pursue storytelling song! Her questions might have been answered in that class. Her questions about her questions, she thought humorously, her mind growing foggy as sleep approached. There was a certain irony to it all, given her reputation during her studies of always asking too many questions.

When Marieke woke, the prospect of appearing before the council drove other considerations aside. After eating the simple breakfast provided to her, she made her way to the audience hall, bracing herself to face the scrutiny of the Council of Singers.

To her relief, however, the ordeal was much less intimidating than she'd expected. Last time, the whole council seemed to have gathered. This time, it was only three members who were waiting, along with Instructor Oriana, Solomon, and a handful of others from the group who'd traveled to Bull

Creek. And they were all seated together around the large table on the floor of the room, the raised seats remaining empty.

Marieke's shoulders had barely relaxed when tension returned to them as she scanned the group and realized that Instructor Rafael was one of the three on the far side of the table. The Academy's Head Instructor was a member of the Council of Singers by virtue of his office. He was also the man Zev had warned her against. He'd urged her not to trust the council completely. *Especially the Head Instructor*, he'd said, offering no explanation whatsoever for his warning.

Typical Zev.

Marieke had come promptly at the time stated on the note, so she was surprised to find so many people already there. After the greetings had been exchanged and Marieke had sat down, however, it quickly became clear that the meeting had been in progress for some time. For whatever reason, she hadn't been invited to attend from the beginning.

Instructor Oriana was giving a report on the team's investigation, but she'd barely started speaking again when Instructor Rafael interrupted.

"Since Marieke has arrived," he said, not meeting her eyes, "how about we hear the information she has to share? Then she can be free to go. No need to take up her whole day when the rest of our proceedings are irrelevant to her."

Especially the Head Instructor. Zev's words sounded again in Marieke's ears, accompanied by the image of his handsome face creased with concern, and something resembling anger.

Zev had apparently read the older man well. Of everyone in the room, the Head Instructor seemed by far the most concerned about keeping information away from Marieke. Why make such a point of secrecy if he had nothing to hide?

But of course he did have something to hide. The whole council did. They were hiding the true details of the coup during which the singers of old had overthrown the monarchies of the two kingdoms. The real question was how that secret could be threatened by Marieke gaining whatever information was being discussed in the present meeting.

"Certainly." Instructor Oriana smiled at Marieke. "I don't mind ceding the floor. Marieke is the only firsthand witness among us, after all." She gave her an encouraging nod. "Go on, Marieke."

"All right." Marieke cleared her throat, wiping her hands on her skirt under the table. Her palms were suddenly sweaty. "What do you want to know?"

"Just recount the events of the fire as comprehensively as you can," one of the other council members chimed in. "We've been given to understand that your observations are of particular interest."

"I'll let you be the judge of that," said Marieke, smiling weakly.

Clearing her throat again, she told her story, doing her best to explain the magical side of her observations in detail. It was gratifying to see that her descriptions made more sense to this audience than they had to her father. The brows of her listeners, which had lowered in displeasure at hearing of the angry magic that had seemed to fuel the fire, rose in surprise when she explained that when the wind finally stopped fighting her control, something magical snapped in the process. They understood the significance of what she was saying.

"So if you're right that magic started the fire, whoever manipulated that magic must have actually been right there," one of the council members said, one eyebrow still aloft. "Close enough to be urging their enchantment to fight yours."

"That was my conclusion as well," said Marieke.

"This certainly casts a different light on the incident,"

mused another council member. His eyes were piercing as they rested on her.

Marieke could feel Instructor Rafael watching her closely as well, but she avoided making eye contact. He certainly wasn't eager to speak and draw her attention.

"It sounds like you did very well, at any rate," said the first council member. "I imagine the local farmers are very grateful to you. It was very fortunate that you were present."

Marieke dipped her head, embarrassed by the praise but also pleased. It was reassuring to think that the whole council wasn't set against her.

"It was fortunate that I happened to focus on agricultural song in my studies," she said. "The skills I learned at the academy were what enabled me to assist."

"Well said." Instructor Oriana's voice held a definite note of humor. "Three cheers for our academy, eh? And I didn't even pay her to say that."

A ripple went around the group as everyone chuckled at the likable instructor's joke. Well, not quite everyone. Marieke noticed that Instructor Rafael remained solemn, his position as Head Instructor apparently not enough to make him join in the praising of his institution. She risked a direct look at him, but averted her eyes quickly when she found him studying her. He didn't look angry, as she'd thought he might. He looked...wary. That was more of a concern, if anything. It didn't seem safe for her to make him feel threatened.

"Fortunate indeed," the third council member said, also studying her closely. "Quite the coincidence, in fact."

Marieke didn't answer, not sure what to make of his tone. Did he find her story suspicious? Perhaps even wonder if she'd had a hand in the incident?

"Thank you for your report." The Head Instructor finally spoke. "We will consider it further."

His words had a clear note of dismissal, but the other pensive council member apparently wasn't done with her.

"I was present the last time you gave a report to the council," he said, leaning forward. "I must say, it's curious that for a second time you found yourself face-to-face with the instigator of a crime that we had been unable to solve. You seem to have a knack for being in the right place at the right time."

His words were innocuous enough, but his tone suggested something else behind it. Marieke's discomfort grew. It wasn't anything as overt as an accusation, but he was clearly suspicious of her.

"In this case, perhaps," said Marieke. "When Gorgon attempted to murder me in the gardens it felt more like the wrong place at the wrong time, to be honest."

The council member inclined his head. "Of course."

"More to the point," interjected Instructor Rafael, not looking pleased with the conversation's direction, "it is reassuring that once again Marieke's evidence confirms that the disaster in question was the act of a malicious individual," his eyes lingered on her, "and nothing broader or more sinister."

A frown crossed Marieke's face before she could smooth her features. Was he really going to argue that the fire—and the storms and other catastrophes Solomon had mentioned—were unconnected with the wider problem facing Oleand?

Unfortunately, the way Instructor Rafael's eyes narrowed told her that he'd noticed her reaction. She should have been more guarded.

"Agreed," the other council member said. "We should dispatch a criminal investigative team to the town."

"There'd be no point," Instructor Oriana was saying frankly. "They wouldn't find anything I didn't find."

"You're very confident." The third member from the council sounded faintly amused.

Instructor Oriana shrugged. "I'm not trying to boast. But as far as I'm aware, no one in Oleand has a higher level of skill in storytelling song than I do. Anything there is to learn from the site, I've learned it. And whoever started that fire covered his or her tracks."

Again the two council members who seemed wary of Marieke directed their eyes to her, but this time Marieke was distracted. The mention of storytelling song had turned her thoughts back to Kaine's words. She considered Instructor Oriana's face, wondering if she dared to ask her about the discrepancy. The instructor loved her area of songcraft, it was clear to every student. Surely she wouldn't have turned Marieke away from the class if she truly had a natural aptitude, like Kaine claimed.

"Thank you, Marieke, you may consider yourself dismissed." Instructor Rafael's voice was crisp, and Marieke cautiously turned to meet his eyes. "The council thanks you for making the journey in order to give us your report. I assume you'll be returning home at once? We will arrange for someone to accompany you, for your convenience."

His eyes lingered on her as he said it, and Marieke felt a prickling sensation on the back of her neck. She was probably being paranoid, but her instincts were telling her not to travel anywhere with an escort of this man's choosing.

You're wise to be guarded and not to trust the council completely. Especially the Head Instructor.

"Thank you," she said mildly. "That's a kind offer, but unnecessary."

"Not at all." He leaned forward. "I'll see to the details at once."

"Yes, certainly." The other council member who'd seemed suspicious of her weighed in. "With such catastrophes hounding your steps, you must not leave the city alone,

Marieke. Stay in your current lodgings until someone is available to see you home."

Again the words were simple enough, but the tone held a warning. They were ordering her to stay put until dismissed? At which point she would be escorted home under supervision? They were definitely suspicious of her, whether because of her presence at the fire or because of her unsanctioned questions, she wasn't sure.

Either way, Marieke didn't like it. She lost no time in making her escape from the council when dismissed. That same prickling feeling followed her, and she found herself heading straight for her room. She wouldn't seek Kaine out for further training after all. And she didn't intend to wait around for Instructor Rafael or anyone else to take charge of her movements. She understood that the instruction to stay put hadn't been intended to be optional, but it had been presented just casually enough that she thought she could get away with defying it if she acted immediately.

But what was she going to do? The question swirled uncomfortably through her mind as she gathered her belongings. She had enough coins to pay her way home, but what then? Join her father's clinic? Wander around hoping to stumble on the next disaster requiring an agricultural singer? It had been weeks since she'd vowed to find out what was happening to Oleand. And she'd achieved nothing toward that end, even as the country battled a new spate of disasters. Worst of all, it sounded like the council was going to spin the fires and storms as random acts not connected to Oleand's bigger problems—and they might even be looking to label her as the instigator. Quite apart from the risk to her, that avenue was fruitless in actually getting to the bottom of things. If the true problem was to be identified and resolved, *someone* needed to be asking the right questions.

The right questions. The thought inevitably brought her mind back to Kaine's words yet again. It was another thing she needed answers about. She wished she could be confident that it was safe to simply ask Instructor Oriana to explain it all, but she no longer felt that certainty. She'd already learned that casual inquiries within the academy had a habit of making their way back to the Head Instructor.

So asking outright about the questioning branch of storytelling song would be unwise, and asking about heartsong was completely out of the question. But she remained convinced that heartsong, whatever it was, had something to do with what was happening to the country. And she'd promised herself she'd get to the bottom of it.

Her bag now over her shoulder, she paused with her hand on the door of her temporary room. She shouldn't waste this unexpected trip to the capital—returning home would put her right back where she started, besides leaving her vulnerable to whatever was in Instructor Rafael's mind. But where else could she go?

She ran through her options rapidly. She didn't want to just run away. She wanted to run toward answers. Answers about heartsong, ideally. She'd heard the mysterious magic mentioned twice. Once in a conversation between the Head Instructor and Instructor Isabel, neither of whom she could safely ask for more information. The other time by Gorgon, right before he tried to knife her.

Which was right before Zev slayed him with his own blade. So no answers would be forthcoming from Gorgon, either.

But Gorgon wasn't a lone lunatic, as the Council of Singers would have everyone believe. Marieke knew better—she knew exactly where he came from. The self-proclaimed monarchists living in Sundering Canyon might have all kinds of answers. It was a risk to approach them, but she was reaching the conclusion that she wouldn't get anywhere without taking some risks. And the fact that going to the canyon would put her within hailing distance of Zev's farm wasn't lost on her, either.

The monarchists weren't singers, of course. They might know something about heartsong, but they wouldn't know anything about a branch of storytelling songcraft that related to asking questions. As she tried to formulate a plan for how to get herself to the canyon, Marieke resigned herself to the reality that she'd probably never find answers on that topic. There was no one she could safely ask in the whole Academy of Song.

The whole Oleandan Academy of Song. Her steps slowed as the thought struck her. If she was going to Sundering Canyon, she'd be most of the way to Tarandon. Perhaps she could find answers at the Aeltan Academy of Song.

The more she thought about it, the more she concluded that she should visit the Aeltan capital before making an attempt on the canyon. Had she wished it, it might be possible to complete her mission without entering Aeltas— she could start at the coast, where the canyon began, and travel along it until she reached the section where the monarchists live. But it would take days to do that journey by foot, through the inhospitable environment of the canyon. Who knew if it was all passable on foot? Or what unforeseen dangers might lurk there? The memory of how the canyon had taken her voice, and thus her access to magic, made her doubly reluctant.

No, she would find a way to get to Tarandon. There she could both provision for her canyon expedition, and make inquiries at the academy about storytelling song. And perhaps from the city, there would be a way to make contact with—

But she cut that thought off before it could grow. Zev might be the first person who'd flown into her mind when she cast around for whom she could trust, but she'd be unwise to place any reliance on his help. He'd made it clear he wanted no part of her mission.

She could worry about that later. First, she needed to find a way to get to Aeltas. It wouldn't be an easy feat, given the bridge was still closed. But there must be some communication between the countries happening. She gave a decisive nod. She knew where to start her inquiries.

Marieke slipped out of the building inconspicuously, feeling a surge of gratitude for her upbringing. Those of her fellow students who were from well-to-do singing families would think that if the council said there was no way between the countries, that was that. But coming from a farming community, she knew better. Trade was the true force that connected different communities. There'd be no livelihood in farming if the produce of the farms couldn't make its way to buyers. The politicians might not be motivated to find a way, but those who made their living from trade would.

She knew where in Ondford the shipments from the northeastern farms were received—she'd hitched a ride to the capital with farming shipments more than once during her years at the academy. From there, she should be able to find a trail outward, hopefully one that led all the way to the neighboring kingdom. Perhaps not farmed goods, but some products were surely still being exported to Aeltas.

She just needed to find a way to get herself exported with them, and ideally before the council noticed her absence.

SEVEN

Marieke

"**A**head!"

Marieke tensed at the call, her eyes flicking uneasily ahead, even though she couldn't see through the covered side of the wagon.

"What is it?" she asked the young boy sitting beside her. "Do you think there's been another storm?"

On the seemingly interminable trip from the capital, they'd already passed through the destruction left by two separate storms, more vicious and devastating than any Marieke had seen before. They'd also seen a vast plume of smoke that suggested Marieke's region wasn't the only one to suffer from fire. It seemed Solomon hadn't exaggerated in what he'd told her.

"I'll check." Her companion, the underage son of one of the merchants who made up the caravan, climbed across crates of goods to peer through a gap at the front of the wagon. "Nah, I think it was a happy call. I think we must be close to—wait! I can see the ocean!"

"Sun and shade, that's a relief," Marieke said, letting her head drop back against the wagon's side. "I can't wait to be back on my feet." She hadn't enjoyed traveling the route to Oleand's western coast by wagon nearly as much as she had on horseback.

That may have had something to do with the company, of course. It was impossible not to think of Zev as she traversed the same route they'd traveled together.

Well, not exactly the same route. Those traders with means enough to establish a water route between the fractured kingdoms had set up their Oleandan base a fair distance north of where Marieke and her group had met their boat last time. They'd still traveled a long way south by land, but she'd been given to understand that the sea voyage would take half a day this time.

With all the merchandise to load and organize, it actually took considerably longer. But Marieke wasn't complaining. She'd been fortunate to barter passage on the journey for a very low rate by offering her assistance. Using her songcraft to keep the goods stable in the wagons and load them more securely on the ships was a small price to pay to get to the southern kingdom.

And to escape Ondford before the Head Instructor and other council members realized that she was gone.

When the ship finally reached Aeltan shores, Marieke felt her tension rise. The stone wharf that provided access to the ruined city of Port Taran loomed ahead. Memories of her last visit to this place swirled around her. She'd thought she wanted answers, but she hadn't been ready for what she and Zev had found there.

She watched her traveling companions as they disembarked, wondering if any of them would have questions of their own when they saw the damaged city. But why would they? Answers were only likely to be seen by those looking for them. And no one showed any tendency to wander off to explore Port

Taran. The group was channeled straight from the wharf along a newly marked route that hadn't been there when Marieke last passed through the town. It led to a small tent settlement that had sprung up just south of Port Taran. It was evidently the new base of trade between the countries, such as it was. No doubt it was intended to be temporary, until a more permanent solution could be found for the deteriorating bridge.

In any event, the new system seemed to be keeping everyone out of the ruined city with its unsettling hints about the past. Even Marieke wasn't tempted to wander through the streets of Port Taran again. She felt no need to check whether Jade's messages were still there. No doubt they were—outlasting their creator, if her guess about what had happened to Jade was correct.

The onward journey from the trading camp to the capital city of Tarandon was smooth, if tedious inside yet another wagon. By the time they arrived, Marieke longed for nothing more than to secure lodgings and collapse. But her funds were limited, and she didn't know how long she would be in Aeltas. She couldn't afford to spend her coins too freely. It was early in the day—she intended to make her inquiries at the academy then leave the city. She knew she wouldn't be able to reach the canyon before dark, but she was guessing that lodging in the countryside would be cheaper than in the capital.

After taking her leave of the trading group, Marieke made straight for the building that housed both the Aeltan Academy of Song and the Aeltan Council of Singers. She felt incredibly free as she looked up at the blue banners with budding trees worked onto them in bronze thread. Here in Aeltas, no one had reason to be suspicious of her or hold her at arm's length. She could ask questions freely, without worrying about who was watching, and who the conversation would be reported to. It was depressing that she felt more wary and unwelcome at her own academy, where she'd graduated not so long ago after giving a good account of herself. When had it become that way? She'd never felt watched or restricted when she was a student.

Pushing these thoughts aside, she tried to look like she was supposed to be there when the guard at the gate asked her business. A slight twinge of guilt went through her as she told him that she was visiting a friend at the academy. Friend might be stretching the truth. But she and Veronica, the student who'd been assigned to show her around on her last visit, had gotten along very well. Marieke was hopeful that she'd be well received.

As Marieke strode across the courtyard, her attention was drawn to a small building just outside the council center. She hadn't noticed it last time, but now it was impossible to miss, because of how much it was buzzing with activity. A long line had formed in front of it, and every so often someone ran in or out of the back area.

Driven by curiosity, she redirected her steps for a closer look. She cleared her throat as she came alongside the person at the back of the line.

"Excuse me. What's this line for?"

"For the new message station," the young man said. "I'm not sure if I've come at a bad time of day or if it's always this busy." He smiled in a friendly way. "Not that I'm surprised it's popular. Anything new always is."

"What's new about it?" Marieke asked, watching with interest as a young woman wearing the blue uniform of an employee of the Aeltan Council of Singers darted out of the building.

As Marieke and her companion drew slowly closer to the front of the line, her ears caught a faint hum of song, and her senses picked up the stirring of magic in the ground beneath her.

"Are the messages powered by songcraft somehow?"

"That's right." The stranger nodded. "Magical communication used to be available only through privately hiring a qualified singer, and it was too expensive for everyday use. But the council has now opened up an official system of song-powered post. It's regulated, and much more affordable."

"That's quite the innovation," said Marieke, impressed. Oleand didn't have anything like that. "Why the change, I wonder?"

"Word is that since the bridge has been out of action, there's been a lot of study and energy channeled into improving magical methods of communication," the stranger said. "This is one of the benefits that's come out of it, I suppose."

"So you can send messages from here into Oleand?" Marieke asked, amazed. That would be very useful to her. "How far can they reach?"

"Not that far," the man said. "But I hear there's a similar station set up near the broken bridge, where they send messages just across the canyon." He jutted his chin out by way of pointing to a sign next to the message station, which they were now close enough to read. "As it says there, fifteen leagues is the current limit. But I think they're hoping to extend it."

Marieke nodded thoughtfully. "I suppose they'll need to set up more bases for stopover points in order to do that," she murmured. "They'll probably send the letters in stages, rather than trying to send them halfway across the country in one go. It would be difficult to ensure the magic remained steady and consistent so far away. And I expect they'll need employees proficient in guarding songs to send protection along with the post." It was all very interesting.

"You seem to know a lot about this topic," the stranger commented, eyeing her.

"No, I'm just guessing," Marieke said absently. "I'm a singer, but I've never been involved with a project like this."

"You're a singer?" he repeated, sounding impressed. "I suppose you could send a letter on your own."

She smiled. "Not reliably. There's a reason private singers charge a lot for communication. It requires the right type of study. Anyway, I'm not sending a letter at present, not if they can't reach into Oleand."

It was a shame—she really needed to let her parents know that she'd left the country and was safe, just in case the Head Instructor sent someone looking for her and scared them with his inquiries.

With a wave at the helpful stranger, she continued on to the only entrance to the academy that was open to the public. She knew there was a welcome desk inside, where she should be able to inquire after Veronica.

She gave her name with a little bit of trepidation, but was gratified only about fifteen minutes later to see Veronica coming down the corridor, looking surprised but pleased.

"Marieke! This is unexpected. Pleasantly so, of course."

"I'm glad," said Marieke, with a slightly awkward laugh. "I know I'm imposing, just stopping by uninvited like this. But I happened to be back in Tarandon, and I thought I'd take the opportunity to look you up."

"I'm happy you did," Veronica assured her. "Do you have time to stop for a bit? You've caught me at a good moment—I don't have any more classes until after lunch. Should I make a tea tray to take to my room?"

Marieke glanced behind her, where sunshine poured in through the open doorway. "Actually, do you want to go for a walk? I need to visit the market while I'm here, and I could use the company to make sure I don't get cheated like the clueless foreigner I am."

Veronica laughed. "No great risk of that. But sure, I wouldn't mind a trip to the markets. Come with me while I grab a satchel."

Marieke followed the friendly Aeltan down the hallway, an unexpected wave of wistfulness washing over her as she took in the bustle of the academy. This was a different building in a different country, but the feel of it was so much like her own academy. Watching students hurry past, chatting as they clutched books to their chests, felt very reminiscent. Life had been much simpler when she'd been a student. The Oleandan farmland had started to show signs of deterioration, but nothing anyone was overly concerned about at the time. And she'd had no reason to doubt those in authority, either among her instructors or the Council of Singers.

She frowned to herself as she waited outside Veronica's door for the other girl to re-emerge. She was now convinced that there was some dishonesty about the distant past in the country's leadership. She was also suspicious of the Head Instructor's intentions toward her. But as she reflected on her years at the academy, she still believed that her instructors had generally been authentic and well-intentioned. She also thought of the times she'd appeared before the council, and how not everyone had been equally reactive to her. Something was amiss, but that didn't mean the whole system was corrupt. For all she knew, most of the council might not even be aware of what she'd discovered about the singers' coup.

The hard part was figuring out who or what was affected.

"All right." Veronica's smile was cheerful as she rejoined Marieke. "Let's go."

The two girls chatted amiably as they walked out of the academy, Marieke deftly steering the conversation to what Veronica had been up to since their last meeting rather than her own adventures. She cast another glance at the new message station as they passed, noting that the line was a little shorter now. Her steps faltered slightly, but she pushed on, scolding herself. She was being silly. He didn't want to receive a message from her.

Veronica guided them past the closest market square, explaining to Marieke that they'd find better prices at the next one along.

"Excellent," Marieke said. "I'm all for being frugal."

"Yes." Veronica looked at her sideways. "So what kind of supplies are you looking for?"

"Well, some non-perishable food, for a start," Marieke said. "And maybe a rope."

"A rope?" Veronica raised an eyebrow, but didn't press when Marieke failed to elaborate.

They reached a smaller market than the first one, although it was still bustling with activity. Under Veronica's guidance, Marieke spent a few of her dwindling coins on a slim but sturdy rope, a supply of food, and a flint. The trading group had kindly given her a water skin, and she filled it at the public fountain in the center of the small square. All of this Veronica watched without comment. It was only after she'd insisted on buying herself and Marieke iced sweets, and they'd perched on the broad rim of the fountain to enjoy them, that she turned to her visitor with a businesslike air.

"So. Marieke. What's going on with you?"

"Nothing much to report," Marieke said lightly. "I spent some time at home with my parents, but I didn't want to stay there indefinitely. Still looking for more permanent work, life of a graduate, you know."

"And you came back to Tarandon thinking you might have better luck finding employment in songcraft here?" Veronica asked, frowning.

Marieke paused, casting her eyes around the pleasant

square. "Not exactly, but it's not a bad thought." She didn't have any growing reputation as a troublemaker to worry about here. And she did like Aeltas. It was still thriving, unlike Oleand.

Guilt pulled her up swiftly at the disloyal thought. She wasn't going to abandon her country, at least not while it was being eaten away at by an unidentified, insidious magic. Maybe if the situation was ever resolved...

But even that thought seemed faithless, so she pushed it aside.

"If not that, then why are you here?" Veronica asked bluntly. "Marieke, are you all right? Are you in some kind of trouble?"

Marieke looked at her warily. "Why would you ask that?"

Veronica's eyes held a rueful mix of amusement and sympathy as they passed over Marieke's form. "Have you taken stock of yourself lately? You seem on edge, Marieke. And, I'm sorry to say it so plainly, but you're a bit of a mess. You look very...travel-worn."

Marieke scrunched up her nose, recognizing from Veronica's delicate tone that the other girl had phrased it more kindly than her appearance deserved.

"Well, I did just arrive with a trading convoy from Oleand," she argued. "I came straight to the academy. I don't even have lodgings yet."

Veronica didn't answer, just regarding her with steady patience until Marieke let out a sigh.

"I don't know if I'm exactly in trouble, but I'm not exactly... not in trouble."

"What does that mean?" Veronica demanded.

"I honestly think you'd prefer me not to explain," Marieke said dolefully. Again she felt that rush of wistfulness for her days as a student, happy and busy and blissfully ignorant that she might be learning a false version of history. "At any rate, I have no reason to think I'm in either danger or disfavor here in Aeltas."

"But you are in Oleand?" Veronica pressed.

Marieke shrugged. "It's a little complicated, and I'm not confident that even I understand what's going on. But it's safe to say our Council of Singers won't be offering me the job I hoped would come from my place on the delegation here."

"I'm sorry." Veronica's brow was furrowed in concern, and Marieke hastened to clarify.

"I haven't done anything wrong. I'm not running from the law or anything."

"I'm sure you haven't," Veronica reassured her. "I wasn't thinking that. But I'm worried about you. You're here all alone, buying provisions for a journey, giving me vague answers... where are you going, Marieke?"

Marieke bit her lip, teetering for a moment before impulsively spilling the beans. "To Sundering Canyon." The words were abrupt. "I suppose someone should know where I'm headed in case I never come back."

Veronica's stare conveyed nothing but bemusement. "You mean the crossing? Why wouldn't you come back from there? You know the bridge is closed, right? You're not going to try to go across it anyway, are you?"

"Not the crossing." Marieke shook her head. "I'm going to try to get into the canyon itself."

"But...why?" Veronica still seemed more confused than concerned. "What's the point of trying to get into a barren gorge?"

Marieke let out a slow breath, stalling for time as she tried to decide how much to tell the Aeltan girl. "Have you ever heard of people living down in the ravine?"

Veronica's surprise seemed genuine. "No, I haven't."

"Well, they're down there," Marieke said. "And I believe their presence is fairly well known in that region."

"How do you know for sure that they're there?" Veronica asked.

"Because when I fell into the canyon on my previous trip, I saw them," Marieke told her. "In fact, I was taken captive by them. One of them freed me, but not to help. He got me to follow him, then tried to kill me."

"Marieke!" Veronica's eyes were wide.

Marieke shrugged. "It ended up all right. I escaped and managed to get out of the canyon."

"With the help of that farmer," Veronica chimed in.

To Marieke's annoyance, she felt her cheeks heat. She'd forgotten that she'd mentioned Zev to Veronica.

"Yes."

"I can hardly believe this," Veronica said, shaking her head. "If they tried to kill you, it should really have been reported to the Council of Singers."

"It was," Marieke said. "I told the leader of my delegation, and she passed it on."

Veronica frowned. "And yet all this time later, I still haven't heard about these people living down there?"

Marieke hesitated. "I guess they have their reasons for keeping the information to themselves."

Veronica didn't look satisfied with this answer, which was heartening in itself.

"What do you know that you're not telling me, Marieke?"

"So, so many things," Marieke said frankly. "But I doubt you want to know half of them. I will say this, though—the people in the canyon hate singers. The one who tried to kill me was so upset about my escape that he followed me out of Sundering Canyon and back to Oleand, where he tried to finish the job."

Veronica looked horrified. "Mari! That's terrible. Is that why you're here? Are you running away from him?"

"No." A shudder went over Marieke as she remembered the sight of Gorgon's body lying in the gardens outside her academy. "He's dead now."

"I don't understand," Veronica complained. "Any of it. Why would the council keep these people's existence a secret? Why would you want to go back down there if they tried to kill you? Why would people want to live in a ravine in the first place?"

"I can't speak for anyone else," Marieke said, smoothly sidestepping the topics she didn't want to dive into. "But I'm going down there because I want answers. There are some things that aren't adding up in Oleand, and I think the people down there know things we don't know up here."

"And you want these answers enough to die for them?" Veronica demanded.

"I'm hoping it won't come to that," Marieke said, a chuckle rising at the look of outrage on Veronica's face. Clearly her friend thought she'd lost her mind. "Remember, the one who tried to kill me is dead now."

"Still..." Veronica twisted her mouth to one side. "Marieke, I don't think you should go into the ravine. Definitely not alone. Maybe I should go with you."

Marieke laughed outright at that. "Veronica, you're a dear, but there's no way I'd let you do that. Don't you have your final exams soon?"

"Well...yes," Veronica admitted. She gave a swift grin. "And to be honest, I don't relish clambering into any gorges." Her expression grew more serious. "But I really don't think you should do this alone."

Marieke shrugged. "I don't have anyone to come with me."

"What about the previously discussed farmer?" Veronica's expression was sly enough to tell Marieke that the other girl hadn't missed her slight flush earlier. She could hardly miss the more fiery one rising after her latest words.

"There's a story there," Veronica pressed, studying Marieke's face. "I guess he made quite an impression in the day he was with you."

"It was more than that," Marieke admitted. "We actually ran into each other again, back in Oleand. We sort of traveled together."

"Did you now?" Veronica was suppressing a grin by the sound of it. "What exactly did this traveling entail?"

Marieke gave her a dark look, but she couldn't sustain her sternness in face of Veronica's twitching eyebrows. A self-conscious smile escaped her, even as her heart ached with the longing to unburden herself—it would be such a relief to tell someone about what had happened with her and Zev. She didn't know Veronica that well, but maybe that was all the more reason to confide in her.

"All right." She raised her arms in a gesture of surrender. "I thought there was maybe something there." She frowned a little to herself. "No, I *know* there was something there. He kissed me, after he...well, saved my life, actually."

Veronica's eyes were as round as coins. "This is all sounding very exciting and very romantic. I hope you don't think you can leave me without details."

Marieke sighed. "It's not so easy to tell details. There's just... so much story behind it all."

"At least tell me what he's like," Veronica pressed.

"He's..." For a moment Marieke struggled to answer. How to put Zev, with all his indefinable presence, into a few words? "He's honestly not like anyone I've ever met. There's this quality to him...this confidence and self-assurance. It's some-thing that needs to be experienced, not told. Judging by his demeanor," she waved her hand in a vague gesture, "by the *feel* of him, you'd say that he's direct, straightforward, solid. No pretensions or affectations. But then what he actually says is so cryptic. He's always giving away as little as possible."

"You've fallen hard," Veronica commented. She said it without mockery, stating it as a simple fact.

"I don't know if I'd say that," Marieke protested, her cheeks heating once again.

"Whether you'd say it or not makes no difference, Mari," Veronica pointed out. "You've obviously spent a lot of time thinking about him since you've been apart."

Marieke stayed silent. That much she could hardly deny.

"Why don't you contact him?" Veronica urged. "Instead of going on some wild quest in the canyon."

"Because our lives are too separate," Marieke said. "He's the one who chose to walk away. His home is here, and my…" she caught herself before saying *fight*, "life is in Oleand."

"And yet…" Veronica let the words hang in the air for a moment before finishing, "here you are. There's a reason for that."

"Yes," said Marieke briskly, ready to turn the topic. "And that reason is that I wanted to ask you something. Or at least to ask someone at the academy." She smiled disarmingly. "And I only really know you."

"What is it?" Veronica leaned forward, protecting her clothes from her iced sweet, which had been neglected in favor of their conversation and was now dripping.

"It's about storytelling song," Marieke said. "Do you know much about it?"

Veronica shook her head. "Not many people do, do they? It's such a difficult area of study. I took an aptitude test—everyone does at our academy—but I didn't have the skills to progress."

"I took a similar test," Marieke said. "And I also didn't progress. But…" She frowned. "But I've recently heard about a new aspect of storytelling song that I wasn't familiar with. Something to do with asking questions."

"Questions?"

Marieke nodded. "Someone told me that for some people, when they ask questions, magic pools toward them. Apparently it's a branch of storytelling song."

"Oh, that does sound familiar." Veronica squinted in an effort of memory. "I think it's called sifting song at our academy. Because you learn to use magic to guide your questions so you can sift through the information and find what's valuable."

"Did you study it?" Marieke asked.

She shook her head. "It's a branch of storytelling song, like you said. We learn what the basic categories are, but we don't learn to actually do it unless we pursue storytelling song as an elective."

"We also learned the basic categories," Marieke said, troubled. "And I don't remember any mention of sifting song, or anything that sounds like it."

"From memory, it's one of the aptitude songcrafts," Veronica said. "One which only a few singers actually have the right ability to pursue. I believe it's quite rare. I'm pretty sure no one in my year level identified it in testing."

"Aptitude songcrafts sometimes happen without training, right?" Marieke said. "The singers with the relevant aptitude can sometimes do it without meaning to or even realizing it?"

Veronica shrugged. "So I've been told, if the aptitude is strong enough. I've never experienced it myself."

Marieke said no more. A short time ago she would have said the same, but now she wasn't so sure. She certainly had plenty to think about. If she came out of Sundering Canyon in one piece, maybe she should see if the storytelling instructor at the Aeltan Academy of Song would be willing to meet with her. Maybe even let her take the aptitude test. She hated to think that Instructor Oriana might have been dishonest about her results, but...it hadn't escaped her notice that there was an irony in her having been constantly ribbed by her instructors for asking too many questions.

Ribbing that had been perfectly amicable until she started asking the wrong type of questions. Or the right type of questions, depending how one looked at it.

How would Jade look at it, she wondered soberly. If she'd known it might cost her life, would she still have pursued her questions?

Marieke pushed these troubling thoughts aside with a sigh. She stood, and Veronica did the same.

"I suppose we'd best get moving," she said. "You need to get back to the academy, and I need to make the most of the daylight. I think I'll try to catch a public coach toward the bridge, if they still run. Apparently there's a message station there where I can send a letter to my parents."

"Yes, I believe there is," Veronica confirmed, leading the way back toward the academy.

Marieke nodded. It would be a good place to start her exploration of the canyon. After all, it was the precise area where she'd encountered the monarchists last time. She didn't voice all this to Veronica. The other girl seemed to have been distracted from Marieke's purpose by the subsequent conversation about Zev and sifting song. No need to remind her.

They parted ways at the academy door, Marieke intending to hurry to the coach house Veronica had told her about. But her steps faltered slightly as she crossed back through the open yard of the council building. The line at the new message station was smaller now.

For a moment, she wrestled with herself. She wasn't any more excited about going into Sundering Canyon alone than

Veronica had been on her behalf. But Zev had been clear that he wanted no part of her fight to save Oleand.

She straightened her back. He might have been clear on his course of action, but she'd been clear on hers, too. Hadn't she promised herself when he left that it wouldn't be the last time she saw him? Hadn't she promised herself that she knew what she was willing to fight for, even if he didn't?

With a purposeful motion, she redirected her steps toward the bustling little stand. If nothing came of it all, it wouldn't be because she hadn't tried.

Zev

Zev strode between the trees, his mind on the supper waiting for him inside the house. Even his orchard, usually a reliable haven, had no comfort to offer him. Not in light of the air of anxiety that had settled over the household since he told his family what he'd discovered about the survey. His father had ridden to Zev's uncle's farm to discuss the development, and Zev knew the whole family was on high alert. Opinion seemed to be split as to whether it was a good thing that the land turned back the questing enchantment, or whether it put them in greater danger. If the council had ordered the surveying team to start in their region specifically because of Zev's earlier encounter with the council member, then surely the anomaly of their property being missed from the survey would be noticed.

If his connection with Marieke caused them to be exposed after all these generations of successfully hiding in plain sight, what would he do?

What could he do? It wasn't as though he could change the past. It wasn't even as though he wanted to.

He cleared the copse of uncultivated trees that stood

between the orchard and the house, rounding the corner of the building with heavy steps. As he lifted his eyes to scan the darkening farmyard, a jolt went through him. Another survey parchment? And this one had managed to get past the land's defenses!

But another look showed that the paper wafting through the air was much smaller than the last one had been, and it wasn't dancing about like a kite on a string. It was moving steadily toward the house, and as he watched, it coasted to a stop outside the front door.

Zev picked up his pace. He was just starting up the porch steps when the front door opened and his mother appeared.

"Zev," she said, stopping at the sight of him. "I was just getting a pitcher from the parlor, and I thought I saw—"

"This." Zev cut her off, leaning down to pick up the parchment. "I saw it, too, from across the yard."

"Is that what the last one looked like?"

Zev shook his head. "No." He turned the small, white envelope over in his hand. "No, this is something different. I think it's a…"

He trailed off, his eyebrows rising as he caught sight of what was written on the other side of the envelope.

"A what?" his mother asked, her voice sharp. "Is it recording information somehow?"

"A letter," Zev finished belatedly. "I don't think it's enchanted like the last one. It looks like an ordinary letter…and it's addressed to me."

"Addressed to you?" He could hear the alarm in his mother's words. "Ordinary letters don't fly through the air, Zev."

Zev didn't respond, his thumb moving across the letters written in a slanting, feminine hand. It was his name all right, and the location of their farm, as clear as day. There was only one way to find out what it was about.

He pulled out his knife and flicked it open, slitting the envelope roughly. There was one folded sheet inside, in the same neat writing. His eyes jumped at once to the bottom, his heart doing a strange lurch when he saw how the note was signed. He would have preferred to read it without his mother present, but there was no way she was going to give him that option. Trying to keep his face impassive, he read through the note from the start.

Zev

I'm back in Aeltas. I thought about coming to see you, but I didn't know if you'd want that. I won't explain in a letter all the reasons I came. I was going to write something about thinking you might want to know my plans, but that's not the truth. The truth is that I want you to know. I don't want to come so close to where you are without you even knowing that I'm here, or where I'm going.

And where I'm going is into Sundering Canyon, or at least that's my plan. I'm hoping to find roughly the same area where you pulled me from the cliff face.

I expect to be there on Thursday. I won't try to enter the canyon until noon. Just in case.

- Marieke

Zev stared at the letter, his heart thumping so forcefully he felt sure his mother must hear it. Marieke was in Aeltas? And she'd written to him.

"What is it, Zev?" his mother asked. "How did it find you?"

Zev blinked at her, struggling to comprehend her question. The contents of the letter had driven out all thought of its method of arrival. What was Marieke thinking, going into

Sundering Canyon? She'd barely escaped from the monarchists with her life last time. Why would she take that risk?

And she was going to wait at the canyon's edge for a while... just in case.

Just in case.

Zev's mind whirled. She hadn't explained those words, but she didn't need to. He understood. She wasn't asking him to come with her—she wasn't going to pressure him after he'd told her so clearly that her self-appointed mission wasn't his fight.

But underneath everything said between them, and everything not said, the simple truth was that she *was* asking him to come with her. Reading her words, he could almost see her hopeful face as it had looked when she'd suggested they unravel Oleand's tangled problems together.

And what would his answer be? Would he turn away again, and leave her to whatever fate befell her?

"Zev?" His mother's voice reminded him of the fact that he wasn't alone.

"It's a letter," he said gruffly, folding it so that the words were hidden again. "For me. Like I said."

He could see the impatience on his mother's face, but she stopped herself from dragging the information out of him, instead ushering him toward the doorway she was occupying.

"Come inside, Zev. Unless..." She paused as she looked at the folded letter in his hand. "Do you think it's safe to bring that thing with you?"

"Of course it is." Zev stepped over the threshold, unenthusiastic about sharing the letter with his whole family, but unable to imagine a scenario where he could get away with anything less. "It's a letter, Mother. Just a letter."

She didn't reply, but he could sense her skepticism without the need for words. He strode ahead of her, all thought of washing up for supper forgotten as he made his way to the kitchen, where the family ate on all but formal occasions. His brother was already at the scrubbed wooden table, and his father appeared moments after Zev and his mother entered the room.

"Did I hear Zev come in? Is supper…" The question petered out as he looked from his eldest son to his wife. "Is everything all right, Narelle? What's going on?"

"A letter came by magical wind," Zev's mother said matter-of-factly. "It's for Zev, from Marieke."

"Mother." Zev ignored the splutter from his brother, who seemed to be choking on his sip of ale. Had his mother peered over his shoulder without him realizing? "You shouldn't be reading a letter addressed to me."

"I didn't read the letter," she informed him. "I didn't need to. I just read you, Zev."

Zev shut his mouth.

"Is it true?" Azai demanded. "You got a letter from that Oleandan singer?"

"Yes." Zev was unimpressed. "You know, pretending that you don't remember her name just makes you look foolish."

"I remember her name," Azai said tartly. "I just choose not to use it."

"Well, that makes you look foolish, too," Zev informed him, lowering himself into a chair across from the younger man.

"Enough with the bickering." Their father was understandably impatient. "Zev, this letter. It was truly carried here by magic, like the last one?"

"I don't know how else it could have gotten here," Zev told him. "I saw it fly to the front door myself. But it's not like the other one. It's not a survey parchment, and it wasn't taking in information."

"How did it get through the land's defense?" Azai demanded.

Zev shrugged. "Weren't you listening to what I just said? This is an ordinary letter. It's not a tool to spy on us, and it's not trying to read or record information. I think the magic was only involved in actually getting it here."

"Oh, how reassuring," Azai said sarcastically.

"Actually, it is," Zev said, his own voice calm. "If the land chose to let it in, doesn't that tell you something?"

Azai looked like he had another mocking reply ready, but their father cut in before the brotherly spat could escalate.

"What does the letter say, Zev?"

Zev tried not to show his tension as he tightened his grip on the folded paper. "It says that Marieke is back in Aeltas. She's planning to go into Sundering Canyon, looking for the monarchists."

His parents exchanged swift looks. "Looking for the monarchists? Why would she do that?"

"She didn't explain her reasons," Zev said.

"Then why write to you at all?" Azai demanded.

"I suppose she thought I'd want to know what was happening," Zev said. "And she was right."

Azai made a scoffing noise, but their father quashed it with a frown. "Don't let your prejudices blind you to the main point, Azai. Zev is showing good sense. The more informed we are, the better. If Marieke's group is searching for an explanation for our land's prosperity, we want to know all developments in that search." His voice turned grim. "I can't say I like the idea of her group searching out the monarchists."

"There's no group," Zev corrected him. "I don't think she's here with a delegation. I think it's just her."

There was a moment of silence as everyone took in this

information. Three pairs of eyes came to rest on Zev, each with varying degrees of suspicion.

"What questions is she asking that she thinks the answers will be found with the monarchists in Sundering Canyon?" His mother's question was slow and thoughtful, and she searched his face as she asked it.

"Zevadiah?" His father's voice held a sternness he hadn't heard since his youth. "What questions is she asking? What exactly did you tell her?"

Zev sighed at the suspicion in the older man's eyes. "I didn't tell her anything. I encouraged her to ask the right questions, and challenged her version of the coup. But I left her to figure out what she thinks." Seeing that his father wasn't satisfied, he added, "She has no reason to connect any of it to us, even if she does accept that she's been lied to about what happened back then."

"No reason other than the fact that you're the one who prompted her to investigate," Azai said.

Zev didn't reply. He wanted to ignore Azai's caustic words, as he usually did, but honesty compelled him to acknowledge that his brother had a point.

"Well..." Their father gave a slow nod. "I suppose there's nothing to fear in her going into the canyon."

"What do you mean?" The words burst from Zev before he thought them through. "There's everything to fear. Last time she barely survived. Those fools down there answer to no one, and they're even more prejudiced against singers than you all are. Who knows what they'll do to her!"

His father's eyebrows were halfway to his hairline by the end of Zev's speech. There was a painful moment of silence before the older man spoke.

"I meant there's no reason to fear exposure. The so-called monarchists know nothing of us. But thank you for making your position clear, Zevadiah. It's good to know that you think us unreasonably prejudiced against singers."

Zev sighed. When his father used his full name twice in one conversation, he knew he was in trouble.

"I didn't call anyone unreasonable."

Azai made a noise in the back of his throat. "So you remain in full agreement with our position on singers, do you?"

Zev ignored the hint of sarcasm in his brother's voice. "You know where my loyalties lie." He kept his eyes on his father. "I will never soften toward the singers who murdered our ancestors. But they earned our contempt. And the Council of Singers earns it by perpetuating lies. But ordinary singers like Marieke are different. Shouldn't they have the chance to show themselves trustworthy before we assume their intentions are evil?"

"No." His father shrugged. "Or maybe they *should*, but they can't. They all go through the academy, Zev, and you know the academy and the council are basically one and the same. There's no real hope of singers forming their own ideas about our country or our past. They're indoctrinated from their youth, surely you understand that."

"Yes." Zev's voice was heavy. "I can acknowledge that it's difficult to be objective about the things you've been taught from childhood."

As he was discovering for himself. He didn't voice that last part aloud, and none of his family seemed to pick up on his double meaning. It didn't sit comfortably to not be aligned with his parents and brother, but he simply couldn't return to the certainty he'd felt before he met Marieke.

"I think I should go with her," he blurted out. "Into Sundering Canyon."

"Why would you do that?" his mother demanded, her brow furrowed. "I know you have a soft spot for this girl, Zev, and truth be told I thought her likable enough. I'm not as convinced as your father that she and others like her are a lost cause. But putting yourself in harm's way seems a step too far."

"Harm's way?" Zev couldn't help the disdainful note in his voice. "I'm not afraid of Sundering Canyon. Or the monarchists. It's true that I don't want to see Marieke hurt, but I'm also thinking of our family." He took a breath, not relishing the need to share this information, then pushed on. "I know the group in the canyon know nothing about our family, but I have some reason to think they might know about heartsong."

"What?" His father was on his feet, and Azai's mouth had fallen open. "Why do you think that?"

"You remember I mentioned that a man attacked Marieke in the Oleandan capital? He came from the group in the canyon, and he said something about heartsong."

"So you're saying Marieke knows what it is?" His father's face was forbidding, not an expression Zev was used to seeing there.

"Of course not," Zev said. "But she's smart, Father. She asks the right questions. I don't think it's true that there's no risk of exposure. If I'm there, maybe I can limit that risk."

"If you can be trusted with the job," Azai said doubtfully.

Zev scowled at him. "What is it that's made you all think I've forgotten everything I've ever believed?"

"We don't think that, Zev," said his mother soothingly.

"I hope not," Zev retorted. "Do you think I don't understand what's at stake? Do you think I want to put all the family at risk?" He waved a hand in the direction of the closest cousins' farm.

"I still don't like it," his father said, frowning.

"Respectfully, Father, you don't have to like it." Zev didn't care that his words were blunt. "I think I should go, and that's what I'm going to do."

He didn't stay to see his father's reaction. He strode quickly from the room, eager for some air and space to think. He was almost at the front door when his mother caught up with him.

"Zev."

"What?" he snapped, still feeling mutinous toward the whole lot of them.

"Well, don't eat me." Her lips twitched a little, and Zev couldn't help softening.

"I know you mean well," he started, "but—"

"We all do," she cut him off. "Every person in this house. And you don't do your credibility any favors by pretending that Marieke hasn't affected your attitude. Dare I say it..." she searched his face, "even your loyalties."

Zev's tension returned. She was touching on the deepest source of his inner conflict, and he didn't know how to respond.

"I'm not criticizing you," his mother said. "I'm not even going to urge you not to go after her. But I worry about you, Zev. I know you care about the family's safety, and you clearly care about hers a great deal. It's too much pressure. What will you do if you can't keep both safe? What will you do if keeping one safe is exactly what endangers the other?"

Zev's eyes were troubled as they met hers. He didn't try to hide it.

"Honestly...I don't know," he admitted, his voice quiet. "What would you do if Azai and my best interests were in conflict?"

"That's not the same," his mother argued. "I'm your mother. It's a different type of relationship altogether."

He raised an eyebrow. "That's not an answer."

To her credit, his mother thought for a long moment rather than giving a snap answer. "I wouldn't have to make a choice between you," she said at last. "Because you would both fight for each other just as tenaciously as I could fight for you." Her eyes were earnest. "I know Azai isn't happy with you right now, but he would, you know. Just like you would for him."

"I do know," Zev said, with the ghost of a sigh.

"But would Marieke fight for the family you hold dear?" Her voice held a definite challenge, but Zev didn't let it abash him. Instead he turned it back on her.

"Would my family fight for her?"

His mother, bless her, was no easier to rattle than he was.

"There's no telling what I might do for you if you asked me," she told him calmly.

Zev couldn't help smiling. "Well, what I'm asking you to do now is to trust me when I say I need to go with her."

"I trust you, Zev," she said. "I always have, and I always will. Just make sure, when the newness of what you're feeling is intoxicating, that you don't lose yourself. Any part of yourself."

"I know I'm part of something bigger than just me," Zev assured her.

She shook her head. "That's not what I meant. This legacy you carry is for others than yourself, but it's also part of you. You wouldn't be the same if you lost it. You wouldn't be complete."

Zev didn't respond, and after a moment, his mother gave a satisfied nod.

"Enough deep talk. Walk it off if you must, but don't take too long. Supper is still waiting, you know."

The same good sense followed Zev when he set out, in the form of a hearty supply of food in his rucksack. He rode his favorite mare out of the gate just after dawn two mornings after receiving Marieke's letter. He should comfortably reach the canyon before noon.

He made good progress, a tangle of nerves and excitement building in him as he neared the place where he'd first met Marieke. He knew the spot—he'd been past there more than once since, his eyes always drawn to the grassy area where he and Azai had pulled over their cart. He was eager to see her again, even though he had no idea what he would say to her, or her to him. When they'd parted, he'd wanted desperately to believe it wasn't for the last time. Yet, drawn to her though he was, he'd made no effort to ensure it. She'd been the one to reach out to him.

He still had a few hours before noon when he guided his horse to a stop on the same patch of grass. He felt a spike of anxiety as he scanned the area, hopping down from his horse to check the cliff's edge for some distance in either direction. There was no sign of Marieke. Surely he hadn't missed her. She'd said she would wait until noon. She wouldn't have gone to the effort of writing to him to tell him that if she wasn't going to honor it. Perhaps she was still on her way.

After an hour, however, Zev was feeling very uneasy. Had she been held up in her travels to the spot? Had she even been able to find the spot? The more he thought about it, the more he realized how unlikely it was that she would actually locate the exact place where he'd pulled her from the cliff. She didn't know the area like he did. There was every chance that she was waiting somewhere else, thinking he wasn't coming.

But which direction to try? It was no more than an hour until noon—probably less—by the time he decided to leave the patch of grass and search along the canyon. Hoping for the best, he chose west, moving toward the capital rather than away from it.

He traveled slowly, keeping to the road, but examining the nearby cliff edge with great care. After half an hour of travel, he had the sinking feeling that he'd chosen the wrong way. But it was too late to turn back now—he wouldn't make it past his starting point by noon.

The sun had only just passed its zenith when he caught sight of something up ahead that made his heart leap. A rope, one end tied to a stake in the ground, and the other end disappearing over the edge of the canyon.

Zev

Zev spurred his horse onward, driven as much by fear as by enthusiasm. What was Marieke's plan? Surely she must know there was no rope long enough to reach the bottom of Sundering Canyon.

He pulled to a stop alongside the stake and dismounted smoothly. In the next moment, he was on his knees by the trailing rope, looking over the edge. All he could see was a dark head of hair, not too far down the cliff face, with a figure mostly hidden. But one he'd know anywhere.

"Marieke!"

Her head whipped up, her eyes widening as she caught sight of him. He watched several emotions cross her face before she settled on a smile.

"Zev." She sounded almost shy, not like her usual self. "You came. I'd given up on you."

"What are you doing, Mari?" His nerves at the prospect of their reunion had disappeared in exasperation. "Are you trying to get yourself killed?"

"Of course not," she said with dignity. "I'm trying to—"

The words were cut off as her foot slipped, a cry bursting from Zev as the rock under Marieke's other foot cracked and fell away. Not stopping to consider the situation further, Zev seized the rope and began to pull it hand over hand. Marieke protested, not walking up the wall like she had the previous time they'd been in a similar situation. The task was considerably harder as a result, and a moment later became impossible as the section of turf on which Zev knelt began to slide. He tried to shift his weight back, but the land under his knees had other ideas. It gave way, and to his horror, he found himself slipping over the edge, only his grip on the rope keeping him from plummeting downward.

Marieke gave a cry of irritation below him, her face bumping against his leg.

"Don't worry!" he called, not daring to look down and risk throwing off his precarious balance. "I can pull myself up and then pull you up as well."

"No, don't. I can't hold on that long." Marieke's tone was somehow still exasperated rather than terrified. "I'm going to have to let go."

"No!" Zev called in alarm. "I can help you!"

Fighting the instinct that wanted to retreat to safer ground above, he walked down the wall toward her, grateful that the rope's knot was holding strong. Before Marieke could say a word, he'd reached her, using his longer legs to push most of his body further from the wall while keeping his hands and the rope right against the stone.

"Can you pull yourself up far enough for me help hold your weight?" he asked, his muscles starting to strain and his head spinning from the awareness of the dizzying drop below him. But he needed to keep calm. "Then I can help walk us both up the cliff."

"Actually—" Marieke's reply was cut off as the rope suddenly loosened. They both jolted down far enough to make Zev's stomach feel like it was trying to leave his body. The stake Marieke had attached the rope to must have bent over. It would surely give way soon.

"That's it." Zev pushed himself out from the wall as much as he could without disturbing the rope. "No more time to argue. Press yourself flat against the rock if you can."

He walked himself down, afraid with every movement that the rope would give way. And not without reason. He'd just managed to edge himself over the top of Marieke when the rope went slack. With a shock too intense for crying out, they both fell.

About two feet.

Zev landed hard on rock, for a moment too winded to grasp what had happened. When he shook off his stupor, he realized that he was lying on a large rocky ledge, the edge of the cliff not too far above him. He also realized that Marieke was somehow encased in his arms, looking as dazed as he felt. He released her hastily—holding her that close was too much for his conflicted heart to handle. Fortunately more complex emotions were quickly overcome by his relief that they were alive.

"You really need to stop dangling off cliffs, Marieke." He found himself holding back a smile, probably born of some combination of the joy of survival and the nearness of the person who'd occupied his thoughts relentlessly for weeks past.

Marieke gave him a disgruntled look. "I wasn't dangling."

"Sure looked like it," he commented.

"I had everything under control," she insisted.

"Didn't look like that." Again Zev was fighting a smile. Was he losing his mind?

"I knew this ledge was here," Marieke told him. "That's why I started at this point. If you actually look at your surroundings instead of panicking, you'll see that this is a huge surface. We couldn't have missed it if we'd tried."

Zev cast his eyes around to see that she was right. More of his tension eased.

"Well, I'm glad you had some kind of plan," he said. "But I still think you should stop dangling off cliffs."

Marieke narrowed her eyes at him for a long moment before her disapproval suddenly gave way to a swift smile.

"Why, though?" she asked cheekily. "Since you always show up to pull me to safety." She flicked his sleeve. "At least you have a shirt on this time."

Zev had opened his mouth to give another retort, but at her last comment he choked on it, feeling the faintest hint of heat rising up his neck. Marieke turned away, but not before her slight smirk told him she knew she'd managed to regain the upper hand.

Zev shook his head at her back, his own lips tugging up into a smile in spite of himself.

"So what's your plan from here, as you supposedly have everything under control?" he quipped.

Marieke was coiling the rope that had fallen nearby. "Well, the plan *was* to use songcraft to detach the rope from up there once I was down here, but it seems the stake did that for me." She turned her head to grimace at him. "I will admit that I had more faith in that stake than I should have. It's a relief that I can use my voice thus far, though. I couldn't talk last time I was in the canyon, let alone sing, remember?"

Zev nodded absently, his eyes on the cliff's edge above. "I'm glad I didn't tie up my horse," he commented.

Marieke slapped a hand to her mouth. "You rode here! Of

course you did. I was dropped by a public coach not far away and walked, so I didn't even think about it."

"Don't worry," Zev reassured her. "My mare will find her way home. She knows these roads well. I just hope the poor thing doesn't wait a long time before heading homeward."

Marieke considered him. "So you're stuck with me on this venture, it seems."

"It seems so." They locked eyes, the silence growing until it had a tangible presence between them. A presence that tasted like the kiss they'd shared in Zev's moment of reckless abandon. A moment he both regretted and didn't regret at all.

He cleared his throat, breaking the standoff with a mixture of reluctance and relief. "I received your letter."

"Evidently." Marieke seemed faintly disappointed, but she didn't call him out for sidestepping the tension between them. "Did you intend to come with me into the canyon, or did you ride out here to try to stop me?"

"Hm." Zev smiled slightly. "The first...if the second failed."

Marieke rolled her eyes, but she also was smiling. "It would have failed." The shyness was back in her voice. "I am glad you're here, though. When it reached noon and there was no sign of you, I thought you weren't planning to come."

"Well, I wasn't planning to come here," Zev said fairly. "I don't even know where here is."

Marieke raised an inquiring eyebrow. "Is this not the spot where you pulled me up last time?"

"Not even close," Zev said dryly. "I waited at that place for a couple of hours before coming searching."

"Oh." Marieke looked sheepish. "Oops."

Zev didn't know whether to roll his eyes or laugh.

"That's a shame," Marieke continued. "Because I was hoping to find the staircase Gorgon took me partway up. It would have made our task much easier, both because we would have much less sheer cliff to scale, and because then we'd know we were in the right area to find the monarchists."

"I hear a lot of *we* in that explanation, but I have no desire to find these self-proclaimed monarchists," Zev pointed out.

"Then why are you here?" Marieke asked.

There was a moment of silence before Zev responded. "You know why I'm here. I'm here because of you."

The silence that followed his words was longer, and more charged. When Marieke looked into his eyes, he held her gaze, wondering if she would put words to whatever was between them, as he'd thus far been too cowardly to do.

But she didn't. After a moment, she looked away, shuffling one careful step closer to the edge of their platform and peering down.

"The more pressing question isn't why but how. We need to find a safe way down." She must have heard Zev's grunt, because she added with a faint smile, "All right, safe might be optimistic, but the safest of our available options."

"What was your plan once you reached this ledge?" Zev asked.

"To figure out a plan once I knew if I had my voice," Marieke told him. "And for now, it seems I do. As long as that's the case, I can tie the rope, then climb down it to another landing point, then use my song to untie the knot and free the rope to fall down to me. Then repeat."

"There are a lot of problems with that plan," Zev said.

"Are there?" She folded her arms. "Name them."

"Firstly, tie the rope to what?"

By way of answer, she swung the rucksack she wore around to her front and pulled out a large metal peg. "To this. Once I've used *this*," she pulled out a mallet, "to drive it into the wall."

"Huh." Zev grunted. "That might work."

"It will work," Marieke said calmly. "Especially if I can use songcraft to strengthen it."

Zev glanced over the edge of the platform as well. "All right, second, your plan assumes that there are enough landing places like this to get you all the way down. That seems extremely optimistic."

"Not all the way down," Marieke said. "I acknowledge that there are some sections directly below us that might be...questionable. But if we can get through them, we should be fine. Further that way," she gestured westward, "the cliff face is incredibly sheer in the top section, but then not that far down becomes much more gradual. Genuinely climbable, I'd say. We just need to get across to it once we're far enough down."

"How do you know that?" Zev demanded.

Marieke moved past him, starting to untie the rope from the stake as she answered. "I have considerable training in agricultural song, Zev. Getting a feel for the terrain around me is rudimentary. And I had plenty of time up there, waiting for you to show up. I did all kinds of assessing songs, and if I say so myself, my reach is pretty good. I have a very fair idea of the state of the slope for quite a while around."

"That is...handy," Zev acknowledged. He was impressed. He wasn't quite willing to admit it to Marieke, but he admitted it to himself.

She stared at him. "Did you just say something positive about magic? You've changed since we parted ways."

Her tone was light and joking, but Zev didn't respond in kind.

"It wasn't the time since we've been apart that changed me. It was being with you."

Marieke bit her lip, probably as unsure what to make of his words as he was. He didn't know what he was trying to achieve, he just didn't seem able to help becoming more intense the more flippant Marieke became. Perhaps it was because inside, he was so torn. Half of him was relieved that she was approaching their reunion with a bantering spirit. The other half was wrestling a desperate desire for them to find their way back to the passion they'd so briefly shared. It seemed impossibly out of reach at that moment, and while his head knew it was probably for the best, he couldn't seem to convince his heart.

"Meeting you changed me as well, you know." Marieke's quiet voice surprised him as she matched her tone to his this time. She gestured at the canyon below them. "All of this changed me. You went back to your old life after you left, but I... couldn't. There was so little of it left to go back to."

Something in the region of Zev's heart throbbed painfully at her mention of him leaving her. She hadn't used the word *abandoned*, but he still heard it. Just as he'd heard it in his own thoughts every day since he walked away from her in that marketplace in Ondford.

"I didn't just go back to how things were before," he said. "I suppose I tried to. But it didn't work. I couldn't just forget."

"So here you are," she said softly.

"So here I am."

For a moment they just looked at each other, the light of their moment of intimacy flickering almost back into life. Perhaps if it had been a declaration they'd shared, it might have been enough to give body to the feelings hovering between them. But it hadn't been a declaration, it had been a mere kiss. Everything that mattered had been left unsaid, and in another moment, Marieke was turning away again.

Clearly it would be left unsaid today as well.

"But here is not where either of us want to be," she was saying briskly. "We need to keep moving if we want to get safely to the canyon floor before dark. We can't afford to spend the night on the cliff face, and we can't afford to rush. So let's go."

Zev followed her lead, silently taking the mallet and peg from her when she'd mapped out their next stopping point to her satisfaction. Muscles straining, he hammered the metal into the rock, not stopping until it was almost all the way in. It took all his strength, and he couldn't help giving Marieke a sardonic look.

"So you were planning to do that part alone, were you?"

"Not alone," she said with dignity. "I was going to use magic."

Zev shook his head, but he had to admit once they'd descended to another, much smaller, ledge that it was mesmerizing to listen to as she used her song to untie the rope above them. The peg stayed lodged in the stone, thankfully having held better than the stake up on the surface.

They repeated this process a few times, some of the landing points precarious to say the least. Zev insisted on going down the rope first each time, and his heart hammered in his chest whenever he saw Marieke clinging to handholds with determination, very little between her and a horrifying fall below.

Thankfully they were on a section of rock wide enough for their whole feet to stand flat when they ran into a new problem.

Marieke raised her face to the landing above, clearing her throat and opening her mouth.

Nothing came out.

"Marieke?" Zev prompted her.

She frowned, trying again with the same result.

"I've lost my voice," she murmured, her own words startling her. "No, I haven't. What's going on?" She cleared her throat again, but nothing emerged when she opened her mouth. "Curious," she said. "I can speak, but I can't sing. Blast."

She bit her lip as she studied the rope. "I suppose I should be grateful that the canyon hasn't taken my voice completely like last time, but this is going to make things a lot harder."

Zev looked around before replying, squinting to his right. "I think I can see the section you were talking about before. We don't have much further to go, and then the terrain should be more passable, right?"

Marieke nodded. "But I don't see us getting over there without a rope. And I don't want to be without one when we get lower down. I couldn't sense all the way to the bottom of the canyon. There may be more sheer sections lower down."

"I'll get the rope," Zev said stoically. "I think I can climb the section we just did without it."

"Zev."

Marieke's voice showed her reluctance, but Zev didn't stop to argue about it. The task wouldn't get easier for being left. Already it was getting dimmer in the canyon, the sun having passed out of sight above them long before.

Pulling himself hand over hand, Zev scaled his way back to the previous stopping point. As long as he didn't look down, it was easy enough. The most dangerous part of it was the thought of what would happen if he fell. He just needed to be resolute in not entertaining that thought.

He untied the knot as swiftly as he could, coiling the rope across his torso before starting to climb down. He'd thought the descent tense enough with the rope—it was a very different experience without it. His palms began sweating at once, and the need to find footholds prevented him from avoiding looking down altogether. The ledge on which Marieke stood, anxiously watching him, wasn't like the one above—if he lost his grip, it wouldn't be wide enough to stop his fall.

Just as he drew close enough to Marieke to start relaxing, the jutting rock he'd grabbed with one hand broke away from the cliff face. Caught off guard, Zev lost his hold and, to his horror, found himself sliding down the rock out of control.

He heard Marieke's cry, and the next thing he knew, she'd thrown her arms around him as he slid to her level, trying to use her body to pin him to the rock.

It slowed him enough to allow him to get his footing on the little ledge, but with him against the wall and Marieke on his outside, she had barely any purchase for her feet. She was still pressed against him such that he felt when her foothold gave way.

There was no time to cry out. Silent and panicked, Zev reached around, gripping her arm just as she jolted downward. It took every bit of his self-control to stay stationary, and every bit of his strength not to lose his own hold on the rock. But he managed it, and once everything was still and he was sure of his footing, he pulled her slowly back to his position, his arms straining with the effort.

"Zev." Marieke's voice was a gasp, but he shook his head.

"We're not secure enough here. Look, the ledge opens up that way. Come on."

Still maintaining his grip on her arm, he started to shuffle along the rock face, not drawing a proper breath until they emerged onto a larger section. With her back to the wall, Marieke slid to a sitting position, her eyes closed and her chest rising and falling rapidly.

"That was terrifying." She opened her eyes suddenly, her gaze piercing him. "Thank you for grabbing me."

"What were you thinking?" Zev growled, his fear making him irritable. "You shouldn't have thrown yourself around me like that."

"What should I have done?" Marieke asked weakly. "Let you plummet to your death?"

Better me than you.

Zev stopped himself from saying the words aloud. They would be far too intense. Even he was rattled by them, by how quickly they'd risen to his lips. Rattled because he felt their truth with simple certainty. Not for the first time, he wondered where this girl had come from, upending his life and oversetting all his priorities. Sometimes it felt like she'd changed his very self.

"We have to keep moving," he said instead, his voice gruff.

"I'm scared to." Marieke's vulnerability made it hard for Zev to keep his own voice even.

"I know," he said. "So am I. That's why we need to. The longer we wait, the more we're risking being paralyzed by fear, and we can't afford to be stuck here. If you fall off a horse when you're still learning to ride, you need to get back on right away."

Marieke drew in a deep breath, then let it out slowly. "That's true," she said, reminding him that she'd grown up around horses. "And I certainly don't want to get stuck here." Her voice became stronger. "All right. Let's do it."

Zev took the lead, scouting the area with his very non-magical sight, encouraged to see that there was a larger ledge not far down. They took the next couple of descents slowly and carefully, always moving in a westward direction where possible, and even sooner than they'd hoped, they found themselves on a section of cliff that sloped outward as it went down, allowing them to comfortably descend without a rope.

In spite of the need for caution, they began to move faster. Zev could tell that Marieke was as eager as he was to get his feet on solid ground again. They climbed for half an hour without saying much, only needing to stop and use the rope once. Zev heard Marieke's breath catch in excitement when the rocky canyon floor came into view. They exchanged a look, then increased their pace. Zev had been going slowly to match

Marieke, but now he outstripped her, reaching the ground with a sigh of relief and turning his eyes quickly upward to watch her progress. One foot on the ground and one on the rocky slope, he reached out a hand, steering her down the last, shaley part of the descent.

Instead of a sigh, Marieke let out a much less dignified squeak when her feet touched the ground. Zev's face froze mid-grin when she turned and flung her arms around his neck. Instinctively, he put his own arms around her, thrilling at her nearness. She burrowed her face into his chest, causing something to roar to life inside him. In that moment, all he wanted was to hold her there forever, safe from the deadly accidents and murderous monarchists alike.

"I won't deny it," Marieke's voice came out muffled, "that was a lot harder and scarier than I thought it would be. There's no way I would have made it down without you, not once I lost my song."

She pulled back, her eyes sincere as they met his. "Thank you."

"Thank you for writing to me." Zev couldn't think of anything else to say.

Drawing a deep breath at last, Marieke stepped back, regaining her composure. Zev let her go reluctantly, his arms dropping limply to his sides.

"We should head eastward, I suppose," Marieke said. "Toward the area where I encountered Gorgon and his people last time."

"And why do we want to find them?" Zev asked, as they started to pick their way across the rocky ground. "They're Gorgon's people. And if you recall, he tried to kill you."

"I do recall." Marieke shuddered. "Vividly. But I also recall what he said to me. I told you about it before you left. He knew something about heartsong."

Zev felt himself stiffen, and tried not to let it show. "And you're still determined to find out what that is?"

"I am." Marieke gave a curt nod. "I'm convinced it's connected to whatever's destroying my country." She looked troubled. "It hasn't stopped with Gorgon's death, Zev, like I hoped at first. We've had floods, storms, raging fires—I came across one myself, and I could feel that it was fueled by magic. Something isn't right in Oleand."

"I agree with you there," Zev said. "But I really don't think that you'll find the answers in heartsong."

He wasn't exactly being forthright, of course—he couldn't be—but he wasn't lying about this issue. Heartsong couldn't be what was causing Oleand's problems. Not when these problems were so recent.

"Why not?" Marieke challenged. "Who's to say it won't provide the answers?"

Zev squirmed inside. He hated that she was so fixated on unraveling heartsong, even while he admired her ability to ask the right questions. But it wouldn't help her solve her current problem, and it was too dangerous for her to explore the concept just from curiosity.

"You said back in Ondford that you think heartsong is connected to the loss of Oleand's royals, right?"

She nodded. "It's my best guess."

"So surely," Zev argued, "whatever effect heartsong might have had should have occurred generations ago, when the monarchs were overthrown."

"I can't answer that when I know nothing about heartsong," Marieke said fairly. "That's why I want to find out more."

"But even if that was the cause of the deterioration of the land, that would hardly be causing raging wildfires or storms," said Zev. "Any more than it could cause attacks on singers like the ones that turned out to be orchestrated by Gorgon."

"Why not?" Marieke shrugged. "Why couldn't it cause storms and wildfires?"

Because that's not how heartsong works. Zev didn't say the words aloud, of course. He fell silent, his certainty more shaken than he'd like to admit. From what he knew of heartsong, he couldn't imagine it causing fires or storms. But then, he wouldn't have guessed it would keep out that survey parchment, either.

"I'm not saying I know it's all caused by the same thing," Marieke said, panting a little as she clambered up a ridge of jagged rock. "In fact, I doubt it can be. Like you said, the attacks against singers were carried out by Gorgon, not caused by the magic of the land acting on its own as I'd started to fear. And the fire I fought a couple of weeks ago was fueled by manipulated magic. A singer must have done it. But even if different magic caused these different crises, I'm convinced it's all connected somehow. And I still think Sundering Canyon is the place to look for answers. This is where Gorgon came from. He grew up among a people who choose to live in the one place in the Sovereign Realms where magic is most potent and least predictable. If anyone will know the link between Gorgon's attacks and the way the magic of the land is turning on Oleand, it'll be these canyon-dwellers."

"Maybe you're right," Zev said slowly.

Truthfully, he'd also be glad to find answers as to how it was all connected—the deterioration of Oleand, the contrasting thriving of Aeltas, the inexplicably magical nature of the attacks Gorgon and his followers had carried out against singers in Oleand, and the recent spate of natural disasters that were apparently not natural at all. If the monarchists in the canyon knew something he didn't know, he'd like to hear it. But it would be a delicate balance, trying to learn new information while steering Marieke away from the information he already knew about heartsong.

A double purpose he hated to be hiding from her. But his own words to his family haunted him.

What is it that's made you all think I've forgotten everything I've ever believed?

He knew what it was—it was Marieke. And here he was, against his family's wishes, accompanying her on her quest to unlock the secrets of heartsong. His family expected him to take every opportunity to steer her inquiries away from the truth. She expected him to genuinely help her search for the answers to every aspect of Oleand's troubles.

How could he possibly do both?

Do you think I don't understand what's at stake?

He'd used those words to reassure his family, and they were true. He did understand what was at stake. But for his part, he felt no reassurance. He had no idea how to walk the tightrope he was on and still maintain his integrity.

"Zev?" Marieke's voice drew him from his thoughts.

He turned his head, realizing that she'd stopped walking and was now a few paces behind him.

"What?"

"I said, do you have any more questions?" Marieke's expression was solemn. "Because I acknowledge that you have the right to some answers about what I'm doing here, given you've now been drawn into whatever misadventure this will turn out to be. But I think we should stop and get it out now, so we can move forward silently. We can't be far from where I encountered the monarchists last time. And this time, I'd rather they didn't sneak up on me."

Zev nodded. "I agree. And no, no more questions. At least for now." He had plenty to think about already. "Let me go first."

He moved ahead, paying more attention to where he placed his feet. He grimaced as he accidentally kicked a rock noisily across the gorge. If they were attacked, he would give a good account of himself, but stealth wasn't his strong point. Although he'd been taught from earliest memory the power of hiding in plain sight, his particular method for doing so was based entirely around getting on with life in a straightforward way and avoiding anything clandestine which might draw attention by its secrecy. That way no one suspected something more was going on. He'd never been taught to creep and hide.

After perhaps ten minutes of quiet walking, he was startled by Marieke's hand on his arm. Looking down, he saw that her gaze was fixed ahead, where the canyon was mostly blocked by a gnarled and twisted tree trunk.

"I think someone's ahead," she murmured, her voice barely audible.

Zev frowned in concentration. "I don't hear anything," he breathed back.

She shook her head. "Neither do I. But there's a concentration of magic that feels more targeted than the chaos in the ground beneath us."

"I thought you couldn't access your song," Zev whispered.

"I can't, but I can still sense the magic around me," Marieke said, her tone suggesting that it was ludicrous to question her ability to do so.

"Well, I don't know how these things work," Zev said, hearing the defensive note to his own muttering.

Marieke just flapped a hand for silence, hoisting her ruck-sack higher up her back as she crept forward. Zev paused to tighten his own pack before placing a hand on the hilt of his sword. Neither he nor Marieke had made it around the bulk of the tree trunk, however, when a high-pitched voice made them both freeze in their tracks.

"Look, this one's lighting up. Someone must be approaching."

Zev and Marieke exchanged a look before Zev shifted to put himself in front of his companion. Perhaps he should have been looking for a place to hide them both, but, again, literal hiding wasn't his way. He'd prefer to fight if it came to blows.

"That's a pain." A second voice responded to the first, the pitch equally high and the words accompanied by a sigh. "Must be a patrol of those monarchists coming. You know what they're like. They'll slow everything down and just be a general nuisance."

Zev kept his eyes fixed ahead, but he could feel Marieke's confusion behind him, echoing his own. These strangers weren't part of the monarchists? There was more than one group hiding out in Sundering Canyon?

"Well, we may as well keep at it until they find us," a new voice chimed in. Again, the pitch seemed too high for an adult, although the voice didn't sound in the least childlike. "Come on, I like the feel of things over—"

The words were cut off as three figures rounded the tree trunk and came into view. Everyone froze—Zev included—as the two groups caught sight of each other. He'd thought himself ready to fight anything, but he had most certainly not been ready for what he was seeing.

"They're not monarchists!" one of the newcomers screeched. "Take them out, Rissin."

The words brought Zev springing back into action. He threw himself properly in front of Marieke, the edge of his sight catching her furrowed brow and open mouth as he drew his sword with lightning speed.

Not enough speed for his opponents, however. He'd barely reached a defensive stance when one of them broke something in his hands with a loud snap. Marieke cried out, and a second later, Zev's whole body went rigid, his limbs completely immobilized by what he could only assume was magic. He had no idea how they'd done it—he'd heard no song.

He keeled over, the impact of hitting the ground causing his sword to clatter out of his hand. The roar that burst from him told him he still had use of his voice, but that wouldn't help him save Marieke or himself from the beady-eyed creature striding toward them with drawn blade.

Marieke

Marieke gasped, her mind whirling with confusion as she tried to make sense of what she was seeing. Who were these creatures? *What* were they? They were human in shape, but they weren't like any humans she'd ever seen. Their skin was unnaturally pale, and although the three of them were clearly adults, they only came up to Zev's midriff—or at least they had, before they'd sent both Zev and her toppling to the ground with some kind of immobilizing magic.

Magic that made no sense, because it had clearly emanated from the middle one of the trio of strangers, but he hadn't even opened his mouth, let alone sung anything.

Marieke lay prone, unable to move thanks to the magic. It was only as Zev let out a roar that it occurred to her that she might be able to speak.

"Wait!" she cried, relieved to hear her own voice.

The member of the miniature trio who was striding forward ignored her. He bent over Zev, his startlingly green eyes glittering as he flourished a small blade.

"This one has murder in his eyes," he commented, his high voice dispassionate. "I'll probably be best to kill him first."

"Don't draw it out," complained one of the others. "We're not human barbarians—don't take pleasure in violence."

"I don't take pleasure in it," the first one said matter-of-factly. "But someone has to do it, and I guess that someone is me."

"Please, listen to me!" Marieke cried desperately, over the top of Zev's growl of anger.

Fear clutched at her when none of them responded. On instinct, she felt for the magic in the ground below, trying to draw it toward her. As always, the magic of the canyon was pure chaos, and she couldn't grasp much. Not that it would help her if she could, given she didn't have her singing voice. She'd tried a defensive song when the strangers approached, and no sound had come out. But she could still feel the magic responding to her reaching. Even if it wasn't pooling around her like she intended, it was definitely moving.

"Whoa. Hold."

The one with the blade raised above Zev paused at his companion's words, looking irked at the interruption but obeying at once. "What is it?"

The stranger who'd spoken, the one called Rissin from whom the immobilizing magic had come, stepped forward.

"Look at that. Look what the magic is doing."

Confused, Marieke followed his gaze to see a cylindrical tool in his hand. It was long and thin, more than twice the size of the small man's whole hand. It was made of some kind of silver metal, save for a strip of gleaming gold running its length.

The stranger raised his head and fixed his eyes—the same emerald green as his fellow's—on Zev. The movement caused his long, straight hair to fall such that the tips of his ears protruded.

Tips that were tapered and wobbling slightly.

Marieke was so busy staring at them, she almost missed what everyone else was looking at. It was Zev's tense voice that reminded her that the stranger had pointed the object ominously toward Zev.

"What is that? What are you doing?"

Marieke gasped. The ground all around Zev was glowing brightly in the dim shadows of the canyon. The light pulsed and shifted, like a fitful gust of wind blowing the long grass on the hill near her home.

"How curious," said Rissin, his alabaster brow furrowed. He ignored Zev's questions completely. "Even for the canyon, this is unusual." His eyes shifted slowly to Marieke, the brightness of their green almost dazzling. "You are an interesting pair. You're the one who made the magic move, aren't you? I saw you open your mouth. When you tried to call out before and no sound came, you were trying to sing, weren't you?"

"A singer, you think?" One of the others cut in before Marieke had decided whether to answer. "A singer whose voice has been taken by the canyon?"

"But the magic still responded to her somewhat," Rissin commented. He sighed. "It would be fascinating to keep her alive long enough to conduct some experiments. It's a rare chance to see a singer interact with the magic of the canyon."

"Stay away from her." Zev's voice was a growl that had begun as soon as Rissin said the word experiment. Marieke found herself in agreement, glaring her displeasure at the cold-hearted strangers.

"They've seen us, Rissin," the one with the blade said. "If they're not with the monarchists, they can't be allowed to live."

"I know." Rissin sighed again. "But it is a pity."

"I want to speak to Svetlana!" Marieke said quickly, as the armed stranger lifted his blade again.

To her satisfaction, all three of them paused, matching alabaster brows crinkling.

"So you *are* with the monarchists?"

"They're not monarchists," another said with a scoff. "Did you see their shock when they saw us? They've never seen elves before. And look at their clothes."

Elves? Marieke had no idea what he was talking about there, but she understood the clothes comment. All the monarchists she'd seen last time had been dressed fully in gray to camouflage with the rock around them.

"I'm known to Svetlana," Marieke said as confidently as she could manage. "And I came here to see her."

"Hm." Rissin considered her. "That changes things. We don't want to upset our human collaborators by killing their friends. That would make our lives unnecessarily harder."

The one with the blade didn't seem convinced, and Marieke didn't blame him. He could probably see the same gleam in Rissin's eyes that she could. She strongly suspected he cared less about offending the monarchists than about retaining the possibility to study her and Zev and the magic of the canyon.

But if it prolonged their lives, she'd take it.

"Will you take us to Svetlana and her people?" Marieke pressed boldly.

"In exchange for what?" Rissin asked, his eyes still gleaming in that discomfiting way.

"Hold on," Zev cut in before Marieke could answer. "Did you say you're elves?"

"No." Rissin turned thoughtful eyes on Zev. "I don't believe we did say that."

"It was said by implication." Zev's voice was hard, his figure unnaturally stiff where he lay on the ground. His eyes flitted to Marieke. "Be careful what you say. According to the legends, elves have magic of their own around them, and words have a force they don't have among humans. They're cold and calculating, and you can bind yourself to a bargain without meaning to."

"You knew about these...elves?" Marieke's voice was a squeak.

"I've heard stories about them," Zev told her. "Bedtime stories. I had no idea they were actually real."

"Real as this sword," said the elf who had earlier been ready to knife Zev. He was examining Zev's blade on the ground nearby. Marieke half expected him to take issue with being called cold and calculating, but it didn't seem to have troubled him. He turned back to his companions. "All right, Rissin, time to make a decision before the freezing enchantment wears off."

"We'll take them to Svetlana." Rissin looked faintly disappointed that he'd failed to get the promise of an exchange from Marieke, but apparently not disappointed enough to order her death. "If she can't access her songcraft, I see no great threat." He nodded at Zev's blade. "But we can't have him armed. Destroy that."

Zev gave a cry of outrage as the elf turned toward his sword. Marieke felt the first tingles of movement returning to her fingertips, but if the magic was lifting from Zev as well, it wasn't doing so quickly enough to save his weapon. The diminutive creature pulled out a round metal disc and placed it on the blade of the sword. Marieke felt a surge of magic, and before her eyes the sharp metal of Zev's weapon turned to dust.

"Hey!" Zev surged clumsily to his feet just as Marieke flexed her sore arms as well. He stumbled once before gaining his balance and snatching the sword hilt from the ground. "What gives you the right?!"

"The fact that I have the magic and you don't." The elf shrugged, untroubled by Zev's fury.

Marieke hurried forward, laying a calming hand on Zev's

arm before he could do something that would ignite the volatile situation.

"Easy Zev," she said softly.

He met her eyes, the mutiny in his gaze ebbing as he searched her face. "Are you all right?"

She nodded, seeing a reflection of her own relief at their narrow escape. "You?"

"Of course."

Marieke wasn't convinced, but she let it drop as Rissin strode toward them. She and Zev stared down at the elf, whose confidence clearly wasn't suffering from the fact that he was half their height.

"We'll take you to Svetlana, but it's too much hassle to move through the canyon with your feet bound. Just know that if you run away, we will kill you."

Marieke saw Zev's eyes narrow, and she cut in again before he could express his opinion of that offer.

"We risked our lives to climb down into the canyon specifically to see Svetlana and the others," she pointed out. "If you're taking us where we want to go, we have no reason to run away."

"So you claim," the armed elf said. "But I'd never trust a human's word. Not unless the human is bound by the magic of a bargain he or she can't control. Otherwise they'll always try to wriggle out of what they say."

"Unlike elves," Zev said in a tone of cold and unconvincing politeness. "Whom all the legends say were trustworthy and transparent, never known for being unscrupulous."

Rissin chuckled. "And here I thought our reputation had been lost. It's nice to know our good name remains known in some corner of the so-called Sovereign Realms." He gestured imperiously toward them. "Now put your hands behind your backs so we can bind them."

"I'd rather not," Zev said flatly.

"Then we'll end it here." Rissin showed no particular emotion with the words, although it was clear to all present that by *it* he meant their lives. "I won't take you anywhere unbound."

"Come on, Zev," Marieke murmured. "Live today to fight tomorrow."

Zev stared at her, something strange in his expression that she couldn't read. It was a common enough saying. He must know what she meant.

After a prolonged moment, Zev sighed, putting his hands behind his back. Marieke could see that it went against his every instinct, and could only be relieved that he wasn't letting his pride get in the way of good sense.

"Elves have excellent hearing," Rissin commented as he stowed his cylindrical instrument into a pack at his side. "Trying to fight us tomorrow will get you killed just as surely as trying to fight us today would have."

Marieke ignored him, instead moving close to Zev and giving his arm another quick squeeze before she put her own hands behind her back.

"I'm sorry about your sword," she told him.

Zev was glaring at the armed elf, who was now chatting with Rissin and ignoring the humans completely.

"It was my favorite weapon," he muttered, still clearly irked.

In spite of the gravity of their situation, Marieke felt her mouth twitch. She quelled the reaction quickly, before Zev's eyes fell back to her face.

"We're no happier about it than you are," commented the elf now tying up Zev's hands with a length of rope he'd produced from who knew where. "That's two powerful talismans we've wasted thanks to you being where you shouldn't be."

"Talismans?" Marieke stared at him, her mind reeling at this mention of items in which magic could be stored for later use. The artifacts were incredibly rare. "You have talismans?"

"You've just seen us use them." The elf's voice was pitying. "Humans truly are dense. Of course we have talismans. Our craftsmanship is the best quality you'll ever encounter," he added proudly.

"Craftsmanship..." Marieke trailed off. "But no one remembers how to craft talismans. That knowledge was lost."

"Lost, was it?" the elf said dryly. "Along with the knowledge of the fact that humans share this continent with real, living elves?"

"Are you telling me that elves were always the ones who crafted talismans?" Marieke asked. She glanced at Zev to see what he made of this new development. He seemed as thrown as she was.

"I'm not telling you anything," the elf said in the contrary way she was fast coming to associate with the miniature species. "I'm talking, and you're drawing your own conclusions." He tugged at the rope around Zev's wrists, studying his own knot with a critical eye.

"I can't make sense of this," Marieke said, raising one of her still-unbound hands to her forehead. "I've never read any record about elves being the ones who made talismans. I've never read any record about elves at all!"

"No, you wouldn't have, would you?" the elf quipped. "Any more than you've read records about the slaughter of the monarchs."

Marieke started, her palms beginning to sweat at this bald statement of the truth Zev had hinted at but never said so plainly. Any doubt she'd retained about what really happened during the singers' coup melted away.

"That's the way it always goes when it comes to conflicts, isn't it?" the elf went on as he nonchalantly tied her wrists so tightly her hands began to feel numb. "Whoever wins the conflict gets to write the records—or *not* write them, as their preference may be. If winning the conflict wins them enough power, they can even get rid of other records they don't especially like."

"So…you had conflict with the singers?" Zev asked. He was studying the elf carefully, his stance back to its usual calm confidence in spite of the bound hands.

The elf gave a snort. "Conflict is a nice way to put it. They tried to wipe us out altogether. Why do you think we're skulking down here?"

"We're not skulking," Rissin cut in reproachfully, strolling up to the group.

The first elf just shrugged.

"What happened between your kind and the singers?" Zev asked, directing the question to Rissin.

The elf considered him steadily, his eyes glittering. "What will you give me in exchange for the information?"

"In asking, I promise nothing, only inquire," Zev said carefully. "What do you seek?"

"I wish to know first, whether you know why the magic pooled around you, and second, the reason it did so," Rissin countered much too quickly and smoothly.

Marieke expected Zev to disclaim any knowledge of the reason, but he just looked back at the elf in uncommunicative silence. Did he not want to engage in a discussion of magic, or did he actually know something he wasn't sharing?

As always, she wished she could read what was in his mind.

The silence stretched out long enough for Rissin to give up.

But Marieke could see the calculating way he assessed Zev as he turned away.

"I wish to reach Svetlana's group before dark," he said to the other elves. "Let's go."

The elves set off, Marieke and Zev following behind. To her relief, they weren't blindfolded like she had been last time, and their packs weren't taken from them. She wished she could retrieve her cloak. Judging by the color of the strip of sky visible to them, the sun hadn't set yet in the world above the gorge. But down at the base of Sundering Canyon, the light was low, and night's chill was already seeping through her light clothes.

They walked for half an hour before the elves turned suddenly sideways, stepping between two offset boulders and onto a staircase that had been hidden from view until they were right upon it.

"They still don't even know we're here. We would have come and gone without interruption if not for these two," sighed the elf with the blade.

But Rissin didn't seem bothered by the change in their plans. "It's good to check in with the humans every now and then. Wait here with the prisoners."

He ducked into an opening above them, leaving them standing for a full quarter of an hour. The light had become so low that Marieke could barely make out Zev's expression. They didn't attempt to speak, just waited in silence until Rissin reappeared, accompanied by a middle-aged woman with gray eyes and grizzled hair.

"Svetlana!" Marieke felt a surge of relief which she knew made no sense. Last time this woman had tried to imprison her. But it was just so reassuring to see a human after the unnerving discovery that another intelligent species existed within the canyon.

The older woman stared at her. "Do I know y—ah." Understanding came into her eyes, a spark of curiosity with it. "You're the one who fell from the bridge! You've got your voice back."

"Not every aspect of it," Rissin broke in. "She's a singer, but seems unable to sing down here."

Svetlana's eyes sharpened, and she looked Marieke over again. She made no comment, however, merely beckoning the group in. "We can discuss this further inside." Her eyes flicked to Zev. "Who's he?"

"My name is Zevadiah." Zev spoke with dignity, but Marieke caught his rueful look—bordering on humorous—in response to the dismissive way Svetlana noticed him.

"I suppose you'd best come in, too," the middle-aged woman said.

Hands still bound, Marieke and Zev followed her and the elves through a tunnel network that eventually led them to a furnished cave. It was much nicer than the cave Marieke had been taken into the previous time. Wooden doors had been built over the various entrances to keep out drafts, and the space was lit by lanterns. Clattering from behind the far door suggested that it might be a cooking area, a realization that made Marieke's stomach grumble. She and Zev had found only minimal opportunity to safely stop and eat on their precarious descent into the canyon.

A glance around the main room revealed several other people clad in the same nondescript gray as Svetlana. One stood by each doorway, and the others hovered not far behind Svetlana, saying nothing but watching the new arrivals closely. Svetlana gave them a subtle nod as she passed, before gesturing toward a number of chairs.

"Sit."

It was more of a command than a sign of hospitality, but Marieke sank gladly into a chair regardless. It was a relief to be off her feet. Two of the elves remained standing, but Rissin approached a chair, putting his hands lightly on the seat and then vaulting himself up onto it. Marieke had to fight a sudden and slightly hysterical giggle at the way his legs dangled above the ground. Like a child at the adults' table.

"What's your name, child?" Svetlana asked her.

"Marieke," she said.

"Is it true you're a singer?"

Seeing nothing to be gained from denying it, Marieke nodded.

To her surprise, Svetlana didn't respond with anger or contempt, instead letting out a sigh. "So that's why Gorgon attacked you on sight, is it?"

"Yes." Marieke didn't expand. Brief answers were probably safest.

"Why did you come to our canyon? Last time, I mean?"

"I didn't come here on purpose," Marieke said. "I really did fall from the bridge. I was lucky to survive." She could feel Zev's tension beside her as his eyes moved between the two speakers.

"I see." Svetlana interlaced her fingers as she studied Marieke's face. "And how did you escape? You did well to find your way through the tunnel network."

"I didn't find my own way," Marieke told her. "Gorgon helped me find a way out."

"Gorgon helped—?"

"Right before he attempted to help me off the edge of a cliff," Marieke added, cutting over the top of Svetlana's astonished words.

"Ah." Svetlana paused. "That makes more sense. I'm afraid he always was hotheaded."

Marieke frowned, finding these dismissive words entirely unsatisfactory.

"I only escaped with my life thanks to my own resourcefulness and Zev's timely help. Otherwise Gorgon would have succeeded in murdering me. And that wasn't the last time. On two more occasions he tried to kill me."

"Yes, I'm aware that he followed you to the surface with his vendetta," Svetlana said heavily. "The whole situation was regrettable, to say the least. If he was here, I would certainly give him an earful."

"Well, you can't, because he's dead," Marieke said bluntly.

"I know that, child." Svetlana's voice was somber, but she didn't seem overly distressed. "I have my sources of information in your capital. In both of your capitals."

Zev's brow crinkled as her eyes turned to him. "How do you know I'm Aeltan?"

"How could I fail to see it?" Svetlana asked. She waved a hand at him. "Your dress, your demeanor, the lilt of your voice. We might choose to live down here, but we know plenty about the world on the surface." Her attention went back to Marieke. "I never received a satisfactory report about Gorgon's death. The details seem to have been suppressed. Was it you who killed him?"

"No, it was me," Zev cut in before Marieke could respond. "I intervened to prevent him from killing Marieke. I do not regret it. But should his family wish to call me to account, I will certainly face them."

Marieke made a small noise of protest, which Svetlana ignored. The older woman was looking at Zev with the first sign of respect she'd given him.

"That will not be necessary. As it happens, Gorgon had no family. I suspect that's why he sought to create his little group of followers." She sighed again. "We all seek belonging, I suppose. In any event, I consider Gorgon responsible for his own death. He did not act with the sanction of our community."

"So you claim." Zev's voice was cold.

"Well then, Svetlana." Rissin was growing bored with the conversation. "If you're satisfied that they're not spies, we'll be on our way. I wish to take this pair with us, and I propose that—"

"No." There was no compromise in Zev's tone, but Svetlana flapped a hand impatiently at him.

"He wasn't asking your opinion, Zevadiah. And Rissin, settle down. You're not taking them anywhere, and I'm not satisfied of anything. How should I know whether they're spies?"

"She asked for you by name to avoid us eliminating her, and you clearly recognize her. Are you saying you're not willing to speak for her?"

Marieke scowled at the elf. *Eliminating?* It was a very bloodless way to refer to the murder he and his fellows had almost carried out. But Zev had said they were cold and calculating, according to the legends.

The thought made her frown again, this time in contemplation rather than annoyance. She looked from Rissin to Svetlana. The elves had seemed calculating in the way they'd spoken with Marieke and Zev earlier. Their manner with Svetlana was different. Was it just because the two groups clearly had some kind of uneasy alliance?

"If you want to take us as your prisoners out of Svetlana's territory, why don't you bargain for it?" Marieke interrupted the conversation between the elf and the monarchist, watching the little creature's face for a response.

But it was Svetlana who snorted in reply. "Bargain for it? Down here? What would be the point?"

"What do you mean?" Zev asked sharply.

Svetlana passed a look of indulgence over the two of them. "Did they pull you in with threats about magically binding bargains? If so, it was a hoax."

"Elf bargains aren't real?" Marieke asked, feeling foolish. She and Zev had taken it so seriously when Rissin tried to bargain with them for information.

"Oh, they're real enough," Svetlana said. "I've dealt with elves up on the surface before—maddeningly slippery they are to communicate with. Down here they're not so insufferable, though. They have to adapt to the environment, and they've learned that the magic of the canyon isn't predictable like it is on the land above. It's wild magic down here, pure magic. It responds to no law, not even the laws of elf bargains."

Rissin leaned back in his chair throughout this explanation, his expression smug and his gaze on Zev. Marieke saw that the Aeltan was watching the little elf with narrowed eyes, clearly irked at having been taken in.

"I see you feel no shame in your lies being exposed," Zev commented.

Rissin was unfazed. "You see that, do you? Such human folly, to imagine that you can see what we feel or do not feel. And to what lies do you refer? We weren't the ones who mentioned the bargain magic," Rissin reminded him with an unrepentant shrug. "That was you. Why would we correct you when your error was in our interests?"

Zev shifted, clearly ready to retort, but Marieke spoke over him.

"I didn't risk my life coming down here to bicker with mythical creatures," she said shortly. After the exertions of the day, her hunger was becoming more insistent, and it was making her irritable. "I'm not interested in an argument about whether lies of omission count as dishonesty."

Zev fell silent, more chastened by her words than she'd expected.

"What did you come down here for, then?" Svetlana asked,

regarding Marieke with interest. "And why did you ask for me by name?"

"To be frank, Rissin is right," Marieke said. "I used your name in hopes it would make him hesitate to *eliminate* me, as he so gracefully put it. But I really did come down here looking for you." She would have waved her hand if it was free, but it was still bound, so she had to settle for making a sweeping motion with her chin. "All of you, I mean. Your whole settlement. I came because I want answers that I don't think I'll find back in Ondford."

"Do you?" Svetlana raised an eyebrow, her reaction difficult to read. "Answers to what questions?"

"Well, the elves are one question," Marieke said, her eyes sliding to Rissin. She still couldn't fully believe that the little creatures were real. "Since you obviously knew about them."

"Naturally." Svetlana was very much at her ease. "We've been doing business with the elves for a long time. But that wasn't really a question."

"Is it true that the singers who orchestrated the coup tried to wipe out the elves?" Marieke blurted out.

"Of course it's true," Rissin said, his affronted tone unconvincing. "Do you accuse us of lying?"

"Spare your mock outrage," Zev said, eyeing him. He was clearly still put out about having nearly been swindled by the elves.

Svetlana ignored all this, her gaze fixed on Marieke. "Do you think it's true, singer Marieke?"

"I don't know what to think," Marieke said frankly. "About a lot of things."

Svetlana nodded thoughtfully, studying Marieke's face for another moment before she spoke. "That's something, at least." Her eyes passed to Zev. "What about you, young man? What do you think?"

Zev let out a sigh, shifting position slightly. He somehow managed to look calm and commanding in spite of being seated with his hands bound behind his back.

"I doubt the elves are lying about it," he said. He turned his head to Marieke, addressing his next words to her. "The very fact that you'd never heard of elves—that I thought them only a story—supports it as well. The first council probably thought they'd succeeded, or they would have tried to paint the elves as evil instead of pretending they didn't exist."

"Like they did with the monarchs," Svetlana said, nodding. She looked quite impressed. "Well articulated, young man. I agree that they likely thought they'd managed to kill all the elves—they wanted the elves to disappear, so that's what they made them do. Once they took power, the singers would be able to get rid of official records of elves. From all I know, they were always inclined to be reclusive when it came to humans, and even back then, most people would never have seen an elf. It would only take a few generations for any surviving stories to devolve into legends and bedtime stories, like the ones you've apparently heard."

Marieke digested this for a moment before responding.

"What do you mean, like they did with the monarchs?" she asked eventually, looking at Svetlana.

But it wasn't the woman who answered. One of Rissin's companions chuckled.

"She means that the singers might have been able to wipe us out of the records, but they could hardly wipe out the monarchs."

Rissin made a noise of disdain. "They wouldn't wish to. No doubt it served their purposes well to keep every record of the old royals' frailties and vices."

"True enough records," the other elf pointed out, and Rissin nodded.

"Indeed." His voice carried the same disdain he'd just shown for the singers.

"So..." Marieke gave her head a little shake, confused. "So the elves didn't support the royals?"

"The pickaxe hung from quite the other belt," said Rissin, again sounding faintly affronted.

"What?" Marieke just stared at him.

"Elf saying," Svetlana interjected. "It means it was the other way around."

"The royals supported the elves?" Zev sounded skeptical.

Rissin's eyes glittered. "The royals...and their courts. They supported our kind financially."

The other elf's eyes had glazed over. "How rich our ancestors were," he said wistfully. "With so many humans willing to spend their ill-gotten wealth on our talismans."

Svetlana sent a swift scowl at the elves. "You're hardly in a position to criticize the monarchs of old. Had your people chosen to do so, they could have defended the royals against the singers' attacks. Some people might argue your kind have blood on their hands as much as singers do."

"Then those people would be imbeciles," said Rissin without heat. "But happily, their opinion would not interest me in the slightest." He stood, the movement unexpected since he pushed himself to his feet right there on the chair, standing for a moment before lightly leaping down to the ground. "If you're determined to keep these two prisoners overnight, we'll leave you to it. We won't return to our ship now, though. We'll camp in the canyon, and if you try to slip them past us, you will regret it."

"Your threats leave me terrified," Svetlana said, the sarcasm light enough not to provoke a reaction from Rissin.

The three elves pattered out of the cave, back the way they'd come.

ELEVEN

Marieke

"**M**addening little creatures," Svetlana commented, her eyes following them. "But at least they're consistent."

She gave a subtle nod to the man standing next to the doorway leading outside, and he melted out of view, in the direction the elves had taken. Svetlana turned to Marieke and Zev, folding her arms over her chest.

"You'll find that human notions of honor are meaningless to elves," she informed them. "They're often considered unscrupulous according to human perception, but they do have their own codes, and they follow them meticulously. Just never expect altruism from an elf. You won't find it."

"Thank you for that wisdom." Zev's voice was just dry enough to convey dignity without being inflammatory. "Does the fact that you're giving us life advice mean that you intend to give us the opportunity to use it?"

"I'm not in the habit of arbitrarily killing people, if that's what you're asking," Svetlana replied coolly, one eyebrow rising as her gaze flicked to Marieke. "Not even singers."

"You'll have to forgive our skepticism," Zev retorted. "Since that was precisely the habit of the only other member of your community we've dealt with."

"I already told you that Gorgon didn't act on our behalf." But Svetlana had the decency to look a little uncomfortable. "I should add, neither do the elves."

"That much is clear," Zev said. "What are they doing down in the canyon, anyway?"

"Back up a bit," Marieke interjected. "The first question isn't what are they doing. It's what *are* they."

Svetlana looked amused. "The first question of many, no doubt. And I have my own. But it can wait until after food and sleep. Your hands will be unbound," one of her silent companions moved to make it happen as she said the words, "but remember that you're not guests. You're captives. Every entrance is guarded, and you won't be allowed to leave. If you try, you will hurt your chances of favorable treatment. And even if you made it out of the cave system, the elves are waiting in the canyon. I don't advise you to entrust yourself to them. Now you've seen them and know of their existence, they won't be eager to let you return to the surface alive."

Marieke brought her hands around to the front of her the moment they were freed, rubbing her sore wrists with relief.

"There's an underground spring in the cavern through that door." Svetlana gestured behind them. "You can wash up before dinner."

She took a step toward the door through which the clattering had come earlier, then paused, looking back at Zev.

"You going to be all right?"

"How do you mean?" Zev asked stiffly. His eyes flicked to Marieke.

"I'm not asking if she's all right, because I can see that she is," Svetlana told him. "She seems level-headed to me."

Zev raised his eyebrows. "And I don't?"

"Well, you wouldn't be the first man whose pride was bruised by being overpowered by critters half his height. It can sting a touch, or so I'm told."

Zev stared at her for a moment before, to Marieke's surprise, she saw his face soften in amusement.

"I wouldn't say my pride is flourishing."

Svetlana chuckled. "Was it being brought to heel, or being outwitted regarding the bargaining that did it? Or both?"

Zev's only reply was a rueful expression, which was enough to bring another chuckle out of Svetlana.

"I'll leave you to tend to your bruises, then. Dinner is in a quarter of an hour through this door, late arrivals depart hungry." She strode through the door, closing it firmly behind her.

To Marieke's surprise, Zev let out a chuckle of his own. "You know, I almost like her." He took Marieke's hand with one of his freed ones, the sudden movement startling her and bringing a touch of heat up her neck.

"Have you forgotten that she's holding us captive?" Marieke asked, swallowing audibly and hoping it wasn't obvious how vividly aware she was of every point of contact between Zev's skin and hers.

"Of course I haven't." Zev's voice held the hint of a smile as he tugged her toward the door Svetlana had indicated. "I just expected her to be different."

"Expected?" Marieke repeated. "Why did you have any expectations at all, since you'd never even heard of her?"

Zev shrugged as, watched by the guards, they went through the doorway and found a well-lit room with a still, underground pool. "Not Svetlana specifically, maybe. But I live close to the canyon. People in my region know the rumors of the monarchists down here. They have their own reputation."

Marieke released Zev's hand to kneel at the water's edge,

dipping in her hands and patting her weary face. "So what did you expect her to be like?"

"Well...like Gorgon, I suppose. Hotheaded and unreasonable, passionate for a cause he knew nothing about. But this Svetlana..." Zev shrugged again, not kneeling by the water himself, his demeanor that of a man keeping watch. "She means well, I think." He smiled ruefully. "Probably. Maybe."

"Whatever that means." Marieke didn't feel in the mood for his riddles, more focused on washing the grime off her arms. Climbing down the steep cliffside hadn't left her tidy or clean, to put it mildly. Her clothes were also the worse for wear, but she couldn't imagine feeling safe enough in the monarchists' enclave to change into fresh ones from her pack.

"Doesn't mean they're not wasting their lives down here, of course." Zev's musings seemed to be as much for his own benefit as hers.

"What should they be doing instead?" Marieke countered. She flashed Zev a grin. "Tilling the soil like good farm folk?"

He laughed. "Yes, actually. A much more productive use of their time."

Marieke stood, studying him. "It's true, isn't it?" she said thoughtfully. "You believe the same as the monarchists do about the singers' coup and the current council. But you don't sit around bemoaning it. You keep active, earning an honest living, helping your country in your own way."

"I like to think so," Zev said lightly. He didn't meet her eye, apparently not as interested in discussing his philosophy on life as she was. With Marieke standing up, he bent, swiftly scrubbing his hands before straightening again. "Come on, I'm famished."

Marieke couldn't argue with that, following him back into the main cavern. Others were streaming into it, a few going past them to the underground spring to wash their hands. They entered the room Svetlana had indicated to find about a dozen people already seated. They all wore the same gray clothes as Svetlana, clearly designed to camouflage well with the rock.

"You do have a point about them wasting their lives," Marieke murmured to Zev. "I mean, what do they all *do* down here? When they're not holding unwary travelers captive, that is."

The corner of Zev's mouth quirked up in the smile that she'd become far too fond of, but he didn't otherwise respond. She understood why. As outsiders, they were clearly an oddity. Every eye found them as they advanced through the room, and it didn't seem likely that speech between them would remain private.

In fact, all speech in the room stilled as they took their seats. Marieke just hoped her stomach wasn't going to growl into the silence. She was hungry enough that she wouldn't be surprised.

They were served up a hot stew, its heartiness surprising her. She glanced at Zev, who'd already begun to eat.

"Where do they get the meat? Surely there can't be enough animals down here to sustain a whole community. Do you think they have a farm somewhere in the canyon?"

Zev considered his bowl for a moment before answering, then ran his thumb along the handle of his spoon.

"Maybe." He didn't sound convinced.

The meal passed in a near silence that was surely unusual for the small community. Judging by the constant looks thrown their way, it was the presence of strangers that stilled everyone's tongues. One girl in particular seemed to be looking at them every time Marieke's eyes rose from her bowl. As the rest of the group started to clear out of the little cave, the girl sidled closer. When Marieke lowered her spoon for the last time, it was to find the stranger only one bench away.

"Hello," Marieke said, holding the other girl's gaze. She expected her to look away or hurry off, but instead she slid closer along the wooden bench.

"Hi."

"And who are you?" Zev's voice was mild, but somehow held too much authority for a captive. The stranger answered at once.

"My name is Trina. What's yours?"

"Marieke," Marieke interjected. "And this is Zev."

The girl, probably no more than about fifteen, nodded. "Is it true that you're a singer?"

"Yes." Marieke folded her hands in her lap, trying to project as much confidence as Zev did.

"Are you from Aeltas?"

Marieke shook her head. "From Oleand. But Zev's from Aeltas."

"Oleand?" Trina looked thoughtful. "Things are bad there, right?"

A defensive instinct urged Marieke to deny it, but she curbed the impulse. She'd come to find answers, and she was more likely to get accurate ones if she provided the truth herself.

"It's not terrible, but it's getting worse."

"Is that why you're here? To figure out how to make it better?"

"One of the reasons," Marieke said carefully.

"Did the Council of Singers send you?" Trina's eyes were wide. "Do they want to know if we can help?"

Marieke let out a dry laugh. "Hardly. They don't know I'm here. I'm not acting on their behalf."

"You're trying to bring them down?" Trina guessed.

"No," Marieke repeated, frowning. "I'm not trying to lead

some rebellion, and I'm not trying to attack anyone. I just want answers. And to help my country."

The girl leaned back a little, considering Marieke. "Very admirable," she said politely.

"Trina." The sharp voice made them all look up to see Svetlana in the doorway.

Trina started as if caught in wrongdoing, and Marieke realized that the three of them were the last ones left in the room.

"I believe you're on clean up tonight." Svetlana's tone made it clear that it wasn't open for debate, and Trina got quickly to her feet.

"Yes, Svetlana." With a final glance at the pair, Trina grabbed a loaded tray from the next table over and made her way from the room.

Marieke grabbed her own and Zev's bowls, adding them to another tray while Zev spoke.

"She wasn't doing anything wrong, you know. She was just speaking with us. Do you have so much to hide that you don't want any of your people speaking to outsiders?"

Svetlana didn't seem troubled by the challenge as she strolled up to their table. "We're not the ones whose main goal in life is to hide the truth."

Zev narrowed his eyes slightly as he considered her. "And what does that mean?"

"It means that it's your Councils of Singers who suppress the truth," Svetlana said, sensing his displeasure and hardening her own features in response.

"Well, this is a nice surprise, really," Marieke commented. She moved to stand behind Zev, who rose to his feet as well. "I expected to be the one under fire, since I'm the singer, but instead the two of you are targeting all your disapproval at each other, just as if you didn't both dislike the councils equally."

"Is that so?" Svetlana didn't seem convinced. "A surprising

claim about a man who's traveling around with an academy-trained singer."

"Just as it's surprising to hear the leader of a secret, subversive community claim that she isn't the one trying to hide," Marieke countered.

"I'm not sure you could call them subversive," Zev said, folding his arms. "I've seen no evidence that they do anything to bring down the authority they claim to hate. Or any evidence that they do anything at all, really."

"You must have forgotten Gorgon's attacks on every singer he could get his hands on, including me," Marieke said.

"I certainly haven't forgotten." Zev's voice was dark, his brow lowered as his eyes remained fixed on Svetlana. "Or forgiven."

Svetlana frowned. "I've already told you he acted without my knowledge or approval. And while we're on the topic of young members of my community easily led astray by outside influences, I surely need give no more reason for not wanting you filling Trina's heads with whatever agendas you came down here with."

Zev seemed like he wanted to retort, but Svetlana didn't give him the chance.

"Much as I'd love to stay and talk, I have other matters to see to. We will speak tomorrow, after you've slept." She nodded to a man who'd just appeared in the doorway. "Someone will show you to a room. I repeat my warning about trying to leave."

The next moment, Svetlana was gone, and the man had stepped forward.

"This way."

He turned on the word, and they had to move quickly to keep up with him. He led them back into the main cavern, gesturing toward the cave with the spring.

"If you go through there, you'll find a small doorway to

another area on the right wall, for ablutions. You won't have another chance before morning."

Marieke shot a self-conscious look at Zev, then cleared her throat.

"I'll go first."

She hurried into the cavern with the spring and found the doorway indicated. She hadn't even noticed it last time. It led to a small cavern, lit with a single lantern. As soon as she entered, she caught the quiet sound of running water. A series of holes had been carved into the floor, and examination of them showed that they'd been cut right through to an underground stream that ran past below.

Handy.

Marieke relieved herself quickly, nervous of someone else coming in. After taking a moment to freshen herself at the spring, she moved back into the main cavern. Zev raised his eyebrows as if to ask, *everything all right?* She nodded and, after a swift and searching look at their companion, Zev strode into the room with the spring.

He was back so quickly, she suspected he was wary of leaving her alone with the stranger. But he needn't have worried. The gray-clad monarchist had stood silently the whole time, staring at the far wall and generally ignoring Marieke's existence.

"Ready?" he asked curtly, when Zev reappeared.

They both nodded, and their guide led them across the main cavern and through yet another doorway. He took them through such a labyrinth of tunnels that Marieke quickly lost track of the way back. She had the thought of trying to surreptitiously form a guiding song to track their path, but then remembered she couldn't sing in the canyon.

Their path got gradually darker as the lanterns mounted on the walls disappeared. Before long, the flickering glow of their guide's lantern was the only source of light. A shiver went over Marieke. It wasn't as cold as she would have expected a subterranean cave to be, it was just eerie.

When they finally came to a stop, Marieke felt her shoulders sag with relief. She was ready to get off her feet again. But that relief dissipated when their guide pulled back the curtain of dried reeds that formed the only door to the space in front of them, and revealed the cavern beyond. It was tiny, with nothing in it but two rolled up pallets, each with a blanket folded and sitting on top of it.

"Is this it?" Zev asked.

The guide's expression was stony in the low light. "Were you expecting luxury?"

"I was expecting something a little more remarkable, given how far we had to walk to get to it," Zev retorted. He glanced down the rough stone corridor. There were no other doorways visible nearby. "Isn't there a second space we can also use?"

"This isn't an inn," the stranger said irritably. "You can't reserve rooms. This is where you're to spend the night, and someone will come and get you in the morning."

He bent down, placing the lantern on the stone floor just inside the curtain, then strode back the way they'd come.

"At least he left the lantern," Marieke muttered. She squinted at the darkness into which he'd disappeared. "Did he just go back into that pitch black maze without any light?"

"Looks like it." Zev's voice was short.

"Well." Marieke shuddered again. "That's a little...creepy."

Zev's face softened slightly in a smile as he looked over at her. "I get the sense that everyone who lives here knows this place very, very well."

"Evidently," Marieke said. "I didn't see any signposts, and he seemed very confident in getting here, in spite of it being so far from the main cavern." She frowned. "Do you think they brought us to a cavern much further away than necessary, to make it harder for us to find our way out?"

"Undoubtedly," said Zev. "We passed plenty of spaces at least as suitable as this one."

"Well, they didn't need to bother," Marieke said frankly. "I'm far too tired to try running away tonight. And maybe Svetlana only said it for effect, but it worked—I don't want to take my chances with those elves."

"Yes, I think we'd be wise to be very careful with them."

Zev followed her as she stepped into the space, an air of reluctance about him.

"I just can't believe they exist!" Marieke said. "Elves. Like something out of a children's story. How did the knowledge of them become lost?"

"I imagine you don't want to hear it, but there's no way every record mentioning elves was lost by accident," Zev said, kneeling down and shifting one of the blankets to get to the pallet underneath.

Marieke watched him for a moment before responding. "You're wrong," she said.

Zev straightened, his brow furrowed as he looked at her. "Marieke, I know it's hard to unlearn everything you've been taught, but—"

"No," she clarified quickly, "I mean you're wrong that I don't want to hear it. I *do* want to hear the truth. That's why I'm here."

Zev held her gaze, something crackling in the air between them. "Yes," he said at last, his voice soft in the deadened space. "You're different from most singers."

"I'm really not," Marieke told him simply. "I just asked the right questions, and even that only happened because of what I saw down here the first time. Many singers would probably have the same reaction I've had if they were exposed to the same information."

Zev didn't answer. Even in the dim light, she could see the conflict in his eyes. It was hard for him, she realized, to accept that his family were wrong in their prejudice toward singers. Maybe even harder than it was for her to accept the lies she'd been told. Both of their foundations had been shaken since they'd met one another, and the realization made her feel more connected to him.

She stepped closer, the silence of the underground cavern suddenly deafening, and Zev's presence electric.

"We can find our way to what's true, Zev." Her voice was whisper-quiet, but it filled the space. "We can find it together."

Something jumped in Zev's jaw, and his eyes were impossible to read as they stared down into hers. Feeling bold in the semi-darkness, Marieke moved even closer. They weren't touching, but she could feel the heat radiating from his chest, inches from her.

"I'm not asking you to solve Oleand's problems," she told him. "All I want is for you to walk with me as I try to untangle the truth from the lies and the lies from the misconceptions."

Still he said nothing, although his eyes stayed locked on her, his demeanor more like hypnotized prey than his usual confident self.

"Is that really too much to ask?" she murmured.

Zev swallowed, swaying slightly toward her as he at last spoke. "It's...it's not that simple, Mari."

Warmed by the use of her nickname, Marieke reached toward him, the movement slow so as not to scare him off. She eased her hand into his, the back of her hand against his palm. His fingers were strong and warm as she slid hers between them.

"Isn't it?" she whispered.

"Mari…" Zev's voice trailed off into the silence with the hint of a groan. For a moment they stood, their gazes locked with an intensity that made it hard for Marieke to catch her breath.

Then Zev closed his eyes, raising their entangled hands in a swift motion and twisting them so that Marieke's palm was trapped against his cheek. She could feel the scruff of his beard against her fingers, and the strength in his hand as he held hers in place. He drew in a ragged breath, his thoughts impossible to read now his eyes were closed against her.

"Mari, I…"

Again he didn't finish the thought. She could feel his tension, but she didn't try to ease it with light words. She wanted him to confront his own heart, to decide what he was willing to fight for. To her disappointment, he seemed bent on avoiding that.

"I'll sleep in the corridor," he said gruffly. "To keep watch in case anyone intends mischief."

"You don't have to be afraid to share a cave with me, Zev." Marieke's tone wasn't quite as light as he was trying to make his. "I'm not going to force you to kiss me again, if that's what you're worried about."

His eyes flew open again at her daring words, his expression startled as his gaze rested on her. Startled and something else, something lurking deeper.

"No one forced me to do anything." His voice was low and husky.

Hope lifted Marieke's heart again, and she tilted her face toward him. One hand was still against his cheek, and she raised the other, tentatively laying it on his chest. She could feel the tightness of his muscles through the thick fabric of his tunic.

"I wouldn't want you to do anything you don't want to do," she murmured.

She saw Zev's free hand twitch, as if wanting to circle her waist, but he didn't do so. Still, he lowered his head, Marieke's heart pounding erratically as Zev's eyes flicked to her lips. She felt her own eyes start to flutter closed, but his lips were still inches from hers when his voice broke the silence, strained and low.

"I'm not free to just do what I want, Mari."

She studied him, her gaze unflinching and her mind clear in spite of the turmoil of her emotions. "I seem to remember you telling me that you're under no one's control but your own."

Zev let out an audible breath, the warmth of it washing over Marieke's skin. "That doesn't mean there are no constraints on me. I wish I could explain it all so it makes sense, but I can't." She could hear his frustration. It mirrored her own as he stepped suddenly back, releasing her hand and running his fingers through his tawny hair. "I can't."

Marieke's hands fell limply to her sides as Zev turned away, dropping to one knee to gather up a blanket and pallet.

"I'll keep watch," he said brusquely as he stood, his arms full.

Marieke put out a hand, laying it on his arm as he moved toward the doorway.

"You need sleep, Zev. Don't try to stay awake all night. You'll just be useless for tomorrow's dangers if you do."

His arm tensed under her touch, but after a moment he gave a curt nod. "You're right. I'll sleep." But it didn't stop him from stepping through the curtain and laying his makeshift bed in the corridor. Apparently he intended any danger to at least have to come through him first.

Marieke sighed, recognizing the pointlessness of further argument. She could use privacy to gather her thoughts, anyway. Zev's nearness had made its usual impact on both her heart rate and her peace of mind. Warmth crept over her when she turned and realized that he'd laid out her pallet and blanket. She didn't doubt for a moment that he cared. Just not enough to surmount whatever barriers were keeping them apart in his mind.

Most likely the fact that his family disliked singers so much, she reflected glumly as she settled on the pallet. But surely that could be overcome with time. Surely if they got to know her, they'd see she wasn't their enemy.

After all, Zev had been hesitant at first, but he certainly no longer saw her as an enemy. Her eyes strayed to the curtain that now separated them, her thoughts wandering back over the day. He might keep his distance in private, but where others were involved, he treated her both as an ally and as someone worth protecting.

It was ironic, because if she had her voice, she'd be much more able to protect him than the other way around. Shifting into a more comfortable position—which wasn't saying much —she tried again to summon her song. She could feel magic in the ground, plentiful and erratic, but it wouldn't pool to her at all this time. And try as she might, she couldn't get any song to come out.

She didn't even realize she'd been clearing her throat repeatedly in the attempt until Zev spoke.

"Are you all right?"

"Yes," she said quickly, embarrassed. "I was just checking if my song is still blocked."

"And?"

"It is," she sighed.

There was a moment of silence, then Zev spoke again. "That's a shame. Your voice is beautiful when you sing."

Marieke felt warmth rise up her cheeks, but she tried to make her tone sound nonchalant. "And here I thought you didn't like songcraft."

"I didn't," Zev said, his voice less gruff. She heard him shifting on his pallet. "That was before I met you."

Marieke smiled into the darkness, her cheeks warm enough to drive away the chill of the stone beneath her.

Surely there was hope yet.

TWELVE

Zev

Zev hadn't expected to be able to sleep, but he'd obviously been more exhausted than he'd realized. Neither the cold stone floor nor the tumult of emotions brought on by Marieke's nearness had kept him from slipping into slumber. He woke not very refreshed, but instantly alert. He needed his wits about him for whatever the day would bring. He couldn't afford to wallow in his guilt over almost kissing Marieke again.

Or his disappointment that he hadn't followed through and done it.

He rolled up his pallet and folded his blanket, stepping quietly into the little cavern. The monarchists must use good oil in their lanterns, since the one left by the guard was still burning. For a moment he paused, studying Marieke's face, so peaceful in sleep. Then he shook off his pensive mood and knelt beside her, gently shaking her shoulder.

"What is it?" She came awake quickly, her voice groggy. "What's happening?"

"It's morning," Zev said, hiding a smile at her bleary expression. "I thought you might prefer to be woken by me rather than by Svetlana or someone coming to get us."

Marieke sat up, hiding a yawn with her hand as she looked around at the dimly lit cavern. "How do you know it's morning?"

Zev shrugged, rising to his feet. "I don't know. I just do."

"Ugh." Marieke looked like she wanted to flop back down again. "Farmers."

Zev let out a chuckle as he picked up the lantern. "I don't think you'll be complaining about farmers when you eat the food we grow."

"I am hungry for breakfast," Marieke acknowledged, patting her disheveled braid with a self-conscious air as she threw the blanket off and pulled her boots back on. "But I'm still confused about where these people get their food."

"I think they must send people up to the surface to trade for at least some of it," Zev said. "They might want to seem totally separate down here, but Svetlana made it clear they know what's going on up there."

"Which means there must be a safe way up out of the canyon," Marieke mused as she rolled up her pallet. "Probably more than one."

"Exactly." Zev nodded. "Having slept on it, what do you make of Svetlana?"

"I'm not sure," Marieke said. "I don't think she's going to attack us, like Gorgon did. But I wouldn't go as far as to say I trust her."

"Definitely not," Zev agreed. He frowned. "Good leaders should take responsibility for the people they lead, but she's very quick to distance herself from Gorgon."

"And what was all that talk about Gorgon being led astray by outside influences?" Marieke added. "As if he needed any influence other than hers to go after singers—the whole purpose of this community is to deny the authority of the singers he attacked!"

Footsteps in the corridor stilled Zev's reply. A moment later the curtain was pushed back, the same guide from the previous evening sticking his head in. With no regard whatsoever for privacy, Zev thought with a frown.

"Svetlana wants you," the man said curtly. He picked up the lantern and disappeared back through the curtain.

"Good morning to you too, sunshine," Marieke muttered, earning a grin from Zev.

They hurried to catch up to the guard, who was already striding down the corridor with their only source of light.

Zev had tried to memorize their turns the night before, just in case they needed to find their way out unaided, and he was pleased to see that his guesses proved correct at each turn. He was glad their lives didn't depend on his memory, though. One wrong turn could have them wandering the labyrinth for days.

When they emerged back into the main cavern, he felt Marieke's tension lighten along with his own. Eager as he was for his turn, he gestured for her to go first through the room with the spring.

"Thanks," Marieke said, grinning sheepishly as she hurried through the doorway. She took longer to emerge this time, and when she did, she'd re-braided her hair. She was, as always, beautiful. Zev acknowledged the fact to himself without hesitation. He'd long since stopped trying to deny her attraction.

Once he'd had his turn, they were shepherded by their guide, not into the eating hall as Zev had expected, but through another, shorter tunnel into a medium-sized room. It was reinforced with wooden beams, and seemed more like an actual room than any of the caverns they'd seen thus far. Svetlana was seated at a smaller table, a tureen of porridge resting on the surface next to a stack of bowls.

"Thank you," the leader said, nodding to the guide. He disappeared back through the doorway, leaving her alone with the pair of outsiders. "Sit." She gestured at the chairs across from her.

Zev waited for Marieke to sit first, his eyes scanning the room as she did so. Nothing stood out as a danger, and he lowered himself into the chair next to Marieke's while Svetlana ladled porridge into three bowls.

"I thought we'd speak in private," she said in her no-nonsense way. "My people don't need the distraction, and Rissin's more curious than is good for him." She pushed the bowls toward them then leaned back. "I want to know what you came down here to ask me. What answers are you looking for?"

"I want answers about the elves," Marieke said.

"I'm sure you do, now you've seen them." Svetlana wasn't to be distracted from her point. "But that can hardly have been your original purpose, given you didn't know they existed."

"True." Marieke seemed to be weighing her words, a caution Zev approved of.

When Marieke didn't expand, instead tucking into her porridge, Svetlana looked at Zev. "And what about you, Zeva-diah? Are you looking for answers as well?"

Zev folded his arms across his chest. "I'm mainly just trying to keep Marieke from getting herself killed in this self-appointed quest of hers."

Marieke acknowledged his words only by a noise of disgruntlement.

"So you're just the bodyguard, then." Svetlana didn't sound convinced as she eyed him. "Or the paramour, or whatever we're calling it."

"He's really neither of those things." Marieke emerged from her porridge, her voice pained. "He's...a friend."

The bland word stung a little, but Zev knew he was unreasonable to dislike it. He was the one keeping her at arm's length, after all.

"If you say so." Svetlana was no fool, but she clearly wasn't interested in arguing with them about the depth of their relationship. "Now are you going to tell me what sent you down here, or do I have to wring it out of you?" She tapped her knuckles suggestively against the wooden table.

Zev lowered his brow, his gaze threatening her to try it, but she just chuckled.

"Relax, bodyguard, it's an expression."

Marieke wisely ignored the whole exchange, taking her time to finish her mouthful of porridge before answering. "You're right that it wasn't the elves who sent me down here. It was Gorgon."

"He told you to come back here?" Svetlana demanded skeptically.

Marieke gave an unladylike snort that was strangely endearing. "Of course not. There wouldn't have been much point giving me travel directions while attempting to stab me to death. No, I meant that he was the one who raised questions. Lots of questions."

Svetlana sighed. "Questions like what happens when the rashness of youth misapplies a desire to see justice done?"

"I was going to say when the rashness of youth is overfed with stories of injustice but given no outlet for useful action to address it," Zev said with deceptive politeness.

Svetlana's jaw worked for a moment as she stared back at him. Eventually she shifted her gaze to Marieke, apparently deciding not to respond.

"What did Gorgon say?"

"It wasn't just what he said, it was what he did." Marieke pushed away her empty bowl, the action reminding Zev to eat his own cooling porridge. "His attacks on singers made no sense."

Svetlana raised an eyebrow. "Maybe not to you. I'm not saying I agree with his method, but I understand his motive."

"That's not what I mean," Marieke clarified. "What I mean is that he used magic in his attacks. But I could have sworn he wasn't a singer."

Svetlana folded her hands on the tabletop, saying nothing. Marieke raised an eyebrow.

"You've become very quiet."

"I have nothing in particular to say."

"How convenient," Zev said dryly. "Well, you're not denying that Gorgon used magic, so that's confirmation enough for me."

"I don't need confirmation," said Marieke, sounding aggrieved. "I sensed the magic myself. Even if it didn't feel quite like any magic I've felt before."

"I imagine not," Svetlana said coolly. "Being a singer doesn't make you an expert on all sorts of magic, in spite of what your academy would have you think."

Marieke leaned forward, eagerness on her face. "Are you talking about heartsong? So you do know what it is?"

Zev felt himself tensing and tried to hide all signs of it. It hadn't taken Marieke long to get right to where he didn't want her to go. Or at least, where his family didn't want her to go.

Zev caught himself up on the thought. He didn't want his family's secrets revealed, of course he didn't. It was far too dangerous for Marieke to find out about heartsong. The growing desire within him to be open with her, to bare every part of his heart, was nothing but foolishness. Dangerous foolishness.

Fortunately for his secrets, neither woman was paying close attention to him. Svetlana was frowning at Marieke, looking surprised by the turn the conversation had taken.

"Heartsong?" she repeated. "What's that?"

Marieke deflated, disappointed. "Don't you know?" She seemed to be trying to read Svetlana's face, probably wondering if the other woman was faking ignorance. "Gorgon did."

Svetlana considered her. "Gorgon spoke about this heartsong?"

"He mentioned it," Marieke said. "He referred to it as some kind of ancient magic, if I recall correctly."

Svetlana shook her head. "It sounds like he made it up to me."

Zev was sure Marieke didn't agree, but she didn't push the point.

"So what kind of magic *was* he using in his attacks, then?" she said instead. "I experienced it myself."

"That may be so, but it wasn't anything ancient or mysterious."

They waited for Svetlana to elaborate, but she didn't.

"Then what?" Marieke prompted. "You don't mean he was a singer after all?"

"Of course not." Svetlana sounded affronted. "We don't have singers in our community."

Marieke still looked confused, but Zev had just caught up.

"But you do have elves," he said. "Or at least, dealings with elves. They provided the magic, didn't they?"

Marieke's eyes widened as she understood. "Talismans! Gorgon and the others used elf-made talismans to carry out attacks that couldn't easily be linked to any person."

Svetlana said nothing, but her silence was confirmation enough.

"But why could singers sometimes feel magic, and sometimes not?" Marieke demanded.

"I can answer that," Svetlana said with a sigh. "I've had

dealings with the elves for a long time, and I know more about their trade than most. They know how to craft talismans that mask the magic they release. But they're very difficult to make, and therefore very expensive. I can't imagine where Gorgon got the resources to buy or trade for them."

Marieke frowned, her eyes glazing over as she sifted through memories her companions couldn't see. "Witnesses reported no magic at the earlier attacks. But I felt it when Gorgon tried to drown me. He must have run out of the expensive talismans by then."

"Most likely," Svetlana said.

"Why are you telling us this?" Zev demanded.

She met his eye unflinchingly. "I wouldn't have if you hadn't learned about the elves without my involvement. We have an agreement, and we're not supposed to reveal their existence to anyone. But since you know already, I'm free to tell you where Gorgon must have gotten his magic. And I'm telling you because I want to prove to you that neither I nor our community had anything to do with Gorgon's plan. He got his assistance from the elves, not from us."

She shifted her attention to Marieke. "Will you tell your council that? I don't doubt you told them where Gorgon came from, and I'm sure someone somewhere is discussing whether they need to eliminate us as a threat. We'll fight if it comes to it, and they won't find us so easy to dislodge. But we're not looking for a fight. We'd rather put the matter to rest and move on. Gorgon is gone, the attacks have stopped, and you have your answers."

"I don't have the ear of the Council of Singers," Marieke told her bluntly. "I don't know if they're thinking of coming after you, and I couldn't convince them not to if they are."

"I doubt you need to be concerned," Zev interjected, picturing the council meeting he'd witnessed. "Revealing your existence risks exposing the truth of the singers' coup, and the council won't want that."

Marieke bit her lip. "I would have said the same before, but..." She looked at Svetlana with furrowed brow. "It's not entirely true that the attacks have stopped. Singers aren't being killed, but a new kind of magical attack is happening."

Svetlana frowned. "What do you mean? What attacks?"

"Fires, floods, destructive storms." Marieke's slight form sagged in her seat. "In some ways it's worse than the earlier attacks, because the effects are wider."

"That doesn't sound like magical attacks," Svetlana said skeptically.

"Well, it is magic," said Marieke. "I know because I fought one of the fires myself, and it was definitely fueled by magic. It's like an escalation of what Gorgon was trying to do."

"But Gorgon is dead," Svetlana said.

"Maybe some of his group survived," Zev suggested.

Svetlana shook her head. "We're a small community here. We know everyone who went missing when Gorgon launched his vendetta. They're all accounted for." The set of her jaw was stubborn. "If someone's using talismans to make fires and storms, it's not one of us."

"So you think the elves are doing it?" Marieke asked. "You think they're trying to punish the singers for what happened in the past?"

Svetlana stood. "I don't think anything. It has nothing to do with us, and frankly, I'm therefore not interested. But I will say this for elves—they're not motivated by revenge. They're strategic creatures, interested in what they can gain, not what they can make others lose."

"And what do they gain from you?" Zev asked shrewdly. "They trade various goods with you, right? Like silverware? You must be giving them something in return."

Svetlana's eyes were slightly narrowed as she looked back at him. "Our business with the elves is just that—*our* business."

There was a moment of silence during which Zev and Marieke exchanged a look.

"Well." Zev stood, mirroring Svetlana's posture. "If you've nothing more to say, we'll be on our way."

He knew before the older woman spoke that it wasn't going to be so easy.

"I don't think so," Svetlana said. "I was going to send someone with you to Ondford, to ensure you passed our message to the Council of Singers there." Her eyes flicked to Marieke. "But since you tell me you have no access or influence when it comes to the council, I'm not sure it's worth it. You'll remain here until I decide what to do with you."

"What right do you have to keep us as prisoners?" Marieke demanded, rising to her feet as well.

"You trespassed on our home," Svetlana said, unconcerned. "You've even admitted that you came here to pry into our affairs and ask questions about our community. We have every right."

She waved a hand in dismissal, and a man moved forward from the doorway. Zev recognized him as their guide from earlier.

Marieke seemed inclined to protest further, but Zev put a restraining hand on her arm. Her eyes darted quickly from his hand to his face, and he gave his head a little shake. They would get nowhere arguing with Svetlana. They needed to come up with their own plan to escape.

Still looking far from convinced, Marieke collected her bag from where she'd put it on the floor. Zev had no need to—he'd kept his on him at all times, not trusting any of the monarchists not to rifle through it. They'd already taken his spare knife when they searched the pair's packs the night before.

And of course, the blasted elves had destroyed his favorite blade.

The monarchist ushered them forward, his eyes sharp and his face grim. When they reached the main cavern, Zev noted that he made a point of staying between them and the entrance that led to the outside world. On high alert, Zev tensed as a young woman jogged across the space, her eyes on a stack of bowls in her hands and her attention clearly not on where she was going. She was heading straight for them, and Zev's warning cry didn't come in time to stop her from colliding hard with Marieke.

Both girls fell from the impact, and Zev hastened to help Marieke up. He noted in doing so that the other girl had somehow managed to hold on to her bowls, none of which were broken.

"Can you go and be clumsy somewhere else, Trina?" their guide said irritably.

The name made Zev's eyes dart to the girl again. He hadn't even realized she was the same one who'd approached them after their meal the night before.

"Sorry," Trina said breathlessly, looking none of them in the eye as she hurried on.

Still muttering, the guard gestured for them to move toward the same route they'd taken the night before, but Marieke stayed still.

"Wait," she said, sounding self-conscious. "I need to relieve myself again." Her eyes passed to Zev. "Do you, Zev?"

He opened his mouth to say no, then paused. Her eyes were suddenly shooting daggers at him.

"Yes," he said smoothly. "If we're going to be locked away indefinitely, I'll take the opportunity."

The guard sighed. "Hurry up, then. I have better things to do than herd you around all day."

"So sorry to hold you up," said Marieke with cold politeness. "If you're in such a rush, we'll go at the same time so as to be faster."

Zev tried to hide his surprise. He saw the guard's lip curl, but he didn't care what the man was thinking about either their relationship or their dignity. Clearly Marieke had some plan.

He followed her silently into the cave with the spring, and through it to the room with the holes in the floor.

"What is it?" he asked as soon as they were alone. "What are you up to? If you wanted to speak alone, surely we'll have plenty of time for that once they lock us up and throw away the key."

"No, it isn't that," Marieke said, her voice barely more than a murmur. He had to strain to hear it above the sound of running water. "That girl, Trina, said something when she knocked into me. She said to convince you to come into this room with me."

"That's all she said?" Zev asked.

Marieke nodded. "I know we know nothing of her, but it seemed worth taking the risk to me."

"Definitely," he agreed, looking around the small, cold space. There was nothing there but a row of half a dozen holes in the floor, the last one blocked behind a wooden sign with an X on it. A couple of lanterns lit the area with a cool, white light, but it wasn't what one might call inviting. It also stank faintly of urine. "I wonder how long we're supposed to wait here."

His eyes had landed expectantly on the entrance, so he was caught off guard when Marieke let out a squeak of surprise behind him. He swung around to see a head poking up through the latrine hole on the end, the one with the sign indicating that it shouldn't be used.

"Oh good. You managed to both come in here at once. That

makes it much easier."

"Trina, right?" Marieke said the name cautiously. "What do you want with us?"

"To help you escape," said Trina. "And we need to be quick if you want to get away with it."

Zev had expected Marieke to jump at the chance, but her voice grew even warier.

"Last time I got that offer, the person tried to throw me off a cliff halfway up the canyon."

"Sure," Trina said practically. "But he wasn't with you that time, was he?"

Her eyes flicked to Zev, and Marieke's followed, her brow furrowed.

"No," she said cautiously, as if expecting a trap.

Trina shrugged. "Well, that was quite a different situation, wasn't it? Of course Gorgon thought he could overpower you. He always was too confident of himself. But have you looked at him lately?" She gestured with her head toward Zev, her eyes passing over his form in a way he found highly amusing. "Those are some serious muscles. I wouldn't be taking him on in a hurry." The girl's face split in a sudden grin, her voice turning cheeky. "At least, not in the sense of fighting him for the right to harm you."

"All right." Marieke sounded put out for some reason. "You've made your point."

"I'm not sure if my opinion counts here," Zev said, still a little entertained by the monarchist girl's manner. "But I'm willing to follow you if it means getting out of this latrine." He felt his voice grow more serious. "But if you're trying to trick Marieke with your assurances, proceed carefully. I really won't let you hurt her."

Trina sighed. "Strong *and* protective. Are all the men up on the surface like that?"

"No." Marieke's tone was hard to read now. "None of them are like Zev, actually."

"That's a shame," said Trina philosophically. "Now come on, let's go." She flashed Zev another grin. "Although I'm afraid you won't be getting out of the latrine so much as going into it."

Zev couldn't quite keep the distaste off his face, but he didn't protest as Marieke lowered herself into the hole from which Trina's head had just disappeared. He followed, his broader shoulders barely making it through. He found himself on a flat stretch of stone, illuminated by a lantern Trina had brought. The space was too small for him to stand as Trina had been doing.

And he'd thought it smelled bad in the room above.

"When they cut the initial holes to align with the underground stream, they missed with this one," Trina explained cheerfully, her voice as bubbly now as the water running through the darkness somewhere close by. "They tunneled through to empty space, but not directly above the path of the stream. People do occasionally ignore the sign and use it if they're desperate, so it has to be cleaned down here periodically. Not enough to get rid of the smell, though."

"So why are we here?" Marieke asked, covering her nose.

"Because," said Trina with relish, "once when I was on cleaning duty with a friend, we were messing around and discovered something cool. If we shift this boulder like so..."

She started heaving on a large stone, and Zev moved forward to help her. He couldn't help noticing that Trina quickly stopped trying, apparently content to watch him lug the stone on his own. In particular, she seemed quite intent on the muscles straining in his arms. His lips twitched again. How old was this girl? Fifteen? Sixteen? He didn't envy her parents.

"Behold," Trina said dramatically, as Zev cleared the boulder from its place with a grunt.

THIRTEEN

Zev

"What are we supposed to be looking at?" Marieke asked blankly. Zev had to agree. He saw nothing but a further small alcove.

"I'll show you." Trina squatted down and crawled into the space. She turned her head back to them, her eyes flashing with mischief in the lantern light. "If he'd like to give me a boost, that is."

"I'm sure Marieke can help you," Zev said unemotionally. "She's stronger than she lets on."

"Shame," said Trina, but she accepted Marieke's help nonetheless. Zev couldn't see much from his vantage point, but the girl disappeared from view upwards.

"And here I am." Trina's voice, faint but triumphant, echoed down. "Connected right through to one of our old, abandoned tunnels."

"Impressive," Marieke acknowledged. "You'd never know it was there unless you crawled right in here."

"Come on, then," encouraged the disembodied voice of Trina. "And bring that one-of-a-kind man of yours, too."

Marieke didn't reply, instead drawing in and releasing a

deep breath as if summoning patience. She lowered her head enough for Zev to see her face through the alcove's opening.

"Well, she's precocious," Marieke said flatly.

Zev raised an eyebrow, keeping a straight face with difficulty. "You really think there's no one else like me?"

"Oh shut it," Marieke said, abandoning dignity as she pulled her head back into the space.

Zev grinned at her legs as he passed the lantern through to her. "Shall I boost you up?"

"I can manage just fine, thank you," Marieke said with a frostiness that didn't fool Zev for a moment.

His grin broadened. "Shame," he said, echoing Trina's earlier reply.

He left Marieke to her splutter of protest as he went to haul the boulder back in place and hopefully hide their route out. By the time he returned, the alcove was empty but for the lantern. He squeezed himself into it, observing with interest the ledge that became visible at about his neck height. Marieke and Trina both knelt at the edge, Marieke receiving the lantern and Trina hauling at his arm in an attempt to help him up that was more eager than actually helpful.

"Let's go," Trina said, once they were reunited. "I'm pretty sure others don't know about this route, but our voices might carry if we stay too close."

She set off at a brisk walk, the others following.

"Does this lead all the way out?" Marieke asked hopefully.

"It does," said Trina. "We're actually not that far from the canyon opening. But I won't take you straight out. I'm just getting far enough from the latrine for us to talk without fear of discovery. I have questions."

"So do we," Marieke said.

Trina nodded as she turned one corner, then another, ending in a decent open space.

"I'm sure. You go first."

"Is it really safe for us to stop here?" Marieke asked. "Won't they come looking for us?"

"I doubt it." Trina settled herself on a rock that looked like it had fallen from the rough arch above, apparently unconcerned about the risk of the tunnel caving in further. "They'll probably think you threw yourselves into the stream to escape. If you had, you'd be dead for sure. It flows quickly, and stays fully underground for a long way."

"Will you be in trouble for helping us?" Marieke asked, the question showing more consideration than Zev had thought to display for the monarchist girl.

"No, I'll be fine." Trina lounged back at her ease. "I doubt they'll realize I helped you, but even if they did, it won't be anything more drastic than latrine duty for a month. She might seem tough, but Svetlana would never hurt one of our own. And I'm part of this community, born and bred." Her eyes passed over the pair of them. "Outsiders are another matter entirely, of course."

"This is all well and good," Zev said. "But why *are* you helping us escape?" He might have found the young girl entertaining, but that didn't mean he trusted her.

"Because I don't think Svetlana is right to hold you," Trina said. "And I'm not even confident she will hold you rather than hand you over to Rissin and his group who, from what I can gather, are very eager to have you. I imagine they'll offer her an excellent trade."

"So your motives for helping us are purely selfless." Zev remained skeptical.

Trina grinned again. "Not purely. I also have my own questions."

"If one of those questions is will Zev carry you off into the sunset, the answer is no," Marieke informed her brutally.

Trina somehow managed to look both amused and aggrieved. "Why are you answering for him?"

"Yes, why are you?" Zev's voice was milder but no less humorous.

"Because I have it on good authority that your family are very picky about your love life," Marieke said tartly. Her eyes flicked back to Trina. "Go back to what you said about the elves. Why are they so eager to have us?"

Trina shrugged. "Something about the movement of magic in the canyon. I didn't really understand what it was all about."

"Well, neither do I, and I'm an actual singer," Marieke said. "There's no rhyme or reason I can find when it comes to the magic down here. But I get the sense we don't want to be passed off to Rissin and the other elves?"

Trina shook her head vehemently. "Rissin is dangerous. Elves are always a bit tricky to deal with, but that one is particularly slippery. Not my favorite of the expedition leaders."

"Expedition leaders?" Marieke repeated, frowning. "What do you mean by expedition?"

"Their forays into our canyon," Trina said matter-of-factly. "When they come to mine."

"So they are miners?" Zev asked. "The gear they had when we encountered them made me think so."

Trina nodded. "Of course. That's what elves do."

"That matches the stories," Zev mused. "In those, elves were jolly little men who loved to mine jewels."

Marieke made a noise in her throat. "Jolly isn't how I would describe them."

"Hardly," Trina agreed. "And they don't mine jewels. They mine magic. Straight out of the rocks. It's why they come to Sundering Canyon. The magic here is plentiful, and the terrain perfect for mining it."

"Come here?" Zev repeated. "So they don't live here?"

"Of course not." Trina raised an eyebrow. "We have an agreement that allows them access."

"And they trade you things from the outside world," Zev finished.

She nodded.

"Where do they live? Somewhere in Aeltas, right?"

"How do you know that?" Trina looked surprised.

"The silverware," Zev said. "It was stamped with a design I've seen before at traveling markets. Supposedly from the south."

Trina nodded again. "That's right. Their community is hidden deep in the jungle. Right in the center, so I'm told. Elves love defined regions. Mountain ranges, forests." She shrugged. "Canyons. Apparently the magic is better."

"Like heart magic," Marieke mused.

Zev shot her a look. Had she meant to say heartsong?

Seeing him looking, she added, "It's a type of magic. Or not exactly a type of magic, more a depth of magic. The principle is that singers can exercise heart magic—as in, they can access the magic of the land to a deeper and more powerful extent—if they have a connection to the land they're drawing it from."

"What kind of connection do they have to have?" Trina asked curiously.

"It could be one of blood, or one of belonging. If it's the land of their ancestors, or if they grew up there, that kind of thing," Marieke explained. "I've never experienced it in much depth, because I come from a spread-out farming region on the coast. That connection to the land is mainly relevant in defined regions like forests. That's what made me think of it. The elves' principle for harvesting magic aligns with our principle for magical connections to the land."

"Interesting," said Trina.

She spoke cautiously, and Zev had a flash of understanding. Her demeanor was too familiar not to recognize. Like him, she'd been raised to think singers and their wielding of magic were to be reviled. But, also like him, when confronted with the reality, she couldn't help finding it fascinating. Maybe even appealing. He knew from experience that it was an unsettling feeling, and he tried to make his tone less combative.

"I don't understand what you mean, Trina. How do they mine the magic?"

"I can't tell you the mechanics of it," she said. "I don't understand it at all, no human does. It's been the elves' trade as long as elves have existed, and they guard their secrets carefully."

"But they can't sing, right?" Marieke said. "They can't form enchantments?"

"Not like singers do," Trina confirmed. "They use the magic to make talismans. They can serve a consistent purpose until they run out, or they can be designed to release a more specific magical function when broken, or otherwise activated."

"Yes, I know what talismans are," Marieke said absently. "We learned about them at the academy. Just without mention of elves. We were told it was an art that had been lost."

"Nope, not lost," Trina said cheerfully. "It remains the exclusive property of the elves, like always."

Marieke nodded. "So if someone is using talismans to cause the disasters in Oleand, the elves are involved, at very least as the suppliers."

"Is it talismans causing the disasters, though?" Zev looked at Marieke. "I thought you said it was a singer."

Marieke raised her hands in a helpless gesture. "I don't know. That's what I thought, but I can't be sure. I have very limited experience with talismans. The discovery that they're still being made changes everything. I assumed a singer was behind the fire, but anyone could have access to magic if the elves are supplying talismans to humans."

"I'd be surprised if they were selling talismans to humans," Trina said. "They don't do that—they couldn't keep their existence secret if they did."

"They sold them to Gorgon," Zev pointed out.

Trina stared at him. "Really?"

"That's how he carried out his attacks on singers in Oleand," Marieke confirmed. "The attacks definitely involved magic."

"Wow." Trina leaned back, lost in thought. "Svetlana has kept that quiet. Gorgon knew all about talismans, of course. But I have no idea how he would have persuaded the elves to sell them to him. He wasn't nearly as charming or convincing as he thought he was." She sighed. "Or at least, I never thought so. Others evidently did."

Her eyes were sad as she looked up at them. "Whatever you think of us, we were all devastated to learn that Gorgon had not only gotten himself killed, but managed to bring down multiple others of our community with him. Most of the ones he recruited were similar age to him, really young. He was only a few years older than me. We were never close, but we still grew up together."

"I'm sorry," said Marieke, her tone subdued.

Zev studied Trina's face, seeing something more that she wasn't saying.

"He tried to recruit you, too, didn't he?"

She started, her eyes darting to him with a wariness that was confirmation enough.

"I wasn't part of his plan to attack singers," she said.

"I didn't say you were," Zev responded calmly. "But did he want you to be?"

Trina studied him for a moment, then let out another long

sigh. "Yes," she admitted. "And I considered it. The thing is, not all of us are happy to live down here forever, cut off from the world outside. I'm loyal to my community," she clarified quickly. "I don't have any desire to serve either of the usurping councils. But..." She shrugged. "That doesn't mean I agree with Svetlana and the other elders, who all bemoan the lies of the councils but don't have any interest in doing anything about it. To them, living apart and refusing to submit themselves to the governance of the councils is enough. I don't see it that way, and I'm not the only one."

"Which is how Gorgon found others like him, willing to take the fight to the singers," Marieke said softly.

"Yes." Trina frowned. "But their plan was no better than Svetlana's lack of a plan. They were just murdering people. That's not the tale he told me when I was considering joining."

"What tale was that?" Zev pressed.

"He said that the murder of the royals had cursed the land —although that part he didn't come up with, to be fair. That was what that girl said."

"What girl?" Marieke asked sharply.

"I forget her name," Trina said, looking surprised by the tone. "I was only ten or eleven at the time. I mean, Gorgon wasn't much older, but I remember him being very taken with her. We were all pretty excited. It's such a rare thing for us to have outsiders come here."

"But who was she?" Marieke insisted.

"She was an Oleandan who said she was sympathetic to our cause," Trina said. "She knew about how the monarchs were slaughtered and how both Councils of Singers were lying about what happened, which got everyone's attention. We thought we were the only ones who knew or cared about that. She claimed that the land had been cursed ever since, and that the existence of Sundering Canyon was proof of it. I guess because we live here, she thought we'd want to help convince everyone about the land being cursed on account of the councils." Trina looked glum. "But as usual, our leaders weren't interested in anything that would get them involved with the world above. They want to be left alone to disapprove from a distance."

"But some of the young people, like you and Gorgon, feel differently," Zev said.

"Yes." Trina nodded.

"But that must have been Jade," said Marieke, her voice excited as these pieces came together.

Trina brightened. "Jade! That was her name. Do you know her?"

Marieke shook her head. "We never met. But I've heard of her."

"Well, she left when she realized we weren't interested, but I'm sure that her talk of the land being cursed is where Gorgon got his idea. He talked more with her than the rest of us did."

"What was his idea?" Zev asked.

"When he first tried to recruit me, he claimed that the curse on the land meant that the magic of the land was rising up against singers, to punish them," Trina said. "I'll admit that caught my interest. He talked as if we were going to find instances of this happening and use them to prove to everyone that the singers were the problem. Then the plan changed to finding a way to actually *cause* the magic of the land to turn on singers. I even swallowed that for a while. By the time I realized that his plan was actually to attack singers in inconspicuous ways and try to make it *look* like the land had turned against them, I was no longer on board. I couldn't work up the courage to tell anyone what I'd been part of, and next thing I knew, Gorgon and the others had left. I'd never fully committed, and he hadn't told me the whole plan. I didn't know enough to stop it, anyway."

There was a defensive note in her voice, but Zev couldn't find it in him to blame her for what Gorgon had done.

"I should have known better," Trina added sadly. "Of course it was too absurd to think that Gorgon could somehow control the land itself. No one could do that, not even singers."

Zev held himself as still as possible, even his breathing feeling strangely conspicuous.

"Yes, that's not how magic works," Marieke agreed. "Or at least, not the magic I know. But Gorgon mentioned a different kind of magic. Did he talk to you about heartsong?"

Trina's confusion looked genuine. "What's heartsong?"

Marieke leaned back, resigned. "Never mind. I thought Jade had learned about it from your community, but that seems unlikely."

Zev silently agreed. He'd reached the same conclusion Marieke no doubt had. Based on Trina's account, it seemed probable that Gorgon had learned about it from Jade, not the other way around. And all that was apparently years ago. The puzzle wasn't making much sense even to him, the only person in the room who actually knew what heartsong was. The magic that tied him and his family to the land didn't seem to bear any relation to Gorgon's plan.

"So Jade was the one who put ideas of cursed land into Gorgon's head," he mused aloud.

"I'm sure she didn't intend for him to use the information to target and kill random people," Marieke said, her voice as defensive as Trina's had just been. Zev raised an eyebrow at her, and she shrugged. "I feel a sense of connection with Jade," she said. "We're on the same path."

"The idea of the land being cursed didn't just come from Jade," Trina reasoned. "It's also just what we've heard. They say that Oleand is dying."

Zev caught Marieke's wince.

"Dying is strong," she said. "But it's in trouble. I don't know if it's under a curse, but something is eating away at Oleand. And that wasn't caused by Gorgon."

"No, it was just a convenient backdrop to make his scheme more convincing," Trina agreed.

"Just like it makes the current disasters—which are also fueled by magic—seem like the land is rising up," Marieke said.

"Current disasters?" Trina asked. "You mean, since Gorgon died?"

Marieke nodded, but didn't expand. "It's a shame it isn't safe to communicate with the elves. It seems likely they know something about what's going on, at the very least."

"It's not exactly *safe* to communicate with elves, but it's perfectly possible if you're smart about it," Trina interjected. "You just have to be careful not to commit to anything with your words, and don't let yourself be swindled into bad bargains. And don't put yourself in Rissin's power. Find a better elf."

"I don't think we can trust any of them," said Zev frankly. "If they answer to no one, how can we rely on their integrity?"

"I don't know if I'd quite say they answer to no one," Trina said. "They have a power structure of sorts. I don't know much about it, but there's some kind of leader—called the Imperator. And of course, they answer to the magic. If you make a bargain with an elf, the elf is just as bound as you are."

Zev considered this information, not certain it was reassuring. He had no interest in being magically bound to anyone, elf or otherwise.

"It must be my turn to ask questions," Trina said. "I want to know what it's really like up there. Is it true that both Oleand and Aeltas are poorly run and the people suffering?"

"Honestly, not really," Marieke said. "Oleand is deteriorating for reasons no one can figure out, and it's definitely making things harder. But that's only in the last few years. Prior to that, we were as prosperous as Aeltas still is." She glanced at Zev. "Well, perhaps not quite as fertile as some parts of Aeltas, like Zev's area. But we were doing fine. And even now, many people's lives are continuing as normal." She looked at Zev. "I can't really speak as to the state of Aeltas, of course."

Zev took a moment to reply. "Our land thrives," he said simply. "I wouldn't say our people suffer. But it's far from perfect. The Council of Singers is not truly representative of the population, and it makes decisions with reference to its own wisdom, not always what's best for everyone."

"I'm not claiming that our council is perfect, either," Marieke said quickly. "Or that its decisions are always right. And I think the decision to hide the truth about how the first Council of Singers came into power is inexcusable. But I truly believe that they generally want to run the country well. They keep order, they do what they can to help the harvest thrive, they make provisions for the vulnerable." She shrugged. "I suppose those who are in power like the position of influence and wouldn't readily give it up. But I don't think they've given any reason to think they're corrupt and power-hungry, at least not in my lifetime." There was a challenge in her eyes as she met Zev's. "Do you disagree as relates to your own council?"

Zev folded his arms across his chest. "No," he admitted. "They do try to run things well. But the whole structure is flawed, with singers far too heavily represented, and not nearly enough opportunity for most of the population to be heard. And while I don't have any reason to think our council members are lining their pockets or anything like that, their authority is still based on lies about the past, which is a form of corruption in itself."

"You have a point there," Marieke said. She sounded too weary for her years. "And I'm not trying to make excuses."

"I know you're not."

Zev's voice was softer, and he found his hand straying to her shoulder. He squeezed gently, trying to communicate without words that he didn't blame her for the crimes of the singers of the past. Ever since she'd gotten her first hint that history had been rewritten, she'd shown over and over that she wasn't like them, that she wanted to know the truth and to make things right.

"Shall I give you some privacy?" Trina's cheeky question made him drop his hand, not sure whether to be irked with the young girl or entertained by the color now staining Marieke's cheeks. "But seriously," Trina pushed on, "would it be madness for someone like me to try to forge a life up there? Would I be dooming myself to poverty or famine, or be persecuted for my origins?"

"Not at all," Marieke said. "You wouldn't have to tell anyone your origins if you didn't want to, and there are plenty of things you could do to sustain yourself, especially if you're willing to learn useful skills and not too proud to take mundane work."

Trina nodded, her expression thoughtful. Zev got the sense that Marieke's words were very different from the picture the community leaders had painted for their young folk of life on the surface.

"Fun as our little chat has been, I think we'd best be on our way," Zev said. "I don't share your confidence that your people won't come looking for us."

"Fair enough." Trina pushed herself to her feet. "I'll show you the way out. If you head eastward, there's another tunnel opening several leagues from here. It's on the other side of the canyon, the southern side, and it contains a staircase that should go all the way up. The entrance to the staircase will be well hidden from the top, but it will be easy enough going up. You might just have to shift some rocks."

Zev nodded. "So we'll come out on the Aeltan side of the canyon," he said. "Like we entered from. That's good."

"Yes," Marieke agreed, her eyes fixed unseeingly on the stone wall in front of her. "Yes, that's best."

Zev didn't ask her what she was thinking. They would have time enough to talk when they were navigating the canyon. He just put his hand below her elbow, lightly steering her after Trina. Marieke came out of her reverie and hoisted her pack up her shoulder, following their guide with Zev close behind.

When they emerged into the tunnel, Zev put an arm over his face. It was still before noon, and the daylight was blindingly bright compared to the dimness of the monarchists' cavern system.

"This is where we part ways," Trina said. "I'd better get back to the main area before anyone connects me with your disappearance. I'm sure there will be quite the bustle." She grinned, apparently enjoying the prospect. She must have faith in her ability to act dumb.

"Thank you, Trina," Marieke said. "We're truly grateful. One night held captive underground was enough for me."

Trina chuckled. "When you're used to it, it's really not such a bad life." A defiant light came into her eyes. "I'm not going to spend my whole life underground, though. Who knows? Maybe we'll meet topside one day."

"I hope we do," Marieke said, offering the other girl her hand. They shook, and Zev moved subtly backward, noting the calculating way Trina's gaze slid to him. No need to give her the opportunity to try to hug him or something.

The next moment, Trina had turned and trotted westward, back toward the settlement.

"Come on." Zev's eyes scanned the area uneasily, painfully aware that he had no weapon. "I don't think we should linger." He felt vulnerable, and he didn't like it.

"Agreed," Marieke said. "I can't see any sign of Rissin and his crew, and that's more ominous than reassuring."

They started walking, moving eastward as quickly as the uneven terrain would allow. They hugged the canyon wall, listening out for any sign that Svetlana's people were pursuing them. A creek bubbled along in the center of the ravine, a few scraggly plants growing alongside it. But for the most part, it was barren rock.

At first they didn't speak, Marieke seeming to feel the tension as much as Zev did. But when a quarter of an hour had passed without incident, they both began to relax.

"So, Trina was a surprise, wasn't she?" Marieke said. "I didn't expect help from anyone among the monarchists."

Zev just grunted. If they knew who he was, he could probably command all the help he wanted from the self-described monarchists. But he'd felt no desire to reveal his identity. They might know some of the truth about the past, but as far as he could tell, they believed—like the original council—that the Aeltan royal line had been fully wiped out at the time of the coup. He had no idea what they would do with the information if they learned their mistake, but judging by their previous record, he doubted it would be anything useful. The last thing he wanted was to see misguided young people like Gorgon burning down the academy and killing people like Marieke in his name.

"She was very taken with you." Marieke seemed determined to draw a response out of him, and he couldn't help the hint of a smirk that tugged at his lips.

"Deplorable taste, I agree," he said solemnly.

Marieke shot him a look, seeming unsure whether to laugh or be annoyed. "You know that's not what I meant."

"Do I?"

"Yes," she said. Zev watched her navigate a shaley patch of

rock as she seemed to steel herself to speak again. "I know you know, because I'm not the one giving mixed signals. It's you who—"

"Marieke, stop!"

She bit her lip. "Too direct? You have to admit that—"

"No, I mean stop!" Zev lunged forward and threw out his hand so that Marieke walked into his arm. Her foot stopped an inch from the netting Zev had spotted half-covered with dirt.

"What is that?" Marieke demanded, her eyes wide as they followed Zev's gaze to see the net.

But Zev's gaze had already flicked upward, searching the area frantically. "It looks like a trap, like a hunter might use in a forest."

"A shame." The high-pitched voice was laced with regret as Zev and Marieke both spun frantically to find it. "I'd really hoped not to need to use up another talisman."

Zev let out a growl as his eyes latched on to Rissin, perched on a rocky shelf above them. His hands balled into fists as he stepped between the elf and Marieke. But he was still out of reach when the little creature raised a metal disc above his head, his hands poised to snap it in two.

CHAPTER

FOURTEEN

Marieke

A shot of determination raced through Marieke as Rissin spoke. The elves had captured them far too easily the day before. Not this time.

As Zev moved in front of her, she bent down, snatching up a rock the size of her palm. Now she was paying attention, she could sense the faint pulse of magic coming from the object Rissin was raising above his head. She didn't want to know what it did.

Drawing her arm back, she sidestepped around Zev, took aim, and released the rock. She'd been aiming for Rissin's head, and it instead hit his torso, but she still considered it a success. Taken completely by surprise by the mundane, non-magical attack, Rissin toppled backward into the rocky slope behind him.

"Come on!" Marieke grabbed Zev's arm and began to sprint along the ravine, still moving eastward. She stumbled on the uneven ground and almost fell, but Zev's hand was suddenly there, steadying her.

A screech of anger behind them told her that Rissin had

recovered himself, and she knew his companions couldn't be far away.

"Got a plan?" Zev asked as he ran beside her.

"There!" Marieke pointed to a fissure in the canyon wall ahead and to their right. "Could that be the staircase?"

"I think it's too soo—" Zev's words were cut off in a hiss as a blade pinged off the rock beside Marieke's arm. "They're aiming for you!" he said, sounding furious.

Marieke didn't reply, instead grabbing his arm and diving into the fissure. It opened into a small cave, and she ran across it, her eyes trying fruitlessly to see into the dark corners.

"It's a dead end," Zev said. "This isn't the staircase."

Marieke's heart was pounding in her throat. She didn't want to accept that she'd led them into a corner they couldn't back out of. She went all the way to the back of the cave, feeling frantically along the wall. Zev was right. There was nothing.

"What are we going to do?" she asked, as Zev appeared alongside her.

He had no chance to answer. At that moment, a small form appeared in the patch of light that marked the entrance, followed by two more.

"You big oafs," Rissin said venomously. "How dare you throw rocks at me?"

Marieke ignored his words, trying desperately to think of a way out. She'd believed Trina when she said they didn't want to find themselves in Rissin's hands. She believed it doubly now she'd managed to enrage the little elf. Her instinct was to reach for the magic of the land in defense, and she started to do so before her mind had time to recall that her voice was blocked.

To her amazement, she felt the magic pool in response. She was vaguely aware that it wasn't moving in the normal way, but anything at all was better than nothing. Hoping for the best, she opened her mouth, fiercely delighted when song was released.

Rissin let out a cry, obviously not having expected her to regain her voice. He lifted the talisman he'd almost used on them earlier, but he wasn't quick enough. Marieke's enchantment hit him first.

In defiance of Rissin's outrage, Marieke's song had directed the magic to do the first thing that came to her mind—to throw rocks at him. Prompted by her songcraft, stones lifted from around her and flew toward him. They weren't large stones— she was limited to those sitting loose on the cave floor—but they were enough to make him throw his arms over his head.

Marieke ignored his shriek, trying to keep focus on her song while also formulating a plan for how best to use magic to get them out of their fix. With her training in agricultural song, her first thought was often to use the terrain itself. But to do so effectively, she'd need knowledge of the landscape in question. She'd had no time to do any kind of analyzing song, and while she had the training to get some sense of the terrain through the magic itself while she channeled it, that training was failing her. The magic of the canyon was so erratic that trying to grasp it was like trying to keep her hold on a slippery fish intent on escaping her grip.

On the other hand, the magic was powerful. Stronger than what Oleandan terrain usually yielded. When Rissin lowered his arms with murder in his eyes, Marieke continued her song, changing its strategy so that the magic was focused on the rocks beneath the elf's feet. Ripping up the ground required more power than lifting objects already loose. But power wasn't the problem. There was enough force in the magic gathering in response to her song to crack the cliffside open. The problem was getting that magic to respond to her direction.

She was relieved when she felt a shoot of magic race toward Rissin, making a jagged shard of rock erupt right next to his feet. It caused the nearest ground to tilt, sending Rissin and his companions toppling.

It bought them another moment, but it wasn't enough. The elves would be back on their feet soon, and Marieke wasn't confident the magic would obey her again. She needed a better plan, but she couldn't seem to make her mind cooperate.

"You can do this." Zev's voice was low and even in her ear, surprising her with his proximity. He gripped her arm, his hold more steadying than any words. "I know you can."

Energy surged into Marieke with his words, and it wasn't just because of his confidence in her. As he neared her, she realized what was off with the magic. It was erratic, but not totally unpredictable. Usually, when she sang, magic pooled to her, gathering around her feet before rushing up into her body. But although she could feel the magic moving in response to her voice, it wasn't pooling around her. It was pooling around Zev. She'd been managing to coax some of it into her to be molded, but it wasn't a direct supply. Once Zev grabbed hold of her, however, so much magic rushed to her that she could barely channel it. She felt lightheaded, saturated with too much power to properly wield. It took all her training to grab hold of only a small enough amount for her to actually manipulate.

It was still more magic than she'd ever drawn in before, with the exception of when she'd fought the fire. And it was all rushing into her at once, not being drawn in bit by bit like it had been on that occasion.

It was both intoxicating and terrifying.

As soon as she was confident she had control of it, she thrust the power outward, her voice growing hoarse as she continued to sing with all her might. She sang of the hardness of rock and stone, trying to work her songcraft around the unyielding nature of the terrain. She'd intended to dislodge more rocks to barrage the elves enough to let them escape, but the magic didn't respond quite as she expected. It was a strange sensation as it flowed through her and out, not like the enchantments she usually molded. It wasn't just the power in the ground that was eager to respond to her—it was the land itself. For a moment she thought she was experiencing an earthquake, her mind misreading what she was feeling and telling her that the ground was surging beneath her feet. Alarm raced over her, the sensation reminiscent of the time the ground had fallen away underneath all the singers in the delegation.

But before she could give in to panic, she realized that it wasn't the ground surging this time—it was magic. The fractured magic of Sundering Canyon, writhing and twisting and racing toward her. It wasn't all coming up and through her, either, as magic usually did. It was pooling around her and Zev, but much of it was shooting straight toward the elves, remaining in the ground.

Trying to think on her feet and adapt her songcraft to this new phenomenon, Marieke changed the words of her song. The blessing Zev had spoken over her when they'd first parted flashed through her mind.

May the land be firm beneath your feet and gentle under your touch.

Marieke turned the words on themselves, singing an invocation to the land to rebel against the attacking elves, to be unstable underneath them and sharp as knives to their hands.

She felt the magic churning forward, eager in its response. It felt like she held a roiling, surging patch of rapids in her mental grasp, and as it raced toward the elves, the ground surged as well. The cave floor where she and Zev stood remained solid, but the strip of stony ground between them and the elves moved like a bedsheet shaken out in the wind. It rose and fell in a rhythmic motion, more unnatural and targeted than any earthquake.

Marieke heard cries of shock from the elves as the ground under their feet cracked and shifted. They darted for the outside of the cave, trying to escape the path of destruction caused by the roiling magic. Shards of rock were lancing upward, and one of the elves let out a horrible, gurgling scream. A shaft of stone, sharper than a blade, had jutted up from the ground and impaled his hand.

Her stomach clenching, Marieke changed her song, continuing to sing her inverted version of the blessing, but leaving out the part about the land being sharp as knives. She'd never imagined the result would be so literal as well as so powerful.

The shard broke away at the base, the rock falling back to the ground and leaving the elf with a bleeding hand. And simmering rage, judging by the look he cast at her.

"Come on!" Zev called over the top of Marieke's song, grabbing her hand and pulling her toward the entrance of the cave, which was now clear.

Struggling to maintain awareness of her surroundings while singing furiously, Marieke stumbled after him, focusing her physical senses on just the firm grip of his hand and trusting him to guide her while she gave the rest of her attention to her magical sense.

The ground stilled under their feet, the patch where they ran not only holding steady, but clearing a path before them from the debris caused by Marieke's song.

When they emerged into daylight, Marieke's song petered out. As she tried to catch her breath, she saw Rissin picking himself up from the ground nearby. Unease washed over her as she realized that his eyes glittered as much with greed as with anger. He knew as well as she did that something remarkable had just happened, magically speaking. He would be doubly eager to get his hands on the pair of humans now. Marieke saw with alarm that Rissin's talisman from earlier lay nearby, only just out of the elf's reach.

Fortunately, Zev had also seen the situation, and his energy wasn't depleted by the song like Marieke's was. He lunged forward as Rissin scampered toward the metal disc.

Remembering what Kaine had said about combat singers using songcraft to strengthen the attack of other fighters, Marieke raised her voice once again. To her relief, the canyon hadn't stolen her voice again—she was still able to sing. The words of her song were simple. She declared Zev's feet to be swift and his arm to be strong, and before her eyes, they became so. Zev reached the elf with dizzying speed, and his fist connected with the little creature's jaw with enough force to send Rissin flying.

Zev kicked the disc hard, sending it skittering out of reach as he turned back to Marieke.

"Are you all right?" he asked urgently.

Marieke didn't answer, once again letting her song die for a moment as she tried to catch her breath. What Kaine hadn't had time to teach her was that using magic to power another person's movements apparently took significantly more energy than using it to affect natural elements around her. It made sense, given that any magical attempt to counter someone else's freedom of movement meant that the singer was battling against that person's will, which was a deep and complex struggle. Not that she was attempting to counter Zev's freedom of movement—that would have depleted her completely, quite apart from being highly illegal. She was enhancing the movements of his own choice, which was perfectly acceptable. It just made sense that it also required significant energy.

There wasn't time to explain any of this to Zev, of course. With her academy training, this analysis flashed through Marieke's head in a moment, but she could see that the elf with the injured hand and the third elf were moving toward them with purpose. Even Rissin was starting to stir on the ground. They probably had more talismans on them, and they would be willing to use whatever force necessary to bring her and Zev in now.

"Come on," she gasped, gathering her voice and her energy. She had to make one final effort to get them out of there.

"Do you have a plan?" Zev asked, following her as she scrambled away from the elves, back down the canyon in the direction they'd come.

"Yes, but it's very risky," she panted, glancing behind her. The uninjured elf was already chasing them, and the others were rummaging in a pack on the ground behind him. "Do you trust me enough to take the risk?"

"Of course." There was no hesitation in Zev's reply.

Marieke's eyes scanned the cliffside on their left, on the southern side of the canyon. "Then start climbing."

She took a deep breath after the words, commencing a new song. Inspired by what had happened in the cave, she sang of smooth paths and gentle climbs. She was barely aware of Zev's hands boosting her up as she grabbed at the stone in front of her. To her delight, the sheer cliff face shifted, surfaces evening out slightly, and the incline changing—only subtly, but enough to mean it was sloping outward a little as they climbed, rather than going straight up.

Zev climbed just below her, encouraging her to keep going any time her voice flagged. At one point her foot slipped, and his hand was on it at once, pinning it in place as she pushed herself up to the next foothold.

"Don't look down," he told her firmly, when her head

started to turn. "Don't worry about the elves. Just keep singing and keep moving. I've got you, Mari."

Confidence swelled inside her, and she pushed her ragged voice on with determination. The ground rippled before her every time she paused for breath, becoming momentarily more treacherous. But as she once again raised her voice, it yielded beneath her hands. Her arms were straining with the effort of climbing hand over hand, and she dug deeper within herself, calling on her training to try to add nuance to the raw power she was wielding.

With her mind and magical sense still directing power to disperse through the ground under her hands, she introduced a new strain with her words. She sent a puff of magic into the air, swirling it through the breeze blowing past her and redirecting the wind.

The chaotic magic of the canyon responded to her more and more readily, and soon a steady wind was blowing up from the ravine, cushioning them as they climbed and urging them onward.

"Keep going, Mari!" Zev encouraged from behind her, his voice again raised over her continued song. "We're out of reach of the elves now. The cliffside is becoming sheer again behind us. They can't follow."

She nodded wearily, fighting the urge to close her eyes for a moment. She needed the use of all her senses. She was glad they'd left the elves behind, but she was still keenly aware of the danger they were in. Sundering Canyon was unpredictable. Last time, when it had taken her voice, it hadn't given it back until she was safe on solid, Aeltan ground at the top. At any moment her song might stop, and then they would be stuck, halfway up a sheer cliff face. And even with her song in play, they were a long way above the ground. If either of them missed their step and fell, the magically enhanced wind wouldn't be enough to stop them plunging into the gorge.

It was tempting to glance down and see just how far they would fall if that happened, but she took Zev's advice and kept her gaze pointed upward. She had a handle on the magic now. It still felt slippery and powerful, but it wasn't like an escaping fish anymore. It was more like a huge rope, one with more strength than she could fully control, but which was traveling through her hands in a predictable direction, not trying to yank to one side or the other. As long as she kept her hold steady, it would continue to pass through her guiding grip, responding to her direction even if not fully in her control.

With that in mind, she dropped the volume of her voice. It was a natural instinct to sing loudly when trying to wield magic more powerfully, but it wasn't actually necessary. In fact, if a singer had sufficient training to handle the magic with the finesse needed, it was much better to sing quietly. It would help the actual voice endure for longer before physical exhaustion forced the song to stop.

Marieke's whole world narrowed to the sound of her own voice, the feel of the magic passing underneath and through her, and the steady presence of Zev following her. Those three things were all her mind could comprehend—she had to just trust her body to do the actual climbing from instinct. The climb felt interminable, her energy depleted long before she could admit it to herself. But eventually, the edge of the cliff came into view above. Marieke's voice wobbled with relief, and she had to remind herself to hold steady. For some time, she'd been feeling the sheer power of the magic lessening gradually as the chaotic canyon floor drew further away. It wasn't a problem. In fact, the smaller volume of magic was a more familiar tool, and easier for her to control. But she'd still like to reach the top before there was a more significant drop.

To her immense relief, her song was still holding steady when her fingers grasped the very top of the cliff. She pulled herself up the incline, getting a final burst of energy that brought her knees up and over the lip. Zev pulled himself up behind her, his clothes filthy from climbing on his belly up the whole height of Sundering Canyon.

Marieke's voice wobbled again, but she kept singing feebly as she crawled further from the edge. Zev followed her, and only once they were a few yards from the drop did she let her voice go silent. It was a good thing they'd moved, too, as the rocky ground shifted a final time before their eyes, the edge of the cliff moving outward as the slope went from inclined to sheer once again.

Marieke's eyes found Zev's, reading in his gaze a reflection of both her current relief and the mark left by the tension that had led up to it.

"We did it," she whispered, barely able to hold her head up. "Do you think we're safe from the elves up here?"

Zev didn't immediately answer. As she watched wearily, he pulled himself toward her across the grass. She didn't even dream of protesting as he pulled her into his arms, pressing her securely against his chest.

She let her eyes drift closed, her cheek against the gritty fabric of his dirt-covered tunic, and her ears full of his rhythmic heartbeat. She could feel his warmth seeping into her, calming her own frantic pulse.

"Yes." His low voice sounded in her ear in belated answer to her question. "You're safe, Marieke. I'll keep you safe from everything."

She didn't doubt it. His arms around her were the strongest thing she'd ever felt, and in the safety of their circle she just let her mind drift, not trying to hold on to awareness of anything in particular, allowing her stretched senses to resettle after the mammoth task she'd just asked of them.

She didn't know what exactly had just happened. But one thing she did know. She and Zev were in it together, as entangled by the strange movement of the magic as they currently were by his arms.

And by her heart, over which his hold was becoming more irrevocable by the day.

FIFTEEN

Zev

It felt like an eternity that Zev lay on the grass, Marieke's sagging form held in his arms. And yet, it was over far too quickly.

Marieke seemed to have relaxed completely, but Zev's heart was still hammering when she started to stir. The climb had been terrifying enough in itself, but more alarming had been the visible waning of Marieke's strength as he shadowed her up the cliff. He'd been afraid every moment that she would suddenly pass out and peel off the surface, dropping like a stone before his helpless eyes.

When Marieke started to push backward, Zev loosened his grip at once, trying not to let his reluctance show. Much as he wished she'd stay in the safety of his arms forever, the last thing he was trying to do was hold her prisoner.

Marieke pushed herself to a sitting position, running a hand over her eyes.

"Are you all right?" he asked, as he also sat up. He brushed grass off his legs absently, his eyes on Marieke's face.

"I will be," she assured him. "I just need to rest. I'm very weak."

He gave an incredulous laugh. "Whatever else you are, you're not weak. Marieke, that was unbelievable. I can't believe how much strength you have."

"I don't, though," she said, shaking her head. "I know the limits of my abilities, and that was far beyond them, trust me. I don't know what happened, but it was something unnatural, even in magical terms."

She leaned back on her hands, her eyes closed as she lifted her face toward the sun. Zev stared hungrily at her features, willing her to speak the truth when she said she'd be all right. Her lovely face was paler than he'd ever seen it.

Not that it did anything to lessen the perfection of the features he'd come to see in his dreams as clearly as he saw them before him now. The straight nose, the high cheekbones, the frame of dark hair—albeit currently disheveled and full of gravel. The soft lips, parted slightly as she breathed in the fresh air of his homeland.

"It's not the climbing that weakened you, is it?" he asked gruffly, trying to redirect his thoughts. "It was your songcraft that used all your energy, right?"

"Hmmm."

Marieke kept her eyes closed as she considered her reply. He could almost see her skin soaking in the sunlight, his eyes riveted to her face as he reveled in the rare opportunity to study her unobserved.

"It's not that I spent too much energy on songcraft, exactly," she said. "It's more that the volume of magic I just manipulated was too much for my body to handle." She opened her eyes at last, blinking rapidly as if trying to clear stars from her vision. "Even the memory of it is overwhelming for my senses."

She gave him an apologetic look. "I don't think I can move from here anytime soon. I passed out when I fought the fire, and this was more intense than that in a lot of ways."

"You don't have to do anything," Zev assured her. "But I do think we should move further back from the canyon. Do you object to me lifting you?"

Marieke bit her lip, a feature Zev forced his eyes not to flick to. "I do not," she said, her tone hard to read.

He knelt on one knee, scooping her slight form into his arms before standing. He relished the warmth of her nestled against him as he strode further from the edge, across the road that ran parallel to the canyon. He recognized the area. It wasn't too much further until the turn off that led southward toward his family's farm.

"Speaking of asking permission," Marieke's soft voice surprised him, "I'm sorry I didn't back there. When I used magic to enhance your attack on the elf."

Zev glanced down at her in interest. "That's what it was, then. And here I thought all those hay bales I lift had paid off."

Marieke chuckled weakly. "Sorry to disappoint. It's a little trick I learned from a friend who's trained in combat song. Normally, though, I imagine the members of a team would have blanket permission from each other to use magic on one another in that way." She looked up at him uncertainly. "Are you angry I did it without checking?"

Zev smiled as he came to a stop under a stand of trees, his grip on her tightening for a moment before he lowered her to the ground. "I'm not."

"Are you sure?" Now standing, Marieke didn't immediately step back, her face turned up to him as she stood still within the loose circle of his arms. "I didn't mean to force you to interact with magic if you didn't want to."

"Marieke." Zev gave a slightly strained chuckle. "Interacting with magic is the only reason I'm in one piece and freely standing back on Aeltan soil rather than being an elf's captive or worse. We may not be in a combat team, but you can consider yourself to have *blanket permission* from me to use magic to enhance anything I'm already choosing to do."

"That's good to know," she said softly. "Because I think we make an amazing team."

Zev drew in a long breath and dropped his arms at last, trying to get enough air to clear his head from the intoxicating nature of her nearness. She wobbled a little, and he quickly put one hand back on her shoulder to steady her.

"Well, let's put our best team effort into figuring out how to get you back to my farm," he said. He flashed her a grin. "Much as I'd like to impress with my strength and romantic demeanor, I can't actually carry you all the way home." There was a hint of regret hiding under the humor in his voice.

Marieke's eyes flicked to his at the word *romantic*, and color crept up her cheeks, but she kept her tone light.

"It's a shame," she said. "Trina's rubbed off on me, and I was entertaining daydreams of you carrying me off into the sunset."

Zev's laugh became deeper and more natural. "She really was precocious, wasn't she?"

Marieke's smile was also more relaxed, the strain of their near miss dissipating, although her form still sagged with weariness. "Just promise you won't run off with her when she's old enough to achieve her dream of leaving the canyon, and inevitably hunts you down."

Zev laughed again. "I think that much I can safely promise you."

Marieke drew a breath as she looked around her. "So your plan is to go back to your farm?"

Zev shrugged. "It's close, and it's safe. Where else would we go?"

Marieke once again worried her lip. "Would I be welcome at your home?"

"Of course," said Zev quickly. "I'm inviting you to come, aren't I?"

"Zev." She met his eyes with a touch of impatience. "I'm not talking about you, and you know it. Will your family be comfortable with you bringing me there?"

"I guess we'll find out," he said, forcing a cheerful tone. "Because that's where we're going." He turned his back to her. "Come on. I can carry you on my back a fair way."

"What?" Marieke sounded aghast, and he swiveled around to see her staring at him in horror. "You're not carrying me like a rucksack."

"Look at you," Zev challenged. "You can barely stay standing on your own. There's no way you can walk all the way."

"Of course I can," Marieke said stubbornly. She shifted away from his anchoring hold to prove it. Unfortunately for her argument, she took only half a dozen steps before she had to stop and lean against a tree, a hand to her brow in a way that suggested her head was spinning from the minimal exertion.

"Not so much," Zev said. "Unless you've got any better ideas, you'll have to swallow your pride and let me give you a ride on my back, Marieke."

"Why don't you just give me a shoulder ride, like a small child?" Marieke said, her outrage making his lips twitch.

"I said *better* ideas, Marieke. That would be harder for me, not easier."

"Zev..." The warning growl in Marieke's voice was more endearing than threatening, but happily the promised squabble was cut short by the sound of hooves.

Zev stepped out into the road, flagging down the approaching wagon with an authoritative gesture. He didn't recognize the driver, who pulled his horse to a stop as he drew alongside the pair.

"Afternoon, friends," he said pleasantly. "How've you gotten yourselves stranded out here, then?" His gaze grew astonished as he took in the filthy and disheveled state of their clothes.

"Just an unlucky mishap," Zev said, keeping his voice light. "Any chance you could give us a ride?"

"Of course," said the man with the obliging manner Zev would expect of anyone in his local farming community. "Where you headed?"

Zev gave the direction to his farm while he helped Marieke climb up onto the seat of the wagon.

"That's not far out of my way at all." The farmer nodded, pleased. "You'll have to ride in the back with the sow, I'm afraid."

Zev eyed his companion calculatingly as he pulled himself into the back of the wagon. She looked docile enough.

Marieke twisted around to look at him. "I'd offer to give you the seat and sit in the back myself, but...I'm not going to." She grinned, the expression infectious enough to make him chuckle.

"No man worth his salt would let his lady ride with the pig while he sat up here," their driver pointed out.

"Oh, I'm not—" Marieke started to protest, but Zev cut her off.

"Quite right. So where were you headed before we interrupted you?"

"Home," he said. "Further east from here, not far south of the canyon."

The farmer was friendly, and having succeeded in getting him talking, all Zev and Marieke had to do was nod politely and rest for most of the journey. Zev was glad of the time to think. He'd projected confidence for Marieke, but in truth he didn't know how his family would respond when he arrived with her in tow. He'd like to think they'd swallow their disapproval enough to be polite and passably hospitable, as they had last time. But things had changed since then. *He'd* changed, and his family were smart enough to know that Marieke was the reason for that change. But he didn't know where else to take her. She clearly needed rest, and if there was a possibility Rissin might pursue them up the cliff face, he didn't want to take any chances.

By the time his farm gate came into view, Zev's stomach was clenching with hunger, and he had no doubt Marieke felt the same way. He could see her form sagging a little on the wagon's bench seat, and he was eager to get her lying down as soon as possible.

"This is it," he told the driver as the gate neared.

"I won't stop," the farmer said. "But I'll come in so I can turn around in your farmyard if that's all right."

"Of course," Zev said.

"What was that?" Marieke had seemed barely awake, but she stirred at Zev's words. "What do I feel?"

"I don't know." Zev edged around the pig, who was watching him lazily. He pushed himself to a crouch in the back of the wagon so he could put a hand on Marieke's back. "Are you all right? Are you going to fall?"

"I'm fine," she said quickly. "It wasn't in my body I felt something. It was something in the land. Magic."

Zev frowned, as much over the stranger's reaction to Marieke's words as over the words themselves. Revealing where he lived had been inevitable, but he'd been hoping to share as little about Marieke as possible.

"You felt magic?" the driver repeated, as he navigated his vehicle through the open farm gate. "Are you a singer, then?"

"Yes," said Marieke, clearing her throat wearily in order to manage the words. "Don't hold it against me."

"Of course not!" The stranger was far too fascinated for Zev's comfort. "It's exciting. I've never met a singer before! They're not common in my region."

"Or this one," Marieke assured him. "Or the area where I grew up, in Oleand. That's a farming region, too, and singers are rare."

"You're Oleandan, as well? I wouldn't have guessed it." The farmer looked her over as though surprised that her country's name wasn't written across her forehead. "Well, what a day." He pulled his wagon to a stop in the yard of Zev's property. "This morning started like any other, and now here I am driving an Oleandan singer around."

"Yes, well, thank you." Zev's tone wasn't encouraging as he vaulted over the edge of the wagon and offered his hand to Marieke. "We appreciate the ride. I'd offer you something to drink, but since you said you can't stay..."

The farmer had brightened at the mention of a drink, his eyes still on Marieke, but when Zev finished the sentence, he let out a sigh.

"I did say that, didn't I? I'd best get this lady home in time for her supper." He jerked his head toward the sow.

"Thank you for the ride," Marieke said, the quiet tone of her voice telling Zev that she was close to passing out from exhaustion. Not knowing her, the farmer had no way to recognize this fact, and he took his leave with the same cheerfulness that had kept him chattering all the way along the road.

Once they'd waved him off, Marieke turned to Zev. "You know," she said, her expression severe, "where I come from, that non-offer of refreshments would be considered downright inhospitable."

"It's inhospitable here, too," Zev said, no remorse in his words. "But what choice did I have? You need to be more careful, Marieke. I don't think it's a good idea to advertise information about ourselves to strangers."

"Being a singer is not something I feel the need to hide," she said coolly. Her eyes flicked to the house and back. "Regardless of what some might think."

"It's not that," Zev assured her. "It's the fact that we just narrowly escaped from two separate groups intent on getting their hands on us. If either the elves or the monarchists sent someone to find us, it wouldn't be hard for them to learn of the Oleandan singer and local farmer traveling together alongside the canyon. You know how quickly any news, big or small, spreads in a community like this."

"Oh." Marieke considered this observation. "I hadn't really thought of that."

Of course she hadn't. She wasn't brought up to value privacy as highly as physical safety. But if she was going to keep asking unpopular and potentially dangerous questions, she would need to learn.

"Hopefully they won't come looking," Zev said, giving his clothes a final slap to try to clear the dust. "Come on."

SIXTEEN

Marieke

Marieke drew in a breath, bracing herself. She was more nervous about seeing Zev's family again than she cared to admit. Considerably more than she had been last time, even though they'd been strangers then and she'd been in their power. It wasn't that she was afraid they would harm her this time. It was that she cared more now. So much more. Zev was... well, important to her. And she wanted his family to like her.

Which made it hard to prepare herself for the cold reality that they were more likely to hate her.

Marieke did her best to appear composed as she climbed the steps, Zev supporting her with an arm. The yellowing light of early evening slanted across the wooden boards, the yard behind them blanketed with the hush of another day's end.

"Mother?" Zev called, as he pushed the door open. "Father, Azai?" They walked through the hall, Zev poking his head into the kitchen before turning back to Marieke.

"They must all be outside. Here." He held out his hand. "Let me put your pack in the room you slept in last time."

Marieke shook her head, clutching the strap of her bag

more tightly. "Not until your parents are at least aware I'm here. Ideally after they've actually agreed to me staying."

Zev gave her a look. "And if they disapprove, you'll hike out onto the open road alone as night sets in?"

Marieke shrugged. "Obviously it's not what I'm hoping for, but I'm sure I'd manage."

"Marieke." Zev frowned at her. "I would never allow that, not even when you're at full strength, let alone now, when you can barely put one foot in front of the other."

Before Marieke could respond, something seemed to catch Zev's eye. He squinted for a moment toward the kitchen window, then strode back out to the porch, Marieke trailing behind. Leaning against the railing for support, she watched as Zev ran lightly down the steps and made his way across the yard. In the fading light, Marieke's eyes caught the figure of Narelle, Zev's mother, walking slowly from the direction of the barn, one large pail gripped in each hand.

"Mother, let me help you with that." Zev's voice carried clearly in the still air. The slightest hint of guilt in his tone made Marieke wonder if the evening milking of the cows was usually his task. One of many, no doubt, that he'd abandoned in order to chase after her again.

"Zev!" The older woman looked up, her face softening in a smile as she caught sight of her eldest son. She didn't seem to have noticed Marieke yet. "You're back."

"Just arrived," Zev said, relieving her of one of the pails. He reached for the other, but Narelle swatted his hand away with a scolding noise.

"I'm not in my dotage, Zevadiah. I can carry a pail of milk." She softened the words with another smile. "I'm glad to see you back in one piece."

Marieke ran her fingers over the painted wood of the porch railing, her eyes riveted on the interaction before her. Zev had something special with his family, that much was clear. It was hard to put words to what she felt when she was with them, but it felt deeper even than the usual bond of family. Perhaps it wasn't so surprising that their disapproval was enough to make him unwilling to dive into anything with her. And yet, what grown man—especially one as strong and confident as Zev—let his parents tell him where to give his affection?

Zev hadn't yet responded to his mother's words when the older woman's eyes flicked up to the house and locked on Marieke. Her step faltered ever so slightly before she recovered her stride, and her expression instantly became neutral.

Marieke sighed, peeling away from the support of the railing with reluctance. All she wanted was to sleep, but she knew she had to make an effort if she wanted even the slimmest chance of Zev's family thinking well of her.

She moved to the top of the steps, but before she could greet Narelle, two more figures came into view, emerging from the field behind the farm's small—and out-of-place—training yard. Zev's father Gideon and brother Azai.

Narelle paused, waiting until her husband and younger son joined them before continuing toward the house. The result was that Marieke found herself confronted with the entire family approaching, three pairs of eyes fixed warily on her where she stood elevated on the porch.

"You brought a guest, Zev," Gideon said mildly.

"Again." Azai's tone wasn't as impassive.

Zev stepped away from his family, walking up the steps to Marieke's side in an unhurried way.

"I did. You all remember Marieke, I'm sure."

"Of course." Narelle smiled. "How are you, Marieke?"

Marieke opened her mouth to reply, but Zev beat her to it.

"She's dead on her feet," he said. "It's a long story, but basically she got us out of a very tight spot with some spectacular songcraft. She desperately needs to sleep, but I'm sure she would welcome some food first."

"I would," said Marieke frankly. Her eyes found Narelle, as the least intimidating of the trio. "But I don't want to impose—"

"I think we're past worrying about that, child," said the older woman, not unkindly. She pushed her milk pail into her younger son's hands and mounted the steps briskly. "Come on, let's get you off your feet. Supper is a little way off, but I have some bread and butter you can eat right away."

Marieke followed her, her stomach rumbling at the mention of food. Realizing that Zev wasn't coming, she glanced back. He was leaning with his hip against the railing, his arms folded and his face calm as he studied his father and brother. They were clearly waiting for her to leave to say whatever they wanted to say, and she wasn't at all averse to missing the confrontation. She picked up the pace, feeling a sense of relief when the door swung shut behind her.

"Poor thing, you do look dead on your feet," Zev's mother said, casting a critical eye over Marieke as she ushered her into the kitchen. "What's happened to your clothes? You and Zev both look like you were caught in a landslide."

"We scaled Sundering Canyon," Marieke said, too weary for subtlety. "Climbed right up the side of it."

"All the way from the bottom?" Narelle was clearly alarmed, and Marieke didn't blame her.

"Yes. It was dangerous," she acknowledged, easing herself gratefully into a chair as her hostess fished out a plate and some bread. "But not as dangerous as it sounds. I was able to use magic to sort of smooth the way." Marieke shook her head. "Well, I had a hand in it. I can't fully claim credit. I've never felt magic behave quite the way it did back there. But they do say that the magic of the canyon is unpredictable."

She looked up to see Narelle watching her shrewdly, and grimaced. "Sorry. You don't want to hear me talking on about magic, do you?"

"Actually, I do," Narelle informed her, spreading butter liberally on a slice of bread. "I'm very interested to know what you and Zev were up to since he left."

Marieke stretched her neck out, trying to relieve the stiffness she still felt from climbing for so long with her neck craning upward.

"I think I should let him tell it his own way. Things got pretty..." She thought of the impossible, miniature elves. "Strange."

"Well, I'm glad you both survived to return to us unscathed," Narelle said.

"Are you?" Marieke had meant the question to be humorous, but it didn't come out quite right. "Having Zev not only reconnect with me, but bring me back here is more or less your worst fear, isn't it?"

She hadn't thought she was capable of taking in more revelations, but as she spoke the words, she felt something strange happen. Magic shifted in the ground beneath her, its signature subtle and unique. It didn't pool to her in a flood...it was more like a gentle trickle, perfectly attuned to her magical sense. It wasn't so much that it was doing anything in response to her words, more that it was alerting her to the fact that it was available to do something should she wish to direct it.

Was it...was it reacting to her question? Without her even trying to sing? Was that what it felt like to have an aptitude for the question-centered branch of storytelling magic?

"Whoa," she said, speaking to no one in particular. "I actually felt it that time." She raised her eyes to Narelle. "What did I just ask you? It must have been an astute question."

Narelle was watching her with one raised eyebrow. "If you say so yourself."

Marieke let out a weak laugh. "Sorry. I suppose that sounded conceited. I'm afraid I'm too tired to be diplomatic. I've had a very confusing couple of days. And it seems the magic of the land has still more surprises for me."

"What does that mean?" Narelle asked, but Marieke's thoughts were already taking off in a different direction.

"I've just remembered my question," she said ruefully. "The one that activated the magic. I asked if Zev bringing me here is your worst fear. I suppose I have my answer." She couldn't quite restrain a wince as she met the older woman's eyes. "Am I really so awful?"

"Of course you're not," said Narelle, sliding the plate of bread to Marieke and seating herself opposite. She looked uncomfortable, but she showed Marieke the respect of meeting her eyes. "We don't dislike you, Marieke."

Marieke was mainly focused on consuming the food as quickly as dignity would allow, but she spared Zev's mother a pained look.

"I know I'm young, but I'm not a fool. I also have plenty of experience being alone in an unfamiliar place, surrounded by people who have the upper hand on me. I know when I'm vulnerable, and I know when I'm unwelcome."

Narelle sighed. "I'm sorry if we've made you feel either vulnerable or unwelcome. We're all a little on edge because of recent events."

"What events?" Marieke asked. "Is everyone all right?"

"Yes," said Narelle. "But our region is under close scrutiny by the Council of Singers, and to be honest, we'd prefer them to leave us alone to get on with our lives."

Marieke frowned. "Why are you under scrutiny?"

"There was a survey," Narelle said shortly. "Never you mind about the details. The main thing is, we're tense for our own reasons. I promise you're safe here."

"I know I'm physically safe," Marieke said wearily. "But that's not the same as being welcome." She met Narelle's eyes with a hint of pleading. "Is my songcraft really so offensive as to make me ineligible?"

"Ineligible?" Narelle's voice was sharp. "What do you mean by that?"

Marieke said nothing, feeling her cheeks heat at her revealing comment. She wouldn't speak so freely if she wasn't too weary and overwhelmed to watch every word. But she didn't entirely regret it. She was tired of playing games.

"Please Marieke, be frank with me," Narelle said. "What is there between you and my son?"

"Nothing," Marieke said, her color still rising but her gaze steady. "Because he's fastidiously holding himself back. But if you want frankness, I'm crazy about him, and I think if he'd let himself, he would feel the same way."

A flicker of something unreadable passed through the other woman's eyes. After a long and silent moment, she leaned back, her expression softer than it had been before. The change was at odds with her words, however.

"I appreciate you being frank. I'll do you the same favor. To answer your earlier question, yes. I'm afraid that your songcraft *is* offensive enough to make you completely ineligible in the eyes of this family."

Marieke winced, feeling as though she'd been suddenly slapped. It was foolish, because she was the one who'd asked the question. And Narelle's manner hadn't been harsh. But Marieke found herself fighting tears.

"Mother!" Zev's voice made both women jump. His form was filling the doorway, and he'd clearly heard the last comment. "What are you doing?"

"Just having a heart to heart with Marieke," said Narelle calmly.

Zev scowled. "It's not your place to—"

"It's all right," Marieke cut him off. "I asked her a question, and I'm grateful for an honest answer." She gave Zev a smile she knew must be unconvincing. "Is it all right if I go to bed now? You'll probably be glad of the chance to talk with your family."

"Of course you can," said Narelle, giving an approving nod. "You're exhausted, no need to stay up on our account."

Marieke rose, picking up her rucksack from beside her chair and making her way to the doorway in which Zev still stood. "Let me past, Zev," she said, her words soft.

"I'll walk you up." Zev's voice and figure were stiff, but it gave Marieke no pleasure to see him offended on her behalf. Driving a wedge between him and the rest of his family was the last thing she wanted to do.

She didn't protest as he led her up the stairs, however. When they reached the door of the room in which she'd stayed last time, he paused.

"Marieke, I..." He trailed off as she held up a hand.

"Not tonight," she said. "I'm too tired for explanations or deep discussions. We can talk tomorrow."

Zev's tense expression softened slightly as he nodded. "Tomorrow." The word was a promise. "Sleep well."

Before she knew what he was about, he'd leaned forward and pressed a quick kiss to the top of her head. Zev turned away without another word, and Marieke retreated into her room, too overwhelmed by it all to even watch him go.

SEVENTEEN

Zev

Zev clenched and unclenched his hands as he walked swiftly down the stairs, trying to regain his composure. He would need it for the confrontation that was coming.

As expected, his family awaited him in the kitchen, three pairs of eyes fixed tensely on him. In a move Zev considered optimistic, his mother had laid out a simple supper. He doubted there would be much eating. She was seated, but his father stood on the far side of the table, and Azai was leaning against the kitchen counter with his arms crossed.

"You all look very somber," Zev commented, lowering himself into a chair across from where his mother sat. He took the chance to swipe some bread, his stomach eager. "Did someone die?"

"This isn't a joking matter, Zevadiah." His father's use of his full name told Zev that he was in for a proper scolding. "Do you not understand the risk you take by bringing her back here?"

Zev took a moment to demolish the bread before he answered, unsure how much chance he'd get to eat once they really got stuck into him.

"I understand the risk," he said at last, keeping his voice even. "With respect, Father, I think it's you who doesn't fully understand what it is you're afraid of."

Azai made an angry noise in his throat. "So now you're wiser and more knowledgeable than Father, are you?"

"I didn't say that." Zev frowned at him. "But none of us know everything. Father is wise enough to know that."

"I am," the older man acknowledged. He rested one fist lightly on the decorative top of the nearest chair. "But my judgment isn't affected the way yours is in this instance, Zev."

"No, it's affected in other ways," Zev challenged.

"Enough of this." Azai pushed away from the counter, impatient. "What have you told Marieke, Zev? Did you tell her who we are?"

"No, I didn't." Zev scowled. "You know I didn't."

"How could we know?" Azai challenged. "I don't even know if I believe you."

"Your brother is no liar," said their mother sternly. "I believe him. Marieke clearly didn't understand why we all disapprove so much of her being a singer. If she knew our full history, she would understand."

Zev turned to his mother, frowning. "About that, Mother, you spoke out of turn."

"I believe I was doing her a kindness." Narelle shrugged. "Pretending things are different from how they are won't help anyone."

"I'm not pretending anything," Zev said, beginning to feel agitated. Part of him wanted to make clear to his family just how real were his feelings for Marieke, but it would only make them angrier. Besides which it was none of their business.

"Then why did you bring her here?" Azai demanded.

"Because she needed help, and we were close by!" Zev kept

his voice from becoming a shout with difficulty. None of them wanted Marieke to overhear this conversion from her room. "This is my home, too, Azai. We'd barely escaped in one piece, we were both exhausted, and we were quite possibly still in danger. Where should I have taken her?"

"Let her go to her own people for help," Azai insisted. "It's too dangerous to keep dragging us into it."

"What are you suggesting, Azai?" Zev demanded. "That I just left her by the side of the road, like you wanted to the first time we met her? Even though this time she could barely walk from the energy she'd spent saving my life as well as hers?"

Azai just shrugged, obviously having no real answer.

"Let me make one thing very clear." Zev's voice quavered slightly with tension. "I haven't ever forgotten my loyalty to this family, and I never will. That loyalty made me walk away from Marieke before, even though I hated myself for doing it. But that was when she was safe and in her own country. No loyalty will make me turn my back on her and desert her when she's alone, injured, and in *our* land. Where would my honor be?"

"Relax, Zev, no one is actually saying you should have abandoned her by the highway," his father said. "But you have to agree that the whole situation is regrettable."

"I don't have to agree anything." Zev could hear the surly note in his voice.

"Let's stop arguing about things that are already done," his mother interjected. "Why don't you tell us what happened while you were gone? You made it into Sundering Canyon, I take it?"

Zev deflated, flopping back in his chair in a gesture of defeat. "Yes," he said. "We did."

"Marieke said things got strange," his mother prompted.

Zev nodded slowly, still struggling to believe all they'd seen. "That's an understatement. And the monarchists were the least of it."

He told them everything he and Marieke had experienced, from the elves to Svetlana's attempt to hold them captive, to their impossible escape up the cliff face. He had the satisfaction of seeing the anger fade from even Azai's eyes, all three of his listeners too astonished by the tale to maintain disapproval.

"The worst of it is," he finished, shoving a slice of apple into his mouth, "they destroyed my best sword."

"I wonder what exactly happened with the magic of the canyon," his father mused. "It troubles me that these elves seemed to take an interest in you as well as Marieke."

"Hold on," protested Azai. "Back up. I'm still caught on the fact that elves are real! They were really like the miniature men from the fables?"

"They were miniature," Zev said. "But they weren't much like the stories otherwise. Except for the bargaining thing. That seemed to be true." He studied his father's face. "You truly didn't know they were real?"

"Of course not," his father said, looking slightly hurt. "Everything I know, I've told you."

"But how could we have such a big hole in our knowledge of the past?" Zev pressed.

His father shrugged. "Our ancestor was only a child when he escaped from the slaughter at Port Taran. And he only survived because his mother gave him to his nursemaid just before she was killed, and the nursemaid got him to safety. He had nothing but the clothes on his back and the documents the queen slid into his tunic."

"The ancestry records, I know." Zev nodded absently. He'd seen those very documents, hidden in their library room.

"Precisely," his father continued. "They were obviously intending to take them when they fled to the continent of Providore, so they could prove their claim to the stolen throne. They would hardly have filled their pockets with documents detailing every aspect of daily life in Aeltas. Most of what we know about life back then was passed down orally, from the nursemaid to the prince, from him to his own children, and so forth. If the elves disappeared after the coup, it's not hard to believe that over time their existence could have become a bedtime story in our family just like it did for everyone else."

"So what you're saying is that we can't fully trust our own version of history any more than we can trust the one taught by the Council of Singers," Zev challenged.

"Of course I'm not saying that." His father sounded shocked. "We have documents detailing our lineage all the way back to the first king of Aeltas, Zevadiah. We know who we are. And the prince wrote his own record of what happened the day of the coup, based on his own memories and on the account of the nursemaid, who was present. Do you really doubt these documents?"

"No," Zev assured him quickly. "I don't doubt either of those things. My point is just that all the other details may have been warped in the telling. Influenced by our own prejudices."

"And you talk about loyalty to our family," Azai said, disgusted. "You're basically siding with the singers now."

"I'm not," said Zev angrily. "But if we're not open to learning that we might have been wrong about things, we're no better than they are. And in fact we're much worse than Marieke. I've seen how much it's cost her to accept that what she thought she knew was actually wrong. But she hasn't shied away from it, or tried to make excuses."

"You think very highly of her, don't you?"

His mother's voice was quiet, the softness of the question cutting through the tense atmosphere more effectively than a raised voice would have done. Zev turned to her.

"I do. She's repeatedly shown me the strength of her character. I wish you could see what I see."

"You care deeply for her. Very deeply." This time it wasn't a question, and Zev didn't offer an answer. His mother sighed. "I wish I could see a way forward, Zev, but I can't. Your heart might be changing, but nothing else has changed."

"She's right, Zevadiah," his father said firmly.

Zev's mother leaned forward, searching his eyes. "It's obvious she cares for you as well. How much does she care? Enough to make sacrifices for you?"

"What does that mean?" Zev asked uneasily. He didn't like where the conversation was going. He hadn't planned on discussing his or Marieke's feelings, and the room felt suddenly much too hot.

"What if she were willing to denounce her songcraft?" his mother pressed on. "To put it aside and embrace a different way of life?"

Both of her sons made noises of protest, although no doubt for different reasons. But it was Zev's father who spoke.

"It's not enough, Narelle," he said. "Singing is still in her blood. Royal blood and singing blood were never mixed, even before the coup. They were fastidious about it, and with good reason. It would concentrate too much power. There's no way that—"

"Enough," Zev cut him off. "Just stop, both of you. We're not talking about this." Discussing his feelings was bad enough. Talking about mingling his and Marieke's bloodlines was way beyond what he was willing to discuss.

"I was only trying to offer a solution," his mother said.

"That's not a solution." Zev's voice was firm. "You don't

understand what you're saying. You may as well suggest asking her to cut off her right hand. Never ever would I dream of asking her to put aside her craft. It's an inextricable part of who she is."

"I agree," said Azai, his tone making it clear that his agreement was nothing for Zev to be excited about. "It's the core of who she is, and it tells me all I need to know about her." His eyes bored into Zev's, his brow lowered. "You would have agreed once, Zev."

Zev shook his head. "Then I would have been wrong, just like you are now, Azai." His gaze encompassed all three of his family members. "We've been wrong about singing. I've seen the beauty of magic. I've felt its power for good."

Azai clenched his fists over the chair in front of him, his eyes furious as he let out a growl. "How can you betray your family like this, Zev? How can you betray your history?"

"Azai." Their father's tone, rarely used, brought both brothers to silence. "Hear him out."

"But Father!" Azai spluttered. "How can you—?"

"Because this is Zev speaking, not a stranger," their father cut him off. "I trust his judgment."

"His judgment is clouded by what he feels for this girl," Azai insisted. "We can all see that!"

"Maybe." His father's calm voice made Azai's bluster seem ridiculous. "But maybe not. I want to hear what he has to say."

"Are you finished speaking of me like I'm not in the room?" Zev asked dryly.

"Yes, for now." His father was unabashed. "So go ahead."

Zev drew a deep breath, keeping his eyes determinedly away from Azai's scowl. He was angry enough with his brother not to care what Azai thought. It was his parents he wanted to convince.

"My perspective may have changed," he said, trying to

speak evenly. "But my judgment has never been clearer. I'm not questioning what happened in the past. I'm just questioning the conclusions we've drawn from it regarding all songcraft. What the singers did back then was evil, no question. But the problem was never magic. It was how they chose to use that magic. You all mistrust Marieke just because she's a singer, but she would never use her magic for evil like they did back then."

"So you think we should just forgive and forget, pretend the slaughter never happened?" Azai asked sarcastically.

"Of course not." Zev shook his head. "The country will always be fractured while our way of life is built on lies. The rewriting of history is almost as bad as the initial crime. But that doesn't mean all singers are complicit. Marieke had no idea of the truth—I doubt the rest of the singers who go through the academy know either. She shouldn't be held accountable for lies told by others—ever since she realized she was lied to, she's been determined to uncover the truth, even though she has nothing to gain from that and everything to lose."

His eyes passed between his parents' faces, willing them to see the truth of his words. "It feels wrong to not care about what's happening to Oleand. Even if it is a result of what was done to their monarchs, how does it benefit anyone for the land to remain cursed?"

"But Oleand has nothing to do with us," his father said.

"It has something to do with Marieke," Zev replied simply. "And that's enough for me to care. I know it's probably not enough for you to care, and I don't blame you. But we're lying to ourselves if we think we can just cut ourselves off from Oleand and be unaffected by its fate. Do you really think there will be no impact on Aeltas if Oleand becomes so barren it can no longer sustain its inhabitants?"

His father didn't look happy, but he didn't contradict Zev's point.

"And it's not just the deteriorating land," Zev pushed on. "There are more disasters happening. Floods and fires and storms. Our neighbor is under attack, and it could very well have something to do with the secret we've been keeping. I want to help make it right."

"How could disasters in Oleand have anything to do with the secret of our ancestry?" Azai protested.

"Not our ancestry," Zev said. "I'm talking about the slaughter of the royals."

"It's the Council of Singers who've been keeping that secret," Azai said. "Both councils."

"We've been keeping it just as surely as they have," Zev said. "We play our part in this mess."

"Our part is to stay in Aeltas," his father said firmly. "Our presence carries a blessing that helps our land to thrive. We're doing right by Aeltas, and that's our duty. We owe nothing to Oleand, and we don't have the power to help it anyway. We have no heartsong there. They killed it when they killed their royal family."

"Maybe so," Zev said. "And I know we can't change the past, or bring the Oleandan monarchs back. But the people of Oleand don't deserve to suffer any more than the people of Aeltas do. It's pure luck for the Aeltans of today that our ancestor escaped."

"I don't understand," his mother cut in. "Are you saying you think that the absence of the Oleandan monarchs is contributing to these disasters? Because how can that be? Their monarchs were killed centuries ago."

"I don't have that answer," said Zev. "And I don't think I have the understanding of magic to figure it out. But others do, and maybe if we were honest about the past, it would be possible to find a solution to whatever is happening. Marieke was smart enough to make a connection between Oleand's sufferings and the true history as soon as she found out she'd been lied to. I want to help her find out the truth of whoever or whatever is behind the disasters. She's convinced they're connected to the land's deterioration, and I think she's right."

"I wish her every success in finding the problem and solving it," his mother said simply. "I just don't want to give my first-born son to the cause."

Zev felt his face soften a little as he saw the genuine fear behind his mother's calm expression.

"You're not going to lose me, Mother. I'm pretty tough, and I have every intention of surviving whatever misadventure I embark on." He searched her eyes. "And you're not in danger of losing me in any other way, either. Not unless you cut me off."

"That we would never do," his father assured him. "But I feel as uneasy about all this as your mother does." He exchanged a look with his wife. "There's a great deal to think about. We can talk more tomorrow."

With a nod, Zev's mother rose. The pair of them bid their sons goodnight and made their way from the room. Zev doubted they would be sleeping any time soon. They were just moving to another room so they could switch from talking *to* him to talking *about* him.

He stared at the empty doorway for a long moment after they left, trying to muster the energy to deal with the most difficult member of the family. But his brother couldn't be avoided forever. Zev turned slowly back to see that Azai hadn't moved. His arms were still crossed, and his eyes bored into Zev's. Zev realized all at once that while his brother's words might be aggressive, his posture was defensive. He was afraid, afraid of what Marieke's presence might do to their family. Maybe even afraid of losing his brother.

"Azai…" Zev started, trying to force his voice not to be combative.

But Azai was having none of it.

"You didn't even ask about things here," he said. "You left a mess behind, and you don't even care."

Zev frowned. "What do you mean?"

"I mean that we're under scrutiny from the council. Someone came by here not long after you left for your little rendezvous with your sweetheart."

Annoyance flickered in Zev, but he pushed it aside, knowing he wouldn't get answers from his brother if he started a fight. "Who came by here?"

"Someone from the Council of Singers. Wanting to know more about us, and more about our property. Apparently," Azai's voice was like acid, "it was a very intentional decision for the survey to focus on our area first. And they were mystified and intrigued that of all the properties in the region, ours was the only one it failed to gather information about."

Zev let out a breath. "That's unlucky."

"Luck had nothing to do with it!" Azai protested. "It was your actions, Zev, yours and that girl's. If you'd left well enough alone, we wouldn't be at more risk of exposure than we have been in two centuries."

"Azai," said Zev impatiently. "You're quick to complain, but you don't have any actual solutions to—"

"Here's a solution," said Azai darkly. He pushed himself up from the counter. "You should have left her dangling from that cliff."

Anger flared in Zev, then abated as Azai swept past him and out of the room. He didn't try to stop his brother, either to placate or to fight with him. What was the point?

Putting his elbows on the table, he rested his face in his hands, staring unseeingly at the barely touched food his mother had prepared for her family. A family that had once been happy and uncomplicated.

Uncomplicated.

It was a word that seemed to no longer apply to any part of Zev's life.

EIGHTEEN

Marieke

Marieke pulled the shawl more tightly about her shoulders to ward off the chill as she slipped out of her room. The garment had been hanging on the back of a rocking chair next to the bed. Hopefully she was allowed to use it.

She'd been surprised when she woke and realized that dawn hadn't yet broken. She'd been so exhausted the night before that she'd half expected to sleep for two days. But after all, it had been early when she'd gone to bed. Apparently her body was sufficiently recovered by a solid night's sleep, because while she still felt overwhelmed emotionally, she felt plenty strong physically.

Stronger than ever, in fact. Or perhaps that was just the memory of the canyon's magic coursing through her. It was the most power she'd ever felt all at once. At the time, she'd been fighting too desperately for survival to fully appreciate it. But in memory, it was intoxicating.

The corridor was hushed as she walked toward the stairs, the creaking of the floorboards making her wince. It seemed she'd risen first, but familiar as she was with farm life, she knew that the others wouldn't be far behind. She wanted to be out of the house before anyone else emerged. She needed fresh air and solitude to clear her head.

The soft cluck of a sleepy chicken greeted her as she crossed the farmyard. The air was bitterly cold, no touch of sun yet having reached it. Marieke made her way through the copse of wild trees, sure of her direction. She'd only been there once before, but that occasion was vivid in her memory.

She stepped into Zev's orchard reverently. Morning mist shrouded the gnarled branches, almost heavy enough to be called fog. It made the air damp, and sent a shiver over Marieke's arms, but the cold was worth it. The scene was impossibly beautiful, otherworldly in its silent stillness. Branches reached up toward the sky and over the rows toward each other, like the trees were greeting one another gently in preparation for another day together.

As Marieke walked, the magic moved in the ground beneath her feet, plentiful in volume and strong in potential. It didn't dance like the magic of a windswept plain, and it certainly didn't surge about erratically like the fractured magic of Sundering Canyon. She was familiar with the powerful ebb and flow of magic near the ocean, and the way magic pooled into regular, invisible wells under a cornfield. The magic in the ground beneath Zev's orchard was different. Its movement was more like the steady, rhythmic flow of water in a deep, slow-moving river.

It was beautiful, and yet for some reason it made her heart ache unbearably. She was aware both of a desire to simply stand in its presence and soak it in, and a desire to throw herself to her knees to get closer to it. She pictured herself digging her fingers into the dirt in a futile attempt to catch hold of the magic and stop it from flowing endlessly, unstoppably on and away from her.

It felt like Zev, she realized. If he could be expressed in terms of magic, that was what he would feel like.

What he felt like physically, she remembered perfectly well. If she closed her eyes, she could believe herself once again pressed against him on the grass near the cliff, his strong arms wrapped around her, keeping her safe from vengeful elves and deathly falls alike.

"Marieke."

The soft voice made her turn, but not start. She hadn't heard him approach, but some part of her had known he would come. Hadn't she come here out of a desire to be closer to him? Where would he be found if not in his orchard?

"Good morning," she said softly, her eyes roaming over his face and taking in the scruffy shadow on his cheeks and his rumpled shirt. He'd dressed in haste, not stopping to shave.

"Are you recovered from yesterday?" Zev asked, his eyes searching her face as unashamedly as she'd been studying his.

"Yes."

She didn't ask the same question. His eyes were a little tired, but she could see at a glance that his form held all its usual strength. He was as solid and unyielding as the timeless trees in his orchard. And as entrancing, at least for her.

Zev seemed to be waiting for her to say more, but Marieke stayed silent. She had nothing in particular to say.

"I heard you leave the house," he said eventually. "Why did you come here?"

"Because I love it here," she said, pulling her eyes from his face and casting them around the orchard. Feeling bold, she returned her gaze to his features. "It feels like you."

Zev took a step forward, the swift movement seeming unconscious. "Mari..."

She felt her heart pick up speed, the shawl slipping a little way down her shoulder as she stood frozen. The light fabric of her sleeve underneath wasn't enough to ward off the chill of the air, and a shiver went over her.

Zev lifted a hand. For a moment she thought he would touch her cheek, but instead he slid the shawl back up her shoulder, using both hands to pull it more tightly around her.

"It's cold," he said.

"Yes," Marieke agreed, her skin tingling as his fingers brushed the base of her throat. She took hold of the shawl with one hand, reaching out boldly with the other to tug playfully at his open collar. "You should know."

Zev gave a chuckle that was lower and throatier than his usual laugh. "I followed you in a hurry."

Marieke's heart skipped another beat, but she kept her voice steady. "I get the sense your family would like you to stop doing that."

Zev's brow lowered, a pained look coming into his eyes. "I'm sorry about last night, Mari. They were taken off-guard, but that doesn't excuse being inhospitable."

Marieke shrugged. "You're not responsible for your family's behavior, Zev. Only your own."

He bit his lip, his discomfort apparently not eased by this assurance.

Marieke's smile held a hint of sadness. "For what it's worth, my parents would love you," she said. She gazed north, toward her distant home. "A strong, intelligent farmer who's unimpressed by academies and songcraft, and works the soil with his own hands?" Her eyes returned to his, the smile more pronounced. "They'd probably lock the doors so you couldn't leave if I brought you home."

Zev took another step closer, his eyes fixed on hers. "I want to meet them someday," he told her.

"Do you?" Her voice cracked a little, but she was past

feeling self-conscious. "Do you even know what you want, Zev?"

By way of response, Zev lifted his hand again, this time tucking a strand of hair behind her ear. Instead of lowering his hand, he brought it to rest on the side of her face, his fingers tangled in her hair and his thumb rough and warm against her cheek. Marieke closed her eyes and leaned into his touch. She scolded herself for her weakness, but even knowing Zev was probably going to once again draw back, she couldn't bring herself to be the one to pull away first.

"I know what I want." His voice surprised her—she'd thought he wouldn't answer. Her eyes flew open to see his gaze fixed on her. "I know *who* I want."

Marieke felt her cheeks warm, her heartbeat once again erratic.

"I want to keep you safe, Mari." Zev's voice was low and earnest. "I want to keep my promises to you, and do right by you. That's what I want. But I also want to do right by my family. It's hard to explain, but the mess I'm in isn't of my making, or my family's. Everyone has their reasons." There was a hint of pleading in his voice. "Please don't think badly of them for it."

"I don't," she told him, her voice a murmur. "They have high standards for you, and so they should. You're special Zev, everyone who meets you can sense it."

"No." By contrast, Zev's voice was sharp. "That's not it, Marieke. It has nothing to do with you not being good enough, I swear."

"Then what?" she asked, her eyes adding a silent entreaty to her words.

"I wish I knew how to explain." His voice was agonized, his hand taut with tension on her face. Did he realize how close his thumb had strayed to her lips?

"Well, you're running out of time to do it," she told him. "I'm not staying, Zev. I have to leave."

"Where are you going?" he asked quickly. "Back to Oleand?"

Marieke shook her head. "Further south." She closed her eyes, relishing the feel of his fingers still on her skin as she took a breath and slowly released it. "I'm exhausted, Zev. I feel like I'm chasing the answer, but every step I take, it remains just as far out of reach. The things we saw at Port Taran sent me to the capital with my head full of questions. All I found was more questions, leading me to the canyon in search of the monarchists. And I found them, but instead of answers, they gave me new questions again."

"And these questions lead south?" Zev pressed, his voice prompting her to open her eyes again. Sudden understanding sent his brows up. "The elves? You want to go looking for them."

Marieke nodded. "Surely this time I'll find the source. If talismans all come from them, they *must* know what Gorgon was really up to, and how the disasters have continued after his death."

"But we only just escaped from the elves," Zev said, his hand tightening slightly in its grip. "Svetlana and Trina both warned us about Rissin."

"About Rissin, yes," Marieke acknowledged. "But they made it sound like most elves aren't as dangerous as him. I want to find their leader, the Imperator Trina mentioned. Maybe he can be reasoned with."

"Bargained with, more like," Zev said. His frown was uneasy. "I don't like it, Marieke. It's a long way, and you'd be at their mercy, even if you did find them."

Marieke gave a twisted smile. "Unlike you, with your farm to run, I have nothing better to do." When he didn't reply, just continued to look at her with a troubled expression, she pressed her palm gently onto his chest. "I can't give up now, Zev. I might be exhausted, but I'm determined. I want to save my country before it's too late to reverse its deterioration. And I can't fix whatever's happening until I find out what's causing it."

Never dropping his eyes from hers, Zev lifted his other hand to mirror the first, so that he held her face in his palms.

"Part of me wants to ask you to just let it go and stay here with me." He gave a wry smile. "But I know you'd never do it."

"Not while Oleand is falling apart," she said, trying not to show how much his touch affected her. "Not to mention the small issue of your family not wanting me here."

Zev made a noise in his throat that might have been protest or acknowledgment, it was hard to tell.

"What about the other part of you?" Marieke pressed.

Zev let out a small sigh. "That part wants to solve the mystery and make things right as much as you do," he admitted.

Marieke beamed at him, her heart swelling. "I'm glad," she whispered. "Having your support means more than you know."

"You'll have more than my support," Zev said. "I'm coming with you, of course."

Marieke bit her lip, pleased but uncertain. "Will your family let—"

"It's not up to my family," Zev cut her off. "We're stronger together, Marieke. I'm not letting you go without me."

Marieke latched on to his words, leaning toward him and pressing her hand more firmly against his chest. "We are stronger together, aren't we?" she agreed, trying not to sound too eager. "I don't know how to explain it, Zev, but something magical happens when we're together."

"I agree." His voice was gruff, and pleased as Marieke was by the admission, she shook her head.

"I'm talking about something practical and specific. You know that I can sense the magic in the ground, right?"

Zev nodded.

"Well, usually, when I'm preparing to sing, the magic pools to me. I can feel it gathering. But in the canyon, try as I might, I couldn't get the magic to behave in the normal way. It was like it was pooling to you, not to me."

"To me?" Zev sounded startled.

"Yes. It's hard to describe, but it was responding to my prompting, yet gathering to you. And once I figured that out—especially once you encouraged me that I could do it—I was somehow able to access it through you."

"The magic came through my body?" Zev asked.

Marieke shook her head. "It's more like it was drawn to you, then obeyed my song without coming into either of our bodies. I mean, some of it came up into me, but some of it just shot straight through the ground to do what I'd asked it."

"That sounds...strange." Zev spoke cautiously, and Marieke didn't blame him. It was all very baffling and unnerving.

"It was," she agreed. "And it's definitely not something I could make happen by myself. I really can't explain it, but it felt like it was something we did together."

Zev was silent for a moment as he thought this over. His hands still cupped her face, one thumb moving absently in a rhythmic circle over her skin. "And this was when we'd run into that cave?" he asked. "When we left the middle of the gorge and went fully under the Aeltan side of the canyon?"

"Yes," said Marieke slowly. "Yes, that's right. I hadn't thought about the fact that it was Aeltan land, but I suppose that's true."

Zev's eyes were glazed over, and he stayed silent for longer this time. Marieke didn't ask him what he was thinking. She was certain he wouldn't tell her, and in any event, she was consumed by her own thoughts. Some idea danced at the edge of her awareness, a suspicion that got its life from the strange secrecy that sometimes surrounded Zev. What was the significance of this new information? How did it all fit together?

"Well," Zev said at last, something in his voice that Marieke couldn't read. "I suppose if we're going all the way to the southern jungle, we'll have time to explore it all more as we go."

"You really want to come with me?" Marieke asked uncertainly. "Your family surely won't approve."

Zev gave a rueful smile. "They won't. They very much want to stay out of it, and in their minds, that includes me."

"Yes." Marieke considered him. "You're not quite a normal family, are you?" Again that suspicion stirred within her, an idea she couldn't quite place.

She expected the familiar guarded look to spring into Zev's eyes, but it didn't. He held her gaze, revealing nothing, but not retreating either.

"But my mind is made up, Mari," he said as the silence stretched out. "We're in this together, you and I. I'll see it through with you."

And then what? Marieke wanted to ask. But she didn't. One step at a time.

They stood in silence, the mist lifting as the sun crept up past the horizon. She could hear a rooster faintly from the farmyard, and knew that their stolen moment, suspended between night and day, would soon have passed.

But for another minute, they remained wrapped in the stillness of the orchard and the nearness of each other. Zev let one hand drop, and she thought he'd pull away. But he twined it loosely around her waist instead. Her breath caught in her throat as he slid the thumb of his other hand across her cheek, brushing it over her lips with a featherlight touch. The desire to kiss her again was clear in his eyes, and she almost believed he would give in to it. But he didn't, and she didn't push him.

She understood, at least as much as she could with her limited information. He wasn't willing to jump off the cliff with her, to tie himself to her in open defiance of his family. She couldn't help but be disappointed by that. She was only human. But he also wasn't willing to let her go. Not anymore. That was what she would hang on to. It was a step in the direction her heart was yearning for. Surely he would find a path all the way to her before long, if she was patient.

But song preserve her, it was hard to be patient! Especially when he stood so close, her lips still tingling from the touch of his thumb. Not quite ready to let go of the moment, she leaned into him, silently claiming him as hers, willing it to be true even though he wasn't yet ready to fully admit it to himself.

Marieke let out a small gasp as she felt the magic move beneath her feet.

"Mari?" Zev's whisper was low and hoarse.

She gave her head a little shake. "I'm all right. It's just the magic."

She didn't explain, too lost in the wonder of the sensation. The steady river of magic still flowed, but now it was interacting with them, even though she'd made no attempt to call it. She and Zev were like a protruding rock in the center of the stream, that the current of power flowed around. Except it was no longer bypassing them completely. Tendrils of magic were wrapping up and around their legs, interweaving and layering and absorbing them smoothly into the flow. It connected them not only to the land but to each other, as if they were tied together by invisible ribbons of power. Marieke's heart sang with the *rightness* of it—it was a certainty she could never have put into words. But it stilled her disappointment and calmed the last vestiges of fear over what Zev would do or leave undone. They belonged together, and she didn't believe for a moment that they were going to drift away from one another, like debris carried in different directions on the surface of the river.

They weren't debris. They were fused to the bedrock, and no turbulence of the water above could detach them.

"It's going to be all right," she whispered, as much to herself as to Zev. "It will work out somehow."

Zev didn't respond, but she felt some of the tension leave his body. For one more moment he held her near, then the rooster crowed again, and the enchantment was broken. He dropped his arms with the tiniest of sighs, and stepped back.

"You should rest while you can," he told her. "I have duties to attend to. It's the least I can do if I'm leaving again soon. We can delay our departure for a few days, can't we?"

"Of course," Marieke said. "If your family will tolerate my presence." She gave a firm nod. "But I don't need to sit around and rest all day. Physically I'm back to full strength. I know my way around a farm enough to be useful."

Zev grinned. "Far be it from me to stop you. If you're determined, my mother will most definitely put you to work. Come on."

He laced his fingers lightly through hers, tugging her back toward the copse of trees that stood between the orchard and the farmhouse. Marieke's lips curled in a private smile at the ease of the gesture, like it was nothing for him to take her hand.

She couldn't help noticing that he dropped it before they emerged into the farmyard, however. One step at a time, she reminded herself.

The next few days were busy enough to keep Marieke from dwelling on her emotions. As Zev had predicted, Narelle had her working hard to help keep things running. It was clear that they'd missed Zev during his brief absence, for which Marieke couldn't help feeling guilty. He would be gone much longer if he came with her all the way to the jungle in Aeltas's south.

At least Narelle seemed inclined to be more friendly than Azai, who generally avoided Marieke. Zev's mother plied Marieke with questions as they worked side-by-side, and Marieke was only too glad to answer openly. If Narelle wanted to know more about the girl her son had brought home, Marieke was very ready to further that goal. Outside the reach of the Oleandan Council of Singers, she had nothing to hide.

As for how the family took the news that Zev planned to leave again with her, Marieke didn't know. Zev told them after she'd retired to bed the second evening—she suspected he wanted to protect her from witnessing the conversation. Azai was particularly surly the next morning, but no one mentioned it to her face.

That didn't stop her from feeling guilty, of course. The more time she spent with Zev's family, the more they felt like real people who cared about him, rather than distant obstacles to their relationship. And she found herself catching a hint of Zev's inner conflict within herself. She hated knowing she was causing tension. She even considered slipping away without Zev late one night. But that would be foolish as well as cowardly. She would be much more likely to succeed in finding the elves and getting to the bottom of Oleand's troubles with his help—as he'd said, they were stronger together.

When the morning of their departure dawned, Marieke was up and ready. She'd slept poorly, which was a shame, since it could be her last night in a real bed for a while.

Whatever their feelings about their son's decision, Zev's parents made no barrier to their departure. When she met Zev in the kitchen, Narelle had not only laid out breakfast, but packed provisions into both her rucksack and Zev's pack.

"I'm off to milk the cow," Narelle said, her voice a little gruff as she embraced her son. "You be safe now, Zev. We'll see you when your errand is done."

Marieke averted her eyes as Zev hugged his mother.

"Where's Father?"

"In the small yard," Narelle said as she moved toward the door. "He's expecting you to say goodbye before you go."

Neither of them made any mention of Azai, who'd clearly decided to skip the farewell scene.

"Take your time," Zev told Marieke, gesturing to the food. "Meet me in the yard when you're ready."

Marieke nodded, but once she was alone in the kitchen, she found she had no appetite. The mood of the house was too somber, like it was losing its son and heir forever, and it unnerved her. After only a couple of minutes, she grabbed her rucksack and made her way out into the yard.

There was no sign of Zev, and she remembered that his mother had directed him to the *small* yard. Where was that? Casting her eyes around, she remembered the training yard where Zev had retrieved his sword the first time she'd been at the property. It had struck her as odd at the time that a farm had a training yard designed for combat practice.

She made her way across the farmyard, stopping at the entrance to the training area. Zev was there, standing next to his father, who was seated and appeared to be sharpening his sword.

"Picked yourself another blade to take with you, I see." The older man's voice carried through the still air, as did Zev's reply.

"It'll do. I liked the last one better, but...it'll do."

Gideon nodded, pausing to examine the weapon he was sharpening. "This became my sword the day my father died. He was taken too soon and too suddenly. A foolish farming accident."

"I know, Father." Zev's voice was low and respectful. "I remember."

Gideon sighed, looking up at his son. "He would have remained strong into old age, I have no doubt. I remember seeing him hold this sword when I was a small child. I thought he must be the strongest man in the world."

Marieke had a good view of Zev's profile, and she saw his lips curve into a smile. "He was still formidable in my childhood."

Gideon smiled as well, standing. Marieke thought he would put the sword back in the storage area, but he strapped it to his side.

"You're my son, Zev," he said simply. "And I trust you. In spite of everything, your life and your happiness are not worth less than any other man's."

"Thank you, Father." Strangely, Zev sounded a little surprised by this statement.

"But," Gideon continued, "they're not all that matters."

"I know, Father."

Gideon nodded. "I know you do. And I trust you to make decisions based on more than what you want." He clapped his son on the shoulder. "And to come home safely to us."

"I will," Zev promised.

His father nodded again. "Goodbye then, Zev."

He turned away, carrying the sharpening stone toward the storage area. Zev shouldered his pack and moved toward the opening of the yard, his step faltering when he saw Marieke there.

"Sorry," she said quickly. "I didn't mean to sneak up on—"

"No, it's all right." He waved off her apology. "Just saying goodbye to my father. Let's go."

Marieke nodded, following him back across the yard. They weren't taking horses this time. The farm couldn't spare them for as long as the journey might take. Zev seemed confident they could hitch rides until out of his immediate region, after which they would look into securing transport in public vehicles.

"You don't want to find your brother and say goodbye to him as well?" Marieke asked, as they approached the main gate.

Zev gave a chuckle that didn't hold much mirth. "Azai? No. I don't think there's much more to say there." He shot her a sideways look. "I invited him to come with us last night."

"You did?" She looked at him in astonishment.

"I suppose I should have asked you first," Zev said. "But I thought we could use his help. He's more useful than he seems, and actually great company when he's not sulking."

"What did he say?" Marieke asked.

Zev's lips quirked to the side. "I'll leave that to your imagination."

They walked for several minutes in silence after that. Marieke could see Zev shooting the occasional look at her.

"Are you all right?" he asked at last.

Marieke nodded, her throat tight. "I'm fine. I just...I feel like I'm tearing a good family apart."

Zev laughed, the sound more carefree than Marieke had expected. "Firstly, you're not responsible for any of this. Secondly, my family is stronger than that. We've withstood worse. We'll be all right."

Marieke glanced back at the farm, the gate barely in view now. She could only hope Zev was right. The destruction of his family wasn't something she wanted on her conscience.

NINETEEN

Marieke

"That was a good one," Zev said encouragingly. "Try again." He held up his hand, palm toward her.

"You didn't even flinch," Marieke said skeptically, although she balled up her fist as instructed. "How good a punch could it be?"

Zev laughed. "You're hitting my hand, Marieke. Did you expect to really hurt me? It's not like you're punching me in the face."

"I'm just saying," Marieke muttered. "If you punched my hand, I'd flinch."

Zev's lips twitched. "Would it help your pride if I did?"

"No." Marieke let out a sigh. "I have no pride in this area. My acknowledged lack of physical strength is the whole reason we're doing this, right? We need to make my punches stronger so that it's more convincing for me to look like I'm physically attacking as misdirection for actually attacking with songcraft."

She would much prefer to keep working on the art of using her songcraft to increase the strength of *Zev's* attacks, but she was mastering that much more quickly than her own punches, so was less in need of the practice.

"That's the idea," Zev agreed. "No offense, but if you punched like you were doing earlier, no one would be distracted by it."

"What makes you such an expert on fighting, anyway?" Marieke asked suspiciously. "Get many bandits attacking your farm?"

"No," Zev said simply. "I have a brother."

"Fair enough." Marieke adopted the stance Zev had taught her, bringing her fists up in front of her. "I'm going to make you wince this time, though."

"All right."

Zev spoke mildly, but she could see the hint of smugness beneath his smile. Narrowing her eyes, she tried to remember what Kaine had taught her at the same time as holding all Zev's tips in her mind. She pulled in a deep breath as she drew her arm back, then released a rapid song as she brought her fist forward.

Her fist connected with Zev's hand as expected, with about as much force as her previous punch. But in addition, power shot through the ground, seizing on the root of a nearby tree and yanking it upward. It emerged from the ground under Zev's feet just far enough to make him wobble. He didn't fall, but he did give a sharp gasp of surprise, his face twisting in a—

"Aha!" Marieke pointed a triumphant finger at him. "You winced!"

Zev blinked rapidly as he stared from the now-docile root poking out of the earth to her grinning face. His surprise changed slowly to amusement, taking his defeat in good humor.

"All right, I did," he acknowledged. "But you cheated."

"Using magic isn't cheating," Marieke said. "It's my primary weapon. My primary tool, really."

"Well, it felt like cheating to me," Zev said. He grabbed his pack from the ground, hoisting it over one shoulder. "Look, there's the coach. Right on schedule."

Marieke made a noise in her throat in acknowledgment of the joke. They'd been waiting by the side of the road for two hours, well past the time the public vehicle was supposed to come by. But at least it had arrived. She'd been starting to think they'd have to continue on foot. And after a week of travel, with the southern jungle finally within reach, she didn't want their journey to slow now.

"If this one is full," she said, as the coach rumbled toward them, "it's my turn to go on the roof seats." She shot him a look. "Don't try to be chivalrous, either. Last time I had a portly woman sleep with her head on my shoulder and her chicken on my lap. I'd rather be up top and risk being thrown off at any sudden stop."

Zev grinned. "Did you expect the journey to be glamorous, lady singer?"

"No, actually." Marieke's eyes were thoughtful as she watched the coach slow in response to Zev's signal. "It's actually been much easier than I expected. Smoother and quicker. Everything sort of falls into place for you, doesn't it?"

"I don't know if I'd say that." Zev sounded startled.

"I would." There was no time for more than the simple reply, because the carriage had come to a stop.

Happily, this far south, the routes were less popular. It was why it had been difficult to find a public vehicle, but it also meant that the lumbering coach wasn't full. They were able to sit across from each other, with only two other passengers for company. Marieke leaned back and closed her eyes. Uncomfortable as the seat might be, she was tired enough that sleep tried to tempt her. It was a relief to be moving while sitting still, at any rate. And with Zev on hand, she didn't feel a moment's fear for her safety with the strangers.

But sleep wasn't actually within reach. Thoughts of their journey kept her awake as much as the jolting of the carriage did. She'd had ample time as they traveled south to observe the prosperity of Aeltas. On more than one journey through Oleand, it had felt as though disasters followed in her wake— the first time she'd returned from Aeltas, it had been so marked that she'd even wondered whether she'd brought a curse back with her.

Traveling through Aeltas with Zev was the opposite. The countryside they'd seen wasn't quite as rich as Zev's region, but there were no storms, no fires, no faltering harvests. On the contrary, it seemed like every second town they passed through was experiencing notable good fortune. In one village where they spent the night at a tiny inn, the residents were attempting to dig a new well, with no success in finding water. When they rose in the morning to continue their journey, everyone was celebrating as a previously discarded site had been found to abut an underwater spring.

In another area, they were stopped for lunch at a tavern when news spread that fishermen at a nearby lake had pulled in a catch that broke all previous records. The owner of the boat was so happy that he bought a round of ale for everyone present, as the town celebrated the weeks of benefit that would follow. It was only the following day that they shared a leg of the journey with a miller's assistant who was full of delight over the unusually high wind that was sweeping through the area, and which he was sure would enable his employer to recover from the backlog that had been caused by his windmill requiring extensive repair a short time before.

Or there was the time they were caught in a heavy downpour, but couldn't bring themselves to complain about getting wet when the locals were so pleased to have a dry spell broken, just in time to remove anxiety about the area's most lucrative crops.

Each time, Zev shrugged off Marieke's comments about the run of good luck following them, but his nonchalance only made her own suspicions grow. It felt like too clear a pattern to be ignored.

The coach moved steadily south as the afternoon wore on. By the time they disembarked at the furthest point south on its route, the thick jungle that dominated the southern part of Aeltas loomed before them. A tiny town was perched only a stone's throw from the first thick-trunked trees, and it was in the town's dusty square that they found themselves.

The other passengers didn't alight, evidently intending to stay on the coach as it turned westward and skirted the forest's edge. But the driver did hop down for a moment to pull out a crate from the storage area at the back of the vehicle. Without a word to them, he deposited it on the grass next to a stone bench, then climbed back onto his seat. Before their bemused eyes, the carriage disappeared around a bend.

"What's that?" Marieke asked, staring at the crate.

Zev looked around. "No idea. But it looks like someone's coming to get it."

Marieke followed his gaze to see a boy ambling around the edge of a nearby building. He whistled as he walked, a pleasant tune that made her want to sing along. But she wouldn't rush to identify herself as a singer before finding out more about their environment.

The boy stopped when he caught sight of them, his initial surprise replaced by curiosity.

"Hello. Did you just get off the coach?"

"We did," Zev answered. "Can you direct us to the inn, please?"

The boy chuckled. "No inn here. We're a tiny town." He strode forward the rest of the way, bending down to test the crate. "Heavy one this time." He cast a speculative eye over Zev. "Care to give me a hand?"

"Sure." Zev lifted the crate absently, showing no great strain over bearing its whole weight himself. "Where am I taking it?"

"To the store," the boy said, leading the way. "Well, store's a bit generous. It's just the front room of me grampa's house. But it's been the only shop in town long's I've been alive. The coach usually drops us off some kind of supplies."

"So there's nowhere we can stay in town?" Zev asked.

Marieke shot him a look. "Do we want to stay in town?"

Zev shrugged. "Not if you're ready to brave the jungle, I suppose. But it'll be dark in a few hours. Do you definitely want to camp tonight?"

Marieke didn't answer, wiping a trickle of sweat from her forehead as she pulled her rucksack more tightly over her shoulder. The climate had warmed considerably as they'd headed south. The air was becoming quite thick, and she wasn't used to it. Given the whole thing was her idea, she didn't want to admit to Zev how nervous she felt about braving the unfamiliar terrain of the humid southern jungle.

"Going into the jungle, are you?" The boy cast another curious glance at them. "No need to be scared about it. A lot of people have superstitions, but it's not so scary, really."

"No?" Marieke pressed, trying not to sound too relieved.

"Nah, if you stay on the main road, you'll be fine. It cuts through the middle of the jungle. Well," he paused, "not *right* through the middle. It's quite a ways west of the middle. But it gets you right through to the southern coast just fine."

"We don't want to go to the southern coast," said Zev. "The jungle is our destination."

"Oh?" The boy eyed him. "Visiting one of the villages along the main road, are you?"

"Aren't there villages away from the main road?" Marieke asked.

He shook his head. "Nope. Not a one. You gotta stay on the main road in the jungle. Or at least near it. There'd be no point straying from it anyway."

"Why?" Zev asked, frowning. "Because we'd get lost?"

"Or eaten by something?" Marieke added. The question had slipped out—hopefully they'd think she was trying to be funny.

"I suppose there are things in there that can eat you." The boy scratched his chin. "But not so long's you stay on the main road."

"You really love this road," Zev said dryly.

The boy seemed surprised. "Not me. I don't go into the jungle much. We're a farming town. We grow avocados, and our grove is out here, not under the big trees. But folk do come through here sometimes, on their way south. The main thoroughfare goes around the jungle to the west, but going through is more direct. Plus you get traders wanting to visit the jungle villages. The main road goes right past them all, and it's enchanted by singers from the council to keep it protected from the jungle. It's safe enough."

He rounded a well, bringing a tidy little house into view. The word STORE was painted neatly on a wooden board above the door.

"So you'll get lost if you go off the road?" Zev pressed.

"Not exactly." The boy pushed the door open, gesturing for Zev to carry the crate inside. "You just won't get anywhere."

Any attempt to get a better explanation was cut off by the boy's yell.

"Pa! Supplies are here. And some folk who want gear for the jungle."

"We don't need gear," said Marieke quickly.

He grinned as he looked them over. "Yes you do."

A gray-haired man appeared in an inner doorway, his wiry frame still upright and strong. He received the crate from Zev, placing it on a nearby table.

"Thanks, lad. I see my grandson found a way to get out of doing any work."

He raised an eyebrow at the boy. Unabashed, their guide took to the crate with a crowbar, obviously eager to examine what the carriage had brought them.

"So you're headed to the jungle, eh?"

"Yes, sir," said Zev. "That's our plan."

"Well, you'll want some salve for the mosquitoes," the shopkeeper said. "Do you have bedrolls? I don't have any for sale at the moment."

"We can make do with what we've got," Marieke said quickly. "But we'd welcome any information you can give us. Your grandson said most people stick to the main road, but—"

"Not most," the man cut her off. "All. Everyone sticks to the main road."

Delivered in a different tone, the words could have sounded like a dire warning. But the stranger didn't seem especially concerned.

"What if the road doesn't go to the town we want to reach?" Marieke asked.

He shrugged. "It does. All the towns are along the main road."

"But there must be some who live deeper in the jungle," Zev insisted. "Maybe at its center?" He was clearly thinking of what Trina had told them about the elves' community.

"Nothing lives in the center of the jungle outside of myth and legend," the shopkeeper said.

Marieke folded her hands behind her back, trying not to show her eagerness. "What kind of legends?"

"Oh, there are all sorts of stories about jungle creatures," the shopkeeper said dismissively. "Stories of forest people who live hidden away among the trees, becoming less like humans and more like the jungle itself. Fireside tales, you know. But there's nothing in them. The magic is too strong in there for people to live. Except for, you know, along—"

"The main road," Zev finished for him. "We get it."

"Well you should be getting that salve," he said. "To spread on your skin. And maybe some nets to sleep under. The mosquitoes get real bad in there."

"We'll take some salve," Zev said. "We won't burden ourselves with nets to carry."

He shrugged. "Suit yourself. Do you have big enough water bladders?" He inspected the one Zev lifted from his rucksack and shook his head. "You should get a bigger one. Long way between some of the villages, and you can't trust the water anywhere else in the jungle. There's magic in it, and it's unpredictable."

He went on to list some more recommended gear. A skeptical part of Marieke wondered whether these items were truly essential or whether the man just wanted the sales. But the prices weren't exorbitant, and she didn't want to be without something they really needed.

"Sure you don't want to stay the night in town before you go?" the shopkeeper asked, once their transaction was complete. "Bessy sometimes lets out her spare room, if the price is right."

"No thanks," said Zev firmly. "We'll push on. Is there somewhere we can buy food?"

"Here." The man smiled. "Not much on the shelves right now, but that's what this is for." He lifted a string of cured meat from the crate on the table. "And we've got plenty of avocados."

It was a good thing they still had food from their last stop, Marieke reflected. They purchased some dried meat and avocados anyway, and filled their new, larger water bladders at the well.

By the time they left town, it was only a couple of hours before dark, and Marieke was wondering whether they'd erred in dismissing the suggestion of seeking lodging with the unknown Bessy. But the shopkeeper had told them that the first town was only a few hours' walk into the jungle, and had assured them yet again that they would be perfectly safe as long as they stayed on the main road.

The road wasn't difficult to find, at least. A path ran out of the town and straight into the trees, a wide space carved out around it. The opening wasn't large enough to penetrate to the canopy—branches still curved over their heads some distance above. But trees had been felled and the ground cleared to make a straight route southward.

"Wow," Marieke said, as they walked into the relative gloom of the jungle. "I can feel what they mean." When Zev tilted his head in inquiry, she added, "The magic. There's some kind of boundary enchantment on this road. It feels sophisticated."

"Is it really enough to keep everyone on the path safe?" Zev asked. "That must involve powerful magic."

"Agreed." Marieke spoke absently, her senses mainly focused on assessing the enchantment. "Although powerful doesn't always mean a large volume. It's often more about finesse. The enchantment probably acts as a subtle deterrent rather than an actual barrier. If it's been in place for a long time, I suppose predators have learned not to include this area in their hunting territory. Maybe it hasn't been tested front on much."

"Reassuring," Zev said dryly.

She laughed. "It's still impressive magic. It must need regular replenishing."

The entrance point of the jungle soon disappeared from view behind them. Marieke felt uncomfortably closed in, but she wasn't sure how much that was due to the thick foliage visible on both sides of the path and how much to the heaviness of the air.

The presence of the magic was comforting, however. And not just the magic of the ground—which was plentiful and eager beneath her feet—but the magic of the boundary on the road. With the familiar sensation of a latent enchantment always nudging at her awareness, it was hard to remember she was in a dangerous and unpredictable environment.

As the light faded away, Marieke began to hum, summoning some of the magic that crowded under her feet. She saw Zev cast her a curious glance, but didn't stop to explain. It took all her focus to draw up only the magic she needed. With less training, she wouldn't have been able to prevent a veritable flood pouring through her in response to her questing songcraft, and it would have been too great a volume to successfully mold. Less was sometimes more with magic.

Once she'd drawn into herself a manipulatable amount of magic, she gave words to her song.

"Light, the darkness gently greet,
Show a path before my feet."

Responding to her prompting, magic issued out from her and concentrated in a ball just in front of her, about the height of her face. She could feel the mass of magic before she could see it, but sure enough, it soon began to glow softly. Marieke hummed wordlessly as the magic continued to pull energy from the rustling leaves and dripping moisture of the surrounding jungle. Soon, she had a glowing ball of light that illuminated the road ahead.

With a final twist, she once again turned the hum into words, in an incantation of perpetual motion that was one of the basic formulas taught at the academy.

"Wow." Zev's eyes reflected the light of the glowing orb as he cast her an admiring look. "That's a neat trick."

Marieke flushed with pleasure. "It's a very simple one, actually. You can always tell that an enchantment is a beginner one if it's set to nursery-rhyme style words. They don't bother with that at a more advanced level."

"Well, it didn't look beginner to me," Zev said. "How did you do it?"

Marieke bit her lip, silently delighted that he was showing such an interest in her craft. "I used the magic's inherent connection with the forces of nature. Magic *is* a force of nature, after all. That enchantment simply sets the magic to collect energy from natural sources and turn it into light. I don't have the strength or training to do it with large sources of energy. But turning a gentle breeze into a source of light is no problem."

"Amazing." Zev was staring at the orb, admiring how it moved in tandem with their pace. "But how is it still going if you're not still singing?"

"Oh, the last bit of my song was a perpetuation formula. A much weaker and more generic version of what's in place with this boundary enchantment. It instructs the magic to keep doing its set task indefinitely." She smiled at him, reveling in the feeling of him looking to her for answers. It so often felt the other way around. "It never actually is indefinite, of course. No singer can harness an infinite amount of magic at once. The task stops when it's exhausted the volume of magic used by the singer in placing the enchantment. A group of singers working together can harness a lot of magic and set up a substantial perpetuation. But just now I grabbed only a little. So I'll need to renew the light enchantment regularly. Which is no problem, of course."

With the bobbing ball of light for company, they continued at a good pace, chatting inconsequentially as they went further into the jungle. The sun had undoubtedly set above the canopy when the promised town came into view, but there was no noticeable drop in temperature.

Marieke came to a stop as Zev put out a hand, lightly touching her arm.

"What is it?"

"I'm just wondering if we should avoid the town," Zev said quietly. "Maybe we should let the light die out and go around it."

"I thought we were planning to camp there," said Marieke.

"We were," Zev acknowledged. "I don't know about you, but I'm less intimidated by the jungle than I expected. Especially with your songcraft at our disposal. I'd be willing to strike out in search of the elves on our own sooner rather than later. And that being the case, I'm not sure we want to advertise our presence to the humans in here."

Marieke frowned. Here again was Zev's obsession with remaining inconspicuous. She didn't relate to it, but it seemed to be deeply ingrained in his thinking.

"You want to strike out at night?"

"No," he said quickly. "I'm suggesting we skirt around the town, go a little way past it, and camp somewhere near the road, near enough to be inside the boundary enchantment but not visible to passers-by. Then strike out in the morning."

Marieke thought it over, then gave a shrug. "I'm willing to risk it. The jungle isn't as frightening as I expected, either."

With a quick song, she dispersed the magic that was still

collecting energy and turning it into light. The glowing orb died away instantly, leaving them in the close stillness of the humid night.

"Come on."

Zev's voice was whisper soft as his hand found hers in the darkness. Tugging her gently behind him, he stepped just off the path, wending between tree trunks. Progress was slow off the road, the undergrowth relatively sparse so close to the cleared zone but still difficult to navigate in the dark.

"Are you all right?" Zev asked, when Marieke stumbled slightly over a root. "Do you want to turn back to the road?"

"No, I'm fine," she assured him. "I just lost my footing. I'm not afraid."

He squeezed her hand. "Good. You don't need to be. Together, we can handle anything this jungle throws at us."

Marieke smiled in the darkness. Yes, they were stronger together, and they both knew it. Walking through the jungle hand in hand with Zev brought to mind their walk from his orchard to his house, and the moment that had come before it. She'd decided to trust that his path would lead him to her if she was patient. And here, alone in the darkness, on a mission no one but them seemed to care about, it felt like every step was bringing him more inevitably to her.

It was worth whatever dangers the jungle might be hiding.

TWENTY

Marieke

Marieke's silent declaration was tested the moment they struck out the following morning. They'd passed a surprisingly uneventful night in their makeshift camp, the boundary enchantment like a comforting blanket over her as she drifted to sleep. But as soon as they crossed the invisible line where the protection ended, all comfort disappeared.

The jungle was like another world, every sense overwhelmed by new experiences. Perhaps most disorienting of all was the effect on her magical sense. The power in the ground under her feet on the path had already been stronger than outside the jungle. But it hadn't prepared her for how it would feel off the path. Magic writhed and twisted through the terrain, so thick in the ground that it felt like it was starting to climb up the trees. The sheer volume of it was uncomfortable. Usually Marieke had to call magic to her to get it to come up through her form. But this magic was almost aggressive—it wanted to pour into her even without being asked, and it took focused effort not to let it.

Not to mention the mosquitoes. They were much worse than Marieke had imagined, even with the warning of the shopkeeper in the village outside the jungle. Thankfully the salve they'd smeared over their exposed skin kept most of the insects from landing on them, but their constant whining buzz still grated on Marieke's ears.

They didn't talk much as they pressed into the jungle. Zev seemed as on edge as she was, the thickness of both the foliage and the air feeling suffocating. The steady dripping of water from the canopy suggested a light drizzle above, and they were soon damp and miserable. Marieke had never been so sweaty in her life, her skin sticky and her pack feeling heavier than its meager contents justified. Zev paused every now and then to score a tree with his blade to mark their route, and each time, Marieke let out a quiet lighting song to make the marks glow.

"It won't last forever," she said after the first such instance. "But if we try to retrace our steps within the day, it should light the way."

"Good thinking," Zev said. He studied her carefully. "Are you all right?"

Marieke nodded. "It's just...a lot," she said. "The magic, I mean. There's so much of it that it's hard to sing."

Zev looked bewildered. "Shouldn't more magic make it easier, not harder?"

"You'd think," Marieke acknowledged. "And to an extent, it's true. But not once you reach this kind of volume. Outside the jungle, the magic is like a steady river running under my feet, and I can reach into it and pull out as much magic as I want for my enchantment, up to the limit of what I'm capable of wielding. But here, it's more like an overflowing torrent which sees me as an outlet it wants to pour through. There's no way I have the strength or skill to wield the volume of magic trying to enter me, and my instinct tells me it would be dangerous to let it come through me at all. The trouble is, it actually takes a lot of finesse to take hold of only some of it. I have to focus hard to manage any songcraft."

"That sounds volatile," said Zev, alarmed. "If it might hurt you, maybe you shouldn't do it at all, Mari."

She shook her head. "It's fine. I just need to pay attention." She saw that he still looked concerned, and she laid a hand on his arm, which was as clammy and hot as her own skin. "Truly, Zev, I'm a fully qualified singer, and I know what I'm doing. Trust me."

He nodded, his expression easing. "I know."

Marieke smiled back as she wiped a trickle of sweat from the bridge of her nose. His faith in her meant more than he could imagine.

They'd walked for another half an hour when Marieke reached to push a vine out of the way only for Zev to reach out with lightning speed and grab her wrist.

"What?" she asked, her heart racing in an instinctive reaction as her eyes darted around them. The jungle was quiet, but as always, she could see only as far as the closest thick foliage. "What is it?"

"That's not a vine." Zev tugged at her, pulling her backward away from her projected path, his eyes fixed on the point ahead.

Marieke followed his gaze and barely stifled a scream as she saw the long-bodied snake looping down from the branch above. Thankfully it didn't seem interested in them, but she still backed away with such haste that she stumbled over a mossy log.

Zev's grip on her wrist stopped her from falling, and she allowed herself a shudder as she passed a hand over her face.

"I don't like this place." The honest words slipped out before she could stop them, but thankfully Zev didn't seem inclined to laugh at her.

"Nor do I," he acknowledged. "Open fields and peaceful orchards for me, thanks."

"I'd even take barren canyons over this jungle," Marieke said. "Come on, let's give it a wide berth."

They'd barely gone a dozen paces, however, when Zev stopped again. Marieke's eyes darted nervously around, but there was nothing sinister in the trees this time. Zev knelt down, shifting a large fern frond with his hand to better reveal a clear print in the mud.

"What animal made that?" Marieke asked, the skin on the back of her neck prickling.

"I don't know," Zev admitted. "I don't know anything about jungle creatures. I could track a wolf or a fox without problems, but this doesn't look like either of those."

"Definitely too big for a fox," Marieke agreed. She knelt next to him, studying the print. "It must be reasonably fresh, if it hasn't been washed away by this drizzle."

"I'll be honest, I don't like the idea of continuing without knowing what's nearby," Zev said. "I wish there was a way to know for sure." He glanced at her. "I don't suppose magic can tell you?"

"Actually, maybe it can," said Marieke. She stared unseeingly at the closest tree, thinking of Instructor Oriana's song at the burned field of wheat. "Storytelling song would be able to tell us what's near."

"Storytelling song?" Zev sounded intrigued. "Is that something you can do?"

Marieke sighed. "No, not really. I learned only the very basics. I didn't get to pursue it. But..."

She bit her lip. Kaine had said she had a strong natural aptitude, at least for one branch of storytelling song. She knew the basic concept. And the magic here was so strong it wasn't as though she'd struggle to find enough for the demanding task. It was worth a try.

Marieke cleared her throat, not trying to form the enchantment until she'd finished pulling magic into herself. It took all her concentration just to do that step. Then she cautiously sent magic out from her. In employing the magic, she copied the formula she used to test the nearby terrain with her agricultural songcraft. But she replaced the words with a simplified version of what she'd heard Instructor Oriana use at the wheat field. Not testing the environment itself, but the temporary elements currently at play within it.

Her song was cautious and short, and when she let it die down, she saw Zev watching her avidly.

"Well?" he asked. "What did you sense?"

She shook her head slowly. "Not much. I mean, there's a lot, but I couldn't identify much. I got a sense of plenty of creatures in the area, but nothing felt big enough to match these prints." She drew a deep breath. "I'm going to try the harder kind, where you ask the magic to tell you what happened rather than what's currently in place."

Zev looked lost, but she didn't try to explain to him. Instead she screwed up her eyes so that her normal senses wouldn't muddy the waters of what her magical sense was telling her. Then she sang soft and low, asking the magic to tell her the story of this patch of land.

Nothing.

Marieke opened her eyes, disappointed. She shouldn't be surprised. It was a complex area of magic, and she had no training. But she'd hoped the land would give her *something*, even if she didn't have the skill to properly decipher it. She met Zev's eyes reluctantly, disappointed to be unable to justify the faith she saw in them.

A memory flashed through her mind, from when they'd

been cornered by Rissin and the other elves in the cave in Sundering Canyon. Zev had gripped her arm and told her that he knew she could do it, and the magic had instantly become more responsive to her.

"Zev," she said suddenly.

"Yes?"

"You believe in me, right?"

He blinked. "Of course I do."

"Can you...can you put your arm around me?"

Zev stared at her, and she fully expected him to ask for an explanation. But he didn't. He just shifted toward her, one strong arm sliding across her back and around her waist, pulling her in just enough so she sat snugly against him.

Marieke was already overheated from the humid air, and the contact only increased that sensation, but it wasn't off-putting. In fact, she was now at risk of a different kind of distraction.

Pulling herself together, she murmured her thanks before focusing back on her song. The magic here wasn't like the magic in Sundering Canyon—it was overwhelming in volume, but not chaotic and unpredictable—and it didn't pool around Zev or travel straight through the ground at her direction.

Still, as she raised her voice in a song, she could feel that the magic was more responsive to her now, in a way she couldn't describe. It just felt...happy with her. Cooperative and malleable. It was bizarre, but useful. An image flashed through her mind, of a dark and sleek shape traversing the same ground they now occupied, its movement silent in the sleepy jungle.

Marieke let out a gasp, her song stopping at once.

"A panther," she said. "It was a panther." She swallowed, nerves rippling over her. She'd seen a drawing of a panther in a book once—it was as close as she had any desire to get to one.

"A panther?" Zev's voice was low and serious, his grip

around her waist tightening slightly. "Are they territorial hunters?"

"I think so," Marieke said. "But I don't know much about them."

"I don't want to find out the hard way," Zev said. "I don't think we should knowingly wander through its territory."

"I agree." Marieke deflated slightly. "We should turn back, shouldn't we?"

"I think it would be wisest," Zev agreed. "I'm not too proud to admit that I wasn't as prepared as I thought for the jungle. If we're aiming for the center, we have a fair way south still to go. Why don't we travel further on the road before trying again?"

Marieke nodded. "That makes sense."

She snuck a look up at Zev. He hadn't released her, and his eyes shifted down to hers. The still air felt even thicker all of a sudden as he pushed a wisp of wet hair back from her forehead.

"You really do have a lovely voice."

Zev's quiet declaration brought Marieke's lips curving into a smile.

"I'm glad, because it's the only one I have," she murmured.

Zev smiled, releasing her at last and casting another glance down at the panther tracks. "Come on. Let's not wait for it to sniff us out."

Marieke nodded agreement, and they turned back the way they'd come. It was disheartening to have wasted the time and effort, but at least the lighted marks made it easy to find their way back to the road. She breathed a sigh of relief when they passed back through the enchanted boundary. It was so much less overwhelming to the senses on the cultivated patch of ground.

They traveled south for the rest of the day, bypassing another village and camping just off the road again. They passed very few other travelers, each time redirecting into the undergrowth to avoid notice.

Marieke was exhausted by nightfall, but even though they were still within the magical boundary, it was hard to relax her mind enough for sleep. There was too much information crowding her senses.

"You can settle, Marieke," Zev said, after watching her toss and turn on her rolled out mat for several minutes.

He sat with his back to a tree, positioned between her and the road so that she was hemmed in by the magical boundary on one side and him on the other.

"I'll make sure all is clear before I go to sleep."

"You need rest, too," she reminded him. She decided not to mention that his proximity in the darkness was as much of a barrier to sleep as their environment.

"I know," he said. "I will rest. But you can relax. Nothing will harm you tonight, I swear."

Marieke didn't know how he could promise any such thing, but the confidence in his voice was comforting nonetheless. She drifted into sleep soon after, and woke to find Zev already up and serving up food from his pack.

Farmers.

Having already stepped off the road, they didn't return to it. They'd traveled a long way south the day before, and it was time to brave the jungle again. They struck out eastward, not talking as they both scanned their surroundings carefully with every step.

They'd barely walked ten minutes into the foliage, their progress painfully slow through the undergrowth, when Zev stopped, putting his hand against a tree and drawing a deep breath.

"Are you all right?" Marieke asked, alarmed. She'd never seen him need to catch his breath just from walking before.

He nodded, letting out a grunt as he gathered his voice. "I'll be fine. It's just...so much pressure." He pounded a fist to his chest, causing Marieke's alarm to grow.

"You can feel it, too? The aggressiveness of the magic?" It hadn't escaped her that the overwhelming intensity of the magic was even worse here than it had been last time they'd tried leaving the road.

Zev stared at her. "That's magic? Surely I can't feel magic the way you do. I never have before."

"Well, what does it feel like?" Marieke asked.

"Like pressure on my chest," Zev said. "Similar to shortness of breath."

Marieke frowned. "That's not how I'd describe the feel of the magic."

Zev straightened. "It's fine. I can handle it. Let's push on."

"I don't like it," Marieke said, keeping pace reluctantly as Zev kept walking. "What if it's killing you or something?"

Zev just made a dismissive noise. "I'm not so easy to kill."

The conversation died out as they navigated carefully around some kind of bog, but after another five minutes, Zev spoke again, his voice more cheerful.

"There, I knew it would just be a matter of adjusting. The pressure is already getting less intense."

Marieke realized he was right. The magic was becoming more contained, its surging power less insistent in its attempts to pour through her.

A moment later she realized why as they pushed their way through some vine-covered, low-hanging branches and emerged onto a wide, well-maintained path.

"There's another path?" Zev said, bewildered. "I thought there was only one main road through."

Marieke sighed. "It's not another one. It's the same one."

"Are you sure?" Zev shot her a look. "What if this is a different road, made by the elves?"

"It's not." Marieke shook her head. "I recognize the boundary enchantment."

Zev frowned, and she understood his reaction. She could have sworn they'd continued in much the same direction for their whole walk. It was a surprise to find that they'd traveled in a loop.

"Come on," she said, striding back toward the foliage. "The bog must have turned us around more than we realized. Let's be more careful of our route this time."

Ten minutes later, they were back on the road, a sign pointing back toward a village they'd bypassed the day before.

"We've made no progress from where we started," Marieke said, disgruntled. "How is it possible for us to be back at this spot? I'm sure we didn't go through the same terrain that time as last time."

Zev didn't answer, just plunged back between the trees, his jaw set in determination.

For an hour they tried in vain to get deeper into the jungle, every attempt leading to the same result. Even the use of the lighted markings didn't help. They couldn't find them when they looked, yet their steps seemed always directed back the way they'd come.

"It's magic," Marieke concluded after the tenth attempt. "Some kind of magic is at work, stopping us from getting deeper into the jungle."

"Why would the boundary enchantment be operating that way here when it wasn't before?" Zev asked.

She shook her head. "I don't think it's the boundary enchantment. It's not any enchantment I can feel. It must be something more sophisticated."

She gasped as a thought seized her. "Something hiding its

tracks. Remember how the elves can apparently make talismans that hide their own magic when they're used? Maybe this is another form of the same craft."

"You think it's the work of elves?" Zev asked. He considered it. "That would make sense, wouldn't it? If they're keeping their existence hidden, they'd have an interest in humans staying on the road." He raised an eyebrow at Marieke. "Why are you smiling?"

"Because if the elves don't want people exploring this part of the jungle, it must mean we're close!" she said. "Come on, we have to find a way around this redirecting magic."

She struck back out, but to no avail. Nothing they tried worked, and by noon, they were both disheartened and weary.

"Any fresh ideas?" Zev asked her.

"I'm all out," she said, groaning as she sat herself down on a boulder. "You?"

He sat down beside her, his expression thoughtful. "The only thing we haven't tried is asking for help."

"From the village back there?" Marieke asked doubtfully. "You think they might know about the elves after all?"

Zev shook his head. "From the elves."

"Sure." Marieke's tone was dry. "Once I find them, I'll be sure to ask for their help in finding them."

Zev grinned. "That's obviously not what I mean. Remember when you sent me a letter, right to my farm? I still have the map that shopkeeper sold us. What if we wrote a message on it and you used songcraft to send it eastward? Would it be turned back by the magic, do you think?"

"Hm." Marieke considered it. "It's an interesting idea. Definitely worth trying."

Zev pulled out the map, and Marieke wrote a clear, simple message, using the nearby signpost as a guide.

· · ·

We are Marieke of Oleand and Zevadiah of Aeltas. We know of your settlement, and we seek an audience with your Imperator. You can find us on the main road, ten leagues south of the village of Firth.

"There," she said, studying it. "Straight to the point, and if it's intercepted by a human, it won't identify the intended recipients as elves."

"Do you know how to do a sending enchantment, or whatever the term is?" Zev asked.

"No," Marieke admitted. "I used an official message station last time. I can't send it to a particular recipient or location. But I can call some wind to carry it eastward. I think I have the required control to make the wind targeted and contained, so it can dodge its way through the trees for a decent distance at least."

"Well, it's better than I could do," Zev said with a shrug.

Marieke rolled up the parchment, casting her eyes around for something to tie it with. She eyed Zev for a moment, then tugged at one of the laces that dangled from the top of his tunic.

"Marieke," Zev said, his shocked tone not fooling her for a moment. "And here I thought I could trust you with my honor, alone in the jungle and at your mercy."

She rolled her eyes, even as she lowered her face to her task to hide the flush his words brought. "Oh, don't be ridiculous. Your tunic is already unlaced anyway."

"It's hot," Zev said by way of defense. "I can't breathe with it all laced up."

The thought flashed through Marieke's mind that *she* found it a little hard to breathe every time her eyes fell on the exposed part of Zev's chest, but she refrained from saying so. His ego was plenty healthy as it was, and she wanted to maintain some dignity, after all.

Having finished tying the parchment up with the lace, she cleared her throat and summoned magic to her. It surged eagerly through the ground, only too ready to take the offered outlet through her body.

Marieke formed her song with care, drawing on the ability to test the terrain that she'd learned in her agricultural songcraft. It didn't reveal much beyond a close radius, as she'd discovered in the morning's various attempts to penetrate the jungle, but it would help her give the parchment a good start.

She and Zev both watched as a light breeze stirred beneath her hand, lifting the rolled-up paper into the air and sending it drifting toward the trees. She kept singing for some time after it disappeared before eventually letting the song die. She could no longer sense where the paper was headed anyway. She would have to trust her enchantment to carry it as directed.

They made themselves as comfortable as they could, setting up a camp a little way into the trees and pulling out some food. They were just on the edge of the boundary, and even though they weren't fully outside it, she still noticed Zev rubbing near his heart from time to time. Her eyes were drawn to the gesture each time, but she didn't comment until they'd been sitting for a few hours.

"Are you uncomfortable?" She told her eyes not to linger on his exposed chest when he lowered his hand.

"I'd be more comfortable if you'd summon another breeze to cool me down," he said. "Can you do that?"

"Yes, I could. But it wouldn't last long."

"I don't know." Zev leaned back against his tree, the hint of a grin lifting one corner of his mouth as he crossed his arms behind his head and closed his eyes. "It would if you kept singing. You could serenade me and blow a nice wind over me until the elves show up."

She gave him a look that he couldn't see. "Shall I also feed you delicacies by hand while you recline at leisure, Your Majesty?"

There was an awkward edge to Zev's laugh, and he sat up straighter and opened his eyes.

"That won't be necessary."

Marieke studied his face, his loss of composure piquing her interest.

"You didn't like that joke," she commented. It wasn't a question, but her next words were. "Why not?"

With the question, she felt the magic in the ground increase in intensity, like the torrent was suddenly bubbling and boiling frantically underneath her rather than racing past.

"Whoa," she said. "Calm down."

"What?" Zev was leaning forward now, his cautious posture the opposite of what it had been before her quip. "What do you mean, calm down?"

"I was talking to the magic," Marieke said, not bothering to explain better. "It seems my question was...particularly pertinent."

Zev looked wary, and Marieke's suspicions swirled as frantically as the magic. She remembered his family's strange reputation and manner, and the way the magic reacted to him in the canyon. Not to mention Rissin's response to that phenomenon. The elf had been as interested in Zev as in her. More interested. And then there was that moment in the orchard, when the magic had seemed to tie them together, wrapping around Zev of its own accord in a way it had no business to when he couldn't channel it.

She opened her mouth to speak again, not entirely sure what she suspected, but feeling like she was on the cusp of a revelation. Then she saw something in his eyes, behind the apprehension.

Conflict.

He wanted to tell her everything he was hiding, but something held him back. And she'd already decided to be patient. She didn't want to pry him open now, like a knife to a walnut. She wanted him to open to her, like a flower responding to sunlight.

Her lips twitched at the image, and bewilderment joined the other emotions on Zev's face.

"What's funny?" he asked cautiously.

"Just my own thoughts," Marieke said, her voice light now. "I'm not sure you'd appreciate them." He still looked uncertain, so she pushed on, changing the topic. "Do you really want me to summon a breeze? I can if you like."

"No." Zev leaned back again, although he didn't regain his earlier carefree manner. "If you're singing, you can't talk, and I'd rather the conversation." He eyed her. "I am surprised how rarely you use songcraft for small conveniences like that, though. It's not what I expected. I imagined singers would use magic all the time to make their lives more comfortable."

"Some do," Marieke acknowledged. "But it's not really encouraged. One of the principles we learn early at the academy is that magic is a powerful tool, and our ability to wield it is not to be taken for granted or used lightly. They teach us that it's not through our own virtue that we were born with the ability to sing. The philosophy is that we shouldn't use that ability to increase our own privilege beyond what nature has already done, or we make the gulf between singers and non-singers wider than it needs to be. We're supposed to use magic to help others, and for substantial tasks that are genuinely worthwhile. Not for little things that make no material difference and only benefit us."

"Well." Zev's eyes had the intensity she always found so captivating as he searched her face. "That's a very different picture from the life I imagined singers to lead before I met you."

She shrugged. "I believe it. But that's the ideal that we're presented with. I'm not saying everyone lives up to it. In fact, many don't."

"But you do," Zev said.

"I try to." Marieke ran her finger through the dirt in a meaningless pattern, a little overwhelmed by his searching gaze.

"I confess I'm genuinely surprised that the academy teaches that kind of mentality, and the council supports it."

Marieke raised her eyes to his again. "I know what you think, Zev. And with what I've learned since we met, I can acknowledge that you have reason. But you don't see the full picture any more than I did before. The council's set up isn't perfect, and the structure makes it too hard for non-singers to have the voice they deserve to have. But in spite of that, I do believe that most of those on the Oleandan council and at the Oleandan academy mean well. They're trying their best for our country, and the vast majority of them aren't evil or power-hungry."

"But they do have power," Zev argued. "And that power is built on lies."

Marieke had no answer, but she didn't need one. A different voice, much higher in pitch than Zev's, responded for her.

"That's an interesting perspective."

TWENTY-ONE

Zev

Zev and Marieke both surged to their feet as a small figure stepped out from between the trees. Zev took a step forward, placing himself slightly in front of Marieke as the elf approached.

"Who are you?" Zev asked, his hand inching toward the hilt of his sword.

The elf's thin lips curved into a smile, his eyes startlingly green as they looked calmly from one human to the other.

"I have the advantage over you. I believe I know who you are, Marieke of Oleand and Zevadiah of Aeltas."

"You got our note," Marieke gasped. The shock on her face told Zev that she'd never really expected their idea to work.

"And you, it is evident, got our attention." The tip of the elf's pointed ears wobbled slightly as he looked her over. "How did you learn of our presence here?"

Marieke opened her mouth to answer, but Zev flung out an arm in a gesture of caution.

"That information has value," he said shrewdly. "Perhaps we don't feel inclined to give it away for free."

The elf chuckled, the sound tinkling but not exactly merry. "You know a little something of our ways, it seems," he said. "But surely you agree I am entitled to know your business with the Imperator."

Zev folded his arms. "Do you claim to be the Imperator?"

"I do not." The elf's answer was swift.

"Then our business with him doesn't concern you."

The elf raised one thin eyebrow, his ears wobbling again. Zev thought there was humor in his emerald gaze, but it didn't make him seem any more approachable.

"That is not for you to say," the elf said in a business-like manner. "But my instructions are to take you to the Imperator."

Zev frowned, reluctant to blindly follow the unknown creature. A glance at Marieke showed both excitement and trepidation on her features. She looked up at him, and he nodded in acknowledgment of all the unspoken thoughts.

It was almost unbelievable that they'd found such a straightforward way around the enchantment that kept the elves safe from humans—unbelievable enough to make him wary—but they didn't know of another way forward. And they hadn't come this far to give up or turn back.

"We'll come with you," Marieke said, turning back to the elf with dignity. "But if you intend to play us false, it won't go well for you."

"Is that a promise?" The elf's eyes gleamed unnervingly.

"No," said Marieke quickly, not needing the warning rising to Zev's lips. "Just an opinion."

"Very well." The elf seemed both amused and a little disappointed. "Follow me."

He turned and plunged back into the trees, disappearing so quickly they had to scramble to gather their things and follow so as not to lose him. Zev expected him to lead them straight into the jungle, but he traveled alongside the road for a short distance before coming to a stop.

"Through here," he said, gesturing to the space between two tree trunks. "It might be disorienting, but it won't harm you."

"What won't harm—"

The question died on Marieke's lips as she, like Zev, got a proper look at the place the elf was indicating. The trees in question were the same as those around them, but the space in between them looked all wrong. The surrounding jungle was thick with lush foliage, but between those trees Zev could see a large clearing. It was like looking through a window onto an entirely different scene.

"Go on." The elf seemed disinterested in their confusion.

"After you," Zev said flatly. He wasn't ready to take the elf's word for it that they weren't at risk of harm.

The elf just sighed, apparently bored by the suspicion of his companions. He strolled forward, his little legs not breaking stride as he went between the trees. He paused in the clearing on the other side, one thin eyebrow raised in impatience.

Marieke started to move forward, but Zev beat her to it. He stepped carefully between the tree trunks, his senses on high alert. He was expecting some kind of magical sensation, but in fact he felt nothing. The air felt slightly different on the other side—less close given the sparser foliage—but that was it. He turned to see Marieke following him through, her expressive face showing all the fascination he was keeping to himself.

"What *was* that?" she asked.

The elf looked like he was debating whether to answer, but thankfully decided not to be ornery.

"We call them doorways." His bright eyes passed between them. "Your kind used to know of them. They helped develop them."

"Our kind?" Zev repeated. "Humans?"

"Singers," the elf clarified.

"I'm not a singer," Zev said. The answer rose a little too quickly to his lips, the thought occurring belatedly that he probably shouldn't offer information for free.

"What?" The elf's gaze sharpened, and Zev realized he'd captured the creature's interest. "Neither of you?"

"I am," Marieke said.

The elf's alabaster brow furrowed as his gaze shifted to Marieke's feet, then flicked to Zev's before flicking back to Marieke's face.

She shrugged. "Don't ask me to explain. I can't."

"Hm." The elf eyed them both shrewdly. "I'll take you to the Imperator." He turned on his heel and strode across the clearing, leaving Zev and Marieke to once again hurry behind.

"What was that about?" Zev murmured to Marieke.

"The magic is pooling around you again," she said. "Not as intensely as in the canyon, but...it's definitely notable."

Zev frowned, not sure what to make of that information. "So you can tell someone is a singer, just by the way magic responds under their feet?" The question was as much to deflect attention from him as to actually satisfy curiosity.

Marieke shook her head as they walked. "Not usually. Magic doesn't normally pool unless the singer is gathering it ready to mold it. At which point, yes, I can absolutely sense active songcraft. It's just that here, the magic is so intense. Remember how I said earlier that it's not waiting for me to pull it to me, it's rushing at me all the time, wanting to travel through me for an outlet? That's even more the case now, and it seems that elf could sense it, too." She screwed up her face slightly. "It's overwhelming."

"Yes," Zev agreed. "It is." He rubbed a hand across his chest absently.

Marieke didn't miss the gesture. "Are you all right?"

"I'm fine," he said. No need to distress Marieke with the information that as soon as they went through the "doorway", the pressure on his chest had increased dramatically. They must be much deeper in the jungle than they had been on the other side.

He cast his eyes around the clearing they were crossing. It wasn't a huge open circle, like he'd at first assumed. It was more like a band of grassy space curving around a central structure. And it wasn't naturally occurring, that much was clear. Judging by the section he could see, it was a perfect circle, the outside of it ringed with huge trees, their trunks as smooth and evenly spaced as pillars.

Lanterns bobbed between them at staggered heights, except they didn't seem to be attached to anything. They were a lot like the glowing orb Marieke had created, but brighter and larger. And their light was the clear white of daylight, not the yellow of a normal lantern. Zev realized that the canopy wasn't as clear as he'd at first supposed. Branches still arched over their heads, but the white lantern light had fooled him into thinking the sky was open.

The trunks were too neat and perfect to look natural. Certainly nothing like Zev's orchard. But the structure in the middle of the space made up for it. It wasn't a building so much as a solid wall of tangled foliage. The branches were criss-crossed so tightly, Zev couldn't even see through it. The wildness of these trees was a strange juxtaposition to the unnaturally smooth pillar trees. The chaos of a jungle and the order of cultivated trees, each taken to their extremes, and combined together.

He didn't like it, he decided. Neither felt natural, and the whole thing was unbalanced. Their elf guide led them toward a path that ran straight across the cleared band from the wall of branches to the pillar trees. As they turned onto it, Zev saw that there was an archway, under which the branches broke for enough space to make a doorway through to whatever was inside. It was evidently designed for elves, though, so he and Marieke had to bend over to travel through it.

They ducked underneath, edging through a short tunnel to emerge into the proper center of the clearing. For a moment neither spoke, taking in the incredible sight with wide eyes.

"What is this place?" Marieke breathed.

Their elf guide glanced back at them, seeming to take neither pleasure nor offense at their amazement.

"The place of our exile."

The words were a quip, his voice dry and his face expressionless, but Zev's eyes didn't linger on the elf for long. He was too caught up in examining the scene.

He'd thought the trees outside of the clearing huge, but they were nothing to the ones on the inside. These trees stretched way up out of sight, the canopy so high above that he had to squint to see it. Instead of lanterns, there were tiny lights sprinkled across every branch. The specks of brightness were reminiscent of fireflies except the light was a warm green, like yellow sunlight coming through leaves. The whole place was bathed in greenness, such that the very air felt alive. And the floor wasn't the hazardous underbrush of the rest of the jungle. It was clear ground, much of it covered with grass, although some patches were rocky.

A number of the trees had structures built around them, not of wood as Zev might have expected, but of some kind of red clay. They ringed the tree trunks, most of them boasting multiple levels. These dwellings, if they were dwellings, varied in height, some so far up he couldn't make out their details, and others almost at ground level. On the closest ones, he could see small elves climbing between levels or leaning from a window to watch the passers-by. The amount of interest they attracted as they continued through the settlement supported their understanding that humans didn't come to this place.

"Look at the roots!"

Marieke's voice drew Zev's attention to the ground. To his amazement, the grassy soil was illuminated by branching patterns of light, each strand thin and wispy, but visible if you looked closely enough. He had no doubt Marieke was right that the light mirrored the roots in the ground below it—the place-ment of the patterns around the trees was certainly consistent with that idea.

"They're coated with magic," Marieke commented, the words directed at the elf. "It feels like...I don't know...a seeking enchantment? It's not unlike the one I use to assess the nearby terrain."

The elf gave a grunt that sounded like grudging acknowl-edgment. "The roots help us identify the right areas for mining."

"Mining?" Zev repeated the word as he glanced around. Nothing about the area suggested it was a quarry in the usual way. The elf must be speaking of the mysterious practice of mining magic.

His eyes traveled over each of the dwellings, looking for one that was larger or more luxurious than the others. Where would they find this Imperator?

"Wow." Marieke's voice brought Zev's gaze to the ground again.

He raised an eyebrow at the bizarre feature they were walking past. At first glance, he'd thought it was a pond, but on closer inspection, he realized that the hollow in the ground wasn't filled with water. It was sealed with a layer of glass. A line of glass even moved out from it like a stationary stream, the surface smooth, but the texture underneath looking fractured and layered as it wound its way around a tree and out of sight. It looked for all the world like a forest spring feeding a stream...except that it was unmoving glass rather than water.

"Surely that's not naturally occurring," he murmured to Marieke.

"I don't think much of this place is naturally occurring," she replied. "The magic in the air is thicker than the air itself." She blew air out of the side of her mouth, unsuccessfully attempting to shift a strand of hair that was plastered to her forehead. "And that's saying something."

The elf leading them, who had ignored their conversation, came to a stop at the base of a large tree.

"Go on." The creature pointed up toward a dwelling, attached to the trunk at about three times Zev's height.

For a moment Zev just stared, then he realized Marieke was moving forward. She'd been quicker than he was to spot the subtle ladder leading upward. It consisted of nothing more than thin strips of wood attached to the tree, easy to miss given they were of the same hue as the trunk. They were set close together, to allow for elvish limbs, so Zev had to skip two out of every three in order to make it work.

He climbed up behind Marieke, his tension not lifting until they emerged safely onto a platform inside the first level of the structure. The pressure in his chest eased slightly as they left the ground behind.

Zev had expected their guide to follow them up, but a glance back down the hole they'd climbed through showed him still on the ground, in conversation with another elf who'd approached.

"This place is quite something, isn't it?" Marieke said, looking around the room in which they found themselves. It was cool within the clay walls, plenty of light coming in from regular windows, and one wall curving away, formed by the trunk of the tree on which the structure was built.

"I never imagined anything like it," Zev admitted. "I'm surprised they settled in this area, to be honest. The trees here are so enormous, even to a human."

"You thought they'd prefer somewhere with more elf-sized flora?" Marieke asked, with the hint of a grin.

"The flora of our ancestral home is as appropriate to elves as anywhere in the forest."

The high voice made them both spin. Neither had heard the approach of the new elf around the curved platform. Zev could see Marieke's flush at being overheard, but he felt no embarrassment as he looked over the newcomer. She looked much older than the other elf had, her face lined and her pointed ears longer than the ones he'd seen before. Her eyes were still brilliantly green, however, and her hair hung down her back in a thick, silver rope.

"Unlike humans," she considered placidly, "we're not daunted by being smaller than the world around us. It doesn't fill us with the desire to conquer. We embrace it."

"I don't think I've ever been gripped by the desire to conquer in my life," Zev informed her.

The elf considered him, her expression thoughtful. "No?"

"We did not mean to offend," Marieke said carefully. Zev was pleased that she'd remembered not to apologize outright, for fear it might be taken to indicate an obligation owed.

"I am not offended, child," the elderly elf said. "I can more accurately be described as intrigued. Only once before in my lifetime has a human sought an audience with me."

"With you?" Zev raised an eyebrow. "Are you the Imperator?"

"I am." She looked him over shrewdly. "And you, I take it, are Zevadiah of this kingdom."

"Well, no one has called it a kingdom in a long time, but yes," Zev said.

"Hmm." The elf was still studying him, her penetrating gaze unnerving. "What humans call the land is of less relevance than they imagine. It is what the land recognizes that has greater impact."

Zev shifted his weight from one leg to the other, his expression carefully impassive.

"Come," the elf said abruptly. "We will sit."

She led them around the curve of the building, traveling through two more rooms before stopping in one that jutted further out from the tree trunk than the others. It was set up with cushions on the floor, onto one of which she sank. Marieke and Zev followed suit, their movements awkward as a result of everything being a bit too small for their frames. Another elf, this one much younger, appeared from nowhere and sat beside the Imperator, her emerald eyes bright and curious as they studied the strangers.

For a moment they sat in silence on the floor before the Imperator's thin lips curved into a smile. "I am not what you expected, am I?"

"Not precisely," Zev acknowledged.

Her smile broadened. "What did you anticipate? A crown? A castle?" She shook her head. "I am no monarch, Zevadiah of Aeltas. I hold a hereditary position, it is true, and my title carries with it a certain power and influence. But my role is more to unite and provide a central point of communication than to actually lead."

She looked to the younger elf at her side.

"Speaking of heredity, this is my granddaughter Kiarana, who will take over my position when I return to the ground and my life is absorbed back into the magic of the land."

Marieke inclined her head to the younger elf, her blue eyes full of the curiosity that Zev had sometimes had cause to rue.

"Well met," she said politely. "I'm—"

"Marieke of Oleand," the Imperator finished for her. "Or so said your note."

Marieke nodded a little awkwardly. "It obviously made its way to you. I had no idea if it would work."

"Well." The elf's smile was a little too calculating to be warm. "It didn't get all the way to me without some assistance. But certainly the penetration of an active enchantment into our protected territory is an event that will secure our attention. It was a sensible approach. Without our assistance, you certainly would never have reached us."

"Just how deep in the jungle are we?" Zev asked. He rubbed at his chest again, unable to help the gesture. Even elevated in the tree where the pressure was less than on the ground, it was so intense it was almost painful.

The elf's eyes lingered on his fist. "Very deep, as you seem to be aware. The magic here is thicker even than the foliage outside our sanctuary. It's trying to crush you from the inside out, from which I surmise that you are not a singer."

"Trying to crush him?" Marieke sat up straighter on her cushion, her alarm clear on her features. "Is he in danger?"

"No." The elf's answer was slow and thoughtful, her eyes never leaving Zev. "He doesn't seem to be in danger. Which is interesting in itself." She exchanged a glance with her granddaughter that filled Zev with foreboding.

"Well, we didn't come looking for you to chat about my safety," he said.

"Your motivations are your own," the Imperator said

calmly. "They have no bearing on my reasons for allowing this audience."

"What are your reasons?" Marieke asked cautiously.

The elf smiled. "The fact that I have reasons does not mean I intend to disclose them."

"Perhaps we can trade answers," Marieke said boldly.

The Imperator leaned forward, interlacing her fingers, which were slim but for the knobbed knuckles that proclaimed her age.

"I feel I'm owed some answers already, in exchange for allowing you passage into our protected realm," she said.

"Your feelings don't create obligation on us," Zev said sharply. "Your choice to allow us entry was your own. It wasn't the result of any bargain."

The younger elf chuckled, drawing Zev's gaze to her. Her grin was more cheerful than the older elf's as she directed her eyes to the Imperator.

"He's sharp, Grandmama, you must acknowledge it."

"I *must* acknowledge nothing," said the older elf, although she didn't appear annoyed. Her eyes were fixed on Marieke's face now. "The simple truth is that it is in my power to expel you from this place and leave you at the mercy of the jungle. If you do not wish me to do so, you must tell me why you sought an audience with me."

Zev was inclined to try harder to drive a bargain of some kind, but Marieke took a gentler approach.

"I don't mind telling you why I've come looking for you. I'll hardly get answers if I refuse to ask questions."

"True," the Imperator agreed. "But that's not the first answer I want. I want to know how you discovered our existence."

"That's easy to answer," Marieke said. "We ran afoul of one of your mining parties in Sundering Canyon."

"You're part of that tribe of monarchists?" Kiarana asked curiously.

Marieke shook her head. "We're not. We were actually looking for them when we stumbled on Rissin's party."

"Rissin." The young elf sighed. "So that's what you meant when you said you ran afoul of them."

Zev raised an eyebrow at her. If Rissin wasn't well liked even among his own people then maybe Marieke had been right to think it worth pursuing answers with the other elves.

"I am aware of your encounter with Rissin." The Imperator's eyes gave little away. "What I'm asking is whether you truly were unaware of our existence prior to that incident."

"We truly were," Marieke said in her earnest way.

"If you know what Rissin tried to do to us, then I would argue that you owe us an explanation," Zev said darkly.

"Your argument would not be sound," the Imperator said. Her posture softened a little. "But as a show of good faith, I will inform you that Rissin's actions were his own." She flashed another of those swift, unnerving grins. "Not that I would have been averse to learning the results had he been able to study you as he intended to do."

"Study us?" Marieke repeated. "That sounds very ominous."

"For you, perhaps." The Imperator's granddaughter once again inserted herself into the conversation. "Grandmama might not, but I want to know why you've sought us out."

"In exchange for what?" Zev asked dryly.

Kiarana laughed in delight. "I said he's sharp, didn't I, Grandmama? He talks like one of us."

"He does no such thing," the Imperator said. "It seems you need more education on humans if meeting one in person has enough novelty to distract you."

"I don't think all humans would," she said fairly. "But he's very handsome, Grandmama. For a human, I mean."

Zev stifled a laugh as both the Imperator and Marieke made noises of resignation in their throats.

"What *is* this effect you have on teenage girls?" Marieke muttered.

"Actually," the younger elf grinned, "I'm twenty-seven. We age differently from humans."

"We have gotten decidedly off-track," the Imperator said. "I believe you were going to tell us why your meeting with Rissin led you to seek us out."

"Is that what you believe?" Zev said politely.

"Relax, Zev." Marieke waved a hand at him. "I came here to ask these questions, I don't want to play games." She turned to the elves. "I'll get straight to the point. It's helpful that you're aware of the monarchists in Sundering Canyon. A few months back, there were a number of seeming accidents that befell singers in my country, Oleand. Some lost their lives. Others, including myself, were targeted but escaped. These *accidents* were ultimately proven to be intentional attacks. They were carried out by a young man named Gorgon, who'd broken off from the monarchist group. And we have reason to believe he carried out the attacks by use of talismans."

Neither of the elves' expressions gave anything away, but at Marieke's last word, Zev saw Kiarana straighten a little. Marieke had their interest.

Marieke cleared her throat, her tone cautious. "I understand that the elves are the only source of talismans."

No answer.

Undeterred, Marieke pressed on. "Gorgon is dead now, and those attacks stopped. But a different kind has begun. Larger scale ones. Terrible fires, unseasonal storms, that kind of thing. And they're definitely fueled by magic." She drew a breath. "And on top of all that, the land itself is deteriorating. Oleand is dwindling away into decay, and no one can figure out why."

There was a long moment of silence before the Imperator responded.

"You said you came to ask questions, but I did not detect a question in your words."

"That's true," Marieke acknowledged. "I suppose my first question is this: are you supplying talismans to whoever is causing these disasters? And the second would probably be—"

"Wait." Zev put a hand on Marieke's shoulder to stop her. The tension in her muscles showed that she was more on edge than she seemed. "One at a time. Even asking a question can reveal information that might have value."

"Very wise," the Imperator complimented him. "What will you give me for an answer to your question? An answer to a question of my own?"

"That depends on your question," Zev said warily.

She nodded. "My question is this: why, according to Rissin's report, did the magic of Sundering Canyon respond to the pair of you in a way he's never seen before?"

Zev studied her shrewdly. It seemed Rissin had made a full report to this Imperator. Zev was starting to suspect that they hadn't been allowed to enter the elves' realm merely because of the letter Marieke sent. If it hadn't identified them as the mysterious pair from Rissin's tale, would they have been left on the road? Most likely.

"I would be willing to make that exchange," Zev said. "If Marieke is also satisfied."

She nodded, and the Imperator smiled. "Good."

"Witnessed," Kiarana said solemnly.

"The answer to your question, Marieke of Oleand, is that I do not know if we've been supplying talismans to whomever is behind the natural disasters you mentioned. It is not possible for me to know given that I am not aware of who is behind the catastrophes. How then could I know if they've received elven-made talismans?"

Zev laughed dryly. "I thought I was being a canny negotiator, but it seems it was a fairer exchange than I realized. Because our answer is also that we don't know. Right, Marieke?"

She nodded. "I know that the magic responded strangely in the canyon. I felt it as surely as Rissin did. But I can't tell you why."

The Imperator raised an eyebrow. "You don't have any guesses or speculation?"

"Our bargain wasn't for guesses or speculation," Zev countered. "It was for an honest answer to the question, and we've given that."

She rewarded him with a smile. "Canny indeed." Her eyes stayed fixed on Zev, even as she spoke to Marieke. "What's your next question, then?"

Marieke didn't answer at once. Zev looked over to see her brow furrowed in thought. "You said you don't know if you're supplying talismans to whoever's behind the attacks because you don't know who it is. But that implies that you have been supplying talismans to someone. If you hadn't, you'd be able to say with certainty that your talismans weren't involved."

It was a good point.

"And it can't be Gorgon like last time," Marieke said. "Because, like I told you, he's dead."

"We never supplied talismans to any Gorgon," the younger elf said. She fell silent at a sharp look from her grandmother, then, after a moment, shrugged. "It's true. And if he was murdering singers, I think we should be forthcoming if the alternative is being connected to his actions."

Like her grandmother, her eyes lingered on Zev, not

Marieke. He felt his skin crawl under the scrutiny, and it was evident that Marieke had noticed it as well.

"I'm grateful for the information," she said slowly, her eyes passing between the elves and Zev. "Although I don't quite understand why you care about our good opinion." Her frown deepened. "Or maybe not *our*. You're more interested in Zev's reaction, aren't you? Why is that?" A curious look passed over her face, although no one answered. She quickly pressed on with a variant of the same question. "I thought you were taking an interest because I'm a singer, but it's Zev's role in all of it that you care about, isn't it?" She gave a surprised laugh. "Whoa. I really can feel it."

"I felt it, too, in my own way." The Imperator's eyes had returned to Marieke. "You've just become more interesting, after all, young singer."

"Felt what?" Zev demanded uneasily. He shifted slightly, not liking how far his cushion placed him from Marieke.

"The magic," Marieke said. "It really liked those last couple of questions. The strength of the response makes me think they were very...pertinent."

"Another questioner?" Kiarana seemed to also be interested now, all of them grasping something Zev didn't understand. "I thought you said they were rare, Grandmama."

"They are," the Imperator replied.

"What do you mean *another* questioner?" Marieke demanded. "Who else have you met with the aptitude for questioning? And what do you mean you never gave talismans to Gorgon? You must have!"

"I will give you a full answer if you will share with me your suspicions about why the magic responds to the pair of you as it does," the Imperator offered.

"I'd rather not," Zev said firmly.

Marieke looked at him, and he could see in her face that it

cost her to turn away from the answers she was so desperately seeking.

"No, we won't make that trade," she said, no hesitation in her voice.

Zev's heart warmed even as he felt guilty that his secrets were impeding her mission. It cost her, but she didn't consider betraying his trust. Not even for a moment.

"Then I don't believe I can help you further." The Imperator leaned back on her cushion, her eyes passing between them with a fixation that made Zev think she wasn't done with them yet, whatever her words might say.

"Please," said Marieke desperately. "We've come so far seeking answers. Please, if you know what's causing the disasters—better yet, what's causing the land to deteriorate—*please* tell us. There must be some other bargain you can propose."

"Not with you," the Imperator said simply. "As intriguing as it is to learn that you have the questioning craft, I don't believe you have anything of value to offer me." Her eyes strayed to Zev. "It's your songless friend I'm interested in. The question is what is *he* prepared to trade?"

"Please don't pull him into this," Marieke said quickly. "This isn't his fight, it's mine. He's not even from Oleand. Whatever's happening to my country is not his problem to solve."

"And yet," the elf said pointedly, "here he is."

"He's only here for my sake," Marieke said.

"Indeed," the Imperator mused. "So perhaps threatening you would be a more effective way to get answers from him than trying to strike bargains."

A growl escaped Zev before he could get himself under control. He pushed himself forward, realizing as he did so that his hand had balled into a fist.

The Imperator chuckled. "Relax, young man. Age mellows

us all, and I'm older even than you realize. Far too old to resort to impulsive thuggery." There was a glint in her eye as she smiled at him. "I'm not sure there's a great deal you could tell me that I don't already know. Or at least suspect."

The words should have alarmed Zev, but he found himself curiously disinterested in the threat to his secrets. His pulse was still hammering at how quickly the elf leader had grasped that Marieke could be used to manipulate him. It was an aspect of his hidden identity that he hadn't considered. The idea of her being threatened, even harmed before his eyes, as a way to get to him was absolutely terrifying.

"Others of my kind are not as smoothed by the passage of time," the Imperator continued. "And you would be mistaken to assume I impose full control over their actions. I know that Rissin, for example, is within the settlement currently, meeting with an associate of his. If you do not wish to remain here under circumstances not of your choosing, I suggest you leave now. I can have you escorted back to the human road."

"Please," Marieke tried again. "Don't send me away with nothing. The answers have been just out of reach at every step. I was sure I would find them here."

The Imperator considered her. "I am under no obligation to do so, but I will tell you my opinion to this extent. I do not believe that the disasters you've described were caused by talismans. And as for the wider problem besetting Oleand..." Her eyes drifted to Zev. "I suspect that answer has been within your reach throughout your whole journey."

Zev's pulse was once again thundering. It couldn't be true. He'd justified his continued deception of Marieke by telling himself that his identity could have no bearing on her mission. The heartsong connecting Oleand's monarchs to their land wasn't the cause of the country's deterioration. How could it be, when the monarchs had been dead for centuries, and the land had only started suffering in the last year or two?

In spite of these assurances, he couldn't bring himself to meet Marieke's eyes, even though he could feel them on him.

"We'll go," she said suddenly, surprising him. "Thank you for your offer of safe passage out of your realm."

The Imperator nodded, her eyes lingering on Zev's face as if she could read his inner conflict. It was an unpleasant sensation. He barely knew what he said as they took their leave, following Marieke back down the ladder without a word.

TWENTY-TWO

Marieke

Marieke wrestled with her disappointment as she climbed down the ladder. She'd been so sure she would find answers here, and the worst of it was that she still thought she could have learned more if she'd been willing to push harder.

But it was clear to her that doing so would be at great cost to Zev, and he didn't deserve to be punished for his willingness to accompany her.

The Imperator had told them to wait at the bottom of the ladder for a guide, and they stood there in a silence that was nothing like their usual companionable one. Marieke cast her eyes around the fascinating settlement, regretful that they didn't have more time to explore it.

A jolt went over her as she looked up at a nearby clay structure. This one was close to the ground, and framed in the window she could clearly see a figure she'd seen before.

"Zev!" she hissed. "Look!"

He followed her gaze quickly, and his face hardened. "Rissin."

Marieke nodded. "She wasn't wrong that he's nearby. I wonder what he—" Her voice died as the elf shifted, and someone else stepped into view.

"That's no elf," Zev said suspiciously.

It certainly wasn't. It was a human woman, her hair as dark as Marieke's but her face proclaiming her to be older, perhaps by twenty years. Marieke was still staring at her when she suddenly turned, her eyes flying to Marieke's and locking on them.

Marieke bit her lip, captured by the older woman's gaze. She could have sworn something passed between them, and she found herself questioning if she actually knew the stranger after all.

Then Zev shifted beside her, the movement undeniably protective, and it broke Marieke's focus.

"Why is she staring at you?" Zev asked, frowning.

"I don't know," said Marieke, unnerved and fascinated in equal measure. As she spoke, the woman turned away, and an unfamiliar elf trotted up.

"I'm to take you back to the human road," he said in a bossy voice. "And I don't want it to take all day, so come on."

They followed him back through the archway, Marieke's skin prickling with the feeling of being watched. Perhaps it was because of how many elves were following their progress with curious eyes.

When they were back in the band of grass between the gateway and the pillar trees, the elf stopped.

"All right," he said, rubbing his hands together. "Back where you were picked up, yes?"

"Actually," said Marieke, "that was a long way south into the jungle. If possible, we'd prefer to be dropped off back at the northern end of the human road."

"That's twice the distance," the elf complained. "We'd have to do two doorways to get there." He looked between them, then gave a huff. "I'd need an extra talisman for that. And I won't be using it unless I confirm it's approved. Wait here."

He'd already started toward the archway when he turned back. "And I do mean wait here. You can't come back through this gateway without one of us, and if you strike out into the jungle, you'll get lost and die for certain."

Marieke raised her hands in a gesture of compliance, rolling her eyes at Zev once the elf had disappeared. "Such friendly, trusting creatures, aren't they?"

Zev just grunted. He seemed on edge since their interview with the Imperator, and Marieke didn't blame him. The intensity of the focus on him was something neither of them had anticipated.

She assumed the elf would take a while to discharge his errand, so was surprised when she heard someone coming back through the archway. But it was a much taller figure who emerged.

"Hello." The woman's smile was a little too careful, but not like she was disguising animosity. More like she was trying to hide how eager she was. "I didn't mean to startle you. You're Marieke, is that right?"

Zev stepped up beside Marieke, his posture not what she would call open. The stranger's eyes shifted to him.

"And you're Zevadiah. Rissin told me about you both."

Marieke raised an eyebrow. "You're Rissin's associate?"

"I suppose you could say that." She didn't look like she relished the title. "He has his uses, but my purposes are my own." Her eyes glinted. "I'm so pleased that you're here. I took a chance when Rissin told me what happened in the canyon. I hoped you would come looking for the elves, for answers. And you did. It was worth waiting for you here. I've been very eager to meet you, Marieke."

"Me?" Marieke asked, startled. "Why?"

"Yes, why?" Zev agreed, the words a growl. He moved closer to Marieke, so that their arms were touching, and she felt the magic swirl under her feet.

The stranger obviously felt it, too. Her eyes lit up as they flicked to the ground then back up again. "I see what Rissin meant. It's remarkable. Fascinating. Like and yet unlike what I've experienced."

"You feel the magic?" Marieke asked, her brows drawing together. "So you're a singer, then." Her eyes widened as realization hit. "You're the other questioner the Imperator's granddaughter mentioned."

"The other one?" the stranger repeated. "So you have the aptitude as well?" She clapped her hands together in delight, the childlike gesture out of place. "I knew it! I knew it couldn't be coincidence that you were following the same course I did, before you ever knew about me." She frowned slightly. "Although I thought they stopped teaching that area of story-telling song after I left the academy."

"After you left the..." Marieke's voice trailed off. "Who are you?" The knot clenching in her stomach told her that she already knew.

"I'm your new best resource, that's who I am," the other woman said. "The progress you've made on your own is impressive, Marieke, but I can take you way beyond. You have no idea what I'm capable of."

"You're...you're her, aren't you?" Marieke's lips felt numb. "You're Jade."

The older woman swept a graceful curtsy. "Pleased to make your acquaintance."

"Jade?" Zev repeated sharply. "The one who left the messages at Port Taran? Who was kicked out of the academy for asking questions about the coup? I thought you said she was dead."

"I was only guessing," Marieke said helplessly. "Based on something Gorgon said."

Jade laughed. "You found my messages at the ruined city? I'm so pleased! Nice to know they're still in place. And I'm far from dead. Gorgon knew that perfectly well, poor thing." Her eyes were indulgent as they shifted again to Zev. "You were a little harsh with him, but I can't say I'm angry. He did *not* act with my authority when he decided to take Marieke out."

"But he did act on your orders before that?" Marieke said, aghast. "You're the one the elves gave talismans to, aren't you? And you gave them to Gorgon!"

Jade shrugged. "Well, I didn't need them, did I? I can sing." She flashed a conspiratorial smile that suggested she was badly misreading her audience. "And yes, I persuaded the elves to trade me talismans. The first human to receive them since the days of the monarchs, I believe."

"You were behind the attacks?" Marieke said. "You're behind the disasters too, aren't you? But you don't even need talismans for that." She gasped. "You were there at the Mosleys' field! You started the fire. It was your enchantment I fought against."

"And very capably, too." The approval in Jade's voice made Marieke sick to her stomach. "I would have approached you then had I felt safe to do so. Later, when you snuck away without a trace, I wished I had."

"You stay away from her," Zev said, his voice low and threatening as he moved forward.

"Oh, you misunderstand me," Jade said. "I want to work with Marieke, not see her disappear."

"Disappear?" Marieke's throat was tight—she could hardly

believe what was happening. "Is that what you call what Gorgon did to the other singers? The ones he killed on your orders?"

"Marieke, Marieke." Jade raised her hands placatingly, her forehead creased in concern. "Don't get the wrong idea. I'm not sadistic. I seek only to right the wrongs of the past. Don't judge me by Gorgon, either. He was young and hotheaded. He and his fellow monarchists were helpful in getting things started, but they were never a big part of the plan."

"Getting things started?" Marieke was almost choking on the words. "What does that even mean?"

"The council has to be stopped," Jade said. "You know enough now to know how vile their lies are. They can't be allowed to continue in power unchecked."

"But the singers he killed weren't doing anything nefarious," Marieke protested. "They were sent out to assess the suffering crops and provide aid to the people of Oleand—doing what good rulers *should* do. You didn't care that they were trying to do their job well. You just saw a good opportunity to target council singers away from the capital."

"A strategist is only as good as her ability to exploit opportunity," Jade said with a shrug. "You must see the bigger picture, Marieke."

"I see just fine," Marieke said. "And I want no part of what you're doing."

Jade groaned. "*Please* don't be so short-sighted, Marieke. We could be unstoppable together. There's so much I can teach you. About the past, about questioning song, about heartsong." Her eyes narrowed as they passed to Zev. "Do you know about heartsong, Zevadiah? Are you feigning ignorance, or do you truly not know?"

"Leave Zev out of this," Marieke cried, anger surging in to at last drive away her numb disbelief. "How can you stand there and admit so coldly to being a murderer?"

"It's exactly that stain I'm trying to wash away!" Jade snapped. She closed her eyes and drew a deep breath, seeming to collect herself. "There's no sense arguing, Marieke. You have a choice to make. Will you help me take on the sins of the singers of the past and make it right?"

Marieke shook her head emphatically. "Not the way you're going about it. I'll never have any part of it."

Jade sighed. "That's a great pity. I took a risk, and it didn't pay off. Sometimes that's the way of things." She looked regretful as she cast an assessing glance over Marieke. "Well, it seems Gorgon had the right idea after all. I'm afraid you'll have to be eliminated."

"Don't you touch her." Zev was in between the two singers before Marieke could blink, his sword raised, clearly oblivious to the magic pouring up into Jade.

Marieke's instinct was to scream a warning to him, but she curbed it, sending the same energy into a rapid shielding song.

The defense was only just up in time, Jade's enchantment crashing against it so hard that Marieke's voice trembled from the impact.

"This is the choice, Marieke!" Jade shouted. "Help me, or be removed from my path."

Marieke raised her own voice by way of answer, adding power to Zev's arm as he lunged forward. The impossible speed of his sword obviously took Jade by surprise, but she threw herself sideways in time, releasing a song of her own.

Zev let out a grunt of pain, and Marieke realized in horror that his sword was heating under his hand. But he didn't drop the weapon, still advancing on Jade.

She sidestepped him again, her focus on Marieke.

"Don't make me hurt you, Zevadiah," the older singer said. "It's her I have a problem with."

Zev ignored her words, his fingers reaching for his belt where Marieke knew him to have a smaller blade concealed. But it wouldn't be enough. Jade's songcraft would overpower Zev's physical strength without difficulty.

Wishing once again that she'd studied combat song, Marieke desperately pulled in magic. She couldn't match Jade for brute strength. She needed to work to her areas of training. Somehow she doubted Jade had studied agricultural song.

Marieke sent magic darting through the air, detaching a large branch over Jade's head. With a splintering crack, it fell, but Jade spun away, her song intercepting the branch and causing it to break into a hundred smaller, less dangerous pieces.

A shout from the direction of the archway told them all that their fight had at last been noticed by the elves. Jade seemed to realize she was running out of time, and in a last attempt, she turned back to Marieke and threw her dagger with deadly force.

Everything happened so fast Marieke could barely keep track. Her own song of defense wasn't quick enough to intervene as the blade soared toward her, spurred on by Jade's song. A flash of movement and a roar were the only indicators that Zev had thrown himself in front of her.

Blind terror gripped Marieke as she tried to cover him with her song, aware she wouldn't be quick enough.

But someone else was. With a note that was more scream than melody, Jade stopped her own weapon, the tip of the blade coming to a halt a hairsbreadth from Zev's throat. Marieke sprang forward, but before she could reach them, Jade was there, her hand on the weapon as Zev and Marieke both froze.

"You're more use to me alive, Aeltan," Jade breathed. "But

this isn't over." Her eyes flicked to Marieke, then back to Zev, malice in their depths. "The next time I see her, I will kill her, and there's nothing you can do to stop me."

Marieke yelled a warning as an incomprehensible volume of magic gathered to Jade—more than Marieke could ever have safely wielded. But the song Jade formed it into was quick and precise, and had no visible effect whatsoever. Before Marieke could blink, Jade had withdrawn her dagger from Zev's throat and plunged between the pillar trees.

Marieke ran to Zev, grabbing his arms and staring blindly into his face. "Zev! Are you all right? What did she do to you?"

She was barely aware of the elves surging across the clearing toward them, her focus all on Zev. She could still sense Jade's enchantment clinging to him, and had no idea what it was doing.

"I'm fine." Zev's voice was low and tense. "But Marieke, you're not safe. She meant what she said. She's determined to kill you."

"Never mind that," said Marieke. "Don't try to be strong and hide it, Zev. She must be hurting you somehow."

He looked genuinely confused. "No, I'm really all right."

"What happened here?" The sharp, high-pitched voice belonged to the Imperator's granddaughter, who'd appeared at Marieke's elbow.

"Jade," Marieke said, dazed. "The human who was meeting with Rissin. She attacked us."

The young elf clucked her tongue. "Search the area," she told the other elves. But she sighed as she turned back to Marieke and Zev. "I don't think they'll find her," she said. "She's far more capable than any human has a right to be."

She made a shooing motion with her long, slender fingers.

"Back inside, both of you. You're not going anywhere in this state." Kiarana didn't let up until they'd accompanied her back through the archway and into the elves' clearing. "In there," she told them, indicating the closest structure, which was wrapped around a nearby tree like the others, but flush with the ground. "Wait there while I speak with my grandmother." She saw Zev's hesitation and gave him a reassuring nod. "You're safe from Jade while inside our clearing."

Marieke saw Zev's shoulders relax slightly, and she grabbed his arm, tugging him into the building. She wasn't satisfied with his assurances. Jade's magic still clung to him, and that couldn't mean anything good.

Mercifully, the building was empty. As soon as they'd closed the door behind them, she turned to Zev.

"Let me look at you," she instructed. She ran her hands over his arms, trying to identify the function of the magic. Bewildered, she placed her fingers over his heart, feeling the steady beat of it and the warmth of his chest, then let one hand rest against his neck while the other traveled up his face and ran through his hair.

"What are you doing?" he asked, his voice gruff.

"I'm checking the usual places a nefarious enchantment would target," Marieke said. "Your heart, your head, even your sword arm. It's not focused on any of those areas. More like... your feet. Which makes no sense."

Zev didn't reply, but she could see his chest rising and falling more rapidly than before. All at once she realized what she was doing, putting her hands all over him without a thought for whether he welcomed the touch.

Not that he seemed displeased. On the contrary, he was leaning in, his eyes boring into hers the moment she dared to meet his gaze.

"Marieke," he whispered.

She swallowed, looking away to give herself time to gather her scattered thoughts. His hair was gloriously tousled from her questing fingers, and she ran them through it again, not really trying to smooth it, just relishing doing something she'd often thought about.

"Marieke." This time his voice compelled her to return her eyes to his. "It's going to be all right," he said. "I won't let her hurt you. I'll die first."

Tears welled up in her eyes, and she fought fiercely to keep them in. "It's all such a mess, Zev. How can it be Jade? I thought she was like me."

"You're nothing like her," said Zev, the words both fierce and simple.

Marieke swallowed. "I thought it was the council who'd become twisted, not Jade."

"Both can be true," Zev reminded her gently.

"I know." Misery washed over Marieke. "But I don't know what to do anymore. I got my answers, but they've only made everything a hundred times more tangled."

Zev hesitated, and Marieke could have sworn she heard his heart pounding faster. "You don't have all your answers," he said, his voice a rough whisper. "You have more questions. I know you do."

She searched his eyes warily.

"Go on," he told her, his expression a strange mixture of tension and peace.

"I don't think I need to ask," she murmured. "I think I know." She swallowed. "The Aeltan royals didn't all die in the coup, did they? At least some survived." His eyes were still locked on hers, their unflinching gaze giving her the courage to go on even as her heart was pounding ever faster at the enormity of the moment. "And you're descended from them."

Zev let out a long breath. He didn't acknowledge it in words, but he didn't need to. Marieke could see the last of his defenses falling away—his admission was clear. For a moment she was silent, trying to take it all in. Unnamed suspicions were one thing. But saying aloud that the farmer she'd fallen for was the heir to the country's ancient, deposed, royal bloodline...that was something else entirely.

"I'm still figuring out what exactly that means, though," she continued at last. "Heartsong is at the center of it, isn't it? It's a different kind of magic, a kind that ties you to your land. That's why Aeltas thrives, because it still has that power. And that's why the magic responds so much better to me when we work together. It's like I have the blessing of the land itself. Or the land has the blessing of heartsong to release magic to me, or something like that."

"That part is as much a surprise to me as it is to you," Zev told her, his voice hushed. "I've never heard of anything like that. We've never thought of heartsong as being magic in the way that songcraft is. It's never been so specific or tangible in its effect before. It's always been more general, and more gradual. Still powerful, don't get me wrong. Under my family's subtle influence, the terrain of our region has physically changed, and the land has become almost unnaturally fertile. But it's functioned on a whole new level recently." He paused. "Since I met you."

"Oh Zev, I'm so sorry." His willing disclosure of information unleashed a dam inside Marieke, and the tears flowed over at last. "I never meant for this to happen. I never wanted to force your confidence. I know you wouldn't have come with me if you'd realized doing so would expose your secrets. But the truth is I'd already started to suspect, and I—"

"No," he cut her off, shaking his head. "*I'm* sorry. I'm sorry I wasn't the one to tell you before you figured it out. Marieke..."

He hesitated, raising a hand to brush it across her temple, where a strand of hair had come loose, and then bringing it to rest on her cheek. His thumb moved across her skin, wiping a tear away.

"Since I can remember, I've been taught to keep secrets like my life depended on it. But there's no part of me I don't trust you with." His eyes drew her in—she was drowning in them. "I'm done holding back from you, Marieke."

Marieke barely took in his words before his arm swept around her. He pulled her flush against him so abruptly that she let out a tiny gasp. A gasp that cut off as he lowered his head and his lips closed over hers.

Marieke laced her fingers behind his neck, her heart overwhelmed with the excess of emotions. Zev's arm was strong and steady around her, and warmth seeped from his chest straight into her. His thumb traced circles on her cheek as she kissed him back with abandon, every fiber of her being surrendered to the embrace.

It was different from the kiss they'd shared after Gorgon's attack—there were no secrets in the way now, and whatever was between them had never felt more natural, more right.

She let her fingers stray up into his hair again, lost in the sensation of his lips moving on hers and the warmth of his closeness. The magic below their feet roared to life, more forceful than the timeless power of Zev's orchard. It wrapped around their legs, flowing into Marieke and out again without her guiding it at all. She wasn't even singing, and yet she felt the magic turning itself into light—tiny flecks that danced around them as they kissed with all the pent-up passion that came from holding each other at arm's length for so long, and from the near miss they'd just experienced.

Zev especially. It was like she could feel him pouring into the embrace every tortured look, every missed opportunity to touch her. And she wasn't about to push him away. Using her grip on his neck to pull herself up, she matched his intensity, wishing the kiss never had to end.

But it did, of course. Zev was the one to pull back, his breath coming in pants as he let out a low groan.

"Are you all right?" she asked breathlessly.

He shook his head. "No. I'm terrified." He pulled her even closer, burying his face in her hair. "A crazed singer is determined to kill you, and we don't even know where she is right now." His grip tightened around her waist. "I don't think I can survive losing you."

"I'm not going anywhere," Marieke told him, closing her eyes and leaning into him. "I know she seems impossibly strong, but we have something, Zev. Something no one else has. Maybe something no one else has ever had. You said it yourself —we're stronger together."

Zev nodded, his face still pressed against her hair. For a moment they were silent.

"Your lineage is why your family are so set against me," Marieke murmured. "I represent the liars who murdered their ancestors."

"Yes," Zev acknowledged, pulling his head back just enough to rest his forehead against hers. She appreciated that he didn't try to deny or soften it to make her feel better. His honesty was the best confirmation of his promise to hold nothing back from now on. "You also represent the biggest threat of exposure we've faced in generations."

"I'm sorry for that," she said, pained.

Zev shook his head, his forehead moving against hers. "Don't be. Don't be sorry for anything, Marieke. I wouldn't change a moment of the time we've spent together."

"Not even the one where you had to strip off your shirt to rescue me?" Marieke asked wickedly, tapping his chest.

"Because if I'm honest, it made you seem like you were trying much too hard to be a dashing knight to the rescue."

Zev laughed, the sound rumbling deep in his chest. "Especially not that one," he said solemnly. He trapped her hand over his chest. "As I recall, you were breathless at the sight."

"I'd just climbed up a cliff face," Marieke said, outraged.

"I don't think that was it." Zev shook his head. "You were overawed by my physique."

She pulled her hand free, swatting him away with a laugh that she hoped would hide the color surging into her cheeks. He might have promised to hold nothing back, but she didn't feel the need to confess that even then, before she knew him, she *had* been a little overawed by his physique.

The door to their sanctuary opened, and they turned to see Kiarana framed in the entrance.

"You're more relaxed than I expected," she commented.

Marieke stepped back, trying not to look guilty as she put a bit more distance between herself and Zev. The elf had a point. In the euphoria of Zev's kiss, she'd almost forgotten that Jade was not only alive, but had tried to kill her mere minutes before.

She threw Zev a wry look that made him raise a brow questioningly. It was a little inconvenient, this habit he'd developed of only kissing her after a barely foiled attempt on her life.

"I'm afraid there's no sign of Jade," the elf told them. "She won't be back here anytime soon, though."

"But she might be waiting for us when we emerge from the jungle," Zev said heavily. Judging by the tension that had returned to his posture, he'd also come out of his blissful oblivion.

"You could stay here," Kiarana said with a smile. "Rissin is itching to conduct some experiments, and he won't be the only one. He will be the most vindictive one, though," she added.

"He's very sore about you escaping him in the canyon, even though the method of escape has fueled his curiosity even more."

"We're not going to willingly subject ourselves to experimentation," Zev said. "Does the offer to provide us safe escort back to the human road still stand?"

"I haven't heard my grandmother rescind it," Kiarana said. She spoke absently, her eyes narrowed on Zev. "What's different about you?"

"Nothing," he said, sounding defensive.

The elf shook her head. "There's an extra weight on you. You don't feel it?"

"I do," Marieke said quickly. "Jade put some kind of enchantment on him, and I can't figure out what it was."

"That doesn't seem good," Kiarana commented, although she didn't seem especially perturbed.

"Never mind that," Zev said impatiently. "What are we going to do about Jade?"

Kiarana shrugged. "That's your own affair. She's no danger to us."

"But she spoke like she intends to start some kind of war with the Council of Singers in Oleand," Marieke said.

Kiarana just stared back, her expression polite but disinterested.

"And she's been using *your* talismans to help carry out her plan!" Marieke said, frustrated.

"Any trades were conducted with full circumspection," Kiarana said. "Her use of the talismans has nothing to do with us."

Marieke ground her teeth in frustration, and judging by his next words, Zev felt it, too.

"And I suppose her threat to kill Marieke has nothing to do with you, either?"

"That is correct." Kiarana nodded, pleased with their comprehension. She tilted her head to one side, the movement making the tips of her ears wobble as she examined Zev again. "I will confess to some curiosity regarding this enchantment, though. It seems sophisticated."

Neither of the humans responded, and after another moment's reflection, she gave a swift nod.

"It's worth the use of power."

With the words, Kiarana pulled out what appeared to be a magnifying glass. It was similar to ones Marieke had seen in the academy's library, except that it was ringed with gold, and magic pulsed faintly from it as Kiarana twisted it. The elf held the glass up to Zev, clicking her fingers imperatively until he bent down so that she could reach his head.

She didn't linger long on the area, moving the glass to his chest instead. She sent Marieke a cheeky wink as the glass hovered over Zev's admittedly impressive muscles.

"It's concentrated on his feet," Marieke said, unimpressed.

The elf shifted her focus down to Zev's boots, her green eyes lighting with interest at whatever the glass was telling her.

"You're quite right, so it is." She frowned in concentration for a moment, then let out a melodious whistle. "That's sophisticated, all right. And powerful. Root and bedrock, she'd better not try to use that on any of us, or Grandmama will expel her permanently."

"What is it?" Marieke demanded, alarmed. "What's she done to him?"

"It's a tracking enchantment," Kiarana said, straightening up. "And it's a work of art, frankly."

"So she is planning to follow us," Zev said, his tone grim but unsurprised.

Kiarana shook her head as she stowed the glass back in her pocket. "Not by use of that enchantment, she's not. This one is much fiddlier. I know a little of your human ways of magic, and I suspect it's part of the storytelling song Grandmama talks about."

"What do you mean?" Marieke asked, uneasy.

The elf folded her arms behind her back, quite at ease.

"It tracks in reverse. It doesn't show her where you go next, it shows her where you've come from to get here. She's probably following the trail right now."

CHAPTER

TWENTY-THREE

Zev

Fear washed over Zev at the elf's words, time seeming to freeze as all the implications broke on him at once.

His family.

"But we came straight from Zev's home," Marieke said, aghast. "Do you mean she can track her way back there using just magic?"

Marieke's eyes flew to Zev's, a shadow of his own fear in them. They hadn't acknowledged it aloud in their recent moment of revelation, but he knew she'd realized the same thing he had.

Jade knew who he was. Or at least, strongly suspected, like the Imperator clearly did. And Jade hadn't seemed surprised by the information. She knew about heartsong already, whatever that meant to her.

"My family." He heard the hollowness of his voice. The same fear that had gripped him when Marieke was in danger held him in its clutches again.

"We have to go," Marieke said. "We have to reach them before she does."

"Unlikely," Kiarana commented. "She won't be traveling by

normal means. From the frequency with which she zips in and out of here, I'd guess she's perfected magical travel."

"You have to help us," Marieke said, seeming just as desperate as Zev felt.

Kiarana raised a thin eyebrow, her tone suddenly frigid. "I do not have to do anything."

"I didn't mean to offend," Marieke said quickly. "I misspoke. I should have said, please help us."

The elf considered her. "I could get you to the coast via doorways and send you north on the ships our mining parties take to Sundering Canyon. They're powered by magic, and probably as fast as however Jade is traveling."

Zev started to thank her, but she cut him off with an upraised hand.

"I said I *could*, not that I will. It would take considerable power."

"And you won't do it for free," Zev finished for her.

"I am an elf," she reminded him.

"But what do you want?" His mind was too panicked to frame his questions more carefully. She would surely ask for confirmation of his identity, and although he'd rather not officially acknowledge it, it hardly seemed to matter much now.

"I want certain assurances from you," Kiarana said, her words directed to Zev. "About the future."

"How can I promise anything about the future?" Zev said. "I don't know what's yet to happen."

"No," Kiarana agreed. "And nor do I, with certainty. But," she gave a slightly unnerving smile that increased her resemblance to her grandmother, "those of us elves with what you humans might call royal blood do have certain gifts, you know. We sometimes see things."

"You see the future?" Marieke demanded.

"I didn't say that," Kiarana said. "It's never so simple."

"So what is it you want from me in exchange for helping us travel fast enough to beat Jade to my home?" Zev asked.

Kiarana held up a restraining hand. "I didn't offer that. I said I could help you travel swiftly. I offer no guarantee that you'll arrive before Jade does."

"In exchange for what, though?" Marieke said impatiently.

Kiarana tilted her head again, her eyes on Zev. "I want you to agree that when you come into a position of power and influence over Aeltas—"

"I have no expectation of ever coming into a position of power and influence over Aeltas," Zev cut her off.

The tips of her ears wobbled in annoyance as she straightened her head. "I want you to agree that *if* you come into a position of power and influence over Aeltas, you will assist the elves to come out of hiding safely, if we should wish to do so, and to protect the secret of our existence if we should not wish to emerge."

Zev frowned. "What if I never have influence?"

"Then the bargain would not be activated."

Zev tapped his fingers against the hilt of his sword, uneasy. "There are a lot of ifs in that bargain which, from my understanding, doesn't make for a safe bargain."

"It doesn't," Kiarana acknowledged. "But it's the only bargain I offer."

Zev exchanged a look with Marieke, who shrugged helplessly. The decision was his.

"I agree to the bargain," he said. "With the *ifs* you added."

"Very good." Kiarana rubbed her fingers together in a businesslike manner. "I will make the arrangements at once."

On the words, she strode from the building, leaving Marieke and Zev alone.

"Are you all right?" Marieke asked, the question tentative.

"I don't know," Zev admitted. "If I've led harm to them…"

"I know," Marieke whispered.

He ran a hand through his hair. "I don't know if the bargain was wise, but I had to try."

Marieke nodded. "I felt the magic that surged up and bound you both when you agreed. It's not something to be taken lightly."

Zev nodded in acknowledgment, not needing the warning. If there had been a safer way, he would have taken it, but not if it might cost his family their lives.

Within minutes, Kiarana was back, surprising them with the information that she would personally lead them through the doorways that would take them to the point where the jungle met the eastern coast.

The journey required more than one doorway, but thanks to the magical innovation, it was completed in a matter of minutes. Before they knew it, they were standing on a cliff, the air tasting of salt, and a wind from the ocean giving welcome relief to the humid stillness. A gull swooped past, its cry more haunting than the birds usually sounded, as if it knew the gravity of their situation.

A rocky path led down the cliffside, and at its base a small boat bobbed in a cove. It would be cramped for the two of them to fit their human forms into it alongside the elven helmsman who would steer them, but they would make it work.

"Thank you," Zev said, turning to Kiarana, who was to return through the doorways.

"Thanks are not necessary when assistance is given as part of a bargain," she reminded him.

"I know," said Zev. "But I also know that you took a chance on this bargain. My end of it may never become relevant. I told you, I don't expect my future to involve influence or power beyond my own life and family."

"I know what you expect," Kiarana said, unconcerned. "But it's not the future I see."

"What future do you see?" Zev asked, frowning.

She met the expression with a smile that was too calculating to be warm. "One in which we work together. Farewell, Zevadiah of Aeltas."

With that she disappeared through the doorway, the anomalous view between the trees disappearing with her until they were looking only at the coastal cliff before them.

"Bye," said Marieke to the empty air, a touch sarcastically. She shot Zev a wry smile. "Good to be reminded of my significance."

He returned the smile mechanically, although he did reach out to squeeze her hand. "You're significant to me, Marieke."

"I know," she said quickly. "My pride isn't really bruised. Much."

Prompted by the elf who remained with them, they hurried down the cliff and into the boat. He wasted no time in pushing off, clearly under instructions from his future Imperator to make the journey as speedy as possible. They headed out far enough for the shore to all but disappear, presumably to avoid detection. Then he turned the boat northward, and activated a talisman attached to the back of the little vessel.

Zev didn't need to be able to sense magic to know that this enchantment must be both powerful and sophisticated. They flew over the water, moving so quickly that the wind whipped his face painfully. And best of all, it didn't require anything from Marieke. She leaned back in the boat, her eyes closed against the rushing air and spray, her voice silent as she conserved all her energy for whatever lay ahead.

They traveled through the night, both humans managing catches of uneasy slumber as the elf guided them silently on. By the time dawn was breaking, they had turned back toward the shore. Thanks to the magic, the journey that had taken them days over land had taken them less than twenty-four hours by sea. Surely Jade couldn't have beaten them there?

Of course, they weren't there yet. Zev's home wasn't on the coast. They still had many hours of travel westward over the land, which Zev knew would feel glacially slow after their time in the boat. They'd debated going through the canyon, but they didn't want to risk being trapped there if Marieke's voice was silenced and they couldn't find a way up.

So instead they pooled their remaining resources to hire horses from the first village they encountered, Zev leaving his smaller blade—an expensive family heirloom—as collateral for their return. He'd never been so glad that Marieke was a competent rider as the two of them thundered over the roads, causing other travelers to pull out of their way with disgruntled expressions.

They didn't even stop to eat, shoving food from their packs into their mouths when they walked their horses. As soon as the animals were rested enough, they pushed them back to a canter.

The afternoon was well advanced when the terrain began to look familiar, and Zev's heart was in his throat by the time they finally reached his front gate. They thundered through it, having urged the poor, weary horses to a gallop for the last stretch of road.

"Mother, Father, Azai!" Zev slid off his horse the moment the animal came to a stop in the dusty yard. He was vaguely aware of Marieke dismounting and taking the reins of both creatures, but he didn't stay to watch her lead them to the barn.

He ran toward the house, stopping in his tracks when he heard a shout from the direction of the field.

"Zev!"

Zev turned, moving swiftly to meet his brother in the center of the yard.

"Azai! Are you all right? Where are Mother and Father?"

"I'm fine," said Azai. "But something's going on. Mother isn't here, the neighbors just slaughtered a pig, and she went to trade for some pork. But some woman just arrived to speak with Father, and I didn't like the look of her."

Fear clutched at Zev's heart, and he grabbed Azai's arm. "Tall, dark-haired, in her thirties?"

"That's right." Azai stared at him. "Who is she?"

"A rogue singer, a murderer," Zev said. "Where is she?"

"Speaking with Father in the smaller barn," said Azai, alarmed. "Father was the one who met her at the gate, and after whatever she said to him, he sent me away and wouldn't let me join the conversation."

"She probably threatened you," Zev said, already running toward the smaller barn, which was set further from the house. "And threatened exposure. I think she knows who we are, Azai. I don't know how, but—"

"Maybe your singer told her," Azai panted darkly as he kept pace.

Zev ignored the surge of irritation at this injustice to Marieke. It wasn't important right now. But it did remind him that Marieke didn't know what was going on.

His stride faltered for one step, then he surged forward. He didn't want to waste a moment redirecting to get Marieke. Besides which, now he knew Jade was here, the idea of Marieke facing her was terrifying. He could still hear the older singer's icy voice.

The next time I see her, I will kill her, and there's nothing you can do to stop me.

He and Azai were only a few paces from the smaller barn

when the stillness of the afternoon was slashed by a cry of agony.

Zev's breath caught in his throat as the brothers burst into the smaller barn together. His worst fears were realized at the sight of Jade standing over his father, who knelt at her feet with his hand clutched to his heart. The posture was just what Zev would imagine for a man who'd had a blade plunged into his chest, but no weapon was visible.

Zev let out a cry of pure rage, surging forward with Azai close behind.

Jade's head came whipping up, her voice raised in a swift song that crashed into the brothers like a solid wall. Knocked off his feet, Zev struggled back up, throwing himself forward again only to meet an invisible barrier. He pounded his fists against it in impotent fury, terrified by the agony twisting his father's silent features.

"You deserve this," Jade told the man at her feet, her voice sad in a detached way. "You had the chance to work with me to make it right, but you've chosen the coward's way."

Azai roared in outrage at the woman daring to call their father a coward, but he was as unable to break through the barrier as Zev was. Zev turned, intending to run out of the barn and find another way around, only to realize that the invisible wall hemmed him in on all sides.

"Turning on...my land...could never make...anything right," their father gasped.

"If you let the land prosper in spite of the crimes of its leaders, they will never be brought to justice," Jade said. She shook her head, continuing to ignore the trapped brothers. "You are a traitor. I betrayed my own to right the wrongs done to your kind. Your choice betrays your ancestors and cheapens my sacrifice."

She turned at last to her audience, her eyes lingering on Zev.

"I don't know how you followed so swiftly. I'm impressed." Her eyes passed between them, her tone almost weary. "I know this is a hard necessity. I hope it motivates you to make a better choice than your father. The future rests with you now. We will meet again, and when we do, I will ask for your decision. I'm not afraid to obliterate your line if it's become tainted by the lies of the councils and paralyzed into inaction."

"Father!" Azai screamed beside Zev, ignoring Jade's words, which must have made even less sense to him than they did to Zev.

Their father didn't respond, showing no sign that he could hear his sons' desperate cries. Perhaps their voices were held in by the barrier just as their bodies were. Their father keeled over as Jade stepped past him, climbing out a window on the far side of the barn. Not until she was fully out of sight did the barrier drop.

"MARIEKE!" Zev screamed, as he threw himself toward his father's form. "MARIEKE, HELP!"

"Father!" Azai cried, carefully turning their father over and searching for signs of injury. None were visible, but the older man's broken moans were becoming fainter.

Marieke appeared at Zev's side, her hand gripping his arm. "I was already coming," she said. "I felt the surge of magic, and I saw Jade."

"Where is she?" Azai's voice trembled with anger.

"She's gone," said Marieke. "She summoned a wind, and it carried her like a bird. What did she do?" Her face was pale as her gaze found Zev's father.

"She attacked him," Zev said desperately. "I don't know how, but I think he's dying. Help him, please!"

"I...I'm not trained in healing song." Marieke's voice shook. "I can do a simple diagnostic song, but..."

Her words trailed off, turning smoothly into a song. Zev's heart twisted in fear at the look that came over her face.

"Zev." Her voice was a whisper. "Zev, I'm sorry. I think she's pierced his heart. There's nothing I can—"

"You must be able to do *something*!" Azai cried, his voice passionate with misdirected anger. "What's the use of magic if it can't do anything?"

"I don't think even a skilled healer could reverse this." Marieke was keeping her tears at bay with a heroic effort. A flash of memory came across her face. "I might be able to take his pain away. It won't fix the injury, and I don't know how to put it in place perpetually. But if I keep singing..."

"Do it," said Zev, his throat tight and his lips numb.

Marieke nodded, clearing her own throat before raising her voice in a soft melody.

"Peace in your heart, peace for your body.
You're home and at rest, all is as it should be."

The tune was low and gentle, the soothing note jarring in the horror of the moment.

Zev's father let out a shuddering gasp, his moans stopping and his eyes fluttering open.

"Thank you, child," he said, as Marieke continued to sing the words over and over.

"Father!" Azai gripped his hand. "You're all right!"

The older man shook his head, but even without the pain, he was clearly too exhausted for explanations.

"I'm proud of you...both," he said, his other hand going to Zev. "I wish this hadn't come...to you. My ancestors got to live out...their lives...in peace. I wish my sons...could do...the same." His blinks were becoming long and slow. "Tell your mother..."

He never finished the sentence. His expression became peaceful, and his eyes drifted shut. To the sound of Marieke's gentle song, he let out a breath that was more a sigh, and his frame became still.

"Father!" Azai sobbed, his grip on the older man's hand tightening.

Zev was too devastated for words or tears. He felt numb, but it was a numbness that threatened terrible retribution when it wore off.

"I'm so sorry, Zev." Marieke's song had petered out—she could no doubt tell that her magic was no longer in use.

Zev didn't reply. He had no voice.

"Where is she?" Azai growled. "I'll kill her for this."

"Jade?" Marieke shook her head. "She's gone."

"Surely she can't be out of reach!" Azai's voice was furious, desperate. "Since when can magic make singers fly?"

"It's not exactly flying," Marieke said helplessly. "It's using the wind—manipulating the basic elements is a common type of songcraft. It's how she started the fire." She half shook her head, obviously remembering that Azai didn't know about that incident. "I doubt she'll be able to sustain it long, but it would be long enough to get beyond our reach."

Azai glared at her, his fist clenching and unclenching in impotent anger.

"Where's your mother?" Marieke's voice was hushed. "Is she safe? Is she—?"

"She's at the neighbors'," Zev said, his voice hoarse. "The next gate down the road to the south."

"I'll find her," Marieke promised.

She withdrew, leaving the brothers alone with their father's body.

Azai let out a low moan. Zev expected recriminations, but Azai surprised him, dropping his head into his hands.

"I should have been with him. I should never have let him send me away."

"No." Zev shook his head, gripping his brother's shoulder with one hand. "You saw how powerful she is. She would just have killed you, too."

"Father was wrong to wish peace for us." The feral anger in Azai's voice cut through Zev's numbness. "I don't want peace. I want to burn it to the ground."

"Burn what to the ground?" Zev asked dully.

"Everything the singers built that brought us to this point," Azai said savagely.

"Then you'd be conspiring with Father's murderer," Zev told him. "That's what she wants. She killed Father because he wouldn't help her do it."

Zev shifted his father's body into a more natural position, laying his arms over his chest. In the process, his eyes landed on his father's sword, lying on the hay-strewn floor beside his body. He would never know exactly what had passed between his father and Jade, but it was clear that the farmer hadn't been able to defend himself against the singer's attack.

Zev drew the sword slowly from the floor, raising it up to his eyes.

This became my sword the day my father died.

He could still hear his father's voice. It was the last conversation they'd had before Zev left. He remembered what else his father had said as well.

You're my son, Zev. And I trust you.

Zev swallowed, his eyes still on the sword as his other hand drew his own from where it hung uselessly at his side. He dropped it to the floor with a clatter, then slid his father's sword into its place on his belt.

He turned to see Azai watching him with a face that looked more numb than angry now, but neither brother could find words. The next half an hour passed in a horrible, surreal blur. Zev couldn't remember much of the scene that followed—he didn't even realize until Marieke returned with his mother that he'd let her go out alone, without even considering whether she was right in her guess that Jade was out of reach. He'd barely been aware of his surroundings...he certainly hadn't considered what a terrible burden it was to expect Marieke to deliver the news she carried.

It was hours later, when his father's body had been moved, a few relatives had gathered, and Marieke was safely in her room, that Zev found himself alone with his brother again. The terrible awareness of their loss was tangible between them, as though the image of their father's lifeless body was held up before their eyes. But the grief hadn't fully enveloped Zev yet. It was waiting, ready to pounce, but he'd found as he replayed the scene in the barn that his thoughts were surprisingly clear.

"You said that Father was wrong to wish for peace," Zev said, finding his voice for the first time in an hour.

Azai looked up at him, his arms straining from the tension with which he gripped the porch railing. "I didn't mean—"

"I agree with you," Zev cut him off. "Father was wrong about this one thing. He wasn't wrong to want peace, but he was wrong to live like it's all that matters. We've let inaction take away too much of our power. But no more. We're going to fight."

He saw the determination flare to life in his brother's eyes. "Yes." It was Azai's turn to grip Zev's shoulder. "We're going to do whatever it takes to bring that woman down."

"She won't be allowed to survive what's coming," Zev promised him. "But it's more than that. She wants to plunge these lands into war, and Father was right to resist that. We won't let her win. We'll fight."

"For our ancestors." Azai curled his hand into a fist, pounding it once against his heart.

"No." Zev shook his head. "Not for the past. For the future." He met his brother's eyes. "For our kingdom."

He could feel the certainty in his own voice, the sense of control which bore no obvious relation to his current situation. And he could see realization flicker into existence behind his brother's eyes.

"Your kingdom," Azai said. "You're the patriarch now. The stolen throne belongs to you. What will you do with it?"

"I don't know," Zev said. "But I won't keep doing nothing. I can't." He gripped the hilt of his father's sword—his sword—so tightly that his knuckles whitened. "Marieke said something to me once, when the elves had us caught in the canyon. She said live today to fight tomorrow."

"I'm familiar with the expression."

"We all are," said Zev. "We live by it. We've been living by it for generations, and for what? We tell ourselves that we live today to fight tomorrow, but when tomorrow comes, we're still not willing to fight. I knew it when Marieke used the expression, but I wasn't ready to admit it yet. Now I am."

Azai was silent for a moment.

"And what about Marieke?" he said at last.

Zev met his brother's eye, his expression unyielding. "I won't give her up. I'll do whatever it takes to keep her safe. And if I survive that, I'll do whatever it takes to be with her, because I love her." His eyes dared Azai to challenge him. "You're wrong about her, Azai. I'm better when I'm with her—stronger. And she's better when she's with me. We belong together."

He didn't wait for his brother to respond. Leaving Azai to his thoughts, Zev strode into the house. Jade was out there somewhere, intent on taking everything from him, and he didn't intend to let Marieke out of his sight. Ever again, if he could help it.

~

Zev closed his eyes, breathing in the cool dawn air and willing the peace of his orchard to settle around him.

But peace eluded him, as he'd known it would. He hadn't really expected anything else, even in his orchard. Not on the day of his father's funeral.

The crunch of a stick behind him made him turn to see his mother approaching down the row of trees.

"I thought you'd be here," she said. She looked up at the branches arching over their heads. "I don't come here often enough. It is a beautiful place." She returned her gaze to his face. "Is it bringing you comfort?"

Zev sighed. "No. Not today."

Her smile was sad. "Nothing will today. And that's all right."

All right wasn't a phrase Zev could relate to at that moment, but he didn't say so. It wasn't as if his mother needed him to tell her how devastating their loss was.

"I'm sorry he wasn't able to say whatever he wanted us to pass on to you," he said. He and Azai had told their mother exactly what had happened in the small barn.

The smile lingered on her face, her eyes unseeing as she gazed at the orchard around her. "He didn't need to say it. I already knew. Every day, I know."

Zev's heart ached so acutely it was unbearable. He shifted his gaze away from his mother's face, wondering if it was his imagination that she looked older than she had a week ago. It wasn't right that she would go into old age widowed before her time. It wasn't fair.

Anger against Jade burned within him, hot and barely contained. He didn't let his mother see it, afraid she would speak words of peace or caution. But it was no less powerful for being hidden, and it fueled him night and day.

A new figure appeared at the end of the row, slimmer and softer of tread than the last. His mother followed his gaze to see Marieke, that sad smile curving her lips again.

"It seems all your womenfolk know where to find you this morning."

"I wasn't trying to hide," Zev assured her.

"I know." She patted his cheek with one weathered hand. "Don't linger too long, Zev. The family will be arriving soon."

He nodded, his focus already on Marieke. He knew he was overcautious, but it alarmed him to see her wandering around alone. He waited with impatience while the women exchanged a greeting he couldn't hear, then Marieke continued to meet him while his mother made her way out of the orchard.

As soon as she was out of sight, he held out his arms, receiving Marieke into them as she leaned against his chest.

"I'm sorry I left the house without telling you," said Zev, laying his cheek on the top of her head. "I thought you were still in your room."

"I was," she said. "And it's fine, Zev. I don't need to be supervised at all times."

"Not supervised," he corrected. "Protected. Jade is out there, and she—"

"I know," Marieke said. "Let's not talk about it. Not today."

Her cheek was warm as she shifted it against his chest, finding a more comfortable position.

"I wish I could take your pain away," she whispered.

Zev's heart ached afresh. If only there was a song to erase

grief, the way Marieke had wiped away his father's pain in his last moments. But he knew it would never be that simple.

"Being here with me is enough," he murmured.

She pulled back and met his eyes. "Are you sure? Are you sure it doesn't make it worse? If it wasn't for me—"

"No." His voice came out harsh. "Don't you dare, Mari. None of this is your fault."

She bit her lip, not looking convinced. But she didn't press the point. Zev drew in a deep breath, letting the flowery scent of her hair envelop him. How he wished he could stay here, in this moment, forever. He didn't want to face the crowd of well-meaning friends whom he wished elsewhere, or the somber family who would now be looking at him with hidden expectation in their eyes. Here in his orchard with Marieke in his arms, time stood still and nothing could touch him.

"Can I ask you something?"

Zev broke the silence at last, cradling Marieke's face in his hands as he searched her eyes. Her warmth seeped into him.

"Are you angry with me for not telling you about heartsong sooner? I never wanted to foil you. I didn't know how to be loyal to my family without betraying you."

She shook her head, cushioned by his palms. "Of course I'm not angry. I understand why you didn't explain it. And we still don't even know if heartsong is the answer to my riddle. At best, it's one piece of the puzzle. I can't see how it can be the cause of Oleand's deterioration. That problem is so recent, and the loss of the monarchs is so old."

"I've been thinking about that," Zev said. "And there's an explanation I never thought of until we met Jade."

Marieke frowned at him, one hand resting lightly on his chest, the other bunched absently in the folds of his jacket. "What explanation is that?"

"That Oleand hasn't lost its heartsong at all." He could see her confusion, and he pushed on. "Something Azai said once has been playing on my mind. He said that Oleand's deterioration means it has no power. Which is much the same as your theory that the land is dying because the royal line is absent."

Marieke nodded in acknowledgment.

"But what if you're both wrong?" said Zev. "What if the land does have the power of heartsong? What if heartsong is being used *against* the land, instead of for it? We've always intentionally tried to bless our land. Even our lifestyle as farmers was chosen with that in mind. Our hands work the ground, which is as direct a way as we know to make it prosper. We didn't know there was a way for our heartsong to interact with songcraft the way it does when I'm with you. But Jade seemed to know."

Marieke frowned. "She did, didn't she? She called the way the magic behaved around us like and yet unlike what she'd experienced."

"How could she have experienced it, though?" Zev pressed. "She didn't know who we were or where to find us until she followed my trail. It can't have been our heartsong she had experience with."

Marieke's eyes widened, her fingertips tightening on his chest as she understood.

"What are you saying? That you think the royal line survived in Oleand, too? And Jade found them?"

"And convinced them to use their power over the land to make Oleand suffer instead of prosper," Zev finished. "I didn't take it all in at the time, but that's the best explanation I can come up with for what she said. She killed him for refusing to do what she was asking. And she didn't just do it out of spite— she must have wanted his power over the land to pass from him to me in the hope she could convince me to yield to her plans. It's why she said I'm more use to her alive."

Marieke's hand went over her mouth, obviously grasping the enormity of it. Whether she grasped the danger she was in, as the most likely target of any attempts to manipulate Zev, was a different question.

"The land really is turning against itself," she said hollowly. "It's being destroyed from the inside. Zev, we can't possibly fight—"

"Yes we can," Zev said. "We have the strength of two kingdoms, and the power of both heartsong and songcraft."

With gentle fingers, he pulled her hand away from her mouth, willing her not to give in to the despair he saw in her eyes.

"This is my fight too, Mari. You won't be alone. We can fight anything if we do it together."

He saw her tension lessen as she took in his words, and the sight eased his own heart. He ran his thumb across her lips, impossibly soft against his weathered skin. Certainty filled him —if nothing else was, the decision to let Marieke in was the right one.

Zev lowered his head, his thumb trailing onto Marieke's cheek so his lips could take its place. She responded in kind, the kiss tender and achingly sweet as he held her close in the stillness of the orchard.

Grief and hope swirled around them in an intimate dance, the power of the moment in no way weakened by the vulnerability it required. Surely no magic could be more powerful than the nearness Zev felt with Marieke in his arms.

For one more moment, the world could wait.

NOTE FROM THE AUTHOR

Thank you for reading *A Fractured Song*. I hope you enjoyed returning to the world of the Sovereign Realms. I would be so grateful if you would consider leaving a review on Amazon—it would really make a difference!

To follow Zev and Marieke on the next and last instalment of their story, check out Book Three—*A Shattered Reign*.

 If you've yet to read the previous adventures set on the continent of Providore, check out *The Singer Tales* today! This completed series includes six connected but standalone fairy tale retellings featuring strong heroines navigating everything from miniature elves to brutish giants as they chase their own happily ever afters.

Join up to my mailing list at deborahgracewhite.com to be kept up to date on new releases, specials, and giveaways, such as bonus chapters. You'll receive some great freebies, too, including *An Expectation of Magic*, a novella which is a prequel to my completed YA fantasy series *The Vazula Chronicles*.

Plus, you'll receive *Dragon's Sight*, an 8,000 word prequel to my completed YA fantasy trilogy *The Kyona Chronicles*.

Again, thanks for entering the world of the Sovereign Realms! I hope to see you back again.

ALSO BY DEBORAH GRACE WHITE

Find a complete list of my published books
and reading order here on my website
deborahgracewhite.com

Acknowledgments

Thank you again to my awesome team for supporting me in this series!

My husband Ray, as always, deserves thanks for his encouragement and patience in listening to me talk myself in circles as I coax the manuscript into life. And it occurs to me that my four wonderful small fry never get a mention in these acknowledgments but totally should! Where would be the fun and magic in my life without them?

Thank you also to my beta readers for all your fantastic help: Adrian, Dad, Alora, Constance, Mum, and Steph. Thanks to Shae for the thorough and professional proofread. Any remaining errors are mine.

Thanks to Moorbooks for the cover and to Becca for another beautiful map.

To you, the reader, thank you for giving me the privilege of being an author.

And most importantly, to God, whose truth can set us free.

About the Author

I've been a reader since I can remember, growing up on a wide range of books, from classic literature to light-hearted romps. The love of reading has traveled with me unchanged across multiple continents, and carried me from my own childhood all the way to having children of my own.

But if reading is like looking through a window into a magical and beautiful world, beginning to write my own stories was like discovering that I could open that window and climb right out into fantasyland.

I cannot believe how privileged I am to actually be living that childhood dream and publishing my own novels amidst the fun and chaos of life with my husband and our four little ones.

I've never outgrown my love of young adult stories, so the genre of young adult fantasy was always going to be my niche. Feel free to email me at deborah@deborahgracewhite.com and introduce yourself! Or subscribe to my mailing list at deborah gracewhite.com for free giveaways, sales, and updates.